The Bulls of Bashan

The Bulls of Bashan

BY

JODI LEA STEWART

Names, characters, businesses, places, events, and incidents are either the products of the author's imagination or used in a fictitious manner. Any resemblance to actual persons, living or dead, or actual events, is purely coincidental.

No part of this publication may be reproduced, stored in a retrieval system, or transmitted in any form or by any means, electronic, mechanical, photocopying, recording, or otherwise, without the written permission of the publisher.

Text Copyright © 2025 Jodi Lea Stewart

All rights reserved.
Published 2025 by Progressive Rising Phoenix Press, LLC
www.progressiverisingphoenix.com

ISBN: 978-1-958640-75-3

Printed in the U.S.A.
1st Printing

Edited by: Chris Eboch

Cover Artwork: "Powerful Bull Charging Through Fiery Dust Storm," by Sandra. AdobeStock ID:1077707454. used under license from AdobeStock.com.

Interior Artwork: Chapter Headings: "Great Detail Illustration of the World Map in Vintage Style With All Countries Boundaries and Names," by pingebat. ShutterStock ID: 601754189, used under license from ShutterStock.com.

Interior Artwork: Lock and Keys: by Mistogane. Used With Permission.

Cover & Interior Design by William Speir
Visit: www.WilliamSpeir.com

Books By
JODI LEA STEWART
Published By
PROGRESSIVE RISING PHOENIX PRESS

TRIUMPH, a Novel of the Human Spirit

SILKI, THE GIRL OF MANY SCARVES SERIES:
Summer of the Ancient
Canyon of Doom
Valley of Shadows

BLACKBERRY ROAD

THE ACCIDENTAL ROAD

THE GOLD ROSE

THE BULLS OF BASHAN

Table Of Contents

PROLOGUE

What if you were finally living what you thought was your best life, a life you dreamed of, worked hard to achieve, and then, one unexpected heartbeat later, found you had outgrown what you always believed was your destiny? What if you kept this changed *perspective* a secret until, ironically, an opportunity more bizarre than *Victor Hugo's eight-hundred-and twenty-three-word sentence* knocked on your door, and you—blindly, impetuously, yes, even ecstatically—jumped in with a fervency that shocked you to the core?

That's exactly what happened to me in 1953; and now, here I am, a member of a four-person team in the middle of a global mystery promising no answers until everything on our mysterious list has been gathered. Whether we're dodging spears and running for our lives in the Amazon rainforest, riding mules into the largest canyon in the world, or traveling through war-torn European cities, I feel compelled to ask how a caterpillar—that would be me only a short time ago—accepts becoming a different creation with a completely new identity—that would be me now. I'm perilously seeking the answer to that question.

– Savannah

THE DINER

CHAPTER ONE

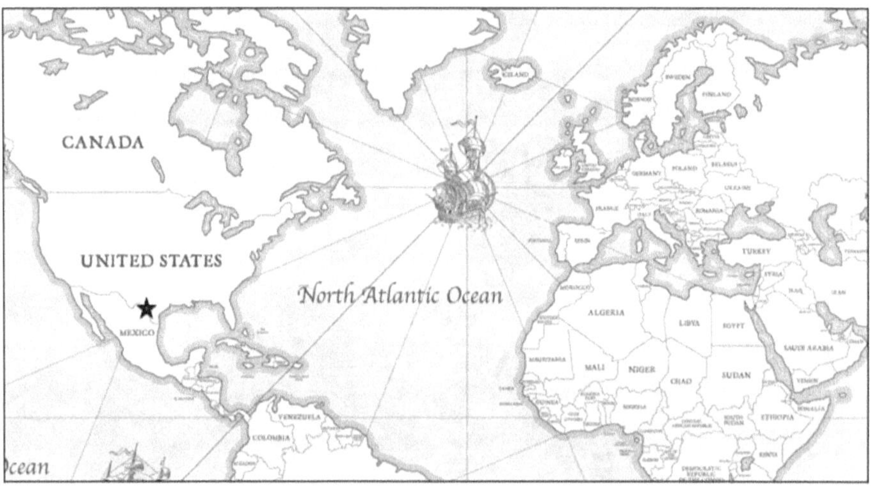

Laredo, Texas, 1953

I was five when my mama ran off to New Orleans with a fake preacher and never came back. I accepted that oddity with more bravado than the secret conflict I was wrestling with the day Shifrah and Malone walked into my life. Before they came through the Dixie Diner doors the first time, I was already emotionally disengaged from my position as the new manager of that eatery. Why is that a big deal? Because the Dixie had previously, like "a minute ago," been my world in every single way. Now, it was putting dark circles under my eyes and fraying my nerves.

How do I explain how everything real and important in my life suddenly wasn't, and that I was in deep distress keeping the *new me* a carefully guarded secret? As it turns out, they, those two strangers, were so confident of who I really am, they already had my passport prepared. When I opened it, there was my photo duplicated from a college yearbook, along with my signature that Shifrah explained "an expert" had *lifted* from a handwritten letter I submitted to the local newspaper last fall.

That's forgery, right? But it's minor compared to how I'm reeling from everything that's happening. Did I say *reeling?* What I really mean is I'm floating on a cloud of such strange euphoria, I feel as if it's no longer me living inside my own body.

A thousand questions blaze my mind into cinders when I lie down to sleep. How did *they* find me? Why did *they* pick me? How will my so-called skills line up with those of Shifrah's and that of the other man, the one they call Reno? Who and what is behind this strange venture?

Shifrah promises she'll explain in depth once we're on the *Aguila Azteca* train bound for Mexico City, and am I really going off with her and that Malone fellow with such sketchy information? Yes, I am, and now I have a mere few days to prepare to leave behind everyone and everything I've ever known. How do I logically explain I'm drifting away from them in a cloud of unanswered questions?

Stable. Steady. Dependable. That's how people have always described me, especially after I completed with honors my two-year college degree a few months ago. Tony, the owner of the Dixie, held a celebration at the diner with our friends, locals, and all the regulars who are like family to me. He gave me a beautiful pin with my name and *Manager* engraved on it. I had yearned to be the manager of the Dixie since I was barely out of braids. At last, I was free to supervise, manage, and work any and every shift I set my heart on—a long-awaited dream.

With Tony's blessings, I jumped right in with plans of updating and redecorating the interior of the diner with shiny silver wall tiles, white and turquoise Naugahyde booths, a new Formica counter, and updated floor tiles and ceiling fans. I posted schedules for the staff on a fancy blackboard installed in the employee room. I hired Yvonne Gonzales, a seamstress in nearby Cotulla, to use *Hannah Troy* patterns to make our new uniforms in matching colors with actual flared skirts. They turned out showier than any eating establishment uniforms this side of Dallas. With Dotted Swiss white and turquoise aprons and geometric caps, our uniforms quickly became the talk of Webb County.

I coasted through each renovation with what I believed was great joy. Yet, in the quiet of my soul—that place where our inner selves tread softly but honestly—ethereal twinges flickered lightly, discreetly. I couldn't grasp them long enough to understand their meaning, so, *practical me,* I pushed them aside. In the meantime, Tony kept me updated on his plan to help me buy the diner when he retired in a few years to take his wife Maria on a long-postponed trip to Europe, especially to Italy and France. Owning my own diner, in particular, *that* diner, by the time I turned twenty-three? What more could I ever want from life?

Then, like a sunny day suddenly interrupted by a surprising streak of lightning and billowing angry clouds, everything changed. I changed. Internally, secretly, painfully. It started one normal afternoon when I was handing out menus to a flock of clucking, cheerful women. An odd sensation came out of nowhere and drenched my insides, leaving me slightly nauseated. I hurried to the employee restroom to scrutinize my image in the mirror. I looked okay. No rashes. No fever. I freshened my lipstick, repined the hairnet over the back of my hair, and downed a few swigs of strong coffee in the kitchen.

Minutes later, I was pouring hot brewed tea over ice chips and enjoying the crackling sound. I looked up and surveyed the redecorated diner—the booths, the curved counter, the jukebox, the ceiling fans, the black and white floor tiles, three waitresses efficiently working the busy room in stylish uniforms. It was beautiful. All of it. It was my world and my future.

In the next blink, my plans, my aspirations, my entire life, shriveled like paper tossed in a fire. Everything became too ordinary, too small, too eaten up by the flames of something I didn't understand. Hands shaking, I set the tea pitcher down on the ledge behind the counter. Had I forgotten to eat? Was I sick? Had there been a cosmic shift in the atmosphere?

Even a ripe peach has sense enough to blush when it's ready to leave the tree. Not I. Volcanoes rumble, emit steam, and unleash earthquakes before erupting. Where were my interim steps, my warning signs, before *hot lava* consumed the old Savannah and left an entirely new Savannah in its mortal flow?

I became an imposter in my own life. It was a daily struggle to keep my new truth tucked away so as not to hurt anyone, especially all our regulars and Tony. With their whole hearts, they have always been there for me, especially after Daddy died in a trucking accident when I was twelve.

The next time Tony mentioned *our* plans about my acquiring the Dixie Diner and that things were *coming along just fine and dandy*, my stomach knotted. I gave him my usual reaction of elation, but it was as phony as a paper rose. For the first time in my life, my reactions to customers became forced, especially with the regulars. Daily dishrag swipes across the new Formica countertop outfitted with a gleaming five-inch silver rim along the edge blurred as I found myself daydreaming of gluing the corners of my mouth into a grin so I could secretly wallow inside my strange discontent.

Then, just like that, Shifrah and Malone walked through the door.

CHAPTER TWO

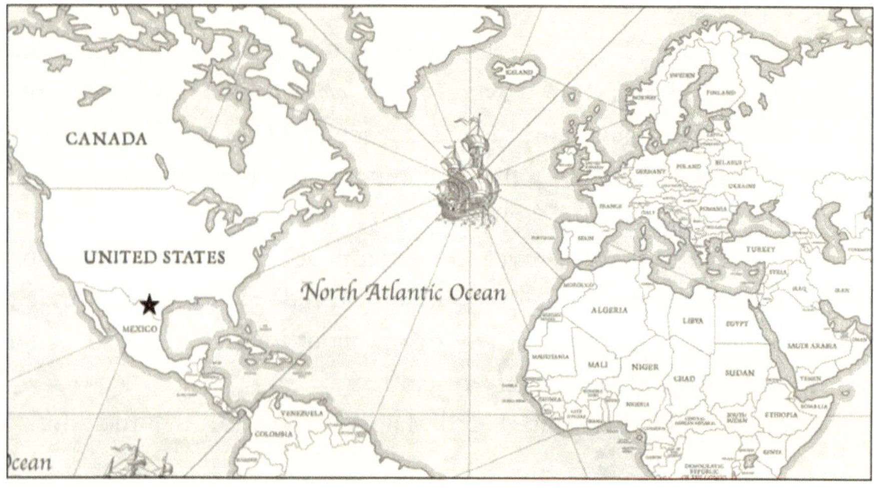

The bell above the door rang for what seemed the thousandth time announcing new customers. Holding menus, I smiled and led the attractive couple to a booth. The man indicated by gesture he wanted to sit on the side facing the door. The woman was young, expensively dressed, and pretty enough to be a starlet. Everything about her radiated wealthy sophistication. The man was tall and wore a suit, tie, and a Fedora hat. Except for migrant workers wearing handkerchiefs on their heads when working in the fields and orchards, all the males in Laredo, Texas, from three or four years old, wear cowboy hats.

The couple seemed, at first glance, like the affluent travelers stopping on their way to California or New York, the ones who order tuna salad-stuffed tomatoes and think chicken-fried steak is a poultry dish. The meticulously dressed man with the starched white shirt and expressive dark eyebrows sat down with his eyes casing the diner. He removed his hat, turning it upside down on the seat beside him. The waitresses whispered in the kitchen he looked like Gregory Peck playing the role of Captain Horatio Hornblower.

The couple came again the next day, and the two after that, at different times of the day, always well dressed and asking to be seated the same way as before. He ate heartily, sometimes requesting a second piece of pie or a malted after consuming either a hearty breakfast or the lunch specialty of the day. *Polite, but on the cold side,* the girls said of him, and *a pretty good tipper.* His Fedora became a matter of chatter with them.

The dishwashers and delivery boys rattled amongst themselves about *the beautiful lady* and how, if they could get her alone, would show her how a real man acts instead of that drugstore cowboy she was with. My frowns stopped their feisty chatter. I was, after all, the boss.

The young woman sometimes sipped hot coffee floating in rich cream, but it was her asking for several slices of lime for her tea that stood out to my gossipy waitresses. That, and the fact she never finished a full meal. After she pushed her plate away, she pulled out a golden pack of cigarettes and smoked a solitary cigarette before leaving. In passing, I noticed the brand on the package as FATIMA, and an illustration of an Arabian woman wearing a scarf over her nose and mouth was on the front of the pack.

We love repeat customers at the diner, no complaints on our part about anyone coming back day after day, but something about those two was off-kilter, and it seemed to center around me. I constantly felt their eyes on me, sensed them listening to my greetings and conversations. More than once, I turned in time to see them exchange glances or nod heads as their eyes followed me. That week ended and, after skipping a few days, they came again around lunchtime. The staff was wildly curious about them, and Tony started worrying they were up to no good.

"Why are they eyeballing you so danged close, Savannah?" he said, and I had no answer. Some of the girls speculated the man was a mafia bigwig planning to kidnap me. The young woman was the beautiful girlfriend of the head honcho of their New York gang and was overseeing the kidnapping. I waved off their foolishness and accused them of reading too many detective novels, but, really, what *did* the strangers want?

Bert, our day cook, said, "If they don't stop keeping such a close account of our Savannah, I'll take that big fella out back and give him a thrashing. I don't throw them hundred-pound feed sacks around like they's bean bags for nothing." He flexed his arms to show off his biceps. "I have a mind to dump their food on the floor before I let you gals serve it to 'em."

I scolded him for his crude talk, but it pointed out the growing uneasiness the two strangers were bringing into the diner. We didn't see them for a couple of days after that, and I assumed they moved on. When they showed up again and continued to scrutinize me closely, I waved Colleen aside and took the tea pitcher from her. Refilling the woman's tea glass, I said, "Excuse me, but is there something I can do for you?"

"Oh, um, yes. Perhaps a few more lime wedges for my tea, if you don't mind. I believe I'll have a small salad and the roasted chicken sandwich—"

"I'm sorry to interrupt you, Miss, but we know you and your friend have been watching my every move every time you're in here. Please don't deny it. We're all witnesses to it. I think it's time you explain what's going on, or, well, since it's upsetting the staff here, I may have to ask you to leave."

The woman looked uncomfortable as she shifted positions, but her unusual brownish-green eyes were clear as she met my gaze. "I understand," she said. She passed a look to the man. He rose and seated himself nearby, flagged a waitress who went behind the counter and opened the pie case. I watched, then turned my attention back to the woman.

"Y'all have been coming in here staring a hole in me for some reason, and—'

"I apologize if we've made you uncomfortable. Would you mind sitting for a minute or two? I have something important to share with you."

"Share with *me?* You don't even know me."

She smiled. "Please sit. I promise I won't bite. By the way, my name is Shifrah."

I sat down on the edge of the booth bench opposite her with my feet ready to take off. I noticed Bert staring at us through the little window above the grill in the kitchen. Darlene and Bonnie were slowly clearing a nearby booth to eavesdrop. I waved them away. Weary with lack of sleep, I felt unusually testy. "Whatever this is, please hurry. We're expecting a large afternoon and evening crowd with the rodeo in town this weekend."

Shifrah smiled, then stared at the street through the window blinds for a few seconds before looking down. I glanced at my watch. "Look, I have a lot of—"

"I'm sorry. I'm trying to find the right words. I'm new at this, so I'll start with a question, if that's all right."

I nodded. She cleared her throat.

"If you had to guess, how many life-changing opportunities do you suppose come along in a person's lifetime—perhaps one or two?"

"I've never really thought about it."

"You've already had a few lucky breaks, along with some pretty tough ones, haven't you?"

I started to ask her how she knew that, but I quickly calculated it was a guess on her part. Everyone has a mixture of good and bad experiences under the belt by the time they're about to turn twenty-one. I was no exception.

"I know what I have to say will sound, um, unusual, but please, bear with me. I, we, uh, we're here for a reason."

"I already figured that out."

"Of course. Well, I'm here to offer you an opportunity that's hard to describe. It's… rare. And different."

"An opportunity? Look, if you're selling something, I'm not interested."

"No, this isn't about selling anything."

"Is it a joke?"

She took a sip of tea. "I assure you, it isn't a joke. And, I take that back. This is about selling you—"

I started to rise from the seat.

"Please don't go yet, Savannah."

"You know my name?" I blurted out, then felt immediately embarrassed. I wear a nametag pinned to my uniform. All our regulars call out my name as soon as they walk through the door and spot me. All the customers hear Bert when he loudly tosses a joke through the pass-through window yelling *this one's for Savannah!* Everyone who comes to the diner quickly knows my name.

She smiled. "I suppose the real question boils down to whether you have a sense of adventure. Would traveling around the world experiencing life as you never have before… does that interest you?"

"Well, I-I don't—"

"Of course, we understand how much this diner and these people mean to you and that running it has always been a big part of your childhood dreams. While that's lovely, might it not be time for different, um, bigger dreams now? Dreams that take you far beyond…" she swept the room with her hand, "…this?"

Was she a mind reader?

"If you sign up with us, you'll travel to destinations most people never get to see, especially people from, you know, small towns like Laredo, Texas."

Sign up? What is this, a military hitch?

"You'll meet people from different cultures, eat different foods, and be part of something that has-has mystery and adventure, to say the least. And, there's more. When your contract is fulfilled, you'll receive a bonus that, by any standard, stands to make you independently wealthy. Naturally, we're prepared to offer that in writing." She held my eyes while she reached into her purse and pulled out a silver case. "Cigarette?"

"I don't smoke."

She smiled. "I know."

How?

She studied the case a moment before taking out a cigarette. "The latch broke recently, and I had to send it back to my jeweler in New York to be repaired. I received it back special delivery yesterday at your post office. I so hate carrying my Turkish cigarettes in their original package. It gets tobacco all over, and…" She smiled, put the case on the table, ran her palm over the front. "The truth is, I'm ridiculously attached to this cigarette case. I've had it ever since I can remember. I was always told it was not only a special gift but also a map to my future." She took out a cigarette, lit it. "Have a look," she said, gently pushing it toward me.

Instinct told me if I looked at it, I would be lassoed into something I wouldn't want to escape from. I hesitated, keeping my eyes on her.

"Please?"

I took a resolved breath and looked down at a silver case with etchings in each corner containing symbols I had never seen before. In the middle was a thick-trunked tree with leafed branches crowning the top. A straight line intersected the middle of the trunk. On the left side of the line was a half-circle of a rounded stadium of some kind. On the right was a split, oval-shaped earth showing all the continents and oceans in tiny etched lines. Underneath the tree were several hefty bulls flinging their heads in the air. I could almost hear their angry snorts.

"It's very unusual. Beautifully engraved. You say it's a map to your future?"

She had me, and she knew it. She leaned back in the booth with a triumphant sparkle in her eyes, blew a ring of smoke toward the ceiling. "That's a discussion for after you join us."

"Who is *us?*"

She nodded toward her companion sitting nearby. "That's Malone. He's, well, kind of my protector and the overseer of our expedition. He's in constant contact with our, shall we say… employer? The other member of our team is Reno. We pick him up in Mexico after traveling by train from Nuevo Laredo to Mexico City. I don't know exactly why we're going there instead of him coming here, but whatever Malone says, that's what we do. Reno's skills, your skills, and my skills make us, along with Malone, the perfect quartet for a job like this. Or so Malone says."

Instead of leaping to my feet telling Shifrah she was crazy, I yearned, no, I ached, to know more. My spirit had been lit by a torch dusted in gasoline. My mouth was suddenly drier than a cactus. I picked up the glass of water Shifrah had not touched and drank half of it, set it down. My pulse thumped in my throat. I took a deep breath and let it out slowly. "Tell me… what makes you think I'd go off with strangers and leave my whole life behind?"

Shifrah leaned forward confidentially. "Because, Savannah—and please don't think I'm being rude because I'm not—but, hon, it's obvious you're bored out of your mind."

If a hissy fit hadn't broken out between Colleen and Rosemary on the other side of the diner, I might have swooned. How could anyone, let alone a stranger, see the deepest secrets of my heart? Had I not done everything to conceal them?

I excused myself and jumped into the middle of the argument, using hand gestures for the waitresses to follow me into the kitchen. As the reprimanded women huffed off in different directions, I rejoined Shifrah to accept a destiny I felt powerless to deny.

Mexico

CHAPTER THREE

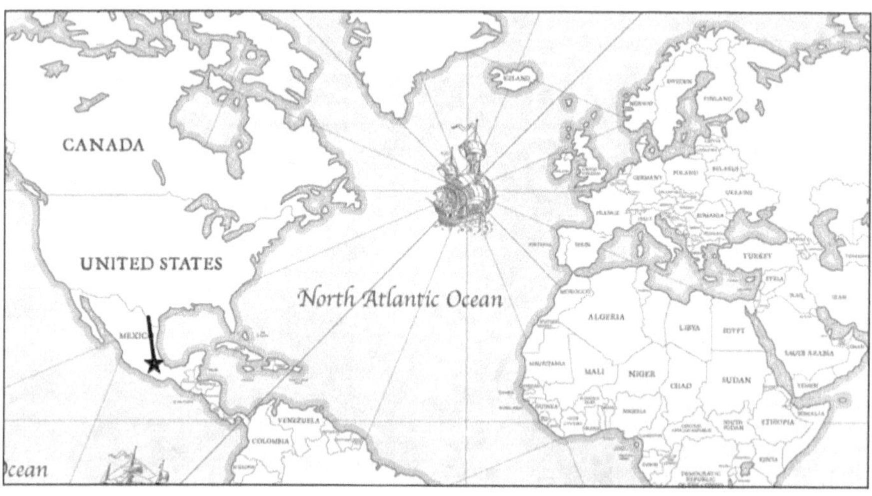

The disappointed confusion written on the faces of Tony and the somber group gathered in front of the Dixie to see me off on a journey neither they nor I understand feels like an icepick jabbing my soul. We've said our goodbyes, hugged repeatedly, and now I'm sitting in the back seat of the car taking me away from them. Keeping my eyes on theirs, I smile the weakest smile I've ever hidden behind and tap the back of the driver's seat.

"Please, Malone, I can't take this much longer."

He nods, puts the car in gear, and drives me away from my life. I manage a few last waves out the open window before burying my face in a handkerchief and allowing my emotions to take over. I fancy this is how it feels going off to war, leaving behind everyone you love and knowing not what the future holds. I give in to my tears.

"Savannah, we're coming to the Rio Grande. Would you care to see the bridge?"

I shake my head without looking up. I've traveled across the International Bridge connecting Texas and Mexico so many times, it's as familiar as the center aisle of the Dixie. A shaky sigh later, and inside the safety of my handkerchief, I ask myself *are you sure this is what you want?* A resounding *YES!* echoes back at me so quickly, I feel my tears drying up. Was I really that bored, or am I merely eager to travel and experience life as I've never known it? I'm not sure yet. I wipe my eyes, blow my nose, and sit up straight. "What time does our train leave for Mexico City?"

"Right before dark. We'll have a few hours to kill," Shifrah says. "I've heard of a famous bar in Nuevo Laredo, something about a car?"

"The Cadillac Bar."

"That's it! Have you been there?"

"Many times."

"Don't they have some kind of famous drinks?"

"Ramos Gin Fizzes."

"Oh, yes, that's what I heard. We simply must try one, Savannah."

"I don't drink."

She clicks her tongue. "Oh, Savannah, you're out in the world now. Life changes." She lights a cigarette and pivots in the front seat, her smiling lips most likely gleaming with one of Max Factor's newest shades of coral-red. Her perfectly applied winged eyeliner, shiny brown hair pulled up, fastened, and turned under in shoulder-length perfection accents her smartly tailored train outfit—a flared olive-green dress with a wide belt, beige accessory buttons, and beige piping around the collar, cuffs, and along the edges of the diagonal pockets. Everything about her is perfect.

I look down at my simple blue shirtdress and plain tan pumps with matching square tan purse holding my passport, cash, a small comb, and a tube of lipstick that I often forget to use. Most of the dresses I've worn since I was a young girl were standard uniform dresses at the diner. Working on engines, fishing, shooting, running track, playing softball… none of those activities called for more than a set of trousers, a tucked-in shirt, boots, or sensible lace-up shoes. I've dressed up for a few occasions, such as graduation parties and auditorium presentations, but not enough to own more than three or four dresses or skirts at a time. Now I realize I know nothing about fashion at this ripe old age of nearly twenty-one, and Shifrah's coifed hairdos, clothes, and perfect accessories make me feel like a country bumpkin for the first time in my life.

"Tell me about Reno," I say to take my mind off myself and my new, self-diagnosed drabness.

"I haven't met him yet," she says, exhaling a long stream of smoke in my direction. "Oh, sorry." She fans the air with her hand and rolls down the front window a few inches.

"Then, how did you select him for this, um, whatever it is?"

"I didn't. Malone did."

Malone nods, offers no explanation.

* * *

Boarding the train at dusk, we push through throngs of smiling Mexican women in long skirts and men in white, blousy shirts and broad hats. The whole train is infused with excited travelers from Europe, New York, and several other states. I've never had a sip of alcohol, but I feel intoxicated with excitement. Already full from eating at the Cadillac Bar, we didn't plan to eat supper onboard. Shifrah is right away dead set on seeing the Schindler Observation car at the back of the train. We make our way through the cars, and I have to admit the observation car is exquisite. It somehow reminds me of the Dixie with its narrowness and sculpted booths.

"He's a big hero in our home," she says.

"Who?"

"Oskar Schindler. See, there's a plaque with his name over the door. His factory makes these train cars. My parents hung his photo in the upstairs hallway, and when I wanted to know what made him a hero, they changed the subject. I know it has to do with the big war, but that's almost a forbidden topic at home, which, of course, is fine by me.

Hilda, our maid and my companion when I was younger, told me on the sly he's an industrialist in Poland who did saintly things for hundreds of people."

"Hundreds?"

"Uh-huh, maybe more, and that's all I know about him. Savannah, my parents are actually my aunt and uncle. Obviously, my real parents are dead or I wouldn't have been adopted by Mommykins and Daddy. My uncle is my real dad's brother. All the facts are muddled about how I came to live with them. I never get a straight answer from them, and, honestly, it never matters to me. Lots of unspoken topics in our house, but I had a jazzy life. My parents doted on me until, um, you know what? My head is starting to pound. If you don't mind, I'll retire to my roomette and get some rest."

"But you promised to shed a lot of light on this mysterious job I've signed up for, Shifrah, and I have so many questions to ask you."

She yawned. "I know, I know, but I'm absolutely worthless when I have a headache."

"But I need to find out—"

"Tomorrow we'll talk endlessly, I promise."

What can I do but nod and watch her leave? What have I signed up for? Where all are we going, and why? Again, it seems almost crazy that I agreed to a job I do not understand at all. Was I that tired of my old life?

CHAPTER FOUR

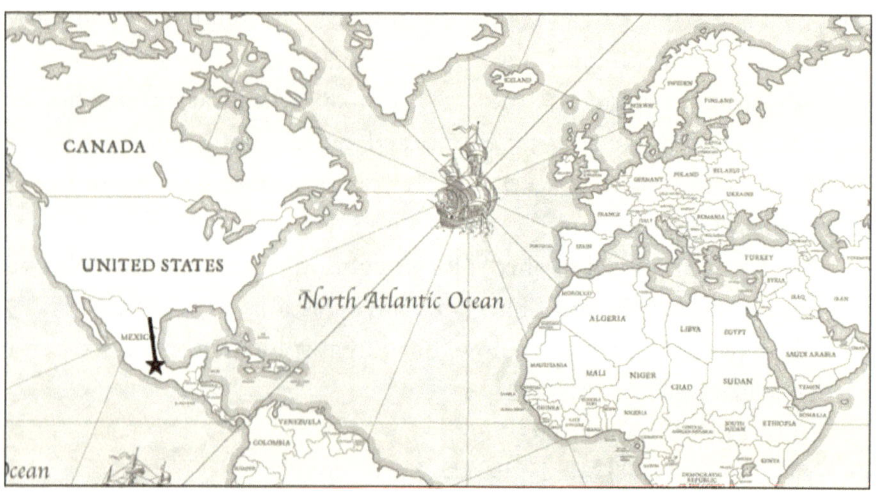

The dark green sleeper cars we saw when we first spotted the *Aguila Azteca* at the depot turned out to have surprisingly comfortable sleeping rooms inside. I slept in a private room for one passenger with seats that transformed into a bed at night with a window and a light on the side. I was too excited to sleep, so I watched out the window for the occasional lights from a Mexican town or village, eavesdropped when there was chatter outside my door, and let my thoughts take over. One thought repeated itself again and again… *what do I think I'm doing leaving my normal life behind and taking off with strangers like this?*

Of course, that question set off a whole slew of remembrances, especially how I became so bonded to the Dixie Diner in the first place. My addiction to it started one evening soon after Mama took off. My daddy quickly realized the only things he knew how to make in the kitchen were boiled coffee, skillet-fried toast, and thick baloney sandwiches with drippy tomatoes and sweet onions. About a week into life with just the two of us, he was standing by the stove flipping our buttery fried toast with a spatula.

I was setting the table for us like Mama had shown me with the silverware on the proper sides when he said in his heavy southern accent, "Sweet Pea, this ain't right. What do you say we head down to the Dixie and have us some black-eyed peas and cornbread? Being this time of summer, ol' Tony probably has some of that blackberry cobbler made up, and I'd sell my chicken for a whistle for us to have us a ration of it. You know, pour some good ol' cow cream on the top and all? Don't that sound fine?"

It sure did, and I wasted no time retrieving my white straw hat with the colorful cloth flowers sewn around the crown and the drawstring underneath the chin. Daddy was waiting for me by the door. "What you wearin' your Easter hat for, honey?"

"'Cause Mama says no lady goes anywhere special without a nice hat on her head, Daddy." That was the last time he said a word about me wearing that hat, and he brought me many more during his truck travels. I never wore a single fancy one, only the billed caps I wore fishing to keep the sun out of my eyes and my Stetson for riding horses or attending the rodeo.

Mama never took me to the Dixie diner, though I often begged to go after seeing the beautiful blinking pink and yellow neon sign on the roof. She had a strange aversion to Daddy hanging out there with the other truck drivers and ranchers, even for a quick cup of coffee. Why, I didn't know, but I heard their arguments from their bedroom next to mine more than once.

At last, I was getting to go inside. Daddy and I climbed the three steps to the door, my eyes taking in every detail. He opened one side of the shiny silver double doors and stood back for me to step inside. *Truck Driver's Blues* by Cliff Bruner and the Boys filled my ears. I knew that song and most of the other popular ones from hearing them on our radio at home. Unless she was asleep, Mama had the radio playing.

She danced all around the house when she cleaned or cooked, sometimes holding a broom or mop like a partner.

Once inside the diner, my eyes were paralyzed by the most beautiful thing I'd ever seen in my life. Taller than me with an upside-down U-shape at the top and lit-up rainbow colors all over it, the magnitude of it rendered me speechless and nailed my feet to the floor. Daddy bent down and whispered, "It's a Wurlitzer, honey—a jukebox. It plays them pretty music records. Let's go sit ourselves down and get us some vitals." He nudged me through the door, but I didn't feel my legs move. I was lost in a wonderland that etched the sights, sounds, and sensations of the Dixie Diner permanently on my mind.

It's strange, but sometimes when I'm drifting to sleep, that truck-driving song and those *etchings* waltz as ghostly dancers across the waters of my subconscious. Last night, they blended into the clickety-clack of the train on the tracks, adding to my sense of awe at choosing to leave Laredo for something I know almost nothing about.

My neck is stiff this morning from, oh, I don't know, probably craning it to listen to the buzz of foreign conversations outside my door as people settled into their private Pullman roomettes throughout the night. I glance in the little mirror above the sink and see both apprehension and excitement in my eyes. Am I crazy to have agreed to this?

I climb back into my plain dress and shoes to meet Shifrah and Malone in the dining car and notice a folded piece of paper shoved under my door. It's from Malone, instructing me to pack my things, eat breakfast, and meet him and Shifrah in the first-class car where we are to ride for the remainder of the trip to Mexico City. My first orders from the man in charge. Why aren't we meeting for breakfast as planned? I don't know, but, one thing about it, Malone has beautiful handwriting.

"Can I help you, Miss?" a porter with a foreign accent I don't recognize asks as I stand with my train case in the aisle of the sleeping car feeling a mixture of aggravation and anxiety. I'm not exactly sure why I've worked myself up into a fit reminiscent of when I'm about to pull rank on a rude waitress, but I have, and I suppose it's because I feel insecure about my surroundings.

"Um, yes. Where are we now, I mean, where is this train inside Mexico?"

"Just south of Saltillo."

"When do we arrive in Mexico City?"

"This evening, Miss."

"Thank you. Can you direct me to first-class car number two?"

He points, and I walk through the sleeping car, passing through two enclosed vestibules and two more cars. I stop in one vestibule to look at the countryside, which happens to be a large, slightly green valley surrounded by rough-chiseled red mountains on one side and rounded ones tinted in purplish-brown on the opposite side.

I first spot Malone sitting tall in the seats behind Shifrah, an open newspaper held to the side so, I assume, he can keep an eye on things. I walk down the aisle and stash my small case under the seat beside the one Shifrah's sitting in. She's dressed in a stylish navy-blue dress with a wide pale-blue belt at the waist and white brocade around the neck. Her hair and makeup are perfect as usual underneath the bright red icepack on her head. She smiles and holds her half bottle of Coca-Cola toward me. "Good morning, Savannah. Did you sleep all right?"

"No complaints. You still have a headache?"

She groans, barely nods her head. "I'm cursed with these ghastly things, get them at the most unexpected times. They last all day, sometimes two days, and I never had a single one until the accid—uh, I mean, until a year or so ago."

"Did you say you had an accident?"

She waves my question off with a flick of her hand, looks out the window while fingering the embroidered collar around the neck of her dress. It's obvious she regrets her near slip of the tongue. I change the subject. "Did you take an aspirin?"

"Several."

I settle into the seat beside her, my *ruffled feathers* beginning to lie back down.

"Savannah?" she says in a faraway voice, still looking out the window.

"Yes?"

"Isn't life the strangest thing?"

Before I answer, I feel a tap on my shoulder, turn, and there's Malone standing in the aisle. His slight nod indicates he wants Shifrah's attention. I touch her arm, breaking her stare at the passing scenery outside the window.

"I'm going for a walk. You need food or more ice?"

She sighs, puffing out her cheeks. "Oh, I don't know. I haven't eaten since Nuevo Laredo last night. A little Melba toast might be nice. Oh, can you check if they have any tomato jam to go with it? If not, I'll take a bit of marmalade. Sweets sometimes help these headaches." She hands the icebag to Malone, hesitates releasing it. "Malone… hold on a minute." She reshuffles her body to face me. "You didn't eat in the dining car this morning, did you?"

"No."

"Are you hungry?"

"Not a whole lot."

"Malone, would you mind asking the porter to bring Savannah a full breakfast—eggs, waffles, cheeses, the works?" He walks away without answering.

"That wasn't necessary."

She smiles, leans her head partly on the seat and partially on the window. "We're on assignment, Savannah, but I haven't heard any rule that says we can't enjoy ourselves. As soon as this headache leaves, we'll talk about our wardrobe for when we depart Mexico City."

"Where are we going after Mexico City?"

"I have a few things I want to say before I answer that."

"Well, what I want to say is I've never seen a fancy red icebag like the one you just handed Malone."

"A gift from Mommykins. My family spoils me terribly, or, at least, they did."

My eyes follow the line of her dress down to her navy and light-blue high heels and back up. "From what I'm seeing, they still do. Shifrah, you're pretty much what we call in Texas *a fancy pants.*"

She chuckles lightly, braces her head. "A fancy pants? That's rich! I love your Texas accent and the way you say things, Savannah. It's quaint and honest. You know, I think I am a little hungry. I hope they have some Melba toast in that train kitchen. Do you know the history of it?"

"Of what?"

"Melba toast."

"I didn't know toast had history."

"Everything has a history. It's just that some of us aren't privy to all of ours, and that's okay with me. Anyway, the companion my parents hired when I was an adolescent—I think I mentioned her last night—she was kind of odd, but fun, and she told me unusual stories like this one about Melba toast. Dear Hilda. She retired a few years ago, went back to Sweden, but she said she planned to travel extensively. She shared oodles of things I never needed to know." Shifrah laughs, winces, presses fingers into her forehead. "You know, I think this blasted headache may be lifting a little, but it's leaving my whole skull sore.

"Back to my Hilda story. Melba toast is named after Dame Nellie Melba, an Australian opera singer who was very popular in the late 1800s. A well-known chef was so smitten with her, he created 'Melba' toast for her to nibble on while she was convalescing from a serious illness. He later created a worldwide famous dish and named it Peach Melba. Imagine foods being named after you! We can only conclude Dame Melba was extremely appealing to this chef, wouldn't you agree?" She concludes her story with a raise of her eyebrows and a playful smile.

I don't know the answer to her question, but I'm captivated by Shifrah's short story. No one at the Dixie ever discussed opera singers, the origin of foods, or anything deeper than the current prices of fuel, conditions for the growing seasons, the price of hay, weather, trucker wages, local gossip, that sort of thing. Discussing interesting topics in a regular conversation instead of reading about them in a textbook or hearing them in the lecture halls of college is a new experience for me.

"Is the story of Melba Toast what you wanted me to know before you tell me where we're going next and why I was asked to join this group?"

She chuckles. "Not at all. I do get sidetracked, don't I? Savannah,

Malone told me only this morning we're flying from Mexico City to Miami and then to Ecuador, and he doesn't have most of the travel accommodations set in concrete yet. He said it might be one of the toughest legs of our journey, so it looks like we're jumping into this expedition—or mission, as he calls it—head first."

"Ecuador?"

"Apparently, and if we can't acquire a certain object there, the whole trip might be canceled."

A wave of disappointment—or is it despair?—hits me like a splash of ice water in the face. "Something we need to get in Ecuador is that important? What is it?"

"I wish I knew. Malone only tells me pieces of the puzzle, no matter how I coax or plead or bat my eyelashes. He's immune to flattery of all kinds. He talks to our employer constantly but keeps most of it to himself."

I had assumed Shifrah was equally in charge of our operation. "You've never met our, uh, our employer?"

"No, I—"

We're interrupted by Malone striding down the aisle with Shifrah's icebag in his hand. Behind him, a smiling porter pushes a cart bearing several cloches, plates, rolled cloth napkins, silverware, and condiments. He pulls up nearly even with us and places a tray with short leg extensions over my lap. He tries to do the same with Shifrah, but she shakes her head.

"I'll share off Savannah's tray," she says. "Oh, look! You have Melba toast and, hmm… looks like a jelly I don't recognize."

"It's *marmelada de xoconostle*, Miss."

"Marma lah what? Savannah, what's he saying?"

"Prickly-pear jam. It's made from the *xoconostle,* a tart cactus fruit," I say.

"Um, okay. No tomato jam?"

The porter smiles. "Oh yes, I can get for you. I must tell you besides the fruit of the tomato, it has jalapeños and chipotles. Very nice, but some travelers do not understand the spicy flavors of Mexico. Shall I bring it to you? We have also a delicious tomato jam made with ancho chilis."

"What are ancho chilis?"

"They have a kind of a sweet raisin flavor," I say. "It's different, but tasty. We sometimes serve it at the diner when Maria gets a wild hair to can a batch of seasonal jellies."

"Hmm, bring both kinds of tomato jam, please." The porter tilts his head in approval, proceeds to fill a plate with some of everything. "Is that pickled herring on toast with cream cheese?" she asks, pointing to a side plate on the cart. Another nod is accompanied by a look of appreciation on the porter's face.

"I'll definitely have some," she says.

When the porter rolls the cart away, Shifrah gets on her knees to peer over the seats. "Write this down and send it to our boss, Malone. Tell him today I am wildly daring, headache and all. Imagine this New Yorker dining on Mexican hot-pepper jam along with pickled herring!"

"Let's save the daring for when we need it," he answers in a bland tone.

Shifrah flips back into her seat and plops the icebag on her head. "Killjoy," she mutters almost under her breath.

"Not much of a talker, is he?"

"Acts like he's still in the military." She salutes the air. "Oh, yes sir, Mr. Military Man."

"He was in the military?"

"Yeah. Army or Marines. I don't remember which, and I don't care. He's all business all the time. My gang and I would have called him a *stuffed shirt.*"

"Your gang?"

"Oh," she waves her hand in the air, "that was a long time ago. Just some free-thinking kids I hung around with in college. Say, let's nibble. I'm feeling slightly famished."

Shifrah's quick change of subject shouts to me she's hiding her past. Maybe that's how it is on the east coast. Where I'm from, folks tell it like it is, plain and simple. Of course, she and I barely know each other, so maybe that's the reason for her secretiveness.

I venture a safe question. "If you don't mind my asking, how old are you, Shifrah?"

She reaches for a piece of the toast topped with herring. Her sleeve recedes, and I see the end of a scar about half an inch wide on the inside of her arm. She sees me see it, pulls her sleeve down.

What is she trying to hide?

"I turn twenty-three in January," she says. "Say, I'd better eat a little before my sleeping pill takes over. I didn't sleep a lot with my head pounding last night. I already have a nice little pillow from the porter." She pulls a small pillow from behind her, places it on her lap. She helps herself to a half slice of wheat toast with herring as the porter brings a small tray with the tomato jams he explained earlier. She puts each kind on the end of a Melba toast and tastes it. "Gads, it's fabulous! Um-um, I'll have to tell Mommykins about these jellies. I wonder if we can buy them in New York? Okay, see you later, Savannah." She smiles, puts her pillow against the window, and closes her eyes.

Oh, great. What do I do now? It's a good thing I brought a book to read because I don't feel like plunging into conversation with Malone. Something about him, well… honestly, his no-nonsense demeanor is a little scary. I'll make sure I get some answers when we get to Mexico City. Shifrah's headache will be gone, and I deserve to know what I'm getting myself into. In spite of being so in the dark about this new job, if you can call it that, I have no regrets about accepting it. At least, not yet. What do I hope to gain from doing this? I think I mostly jumped at the chance to escape the small-town structure of my entire life. That's okay, right?

CHAPTER FIVE

We pull into the Mexico City train station at eight-fifteen p.m. Malone hails a taxi to take us to the Hotel Ritz, and I'm surprised how light Shifrah is traveling with one small suitcase and a matching train case. I brought more than she did, and that makes one more thing I'm curious about. I'm handling most of the communications in Spanish, which tells me that's most likely one of the reasons I was selected. Mexico and now Ecuador—two countries mostly speaking Spanish. Will there be more?

Outside the hotel, our baggage is handed to a grinning porter who can't take his eyes off Shifrah. Malone speaks to the hotel clerk inside, who is obviously bilingual, signs the registry, and brings us keys. "You two are bunking together from now on. Here's a key for each of you. I want you settled in before I pick up Reno."

"Oh, no you don't, Malone. Don't treat us like old ladies. My headache is gone, and the night is young. We're going with you to meet Reno, aren't we Savannah?" Two pairs of eyes stare at me, two in a scowling face and two silently beseeching me to agree.

"I, uh, I, sure, I'd like to meet our new partner tonight."

Shifrah graces me with a beaming smile. Malone rolls his eyes. "I leave this lobby with or without you in twenty-five minutes," he says, glancing at his watch and striding off toward the row of telephone booths across the lobby.

"You certainly are traveling light. It's not what I expected," I say to Shifrah once we're in our room.

"Isn't it disgraceful? If I had been allowed to bring what I wanted, I'd have at least ten giant suitcases brimming with clothing and accessories."

"You didn't mention any limits to me."

I didn't want to discourage you from bringing whatever you're comfortable with. I see that you packed very light anyway, Savannah."

I brought more clothes than I thought I'd ever need, more than I've ever shopped for at one time, and she thinks it's light?

"To be honest, it really makes no difference. Malone will be advising us on what we need for each destination and circumstance. Then, we'll most certainly shop excessively."

"Are you saying you're mostly in the dark about this, uh, whatever it is?"

"I know some of it, of course, but Malone is the communicator with the person he calls Mr. A. Facts have been doled out to me in pieces. Rest assured, all that I told you in the beginning is true. We are traveling to exotic locations to accomplish tasks that happen to be picking up some kind of artifacts that are crucial to something important, and we'll know what that is at some relative point, Malone promises. We'll be meeting a variety of people, and it's true after you fulfill your contract, you will be considered wealthy when you receive your bonus, which, because of its investment potential, will provide dividends from now on. That part I understand very well. My parents are into multiple investments."

"I have to say this is a little disturbing, Shifrah. I was under the impression you knew where we were going and why."

"If it were something to worry about, my parents would not have, I mean, Malone, uh, please don't worry about it. Malone is a very capable man. He won't lead us astray."

I ease down on one of the beds. "I hope you're right. Anyway, I've never thought about being a wealthy person."

"Money makes the world a better place, so it's fine to care if you have it or not. I love clothes, so I may care a bit too much. Hey, you look a little upset."

"I'm wondering if leaving Laredo was cruel to the ones who always looked out for me."

"Cruel? Savannah, consider this. When you return, you'll be a world traveler with astounding stories to tell anyone who wants to listen." She looks at herself in the mirror, combs a piece of hair with her fingers. "We'll be going back to the states for some of the *retrieves,* as Malone calls them, and we're also sailing on an ocean liner to somewhere after that. I haven't been on a cruise for oh so long, and won't it be exquisite to travel the seas? We'll buy the chicest clothes, have facials, massages…"

Her voice trails off as she lists all we'll do on a cruise ship. She shrugs. "I admit the Ecuador destination took me by surprise, but Malone said it was always the plan to go there first. All our other arrangements and timetables are subject to change depending on the people we have to engage with at different destinations."

"So, let me see if I have this right. We're traveling to places that you don't know, to pick up items Malone calls *retrieves,* but you don't know what they are, and we don't know how long this will take, and you don't know the final purpose or destination of our trip. Do I have it right?"

"Well, when you put it that way, um, yes."

I smack my forehead with my palm, shake my head. "Why am I not more rattled about all this?"

"Because it's mysterious and full of intrigue. Come on, admit this is more fun than pouring coffee and serving pie!"

Her eyes shine with fun. She's right, and I wouldn't go back to Laredo for anything right now, not until I get to live out all that she promised. I smile and nod.

"I knew you were the perfect one for this adventure. By the way, Malone told me the *retrieve* in Ecuador genuinely sets the pace and nature of our entire expedition, or mission, as he calls it, so it's critical for it to work out. More mystery!" She glances at her watch. "Oh, gosh, we have fifteen minutes before Malone leaves without us, and trust me, he will. Let's hurry!"

I open my train case, take out my toothbrush and paste.

"What are you wearing?" she asks, hurriedly slipping into grey slacks.

"You're changing clothes?"

"Of course, darling. We simply must wear our fancy lovelies and look like ritzy tourists out on the town in Mexico City! We'll be eating a late dinner, so we'll be rubbing elbows with the local sophisticates." She steps into the bathroom for a minute and returns wearing a sheer organdy blouse in mixed pinks and burgundies with lantern sleeves and a layer of material around the shoulders that appears to take flight with her slightest movement.

Watching her, I feel more like I should be milking cows and pitching hay instead of participating in some kind of international mystery mission. I bought several new trousers, tailored shirts, and four blouses before I left, but I'm not sure they're what Shifrah will call *fancy*. I take my two clothes items into the bathroom thinking how no one at the Laredo College dressed up for classes. In high school, I guess I didn't bother with anything that kept me from doing the things I loved—playing sports, engine mechanics, going hunting or fishing with the regulars. Maria, Tony's wife, wore colorful, embroidered shifts from Mexico and roses in her hair when she dressed up. Pretty, but not my style. Nifty uniforms, a dab of lipstick, and hairnets covering at least part of our hair at the Dixie have been my fashion totality in my other life. So, here I am ignorant of fashion and walking out of the bathroom feeling self-conscious beyond words. Shifrah is fluffing her hair, stops, smiles.

"That blue blouse looks nice with your blond hair, Savannah, but it's a teeny bit plain. I have just the thing to spritz it up, but we really must hurry. The clock is ticking!" She digs in her suitcase and brings out a scarf with small white feathers sewn around the edges. Before I can protest, she steps behind me and ties the scarf around my neck. She pushes it to the side with the knot below my right ear. She fusses with the creases and feathers until she's satisfied, stands back, smiles. "Perfect," she says. "You brought flats to wear with your trousers, right?"

"I brought the high heels you've already seen, hiking boots, and a pair of walking shoes. Shall I wear the walking shoes?"

"Let me see them."

I dig them out and hold them up.

"Hmm. I bet we wear the same size." Again, she plunders in her suitcase and pulls out a pair of cloth-covered royal-blue flats with a crystal flower on top. "I brought these to wear in case my heels were too uncomfortable on the train trip. I didn't realize we'd be sitting for so long."

"You mean sleeping, don't you? Thanks, but I can't wear those."

"Why not?"

"Well… they don't match?"

She chuckles. "You're wearing dark blue trousers, a pale blue blouse with a white and blue scarf. They match perfectly! But, listen, I know Malone won't wait one extra second for us. He's like that. Punctual to a fault. You can add more lipstick on the way to the lobby. I don't see a smidge of it left on your lips."

Maybe because I'm not wearing any.

I reluctantly slip on the prettiest shoes I've ever seen in my life. Stepping into the hotel hallway, I feel like a goose wearing a fancy bib and Cinderella's slippers, and the oddest part is I love having someone fuss over me like this. Is this what it's like to grow up with a mama, someone caring how you look and what you wear?

CHAPTER SIX

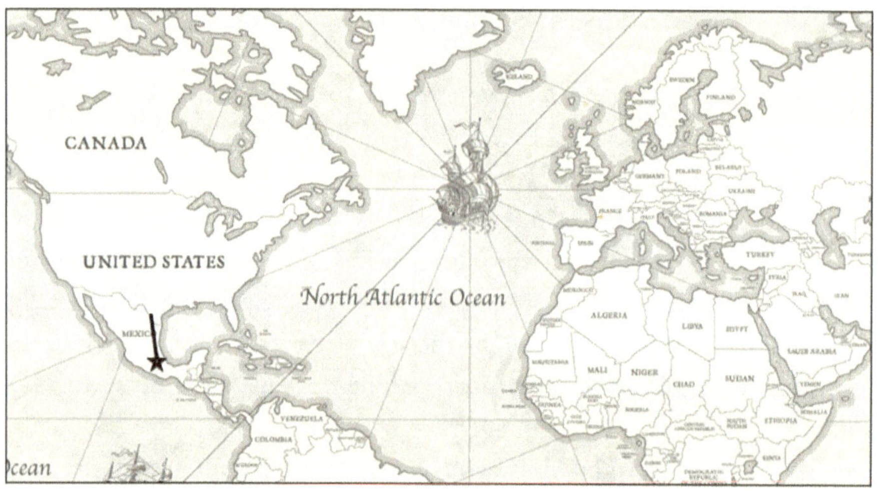

Shifrah told the truth when she said Malone wasn't susceptible to her feminine wiles. She's been working on changing his mind ever since we left the hotel, but he hasn't budged an inch.

"But why can't we go inside with you, Malone?"

"I already told you. Women are not allowed in Mexican cantinas."

"That's absurd. This isn't the Stone Age."

"I don't make the laws in another country. You two wait here in the taxi while I go inside and get Reno. I imagine he'll be plenty hungry after riding broncs and bulls in that big rodeo today."

"Rodeo?" both Shifrah and I say in unison.

"Well, shoots, I mean, shucks, Savannah. It appears we have an authentic cowboy joining us as a companion," she says, trying hard to sound Southern but failing miserably with her east-coast enunciation.

"Shifrah, don't try to talk like a Texan, please," I say, laughing.

"I thought I did quite well. How would you say it?"

"Like this… 'Well, now, it shore looks like we got us a gen-you-wine wrangler for a pardner. Isn't that somethin' to write home about?'"

"Oh, all right. I'll leave the Texas talk to you."

Malone stares at us like we're crazy, mumbles, "Stay put," and steps out of the taxi. Shifrah rolls down the window to say something to him, most likely a jab aimed at his restrictions, but our attention is drawn to the sound of shattering glass across the street. Two men just crashed through the large picture window in the front of the cantina. They awkwardly stand up, charge into each other, fall to the ground grappling and throwing punches.

Four men barge out the front door, and Malone is not trotting, but running, across the street. In what looks like a sped-up movie film, he punches the jaw of a man wielding a piece of pipe aimed toward the wrestling men. He whirls, punches another man in the stomach, grabs another by the collar and throws him several feet. The two ground wrestlers break apart and stand up. One wipes his eyes with the back of his hand and hurries to Malone's side. The remaining standing man and the other ground wrestler beat a quick retreat inside the bar. The ones Malone flattened earlier hurriedly follow suit.

It's hard to make out details under the cantina lights, but we see Malone and the standing man shake hands, talk animatedly. The man pulls a handkerchief from his pocket and wipes his face as he and Malone cross the street and walk toward us.

"Good gosh, Savannah! I believe that ruffian with Malone is our Reno," Shifrah says.

Reno's quick introduction to us is followed by a mumbled *Nice to make your acquaintance, ladies* as he mops dirt and blood from his face with an oversized handkerchief. His hair is full of dust, dried grass, and slivers of glass. Following Malone's unspoken directions, he climbs into the front seat with the taxicab driver. Malone scoots us over to ride in the backseat. No one says anything on the short ride to a saggy hotel hemmed in by a sea of wild blue agave cactus plants and outlined by dull amber lights.

Reno goes inside, and we sit in silence until Malone says, "That fight might have been a bit unsettling to you girls."

"We're not girls," Shifrah says.

"Excuse me… ladies." He clears his throat." I suggest you toughen up, starting tonight."

"Oh, I see, like shoe leather?" Her tone drips with sarcasm.

"Why not? You might see more of the same before our mission is completed."

Other than a few minor scuffles breaking out on the football and baseball fields in high school, or the time Tony physically threw a drunk hitchhiker out of the diner, I've never seen a real fight until tonight. Judging from Shifrah's demeanor after the brawl, I don't think she has either. Malone's capabilities in a conflict elicited a new brand of respect from me, and a little healthy fear at the same time. Let's just say, I wouldn't want to cross him.

Reno comes out of the seedy hotel carrying a tooled leather duffle bag and a canvas bag slung over his shoulder. When he opens the cab door, light finds him freshly cleaned up. His dark hair, vivid blue eyes, and wide smile showing rows of nice teeth shine through despite the cuts, bruising, and swelling on his face and neck. Shifrah and I swap looks that seal our mutual agreement of his surprising good looks.

CHAPTER SEVEN

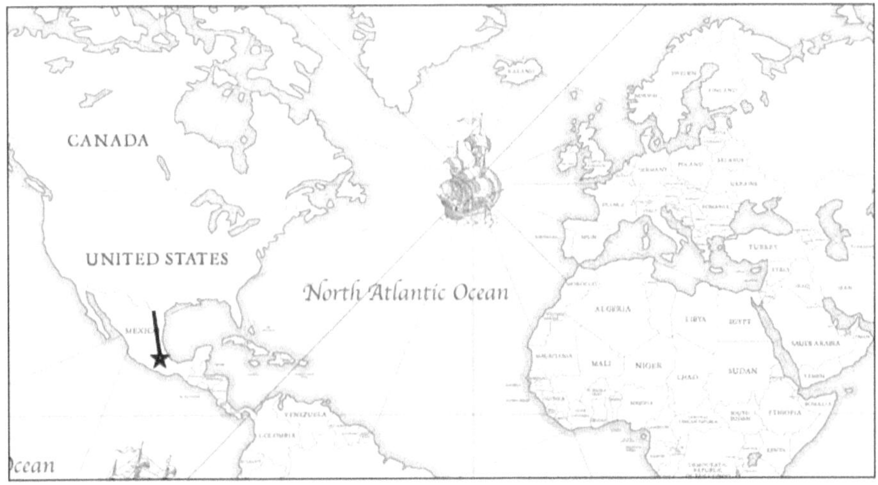

If I had met Shifrah only this evening, I would classify her as a New York snob. She's glancing around the restaurant making no eye contact with the rest of us sitting at the table. She takes long, dramatic draws of her Turkish cigarette and slowly blows smoke circles with her face pointed upward. It's the first time I've seen her using a bejeweled cigarette holder, and she does it with such elegance, it almost makes me want to take up smoking.

She's nursing a glass of imported wine and looks beautifully cold and perfect. Her level of citified sophistication bewilders me, and now I'm wondering if all this *show* is for our new and handsome companion, or if this is the way women *in the know* act in a public setting. So far, my small-town background isn't serving me very well out here in the world.

Malone, wearing his black-rimmed glasses, which I've noticed he puts on when he's all about the business at hand, is scratching out notes on a small pad of paper, purposely oblivious to all of us. Reno takes sips from his glass of 7-Up, puts it down quickly. He looks around the table to see if anyone is going to start talking, then pretends to study the various cuts and injuries on his sun-browned hands—hands, we have learned, that can manage bucking horses or crazed bulls. Hands that bust jaws, and, from my own personal imaginations, hands attached to arms that surely know how to hold a woman.

My last thought burns across my face. I sip my cold glass of Coke and reprimand myself. I have a strange history with the opposite sex, mostly none at all. After Daddy died, most of the regulars at the diner tucked me under their wings as tight as if I were their own kid. In time, they became overly protective. Did I have boyfriends? Not a chance. I wasn't really interested until my last few years in high school, but, by then, it did me no good. My self-appointed resistance squad was like a colony of bats with radar. Oh, they were plenty nice about it, informing any young man who started hanging around me that sort of attention aimed at Savannah wasn't allowed.

She's focused on her "edge-uh-cation" and her future, so you best be forgetting about those flirtations, son, they'd say in a hundred different ways. No mouse hightailing it across a field under a falcon's gaze was more watched than I by my regulars. Did I mind? I'd be lying if I said no because many times, it made me furious. I never stayed mad long. They showed up and rooted for me at all my competitions and taught me the *essentials* they thought I needed in life, things like hot wiring a stubborn truck engine that wouldn't start and the finer points of not losing a finger when catfish noodling. Every one of them would stand on his head for me, and I loved them even when they nearly suffocated me.

I step out of my own thoughts and look around the table at our group. Who are we? Will we ever feel like friends, or is that allowed? I've never eaten my last meal of the day this late before. Staring at the bubbles in my soft drink, I think how the Dixie Diner's second shift came through the back door in the kitchen hours ago, noisily visiting and calling out greetings to the kitchen staff. If I had been there, I would have given last-minute instructions to my night manager before going home to the little cabin behind Tony and Marie's home located a stone's throw from the diner. If a worker didn't show up, I subbed for him or her no matter what the job, and I never cared that I was sometimes so dog-tired I could barely see straight. It was the Dixie, it needed me, and that was all that mattered.

How did I release it so easily? I don't know, and the scariest thing is I don't seem to be missing any of it. What does that say about me?

Our waiter steps in to refill and replace our beverages. My Texan upbringing makes me want to start yapping my head off. Instead, I bide my time and scooch further back in my chair, smile at whoever catches me looking, then resume glancing around the restaurant. Are we the perfect quartet as Malone suggested to Shifrah, or will we turn out to be a pack of misfits?

"Look here," Reno says out of the blue. Shifrah jumps at the same time I choke on a mouthful of cola. She turns her head toward him with a practiced combination of both detached interest and tranquility on her smooth features.

How does she know all those beautiful mannerisms?

"I'm thinking I might ought to apologize for that barroom scuffle y'all saw outside Greg's little cantina. I don't believe in fighting when there's women around, but that fellow was in sore need of learning some manners. See, first, he accuses me of cheating in our little card game we had earlier, which was an out and out lie. When I told him so, he got his pants all bunched up and calls me a few names. Shoot, I can take that, I mean, I been through far worse, and besides, I was a little tired out from riding those two broncs and three bulls today at that *Rodeo Grande de Mexico* I promised an old friend I'd show up for. Boy howdy, that last bull was the meanest can of kerosene I ever met! He's the one did this to my face, planted my nose right in the dirt, the ol' scoundrel.

"Anyways, a little card playing and *dos cervezas* had me feeling about as mellow as a cat chasing a two-legged mouse, you know, so I ignored ol' smarty pants, figured he had too much to drink and best to let him stew in his own juices. That's when Juanita, the cantina owner's daughter, well, she comes from the owner's living quarters behind the barroom, you know, and she's just come out to tell me some guy by the name of Malone called on the phone and said he's coming to pick me up shortly.

"I'm mighty glad to hear that, so I mosey up to the bar for one quick shot of Jose Cuervo, my most favor-ite tequila, and that clown starts grabbing and kissing on Juanita when she walks by. I'm telling you this, she isn't but fourteen, sweet and innocent as all get out, and that gets my dander up real good. I tell him to lay off, and he insults my mama. I don't know about y'all, but where I'm from, that's a call to action. I just want to say I apologize you had to meet me first thing in such a commotion. I'm usually a real peaceful guy."

Shifrah has bent so far toward Reno while he talked, she's almost lying flat on the table. Her cigarette ash is more than an inch long, and her expression is pure dumbstruck. I'm used to rowdy male tales, but I don't think her big-city background has exposed her to anything like what she just heard. I stifle a laugh and decide she's what we call in Texas a female dude, that is, a *dudette—a female who puts on cowboy boots but can't walk in them.* I'm also thinking Reno's talent might be hypnotizing his audience with his handsome face and vivid storytelling.

"Reno, you know trouble follows you everywhere you go. You walk through a door and half the men inside get an urge to smash your face in. Good thing you were on the right side in the war, and now you know why I kept you on such a tight rein."

"Seems pretty dang true, doesn't it, Major. Anyways, if someone starts it, you know I'm up for finishing it."

Major?

Malone shakes his head as though remembering past experiences, puts both elbows on the table like he's about to huddle up and finally give us some facts, but our arriving dinner service interrupts the moment. When the waiter leaves, Malone says, "Okay, a few facts to chew on. Our entire mission will always be subject to change depending on weather, accommodations, that kind of thing. It's mostly maneuvered by headquarters and myself contacting, recontacting, and consulting with certain people for our *retrieves* in different destinations. You know that, right?"

Shifrah and Reno nod.

What do I know? Nothing, and where is headquarters? "Can you please tell me what the mission is? The purpose?" Every face turns toward me.

"In due time, Savannah, in due time," Malone says. He clears his throat. "As I was saying, our contact, um, DD, in Ecuador, is a difficult contact, to say the least. He's been in Ecuador so long, I believe he thinks differently than we do. I hear he's been living out that way for seven or eight years. Mr. A had a hard time locating him for most of those years. Anyhow, we can't leave Mexico until we have assurance DD can meet us in Quito, the capital of Ecuador. I figure we'll probably fly out of here to Miami since Pan American has a flight from Miami to Quito. Naturally, for safety reasons, we want DD to go with us to his village.

"Once we get to Quito, we'll fly small planes out to DD's village located in the rainforest. Our pilots may turn out to be the ones working for some of those jungle missionaries." He shakes his head. "Those guys are going to get themselves killed trying to westernize those tribes deep in the Amazon. Seems a fool's mission at best. You can't change what doesn't want to be changed, and that goes for people, too. Guess those guys are guided by something we don't understand. I give them credit for that.

"I tried to convince some of those CIMA people in Ecuador to give us a ride in one of their cargo planes once we arrive in Quito, but it was a no-go. That would have worked out real fine. Probably not enough airstrip for one of those things to land anyway."

Shifrah has extinguished her cigarette, sits up straight, still looks a little waylaid from Reno's action story. She clears her throat, "What's CIMA, Malone?"

"A mining company. Stands for Consolidated Industrial Mining Company, or something to that effect." He delivers a fork and knife so brusquely to his stacked enchiladas, it pushes the plate back a few inches. He moves the plate back into position and saws the tortillas at a more reasonable velocity. "Been working on that deal for a while. Got me nowhere. The last fella I talked to told me about the pilots bringing in supplies and whatnot to the missionaries, and suggested I contact them. I hope to find out something solid tomorrow. Now if I can just keep DD in one spot long enough…" He shakes his head, frowns.

"He giving you problems, sir?"

Malone raises a hand in a gesture that says the subject is now closed, then he concentrates on his food.

"What's it like to fly in a cargo plane? Cargo is big, so they must be large planes. Do they have stewardesses?" Shifrah asks.

"No, and I haven't secured us a ride in a cargo plane yet, Shifrah. Most likely, we'll wind up in Piper PA-12s. They're-pilot-plus-two-passenger planes. Small. Rough flying in certain weather conditions. Dangerous if not expertly handled, but we'll be all right. Might get us a PA-14 if we're lucky. They carry a pilot and three passengers."

"That's not big enough for all of us, either."

"That's why we'll need two planes."

"You really expect us to fly in a little tin can with wings with no stewardess or any amenities?"

"Absolutely, and this is your chance, all of you, to shop for clothes suitable for the rainforest while we're here in Mexico City. Our stay in Miami might consist of a quick plane change, so you best get your gear here. Nothing fancy. I'll give you Mexican cash in the morning at breakfast. Get you some sturdy lace-up boots for one thing. Tough leather, something a fang can't easily penetrate. Buy some waterproof rubber ones, too, if you can find any. Stick with khaki and greens. Tan and brown are okay. Black is too hot. It's going to be humid and wet there, so think about that when you buy your gear. They call it the dry season, but it still rains every day."

By now, half of his enchilada stack and part of his beans are gone. No nonsense. No time wasted. That's Malone.

"Did you say we need boots a fang can't penetrate? You mean like a snake fang?" Shifrah asks.

Malone nods.

"You're saying we're flying on Pan American Airlines to Quito from Miami and then taking squatty little planes into an Amazon Forest village where there are reptiles? Is it possible they have snakes as big around as this table in that jungle? I think I saw that in a Tarzan movie one time."

Malone stops eating for a few seconds, doesn't look up, resumes eating.

Shifrah sighs noisily, I think, to get Malone to look at her. He doesn't. "So, Malone," she says, "you're leading us into the depths of danger and yet you want us dressed in ugly colors like browns and khaki? That's a lot to ask of a woman, even for you."

"Safety first."

She sips her wine, studies her food, looks up. "I never thought we'd be contending with reptiles. You understand, don't you, that I cannot endure frightening creatures like snakes or spiders? I-I just can't. You wouldn't believe the terrifying experience I had in Saks Fifth Avenue one summer a few years ago. Is anyone up for hearing a real horror story?"

Both men eye her curiously. "I sure am," I say, and I mean it.

She smiles, leans back in her seat. "In a way, it was my own fault. I was desperate to find a Hermès Carré scarf before we left for the Hamptons for our annual vacation because you know what the wind does to your hair when you go boating, right? Frightful! Honestly, I don't know how I ever let it slip my mind that I hadn't purchased the perfect summer scarf to match my yachting outfits, and there I was in the accessory department of Saks, urgently shopping at the last minute. Traffic, time restraints, and the fear of not finding the right accessories are enough to make anyone swallow a tranquilizer or two, you know?"

She leans forward. "Thankfully, quite soon, I spotted the perfect scarf tied beautifully around a mannequin's hair, hair the same color as mine. What a relief! I put my hand out to feel the scarf, and there it was… a spider, just an inch from my hand! I nearly died of shock. Naturally, I screamed, and that brought salesladies and the manager, Mr. Briggs, running to my rescue. I couldn't talk, merely pointed at that horrid, hairy thing almost two inches long sitting on a fold of that lovely silk scarf. The manager valiantly flicked it off and crushed it with his shoe when it hit the floor. He said not to worry, it was a harmless spider, but that didn't help my nerves, not in the least."

She fans her face. "They escorted me to the lounge to recover and brought me a cool glass of tea from the famous tearoom across the street. Afterward, they gifted me the Hermès scarf I had admired, and well, I honestly think I deserved it after suffering such an ordeal. Besides, I'm a constant customer of Saks, or, at least, I was until-until lately."

She coughs lightly into the back of her hand. "You can well imagine my dilemma of forgetting the image of that spider before I tied the scarf around my hair for the first time, but I'm a trooper and, after all, it was a perfectly divine scarf that matched all my boating outfits. Oh drat, can you believe my heart is beating out of my chest right now simply from recalling that terrible experience?" She pats her chest and smiles a brave smile at us.

The dumbfounded expressions on Malone's and Reno's faces are so comical, I put my hand over my mouth to stifle a laugh.

"What, Savannah? 'Fess up, won't you?" Reno says, fighting to keep a grin off his face.

"Oh, nothing." I look at my hands.

"Savannah?" Malone says.

"Well, it's just that the only spiders we kill on contact in Laredo are black widows and brown recluses, but we rarely see any. The big wolf spiders or the jumping kind or whatever else, we just ignore them. Shifrah mentioned snakes, and I bet I've killed at least twenty copperheads, rattlers, and a few cottonmouths with my .22 pistol. Never give it a thought."

"You actually shoot snakes?" Shifrah asks, wide-eyed.

"Only if they look at me cross-eyed."

Everyone but Shifrah bursts out laughing. I feel I've earned some respect from the men, and that feels pretty good. Maybe I don't know how to dress and act like a New Yorker, but I sure as thunder know how to survive like a Texan.

CHAPTER EIGHT

Malone finishes his meal first, stirs restlessly in his seat, eyes us with a serious expression. “Eat up, crew. I have calls to make and wires to send tonight. The reception and service are usually lousy down here. We’ll meet in the morning for breakfast and a quick gab at 0600. That’s six o’clock for you civilians. That little café down the street from the hotel is walking distance, so we’ll meet there. Reno, you’re with me after we get the ladies back to the hotel. We’ll get that other matter, uh, squared away. Don’t forget to steer clear of the water down here everyone. Drink sodas or beer.”

“Or wine,” Shifrah says, draining her glass. She takes a few more small bites of her lobster tail. Malone pushes his empty plate to the side. He wipes his mouth with a napkin, places it on top of his plate, leans back in the chair. Shifrah pushes her uneaten food away, waves the waiter to our table and asks for a container to take her dinner to the hotel.

It's exactly how they were in the diner. She barely eats, and Malone has a voracious appetite. Total opposites.

"Sir, what's the plan when we get there to, uh, where is it?" Reno asks between bites.

"Quito."

"Yeah. That place, Uh, sir—"

"Just call me Malone, buddy. We're all on equal ground here."

"Are we, though?" Shifrah says sarcastically. "You get to tell us where we're going, what to wear, and everything else. You know I'm not used to this kind of life, Malone."

For a brief second, I notice a softening pass across his features, watch it dissolve the next instant. "Mr. A gives the orders. I carry them out," he says.

"Mr. A? Is he the guy with that locked—" Malone's furious look quiets Reno instantly. "Sorry, sir, uh, Malone. Yeah, uh, that won't happen again."

"The guy with what?" Shifrah asks.

Malone waves a dismissive hand at her, pivots to signal the waiter to bring our check.

"Excuse me, Malone, did I understand you to say we'll discuss everything in detail in the morning?" I ask.

"I said we'll talk over some things in the morning."

"But—"

"We'll know what we need to know when the time comes."

"I second that," Reno says, lifting his glass in the air with a smile that's surely broken a thousand hearts.

Outside the restaurant, the scene has drastically changed. The streets were filling up with people and cars earlier when we went inside, but that didn't prepare us for the throbbing mass of party-goers that gathered while we ate. People are dancing to street musicians, eating street foods, waving flowers and crosses in the air, carrying painted signs sporting likenesses of famous Mexican freedom fighters, and waving banners honoring the Virgin of Guadalupe, the Roman Catholic version of the Virgin Mary as she appeared to an Indian peasant in the 1500s, or so the legend goes.

"What in the—" Malone says, taking in the scene. "I saw some handbills posted in the hotel lobby about a parade or something tomorrow, but I didn't expect this. Why start so early?"

"I sure don't know, sir."

"I do," I say, and all eyes turn toward me. "Mexican history says that on this night, September 15, 1810, at 11 p.m.…" I glance at my watch, "…right about this time, Father Hidalgo walked into a parish church in Dolores, Mexico, and rang the bell. When the villagers came running to the church, he told them the time was ripe to revolt against the Spaniards. That started the revolution. Poor Father Hidalgo was later beheaded, and his little army of peasants, women, children, and grandparents, went back home. More brave priests later took up the fight, and the battle continued for ten bloody years before they finally gained their victory. Tomorrow is Mexico's Independence Day, and the festivities begin the night before."

"It's true," Shifrah says, staring at me.

"What's true?"

"What the communiqué says about you. You really are a history genius."

"I'm far from being a genius. I just happen to know a few things about certain countries, especially Mexico. Hey, what's the communiqué you're talking about?" I don't miss the quick look passing between she and Malone.

"Let's talk about it later in the hotel, okay?"

I start to mouth a protest when a series of pops sends Malone's hand sliding inside his suit jacket. A cluster of boys dragging strings of exploding firecrackers runs by us, brushing hard against Malone's legs and leaving a blue, smoky smell in their trail. Malone curses and slaps the dust off his pant legs. The sky lights up with a burst of fireworks to our right, and I watch the reflection in the eyes of the three people I am now linked to. Any lingering and idealistic notion that this expedition is a peaceful trek around the world dissolved a few seconds ago when I realized Malone is armed.

Is that bad?

Not to me. Whatever this is, it's already more exciting by a thousand volts than what I was doing day after day for years. But why is Malone carrying a firearm? Are we sort of like spies on a mission?

CHAPTER NINE

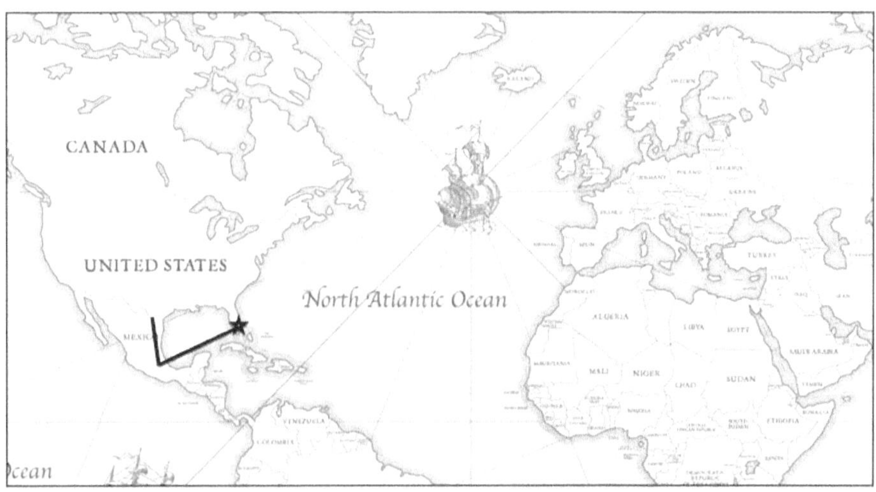

We end up being delayed in Mexico City for several days. We didn't attend a single bullfight, even after nearly everyone insisted we should. It seems to be the biggest draw for tourists in Mexico City, but seeing a bull stabbed to death isn't something any of us wanted to do. Besides shopping for clothes and boots, Shifrah and I found a bookstore. She bought six novels written in English and hasn't opened one. I bought a book written in Spanish about Ecuador, and I've been reading parts of it aloud to her every day.

At last, we get the green light, and here we are aboard a plane from Mexico City to Miami. Shifra and I nap, drink a lot of safe water, and chatter. She tells me she already decided I was the right person for the mission before she ever set foot in the Dixie Diner.

"Why?"

She shrugs. "I knew you were perfect from the, uh, the information we had, and when I saw your photo, I was entirely convinced."

"From my photo?'

"Uh-huh."

"That doesn't make sense."

"I'm psychic."

"You are not."

"Maybe not, but I'm very intuitive. I knew you were the right choice, and I was right. Malone agrees with me."

"When?"

"All along."

"Okay, so can you tell me how—"

"Oh, please excuse me, hon. I'm desperate to use the restroom," she says, rising from her plane seat. When she comes back, she feigns exhaustion and closes her eyes for a nap. Consequently, that's all I learn about why and how Malone and she were at the Dixie to offer me this opportunity provided I passed all their checkpoints. Why does she sidestep every opportunity for me to know why I was hired, and when will I feel like cornering Malone and asking him myself?

* * *

Shifrah didn't follow Malone's clothing rules, and I can't imagine what he'll say or do when she shows up wearing her new blouses in purples, yellows, corals, and bold prints. She bought fashionable leather boots with a slight heel and a pair of maroon galoshes. I'm wondering why she seems to purposely do things to annoy him, but I learned working in the diner to keep my nose out of other people's business unless something involves me or someone close to me. Whatever happens concerning those outfits is between them, and to be truthful, I can't wait to see his reactions.

Right now, she's leaning so far over my shoulder to look at the photos in my book on Ecuador, I'm about to fall out of my chair.

"Tell me more about the pirates."

"I'm going to fall on the floor if you don't back up an inch or two, Shifrah."

"Of course. Foolish me." She exhales loudly. "I'm so bored, Savannah. Malone has to locate that DD man again so we can leave this Miami hotel room. All these days literally locked up when there's an exotic city outside this hotel calling my name." She steps to the window. "Look at those palm trees swaying in the ocean breeze. I should be walking along the sandy shore in my purple kaftan, a Mai Tai in my hand, admirers asking me to join them this evening to dine and dance on the beach. This is cruelty."

"If he suddenly reaches DD, how will he contact us so we can quickly catch our plane, Shifrah? That could mess up the whole plan."

"You're always so logical. So painfully logical."

"Managing a diner and staff made me this way. Didn't the communiqué tell you that, too?" I never miss a chance to throw the communiqué up to her because she still isn't giving it up. I did find out I'm supposedly one of many candidates considered for this expedition of mystery, and she explained she and Malone were checking off a list of my behavior traits and abilities when they visited the Dixie so many times.

One question *partially* answered. So many to go.

"Please read about the pirates again," Shifrah pleads from the bed.

"Unless you want me to make something up, there isn't much else to say except English pirates used the Galápagos Islands to hide out and rob Spanish treasure ships. Sometimes the English were successful, and sometimes they suffered the biggest losses."

"Serves them right. I wish we could go see the Galápagos Islands when we travel to Ecuador. I want to see turtles that live a hundred and fifty years, iguanas, and exotic birds of every color."

"We'll probably see plenty of exotic birds and animals when we go into the rainforest."

"That's what I'm afraid of, but they might be the dangerous ones. She sighs, flips onto her stomach. "Why didn't we plan to meet our contact somewhere besides Quito? You know I'll surely get one or ten of my headaches there. What's that elevation again?"

I thumb through the index, open a section, and read, "Quito sits in a mountain valley at 9,350 feet above sea level."

"Oh, groans. You know what happens to people at those heights, don't you? Dizziness, breathlessness, and headaches. I hope we won't be there long."

"You know what Malone said, that if everything goes according to plan, we're leaving Quito right away and flying to DD's village in the jungle where there's a strip cleared for small-plane landings. Our contact keeping a mysterious *retrieve* in an Ecuadorian rainforest is making me wildly curious about it."

"Me too. Maybe it'll help us figure out the ultimate objective of all this traipsing around."

"You honestly don't know, Shifrah?" She shakes her head. "Why did you agree to tag along if you didn't know what it was?"

"I-I, well, I'm along for different reasons."

"Like what?"

"Nothing to bother you with right now. Obviously, Malone knows everything, and I half way believe Reno does too, but he's as impenetrable as Malone. I've already tried to wheedle information out of him. He only gives me that sumptuous smile and busies himself doing something else. By the way, have you noticed how ridiculous women act when he's around? It-it's foolishness."

"And you're immune to his charms?"

"He's a flutter bum, for certain. No, I'm not entirely resistant, but I-I, well, I gave my word I'd finish this-this mission. I think it's best if the sexes stay on the formal side with one another during this ordeal, don't you? You and I can be best friends if we want, but that's completely different."

I've already had that talk with myself about our handsome companion, and I made up my mind I'm not succumbing to any of his charms or looks if he sends them my way. He isn't a flirtatious man, which is honorable and makes it easier. I've seen and met a lot of men in the diner over the years, but never one quite like Reno. He doesn't seem the least bit prideful, and that makes him even more attractive. The poor guy can't win. I'm not so sure Shifrah is being completely honest. She gets a little on the giddy side whenever he's around.

"What's a flutter bum?"

She laughs. "Oh, that's my friend Zellie's lingo for a handsome guy. She was in our gang, er, I mean group, and she used so much street slang, it was like deciphering a code trying to understand her."

She moans and turns on her side. "Oh, Savannah, I want to go out dancing and sip exotic drinks by the ocean. We're in Miami, for Pete's sake!"

"When this is over, you're free to go and do whatever you want, right?"

"Of course. I'm, uh, free right now. I'm doing this because I-I… look, I'm sorry, Savannah. Don't listen to my complaints. I'm spoiled. That's the truth of it. Breaking out of my regular habits is hard."

"What do you mean?"

"Suffice it to say, I made some mistakes and I'm paying for them."

If she didn't look so sad, I would have bombarded her with more questions. One thing is clear… she has a lot of secrets. My biggest question is why a delicate woman like Shifrah is on this mission at all.

Why are any of us on this mission?

Malone has obviously been hired at a substantial rate of compensation, I presume, and he's merely doing his job. Reno served under Malone in the Army, we all see that, so he's doing it from loyalty and, most likely, for the money, too. Let's face it, you don't get rich doing rodeo favors and hanging out in Mexican cantinas. Shifrah's motives remain a mystery.

And you, Savannah?

All I know is something in my nature was waiting to be released, and this opportunity was the exit door, or something like that. The idea of being financially set isn't too bad, either.

As usual, Reno and Malone meet us for dinner in the hotel restaurant. I've stopped calling it supper because Shifrah says supper is a post-midnight meal after dancing and clubbing. That's a foreign concept to me, but I stopped calling the evening meal *supper* immediately.

Along with our menus, we are served iced water we can safely drink, and I never realized how wonderful that is until after our extended stay in Mexico. Malone and Reno order tall beers in frosted mugs. Shifrah orders wine with a French name. I order a soft drink, and I don't like how they all look at me every time I do that. I'll try an alcoholic drink when I'm good and ready, and they don't need to pressure me. I've been calling my own shots for a long time, and I'll be the one to decide when or if it's time for my next steps.

"Damn, that fellow can't sit still five minutes," Malone says as soon as we open our menus. "He's been in Quito twice since we were in Mexico. Once, he left for the village where he lives, I think it's in, oh, I don't recall right now. He came back to Quito real quick, I line up pilots ready to fly us to his village, and off he goes again taking a group of Hungarian scientists to some remote location. Left word he'll most likely be back tomorrow. Yeah, I'll believe it when I see it." He takes a long swig of beer, draining half his mug. "Needs a hard lesson in punctuality," he mumbles, staring at the menu.

"Or a good punch in the nose," Reno says, which makes Shifrah and me chuckle.

Malone's austere look quells our laughter. Before our food is served, he's paged for a phone call. Returning, he says, "We're set. A change in geography, but it'll work. Be in the lobby with your gear ready to depart at 0500. Dress accordingly as we previously discussed."

CHAPTER TEN

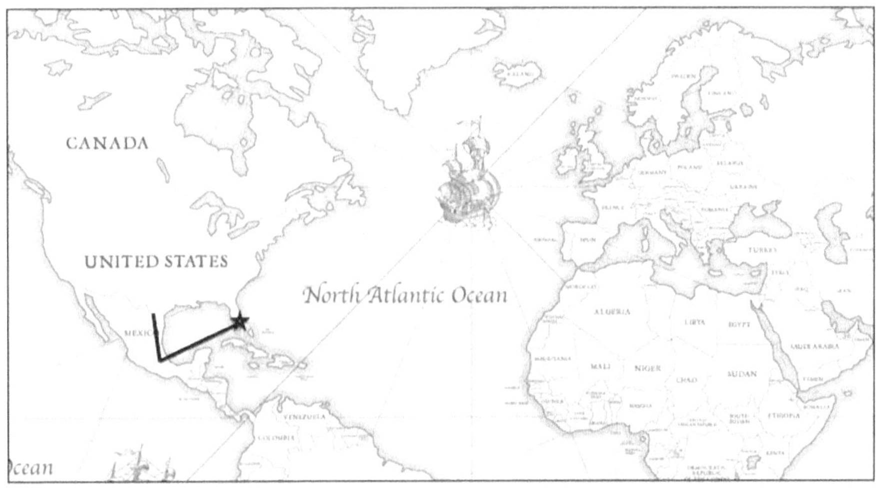

Imagine me with my head wrapped in tin foil. No, I don't have silver foil on my head but I do have round pin curls with bobby pins sticking out in every direction. It's Shifrah's doing, and she tied a scarf around the whole mess so the pins won't fall out while I sleep. She laughed when I asked her if she thought a woman should look glamorous even when she's going to a jungle the next day.

"Doesn't everyone think so? We owe it to the world to always look our best, Savannah. Besides, I'm taking oodles of photographs with my fancy Zeiss-Ikon Contessa 35 camera Daddy bought me for Christmas. I need to practice with it before I forget how to use it. It's quite complicated, you know. Don't you want to look your best in my photographs?"

"You've taken too many of me already."

"I'm just getting started."

"I look like one of those ridiculous characters in a space helmet in that terrible movie I let Darlene and Bonnie talk me into going to last year."

"Oh, what was that?"

"You've never heard of it, I'm sure. It's so dumb."

"Sometimes my friends and I went to dumb movies just so we could have laugh fits. What was it?"

"Destination Moon."

"Hmm. I must have missed that one."

"You're lucky."

She turns her attention back to packing her suitcases, and I decide that since I'm the one from the small Texas town, maybe she's right. I'm just glad none of my regulars from the Dixie can see me like this. I think about what I'd be doing at home in Texas tomorrow morning instead of flying at the crack of dawn to the country of Ecuador. I'd be unlocking the diner's front door and turning the OPEN sign outward after checking, and probably helping with, the morning activities in the kitchen—activities that start at 4:00 every morning. That's when Tony and Bert start rolling out pie dough, baking bread, assembling lasagnas, stews, and casseroles, cutting pounded round steaks into strips for frying into steak fingers, and doing whatever else is required for that day's menu.

A pang of missing Tony hits me. I nurse it only a few minutes, then push it aside. He's all right. Everyone is all right. No need to let myself get emotional right now.

"It's proper that we toast our departure tomorrow. Let's toss a coin to see who goes to the lobby for Cokes," Shifrah says when we finish packing.

I lose, give her a false frown, and dip into my coin purse for the money. "Wait a minute. I can't go to the lobby with this mess on my head. I look crazy."

"You're wearing one of my favorite designer scarves over that so-called *mess.* No one will see you, no one important, anyway. You lost the wager, Savannah, you have to go," she says with an impish smile.

Never in my life did I dream I'd be seen in public with pin curls and a scarf on my head. I hurry down the hall, press the elevator button, and wait to die of shame. The doors open, and no one is inside. My face is hot as I step out of the elevator into the lobby. People are going in all directions, but they don't appear to care what I look like, or even that I exist. I pretend I'm Shifrah with an uplifted chin and a detached look on my face and head for the thick row of decorative potted palms and ferns indigenous to Florida. Behind the plants is a short hallway with a row of vending machines selling soft drinks, candy, and gum.

My coin poised above a slot in the soft drink machine, I pause to listen, wondering if it's Malone's and Reno's voices I hear. It is. As their voices grow louder, I duck behind the last machine in the row of machines. I refuse to be seen like this.

Darn you, Shifrah!

"Coke or 7-Up?" Reno asks.

"Coke. Yeah, anyway, I tried, but he seems dead set on them going everywhere with us on the mission, and I do mean everywhere," Malone says.

"He knows how dangerous that bunch of trees and water can be, doesn't he?" Reno asks.

"Sure he does, but I'm getting the idea that's the point."

"What is?"

"That he wants them tromping through the thick of everything, no matter how difficult."

"Really?"

"Yeah," Malone says with a sigh. "My gut's telling me that's the way it's going to be. We discussed this a little at the beginning, but I didn't think he was really serious. I mean, the rainforest? One thing about it, we have to keep Shifrah away from DD. That's crucial. I tried explaining things to him on the phone, but with the bad connections and static, I had to stick to the facts. We can't have him spouting off if I haven't had a chance to talk to him first. I'm leaving the gals in the planes while we get the *retrieve*. That'll keep them above and around the forest but not in it."

"But you had them buy all that gear for going in the jungle."

"Yeah, I know. It'll come in handy other places we go. Besides, Shifrah has to shop real often or she gets down in the mouth. Just her nature."

"Bet that's right," Reno says with a chuckle. "You kind of like ribbin' her, too, don't you?"

Malone chuckles. "Let's just say I don't mind."

"Sir, how big is that *retrieve* we're getting from DD?"

"About the size of a piece of typing paper, I'd say, maybe a tad smaller. Mr. A wanted it placed in a leather pouch for shipping, and he gave me the dimensions for buying one. Found a good one in Mexico City. We're shipping it to him special airmail as soon as we can from the States. He doesn't want us carrying it around while we're getting the other *retrieves*. Makes sense. He's made it clear it's the one object we must have or the mission fails."

"Shoot, that's interesting, isn't it? This is stacking up to be a mighty exciting deployment, sir. I appreciate you letting me join in."

"Have to keep you out of trouble somehow, Reno. Anyway, you'll have your work cut out for you. Count on it. Keep your eyes peeled, too. I'm hearing a little rumble about some things that might concern us. I'll let you know when and if we need to be more cautious. And, Reno, for lord's sake, don't get yourself in any more tight squeezes like that one in Mexico City."

"Ah, sir, that was a pure-dee ol' accident. I never promised to marry that girl, honest to Pete I didn't. Never mentioned any such thing. I only told her she was pretty as a picture and that I liked her family. She's the one who invited me to supper at that big fancy house of theirs. How did I know bringing her some roses and accepting a supper invite meant I was proposing marriage? Her daddy is an official of the city, so you'd think he'd have more horse sense than that, wouldn't you? Anyways, thanks for getting me out of it, sir."

"Like I always say, Reno, trouble follows you like a shadow. Keep your wings tucked in real tight, uh, with everyone, while we get this mission accomplished, okay?"

"Yessir, I sure will."

"And Reno?"

"Yessir?"

"Drop the *sir.*"

"Huh? Oh, yeah. Sure is hard, though, after what we been through, and you being my commanding officer and all. I don't talk about it to anyone, sir, uh, Malone, but I-I still get a little, uh, you know, mixed up sometimes. I hear things when I don't know if I'm sleeping or awake. Worse one is that whine, that sound, of a plane nosediving to the ground or into the ocean. Machinegun fire might start ringing in my ears any ol' time, even when I'm getting myself cleaned up or riding a horse or...

"Anyways, sometimes I hear orders barking out of nowhere and getting cut short right in the middle. Men screaming. That stuff goes to circling around in my noggin and—."

"I know. I know." Malone says in a low voice. He clears his throat. "It's tough, damn tough, Reno, but you're tougher, son. I've seen it time and again. I have no doubt you'll be fine. Hey, we whooped their asses, didn't we?"

"We sure did, sir! Heck, that makes it all worth it, doesn't it?"

"You bet it does. We went in there and did what we were supposed to do. Got the job done."

Reno whistles. "You ain't just a'whistling Dixie. You know, none of that commotion over there makes any sense, people so danged eat up with meanness…"

Their voices recede. I ease out of my hiding place and drop coins in the vending machine in slow motion. It's going to take some time to absorb everything I overheard, and I already know I'm keeping it to myself. One thing I'm positive about, I'm proud to be in the company of men like Malone and Reno. I don't know much about the military or war, but I'm pretty sure I know a couple of war heroes now.

THE AMAZON

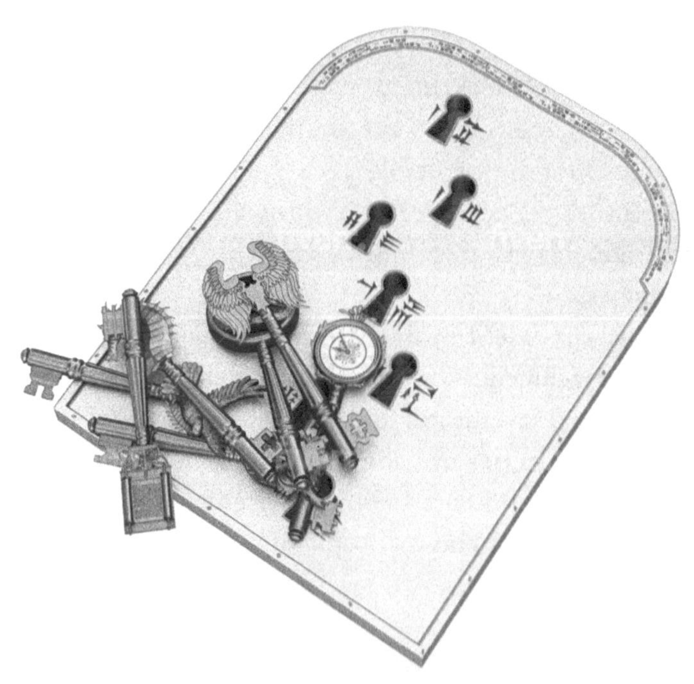

CHAPTER ELEVEN

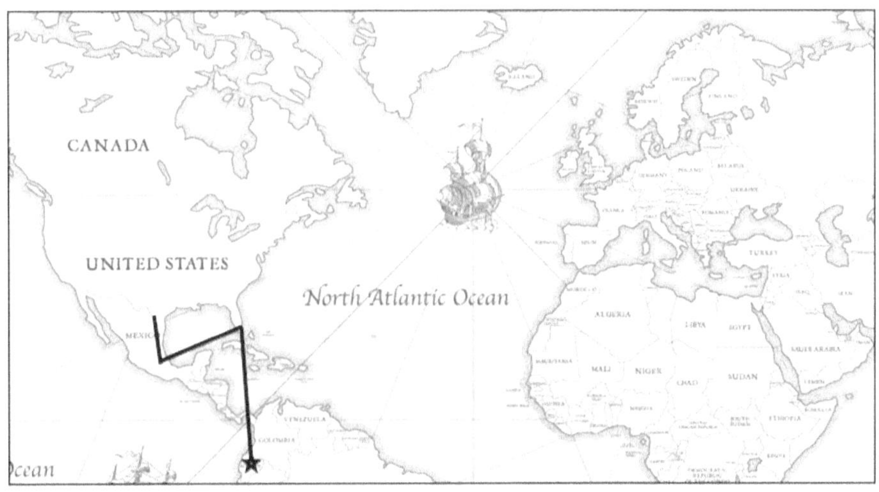

A popular saying in Texas is someone is as *mad as a hornet.* I personally never encountered hornets in Laredo, but I think I'm seeing someone as mad as one right now. Malone is buzzing around the airport terminal, back and forth, in and out of the exit doors, and I'm pretty sure if DD were here, he'd happily sting him repeatedly.

Malone was being paged as soon as we came through the terminal doors at the *Mayor Galo de la Torre* Airport here in Tena, the capital city of the Napo Provence in Ecuador. The message over the loudspeaker was in Spanish, but there was no need for me to interpret it.

"That better not be DD messing us up again," Malone muttered before heading toward the customer assistance area. We watched the uniformed employee hand him a piece of paper. The way Malone slung his head after reading it reminded me of Bert's ornery bull, *Cisco Kid,* and how he slings his head right before charging, even charging Bert when he scatters hay or feed for the crazy thing.

Malone hustles out the entry door, back in, makes a line or two back and forth in the lobby, then walks toward us. One look at his red face and Reno, Shifrah, and I know to take cover. We quickly obey—as people do when there's an angry person in their midst—his unspoken directions as he herds us away from the sparse crowd.

"Damn that guy," he spews as soon as we were off by ourselves. "I changed all the tickets to get us here from Quito, closer to his forest settlement for his convenience. Yeah, his convenience, and now he's gone again!"

"He isn't here?" Reno asks, frowning.

"I have pilots and planes waiting for us right now, and that son of a..." Malone catches himself, presses his lips together.

"Where is he?" Shifrah asks.

"The wire says he went back to his village. He couldn't wait a few more hours for us to get here? When we were in Miami, I tried talking him into bringing the *retrieve* here to Tena, but he was dead set against it. Said I'd understand when I see where he's been keeping it. Sure as hell would have saved us a lot of trouble."

"Did he offer any explanation for not waiting for us?" I ask.

"Says his wife took ill."

"That sounds legitimate."

"Not when he's already held up our operation this long. We have a schedule to keep, but I guess he's too acclimated to his jungle life to give a damn." Malone takes off walking again, this time back and forth in front of the windows, constantly looking outside at the airstrip.

"I've never seen Malone like this," Shifrah says. "I almost wish I had on a drab khaki shirt instead of this delightful mint-green one. Maybe he'd be less upset if I had followed his dress code."

"Nah, he'll be okay in a minute or two. He doesn't give two shakes about you wearing your pretty little shirt, Shif. That guy throwing a wrench in his schedule, well, that's another thing. You don't ever want to get Malone too riled up," Reno says, shaking his head. "It, uh, doesn't bode too good."

Shifrah lights a cigarette, blows out a stream of smoke. "I'll keep that in mind," she says. "Frankly, I thought he'd at least mention this shirt, get piqued at me or something."

It's becoming clear to me Shifrah needs Malone to pay attention to her, and he isn't complying. Does she miss her dad that much, or does she merely need gobs of attention from everyone around her? One thing about it, she looks elegant today wearing light-tan dungarees, a matching jacket that extends below the waist and a pale-green collared shirt underneath the jacket, knee-high leather boots, and a wide, camel-colored leather belt circling the jacket and accenting her slender waist. Her hair and makeup are, as always, flawless.

Every morning, she has me going in circles. I'm used to starting my day by brushing my teeth, washing my face, fastening my hair in place, and dressing. That's all, except for an occasional touch of lipstick. Shifrah was horrified when I explained my usual daily routine to her.

"Oh, Savannah, how primitive!" she'd said, eyes wide and peering straight into my fear of being a country bumpkin. That resulted in us spending at least forty wasted minutes every morning *making ourselves beautifully presentable,* she calls it, and that causes us, with Malone's propensity for early meetings, to rise earlier than I ever did for early-morning fishing trips with my regulars and even earlier than when I opened the diner for Tony when he took his annual vacations.

She still hasn't convinced me to wear eye makeup, but she says she will soon. I figure she might have a comeuppance on that. I may not be sophisticated, but I'm nobody's pushover. I keep agreeing to what she wants me to do because, to be honest with myself, I love the way she fusses over me like a sister might. Or a mama.

True to what Reno said, Malone joins us in a few minutes noticeably calmer. "Listen up. Go use the latrines. Splash some water on your faces. Don't drink any, though. Get yourselves a bottle of soda pop and a bar of candy or something out of the vending machines. If we hustle, we'll be back here in Tenu in time for dinner." He checks his watch. "You got fifteen minutes." He half folds, half crumples, the paper with the wire from DD and stuffs it inside his shirt pocket. "DD sent navigation instructions for the pilots…" he says to Reno as they stride toward *el baño des hombres.*

Sixteen minutes later, we exit the terminal and head toward a cluster of small planes parked next to a row of hangers alongside the airstrip. A man standing by a plane larger than the other small planes is holding a sign with Malone's name written in large letters.

"What the…?" Malone says. "Where are my two pilots with the Piper PAs? That can't be our plane and pilot."

The man steps forward with his hand outstretched. *"Bonjour, monsieur!* You are Malone?" He has a heavy French accent, gray hair, a silver moustache, and a slight bow in his back, but his face is shiny with friendliness.

Malone shakes his hand. "I'm Malone. What happened to my other pilots and the Piper PA-12 and 14?"

"Ah, it is regret your Piper PA-14 pilot had *d'urgence* in his family and he flies back to Columbia."

"What happened to the other plane and pilot?"

"Heureusement pour vous, monsieur, je connais ces pilotes. Frères. Ils ont étudié pour devenir pilotes au Canada. They are my friends. De bonnes personnes, mais un frère ne volera pas dans la jungle sans l'autre frère parce qu'ils sont superstitieux. Très stupide, right?"

"What the hell is he talking about?" Malone says, his former irritation slipping back on his features.

"He says the two pilots are brothers, and they became friends of his when they took pilot training in Canada. One brother won't fly into the rainforest without the other because they're stupidly superstitious," Shifrah says.

"You speak French, Shifrah!" I exclaim.

"Everyone speaks French in my, uh, *neck of the woods,"* she says with a wink.

Malone points at the plane. "A DHC-2 Beaver made by de Havilland, right?"

The man shakes his head vigorously and launches into a whole stream of French conversation. He smiles, gestures, turns back and forth toward the plane and us. Shifrah listens, nods, touches him on the arm as a gesture of interruption. She turns to Malone, the breeze lifting her hair slightly.

"I'll try to interpret what he says, but it's almost Greek to me. His name is Jacque, by the way. I gather he thinks this is the greatest plane in the whole world, Canada's pride and joy. He says it has amazing lift power. It can take off and land on a 1,000-foot dirt airstrip. He says the stall is unequaled by any other small plane. What's a stall?"

"I believe he's saying *STOL*, Shif, and it means Short Takeoff and Landing," Reno says. "If it can take off and land on a 1,000-foot airstrip, he's right. Malone, you heard about those Beavers used by the Army in the recent Korean theater, didn't you?"

Malone nods, still looks perturbed. "Yeah, beat out the Cessnas by a mile.

"Is this really one of those babies?" Reno walks to the plane and runs a hand along the side of it.

"US Army ordered more than nine hundred of them," Malone says.

Reno whistles. Jacque breaks into more French.

"He says they're made of all metal, they carry six people, and they can be amphibious," Shifrah says.

"Amphibious?" I ask.

"They can land on water," Reno says. "Say, how long is that cleared airstrip in DD's village, Malone?"

"I'm headed back in the terminal to borrow their short-wave radio. I'll let him know we're on our way and he damn sure better have enough airstrip for us to land this plane. Reno, get our gear loaded up so we can take off pronto." He pulls out the folded paper from the shirt of his bush jacket. "Give this to the pilot, er, Jacque, Shifrah."

CHAPTER TWELVE

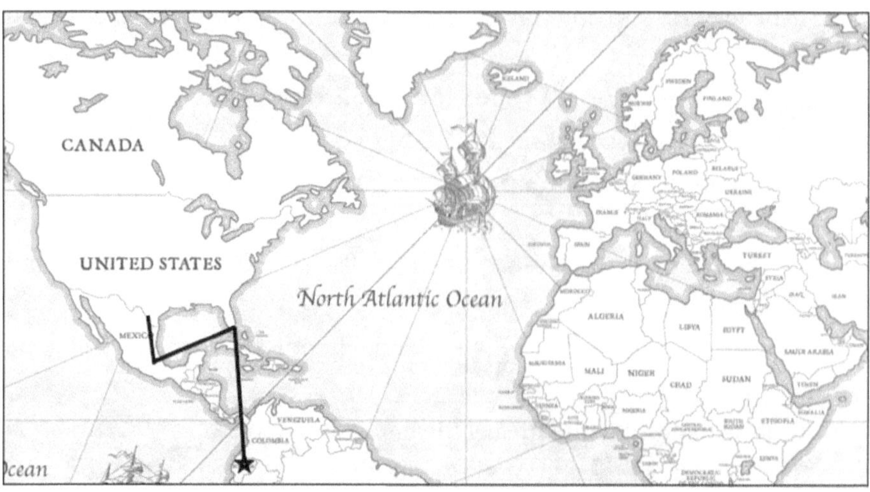

From the look on Reno's face when he turns to grin at us, which is often, he's in hog heaven in the copilot seat. Shifra and I took the two seats behind the cockpit, and Malone is behind us with a leather pouch on his lap—I assume the one for the *retrieve*—maps and papers scattered on the empty seat beside him. He's wearing his black-frame glasses, and from my own interpretation, he is, as usual, intense.

I'm not used to a man like him, a hound dog on the hunt leaving no stone unturned. No nonsense, no distractions, and nothing like my daddy was or how Tony and my trucker and rancher regulars are at the Dixie. Their way of handling pressure is to go fishing, take a horseback camping trip with their buddies, or drink coffee and gossip over a big plate of chicken-fried steak and gravy. Maybe Malone is carrying a load bigger than the rest of us realize. Something sure keeps him in a stew.

The view outside my plane window is startlingly beautiful. I still have a hard time believing this gal from Laredo, Texas, is now buzzing around seeing parts of the world most people will never see. I wish I understood more of why I was chosen and what this mission is about, but not knowing is okay as long as I get to do what I'm doing. At least for right now.

"Have you ever seen so many trees in all your life, Shifrah? They remind me of a giant bunch of broccoli heads all squashed together good and tight. I wonder how any sunlight breaks through that canopy of green?"

"What?"

I say the same thing again, louder. Shifrah peers out the window, leans her head back against the seat.

"Do you know how many things you equate to food, Savannah?"

"What?"

She repeats what she said.

"Do I?"

She leans close. "Yes, a lot. I suppose it's to be expected since you've been serving food your whole life. To answer your question, it only looks scary to me. It doesn't look anything like flying over Florida or Hawaii."

"Hey, Shifrah," Malone says loud enough for us to hear without his leaning forward. "Ask our pilot if he thinks he can get us to DD's Pastaza River settlement in less than an hour. Says here on the map, it's a little over eighty flight miles from Tena, and it's located less than a quarter mile north of the river at the navigational points DD sent me in the wire. Reno already gave him the points, so—"

"Malone, what in the world are you talking about?"

"Just ask him the ETA."

"The what?"

"Ask him how long before we land."

Shifrah leans forward and speaks French to Jacque, leans back, says, "About twenty minutes."

"Not bad, not bad," Malone says, barely loud enough for me to hear him.

"This little Beaver sure is a dandy, Malone," Reno calls from the front. "I'm getting why the Army bought so many. Bet they do the trick for search and rescue or flying into about anywhere you fancy. It's a funny thing how I'm more at home here in the sky than anywhere on the ground. You ever feel like that, sir?"

Malone doesn't answer. Reno turns back in his seat, and again, Shifrah and I exchange looks that solidify our mutual admiration of his looks. Today, he's wearing chocolate-brown bush pants with a matching over jacket belted at the waist like a real jungle outfit you see in the movies and dark-brown cowboy boots. His eyes are startlingly blue above those brown clothes, and when he puts his cowboy hat on, all you see are blue eyes and dark eyelashes—except when he flashes that smile with all those white teeth, of course. Shifrah and I have discussed the mystery of why he hasn't been claimed yet and came up with the idea that he probably enjoys playing the field. Lord knows he most likely has a field bigger than the state of Texas to choose from.

Malone taps Shifrah and me on the shoulder at the same time. We turn and see him scooted close to the back of our seats. "You two stay in the plane when we get to the village. We'll get the *retrieve,* load up, and be on our way. We'll eat in Tena tonight, fly out of there in the morning. Next stop in our mission is going to surprise you. We'll talk about it over dinner."

"You're kidding, right?" Shifrah asks, twisting all the way around in her seat.

"I don't kid about anything important."

"You can't expect us to not see that village or meet that DD character or anything else after all we went through to get here. We're in the Amazon jungle, for Pete's sake, and we want to see it."

"I do expect it. Both of you stay put." He settles back into his seat, and I think about the conversation I overheard in the hotel when I was getting Cokes for Shifrah and me. A red tinge swirls across Shifrah's face like a tiny dust devil. Her flashing eyes and pressed-together lips reveal she has no intention of following Malone's orders. That puts me in a bit of a predicament. Do I go against Malone's orders, too? The idea of not meeting DD and missing the only opportunity of my life to see a remote Amazon village makes me sick with disappointment. I'm already so curious I can barely stand it about why Malone told Reno it was critical for DD and Shifrah not to meet. Why should it matter? What secrets are being kept from us? What do I do about needing to answer the call of nature?

Malone senses mutiny in the air. He leans forward again. "Girls, excuse me, uh, ladies, do you know anything about the Achuar people Dietrich Detzer has chosen to live amongst?"

"Who's Dietrich Detzer? Shifrah and I ask simultaneously.

"DD."

"You knew his name all along?" I ask.

"Safer to use the code name in public."

This time, Reno turns in his seat. "Did I hear someone say DD is a code name?"

"It stands for Dietrich Detzer," I yell.

"What? Dietrich Detzer? Sounds like a writer or a scientist," he yells back.

"I asked you a question, ladies," Malone says. "Do you know anything about the Achuar tribes?"

"Of course we don't, but I'll wager my bottle of *Windsong* perfume you're going to enlighten us," Shifrah says sullenly.

Malone leans closer.

"DD, uh, Dietrich, got inducted into this settlement when he married a woman originally from the tribe. She was working in Quito when they met."

"How did you find this out?" I ask.

"Headquarters. I was told he lives in a settlement, a village, and the people there are Achuarians, or however you call those Achuar people. He lives there part-time. Probably because of his marital ties. Anyhow, I did a little studying about those people before starting the mission. Visited some universities, a museum or two. Called an anthropologist friend of mine. Found out what I could, which isn't much. Not a lot has been written about the primitives in the Ecuador Amazon. Anyway, I think you should know why you're staying on the plane."

"Why?" Shifrah asks, lighting a cigarette. The protesting racket from the pilot and Reno is immediate. She quickly douses her cigarette in the last remaining swallows of her soft drink. "Geez, you'd think I tried to rob the treasury," she says. "Go ahead, Malone, tell us why we never get to have any fun."

"Each Achuar group, or settlement, has maybe five or ten households. Dietrich's village will be about that size, too."

"That's certainly terrifying," Shifrah says, rolling her eyes. "I may never sleep again after hearing such a tale of horror."

"Uh-huh, well, there's more. The Achuar people are closely associated with the Shuar people. Know anything about them?"

I shake my head.

"Ever hear of shrunken heads? The Shuars were famous for head shrinking. They thought by shrinking their enemy's heads, they trapped their souls. Still goes on, but not as much."

I figure from the look on our faces, he knows his words are hitting their intended mark.

"The Achuar women deliver their babies in special gardens where they believe, uh, what was that name?" He rifles through the papers on the seat. "Oh, here it is… *Nunki,* a protective spirit watches over them in those gardens when they have their children. For more fun and games, they drink something they make from vines called…" he studies a paper, "…*Ayahuasca.* Serious stuff. Sends them into a trance so they can talk to their dead ancestors, become animal spirits, that kind of thing."

"Malone, are you serious, or are you trying to scare us?" Shifrah asks.

"I'm dead serious, but that's not the only reason why it pays to be cautious in this part of the world. The forest itself is something none of us has ever experienced before."

"Which is why we want to," I say.

Malone looks at me with a patient expression. "Savannah, some of the Amazon rainforest is not impossible to manage if you are well equipped, have experienced guides, compasses, all that, but Dietrich's settlement is not far from a river in the deepest, darkest parts of the forest. Lots of rain and being located near a river turns everything into marshlands."

"What difference should that make?" Shifrah asks, sounding confrontational. "I mean, what those primitives did in the past shouldn't affect us now, and so what if this Deeter character lives near water?"

"You really want to know?" he says. They have a thirty-second mutual glare before Malone says, "Marshy land has Green Anacondas, which happen to weigh as much as five-hundred pounds and can be thirty feet long. They kill their prey by wrapping around them and strangling the life out of them, swallow them whole. But, that's not all. Blue Poison Dart frogs, deadly coral snakes, and pit vipers. The pit vipers have triangular heads and catlike eyes, and their bite, naturally, is fatal. They love to hang from a branch and look exactly like a dangling vine, stay perfectly still until something rubs up against them, then… they strike!"

"Oh, my God! Who in their right mind would live in a place like that?" Shifrah says, shuddering.

"There's more. Jaguars, electric eels, blood-sucking leeches, stingrays with venom-laced tails, swarms of mosquitos carrying diseases, huge insects, billions of large ants that sting or bite or both, spiders the size of grapefruits, scorpions, centipedes larger than your two hands, vampire bats that sneak into huts at night and suck a person's blood from their face and feet—"

"Stop! Not another word!" Shifrah says, covering her ears.

"You wanted to know. Still want to get out of the plane when we land?"

She shakes her head, turns her head to stare at the raindrops starting to cover the windows.

"Préparez-vous á atterrir! Jacque calls in a loud voice.

"I can interpret that myself," Reno calls out. "Prepare for landing!"

CHAPTER THIRTEEN

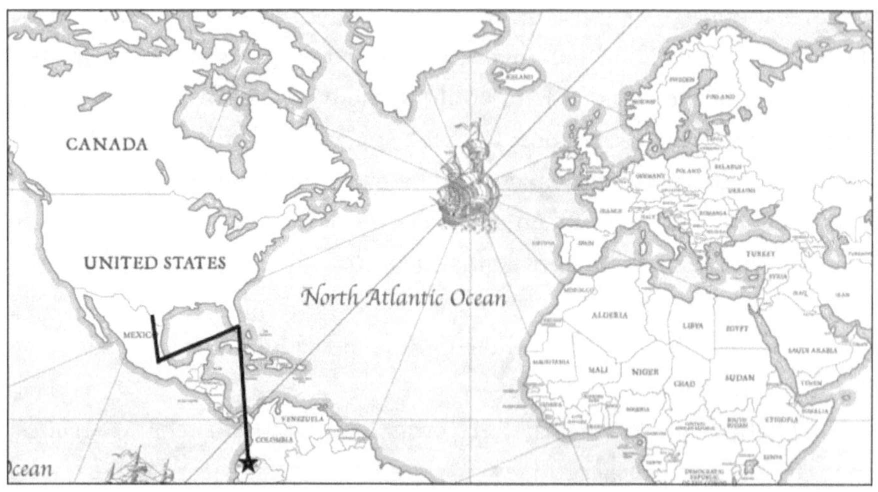

My arm aches from Shifrah clasping it in a death grip from the moment our wheels touched ground. Loud bumping, grinding, sliding, and shaking scared me, too, but my years of hanging out with rough-and-ready guys who have no time for the *faint of heart* trained me to keep my "girly" thoughts to myself.

Reno looks back at us smiling big. "Shoo-ie, now that's livin', isn't it? Everybody still got your teeth?" He laughs at his own joke, but it really did feel like my teeth would fall out of my head during the landing.

"Not what I'd call a real airstrip," Malone grumbles as we come to a rocking stop. "Must have cleared the last five hundred feet with a kitchen knife."

"I need a glass of wine," Shifrah moans, fanning her face with her hand. "Make that an entire bottle."

In front of the plane's nose is a shocking mass of green with trees so tall I can't see the top of them from inside the plane. I'm stretching in every direction to stare outside at shorter, wide-trunked trees, scissor-sharp, low-lying palms, ferns, and crisscrossing vines beckoning, no, daring one to enter the darkened forest they greedily own. Raindrops lightly dust the plane windows. Monkeys swing in crazy patterns from branch to vine to branch in a giant tree completely surrounded by thick, grasping vines.

"Care to go for a stroll by the river? I hear the black crocodiles come out early when it's raining," Malone says.

The dagger eyes Shifra aims at him would kill a weaker man.

"He's turning us around for the trip back," Reno yells from the front, but we already know that. More bumps, thumps, engine whines. Sludge spatters our front window as we hit a slick spot, sending us into a short slide before Jacque cuts the engine. The strange silence after the engine is turned off feels as if we're wrapped in cotton. Harder raindrops begin pelleting the plane, creating an eerie hollow sound.

"Is it all right if I use the lady's room before we take off again?" I ask in the strange dead air surrounding us. The Coke I drank plus our *milkshake landing* has me on the desperate side to use a bathroom.

"Lady's room? It's probably those trees over there or nothing, hon," Malone says. "Sure, help yourself, but keep your eyes good and peeled. I'm serious. Make it quick."

"So, it's okay if Savannah leaves the plane, but not me?" Shifrah says.

"You want to go squat in the trees, be my guest," Malone says, bent almost double to move past us and out the side door. The rain shower abruptly ends as I follow him outside. My nostrils are immediately filled with the pungent odor of warm soil and vegetation, a smell I remember from visiting Martha's Greenhouse in Laredo. It's not unpleasant, but a little goes a long way. Sticky, humid air reminds me of San Antonio, Texas, in August—a suffocating, sweat-producing air. Serious, unsmiling faces peer at us from the trees and unusual huts topped with cone-shaped thatched roofs.

I poke my head back inside the plane. "Please come with me, Shifrah."

"Not on your life."

"It's our only chance to see this forest up close. Don't you want to take some photographs?"

"Not in this wretched place. I'd snap a few through the window, but they won't turn out with that rain on the glass. Listen, Malone telling us there's grapefruit-sized spiders out there is more than I can bear. And look at those faces staring at us! I don't see a single friendly one. I-I can't do it. I'm staying right here."

"Okay. Guess I'm headed into the jungle alone."

"Be careful, Savannah," she whispers, shooting me a worried look.

I cross in front of the plane and aim for the thick foliage, not at all certain I will live or die from all the dangers Malone foretold in the airplane. Strange as it is, the human urge to empty one's bladder overrules all potential dangers.

"Young woman! I say… young woman!"

I turn and see a tall man with dark hair, gray at the temples, sporting a thin moustache and standing at the end of a raised-plank platform encircling a large hut with three connected thatched roofs. He looks smartly dressed in khaki matching shirt and pants.

Is that DD, and is he talking to me? I point at myself, and he nods. Malone and Reno are making their way toward him, but he's eyeing me. They shake hands, talk, and I stand like a dumb cluck not knowing what to do next. Now they're all looking in my direction. Reno jogs back to me.

"DD, er, Dietrich says not to go in the forest alone. If you need to, uh, you know, use the latrine, he said he has a nice setup in his hut and you're welcome to use it."

This awkward attention to my urge to answer the call of nature burns my cheeks. All those men focused on knowing my personal business—whoever heard of it? When I'm out fishing or hunting at home, I merely disappear into the woods a few minutes, and nothing is ever said about it. If we're in a small boat, I simply remark I need to check something on shore. That's the cue for them to let me out to relieve myself. This… is humiliating.

I nod and follow Reno, hot face and all. The closer I get, the more Dietrich reminds me of the movie star Clark Gable, and that truth embarrasses me to the core. I had worked up my own image of a short, neurotic man with Albert Einstein's frizzy hair, a wild, disoriented look in his eyes, perhaps even wearing a loin cloth like Tarzan. Now, my assumptions seem absurd, though I am more confused than ever why someone so elegant would give up a normal life to live in a jungle hut, especially here in the Amazon.

"Hello there! It's Savannah, isn't it?" he says, smiling and offering his hand to me as I climb the three steps to the platform. I don't know what to say, unsettled as I feel, so I simply smile closed-mouthed and extend a hand. He leads us along the walkway to a closed door, turns and faces us. "If you will kindly indulge me, there are a few things I must explain before we enter."

We all nod, and he continues. "The Achuar people have long-standing customs I attempt to follow as closely as I can. I don't abide by all of them simply because my wife and I are a little different than them. In actuality, we're quite different, to be more specific, but we make all efforts to exude peace and nonjudgment in our work here."

His foreign accent makes him even more handsome.

"When we go inside, you will see two young women, twins, lovely girls, only sixteen years old, who were given to me by a neighboring community a few weeks ago. The other settlement was grateful to me for the work I'm doing with the Ecuadorian government to help them gain status and security with possible far-reaching financial opportunities. I was a medical doctor with experience in the field of law in my past life, and I try to use whatever skills I have remaining to help the indigenous tribes of this country. It's a bit of a calling."

Watching this well-spoken, charming man, I'm mesmerized.

"Try not to be shocked when I say I had to accept the girls as wives. A refusal of such a gift would be considered highly insulting and might have incited a disastrous midnight raid on our community here. That would never do, of course, so my wife and I agreed. The girls will live with us as part of our family, daughters, if you will, but I am married to one woman only. Most tribes here are polygamous, but, of course, Alwine and I have our own belief system, and I assure you, it does not include multiple wives."

He points to the hut before us. "I'm used to our large home in Columbia and our apartment in Quito, so I've made architectural changes to our hut lifestyle here to make it more like home. I suppose you could say Alwine and I are spoiled, but we divide our time between residences and try to be here to help as much as possible."

He smiles, and I focus on the dimples on each side of his mustache and think *I could get lost in that smile,* then seriously reprimand myself because, *my gosh, Savannah! He's a married doctor.* In my opinion, he could pass as Mr. Clark's *almost* twin brother, and the former image of him in my mind has dissolved like sand under a hoofprint. How I wish I had more experience with males from my high school and college years so I felt more mature in situations like this.

"You might be interested to know no nails are ever used in hut construction by the Achuar people, only vines. All three of the huts you see here are interconnected, and the first hut serves as our visiting room. Now, the visiting room has specific, native-inspired purposes."

He smiles directly at me, and I feel weak in the knees. "I'm sorry, Savannah. I know you are seeking relief, but it's customary, and might I add, required, that we sit in the visiting room a few minutes. We can talk or sit silently. It doesn't matter as long as we pause there momentarily. The young women might stare, but don't let it bother you; it's merely curiosity. In a few minutes, I'll have them take you back to our sanitary accommodations located in the second hut."

He faces Malone. "I sincerely apologize for not meeting you in Tena, and for all the interventions we've had to your schedule. My life is complicated, I must admit. I had every intention of escorting you here personally, but, you see, my wife was bitten by one of our most unpleasant forest insects, a centipede. Usually, though most unpleasant, the intense pain is accompanied merely by swelling, fever, and weakness—not really a serious threat."

"Not a serious threat? How big are those things, those centipedes?" Reno asks.

"About 30 centimeters. Oh, that's approximately eleven inches."

"Gosh-durn, that's a Texas-sized bug no matter how you twist it," he says, slapping his thigh. Sir, what made it worse for your wife this time around? Seems like it'd be a calamity any time one of those bugs got hold of you."

"Alwine is still recovering from a bout of malaria, so this bite constituted a greater risk to her health. The Achuar tribes are, arguably, the most resilient people in the Amazon Forest. They have medicines and elixirs made from plants and trees that cure almost anything. Sometimes we use those, other times we use our own medicines. This time, Alwine didn't respond to any of the usual remedies, and the elders were scared with her malaria struggles, she might, well, she might die.

"Ontwao, my assistant when I'm here in the village, notified me, and I hurried to her side, praying all the while, and when I got here, thank God, she was showing signs of improvement. After a few days' rest, we feel certain she'll fully recover. Nothing holds my Alwine down for long. Had her condition worsened, I'm afraid I would have been forced to cancel our rendezvous once again.

"That's good news, Dietrich," Malone says, clearing his throat. I get the feeling he's a little ashamed of how he prejudged this man who turns out to be highly educated, humane, and not the least bit deranged. His perfect English, along with his accent and admirable looks, have captured my attention, to put it bluntly, and Shifrah should have come with me out of the plane. She'll kick herself when I tell her about him.

"Oh, please call me David, if you don't mind. David Diamond is my real name. Practicing as a medical doctor in Germany, I went by Dietrich Detzer for obvious reasons, though that contrived name obviously didn't stop—"

"Dietrich, uh, excuse me, David, can we talk privately for a minute?" Malone says, his brows almost meeting above his eyes.

"Of course. Excuse me, please." He nods at Reno and me, takes Malone by the elbow and guides him away from the front door along the curve of the raised walkway. They stop outside the door on the side of the second connected hut. Whatever Malone is telling him, he's using lots of hand gestures to do it. He points to the plane a few times, then at Reno and me.

"Man oh man, if this isn't a plate of fancy calf fries," Reno says, leaning on a walkway rail. "I didn't expect anything like this hombre. Ace-high for sure."

"He defies logic. Do you see how much he resembles Clark Gable? I can't understand how he wound up married to a primitive woman from a jungle tribe. It doesn't make sense."

"She's no primitive, Savannah. She's a medical doctor like him. Seems they met in a hospital in Quito, and if I have it right, he was her patient at first. She's a looker, too, I hear. Don't suppose we'll get to meet her with her laid up sick in the bed."

"How did she become a doctor?"

"Malone says he intends to tell y'all the rest of what he knows about it on the trip back to Tena this afternoon, so I'll go ahead and tell you some of it. DD's, um, David's wife was adopted by a visiting missionary couple who barely survived their own assigned mission here in the jungle. Most of their mission group didn't.

"The girl's whole village had been wiped out in a raid from another village. An old woman who survived the raid but was on her last leg, took the baby girl, Alwine, to the American missionaries planning to return to the States. The rest is history."

"How does Malone know all this?"

"Mr. A, of course. His team spent years searching for and learning about the folks we're planning to meet up with on our mission. This one, DD, I mean, David, was a hard one to nail down, Malone says, since he doesn't show up on the radar screen much. That's how he wants it, you know, and I can't, uh, well, I can't blame him. Eventually, Mr. A found him, and I hear he, David, that is, was real eager to help. In fact, he was searching for Mr. A long about the same time."

"It almost sounds like he wants to stay hidden. Do you know why?"

"I guess his past makes him careful not to stand out. I think he goes by another name when he's in the cities, too. Something altogether different."

"But, Reno, why? I don't understand. Who is Mr. A, and where—"

Reno holds up a hand. "Hon, please. You know how it is. You have to get your information from Malone. Whatever he tells me is confidential unless he says otherwise. I hope you understand."

That kind of hurts my feelings, but I don't get to dwell on it because I'm about to float away needing to use the bathroom. When David and Malone rejoin us, David smiles at me in a way I know he knows some things about us he didn't know before. We follow him inside, and true to what he told us, two young women are sitting on a mat across the room from the scariest-looking carving I've ever seen in my life—a ferocious monkey about three feet high, teeth bared, eyes bulging with threat. He occupies a low bamboo table placed near a wall of the hut. The women seem preoccupied with a large basket they're weaving and don't look up as we enter the hut.

We sit in silence for about ten minutes, and I'm needing a bathroom so bad, I feel close to having an accident. Most of the time, I stare at that monkey carving and wonder why a refined man would own such a hideous sculpture. Finally, the girls look up from their weaving, smile at us, then say a few words in a language I have never heard before.

"That's an Achuar greeting and a welcome to our home," David says, smiling. "Atwine and I will have them speaking Spanish and English by this time next year." He talks to the girls in their language. Both rise, give a quick side glance toward the carved monkey, and come to stand in front of me smiling. "They'll take you to the lavatory now," David says.

Both of them?

If I didn't know better, I would think they were instructed to delay me after I finish using the bathroom. When I come from behind the woven palm frond curtain providing privacy to a chair with a pan affixed underneath a hole cut out in the middle of the seat—a most embarrassing situation, in my opinion—they chatter and point to various artifacts inside a long glass case. Petrified bugs, rocks, little woven straw figures and animals, beaded jewelry, maracas, and black and white photographs litter the inside of the case.

Studying the photos, I see that Reno was right; Alwine is an exotic beauty with flowing wavy hair down to her waist in some photos, then smartly fastened into a bun when she's wearing street clothes or her white doctor's tunic. I don't know what to do but smile and nod at each thing the girls point at. This goes on until I take a step toward the visiting room. One of them touches my arm and points to a shelf of books. Thick, scholarly books, occupying a shelf clearly affixed to something sturdy on the outside of the hut wall. Okay, books. Now what? After several more minutes of this, I decide to break free from the tour of Hut Number Two, with or without them.

My instincts were right. I was purposely detained. All three men are standing close to the table with the angry monkey sculpture on top. Malone is placing something inside the leather pouch he's wearing crisscrossed over his shoulder. The *retrieve,* and I missed where it was hidden. What did it have to do with that sculpture?

David has his shirt sleeves rolled up; a small crowbar tool is in his hand. My big frown catches his attention. "Thank you for detaining my girls so I could recover this for… for…" He glances at Malone, "…for Mr. A without them observing the procedure. I've kept this *key to the keys* a secret for many years. Only Alwine and Ontwao know of its existence here, and I can't tell you what a magnanimous relief it is to know it will at last be utilized as it was originally intended for all of us. I was afraid the entire effort had been abandoned and, let me say, my prayers are with all of you as you finish this important undertaking and restore things as they should be."

What is he talking about?

My eye catches a hint of dark on the outside of his left arm before he rolls his sleeve back down. A birthmark?

Our pilot looks slightly prune-faced when we return to the plane. "Everything all right?" Reno asks him. He nods and steps into the cockpit. Maybe he wanted to go inside with us?

Shifrah is spitting mad because I was inside David's hut with the men, but the truth is, it's her own fault. If she'd agreed to answer the call of nature with me, she would have been with me when I was stopped from going into the forest. As it was, with David's extension of courtesy, Malone had no choice but to let me tag along.

I can only assume his private conversation with David was warning him not to say certain things in front of me. I wish I knew the whole truth of this mission, but at least Malone has agreed to show all of us the *key to the keys* tonight at dinner. I want to know more than what it looks like. I want to know what its purpose is. In short, I want to know everything.

"I waited for you to come back, Savannah. I even stepped out of the airplane. That took all my courage because I expected one of those crazed, shrieking monkeys to land on my head or a jaguar to come running out of the cluttered vinery to eat me. I was already shaky when I lit a cigarette outside the plane, then *El Capitan* up there scared me half to death by having a conniption, jumping up and down yelling about the fuel and flames and I don't know what else because his French took on a whole new version with him so flustered about one little ciggie. He made me walk down that dirt runway to smoke, and I took two drags and put it out. I wasn't about to stand down there alone with savages and wild animals everywhere.

"I didn't get to photograph a single thing, and you'd have to murder me to ever get me back here. I was sure you'd come see about me, but you didn't. Do you know you were gone more than twenty-five minutes?"

I want to laugh, but I don't. She's such a city girl, and that constantly puts her on the losing end when she's out in the wilds. I'm sure I'd be the same way in a big city. "Was it only twenty-five minutes? It felt more like thirty. Listen, I couldn't leave. These folks, let's see, the Achuar's, have a strange way of greeting folks. You have to go inside into what they call a visiting room and be quiet until someone says hi to you. Then, you get to smile and talk and have a grand old time. By the time those two new wives of David's came alive, I was about to float down my own river, if you catch my drift."

"Two new wives? David? Who's that?"

"Hang on, Shifrah, I'm coming to it. First thing is…" and in no time at all, I have Shifrah's full attention, wide eyes, smiles, gasps, and everything else that makes her such an interesting companion on this journey.

CHAPTER FOURTEEN

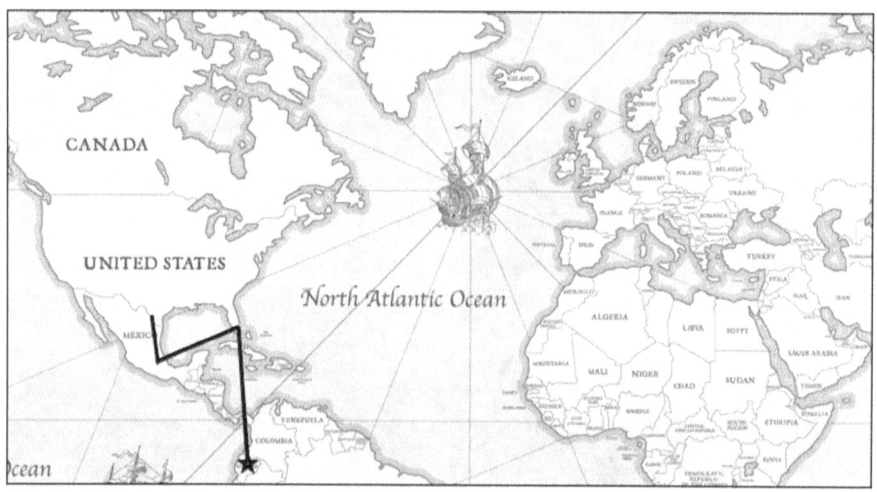

We're heavy into our conversation when the plane jerks, then dips down slightly in the front. It happens again, weaving a little side to side.

"Hey, Jacque, you all right, buddy?" we hear Reno shout above the sound of the engine. In the next few seconds, we know Jacque is far from all right as he slumps forward. "Hey pal, what's going on?" Reno shouts.

"My-my medicine. Pills…" Jacque says.

"Where are they?"

"In the back if I brought…" he leans forward, his face on the steering mechanism. We begin a nosedive downward.

"We're going to die!" Shifrah screams.

"Reno, grab the yoke!" Malone shouts, but Reno is struggling to wrestle Jacque's slumped-over form off the steering device. He manages to shift Jacque to the side, grabs the yoke—a new word to me—in front of the copilot seat. The cabin fills with a spirit of relief as the plane levels out. Reno's wrestling now has Jacque leaning sideways and partly positioned between the two pilot seats, his face turned toward us.

"He's turning paler by the second. He's starting to sweat!" I yell. I scoot forward and pat his cheeks. "Jacque! Jacque! Where do you keep your medicine?" He mumbles something, but I can't understand him. "He's speaking French!"

Shifrah moves closer, speaks to him in his native language. She puts her ear to his mouth, leans back with a fearful face. "He thinks they're in the compartment at the back of the cargo hold in a small brown case if he brought them. Says he sometimes forgets to pack them. If he doesn't get them quickly, he said he'll die. It's his heart."

"Oh, good lord," Malone says. "What's this guy doing flying with a bad heart? Reno, find us a sandbar and land this thing. If we don't get some medicine down his throat asap, we'll have a corpse on our hands!"

"Roger that, sir!"

Shifrah clasps my arm, shakes her head. "I thought living in New York City was dangerous, but it's a waltz on glass compared to this-this whatever it is," she says. She sticks her face between our seats to look at Malone. "Are we going to die?"

"Reno's an ace. None better. Landing this little bird is nothing to him."

"I see something, sir! Going down," Reno says, and we begin an instant descent.

What in the world are you doing in a small airplane making an emergency landing in the Ecuadorian Amazon Forest? I ask myself and start laughing, laughing so hard tears roll down my cheeks.

"She's gone hysterical! Shall I slap her?" Shifrah yells.

I put a hand up and try to get my breath. "Don't slap me," I say, laughing still. "I just thought about how we used to think running out of eggs or coffee at the Dixie was a genuine emergency, a catastrophe," I say, wiping tears off my cheeks. "This trip is making me see things in a whole new light. I'm okay now."

"Buckle up! Prepare for landing!" Reno yells, and it seems only a minute before we're rolling along the ground with rainforest scenery and water on all sides of the plane. The landing is much smoother than the one at David's settlement, and when we stop, we all sigh with relief. Again, the silent air moments after the engine cuts off makes me feel disconnected.

Malone is immediately maneuvering to get out of the door on Shifrah's side. His hand on the latch, he yells, "Reno, help me throw aside all the heavy stuff in the cargo hold and look for this man's brown case."

"Shall we lay him out flat on the ground, sir?"

"Not unless we can't find his pills."

"Malone?" Shifrah says as he steps out.

He sticks his head back into the cabin. "Yeah?"

"I have to use the bathroom."

"Well, uh, all right. You and Savannah go together."

"But there's no trees on this sandbar. Is it safe for us to cross the river?"

"Hell no! Don't go anywhere near that water. That's an order. Go squat in front of the plane. We'll be throwing stuff around in the cargo hold. Make it quick. We have a dying man here."

The stunned look on her face almost makes me laugh again, but I understand her feelings about such a lack of privacy. I wouldn't like it either. "Shifrah, it's okay. I'll stand between you and the plane while you do your business. No one will see you, not even me. How's that?"

Her voice trembles when she answers *okay,* and I feel genuinely sorry for our city girl. We walk about twenty feet from the front of the plane, and, as promised, I turn away while she begins the entirely new experience of squatting outdoors to relieve herself.

Earthy smells of wet foliage, still water, and sand make my nose tingle. The clammy air gathers me into its suffocating, vapory arms, making it hard to get a deep breath. I fan my face with my hand, cooling the sweat on my forehead. Exotic noises fill the trees around us—screeching monkeys, bird squawks, and peculiar trilling and buzzing sounds. A cloud of flying insects invades my face for a moment, but thankfully, moves on. I scrutinize the water's surface on both sides and don't see any of those black crocodiles Malone told us about. Some of the trees look creepy with strange, gasping roots growing horizontally from the lower sides of the trunk. On my left, I spot a flock of richly colored birds, ten or more, occupying a branch of a tree that appears to have been taken prisoner as it is slowly encircled by another tree.

"Shifrah, check out that flock of birds on the left. They have the brightest royal blue bellies, and the light green around their eyes makes them look like they're wearing masks. So vivid and beautiful! I wonder what they're called?"

"You really think I have time for birdwatching at a time like this? Darn that clothes shop we found in the alley off the square in Mexico City. I knew those prices were too good to be true. My stupid zipper isn't working."

"Need help?"

"No, I think I got it. Just in time, too."

And that's how it is that Shifrah has her pants down when the first spear whizzes through the air. It lands inches from my right foot. I turn in shock to stare at the jungle foliage across the river opposite of where I spotted the birds. Several brown-skinned warriors have gathered along the bank of the river. They have red masks painted around their eyes and black vertical streaks on their chins. They furiously wave spears at us. I let out a scream that leaps to the tops of the trees and hangs there.

I run to grab Shifrah as she's rising to her feet. I lift and drag her the best I can, and I'm grateful for my field-track training because, even with her trying to zip her pants and squealing like a cat with its tail in a wringer, we're back at the plane in moments. Another spear lands close to the wing of the plane.

"In the plane! In the plane!" Malone shouts, literally lifting and throwing Shifrah through the door like cargo. Reno jumps into the cockpit, starts the engine. Malone lifts me off the sand by my waistband and tosses me into the nearest seat and disappears. The whiz of the spears flying through the air and the dull sound they make hitting the sand reverberates through the open door. I scream at Reno not to leave

Malone behind. Malone falls through the door in the next few seconds, a brown case in his hand. He quickly closes the door and shoves the case toward our feet.

"Strap in!" Reno shouts, and none of us move so much as a muscle as the plane rolls down the sandbar with the clunk of spear tips hitting the plane.

"Good thing this baby is all metal!" Reno shouts.

Malone crawls on all fours into the seats behind us, breathing hard. "Hurry, Savannah, open the case and check for his pills," he says wearily, and I come out of my shock to fumble with the latch. One glance at Jacque's face hanging between the seats and I'm not sure any medicine will help him. Among small tools, a razor, and a tube of toothpaste, I locate a bottle of pills and read *Digoxin* on the label.

"I don't know how many to give him!"

"Give him three tablets and see if he comes around," Malone says in a calm voice. I shake three out and stuff them into Jacque's mouth.

"Make sure he swallows them. Quick, now." Malone orders.

Talk about a new experience, poking pills down a possible dead person's throat. Nothing happens. I steal a glance at Shifrah. She's preoccupied with getting her shirttail unstuck from her pants zipper.

"Shifrah, stop fiddling around and hand me my Coke bottle!" She looks at me with a faraway expression, stares, doesn't move. "The Coke bottle, behind the copilot seat. Give it to me, and hurry up!"

She looks at Jacque, drops to her knees on the floor, hands me the bottle. "What can I do to help?"

"Cradle his head! I'll see if we can get him to swallow what's left in the Coke bottle. I think I got the pills a little ways down his throat, but I'm not sure. The soda pop might push them down his gullet. I-I'm not even sure he's alive."

We pour liquid into his mouth. It runs out. "This is our last chance," I say, looking at the little bit left in the bottle. "Let's turn his head toward the ceiling and tilt it backward." I pour the last swallow of soft drink into his mouth and clamp his lips together, shake his head back and forth. I lean back as he chokes and spews. He coughs again, dry-heaves, coughs, breaks wind, burps loud and long, breaks wind a second time.

"This is appalling!" Shifrah squeals, her hand cupped over her nose.

He opens his eyes. *"Merde, tu essaies de me tuer?"*

"What's he saying, Shifrah?"

"He's cursing," she says, "and he wants to know why we're trying to kill him. If he emits any more disgusting body sounds, I might murder him myself."

Jacque twists his head and sees Reno piloting the plane. He smiles, looks back at us with moist bloodshot eyes, appears to fall sleep.

"Well, damn, that's good, ladies. Real good. Nothing like *not* arriving at an airport with a dead pilot. I guess you realize that band of warriors didn't intend to kill us," Malone says.

"What? They threw spears at us!" Shifrah says. "They wanted to shrink our heads!"

"Nah. You think they'd be such terrible shots when they hunt food with spears and blowguns every day of their lives just to survive?"

"He has a point," I say.

"Damn right. We lucked out, that's for sure. Not all the natives in that forest are dangerous. Some are, but others only want to let visitors know they aren't welcome. That's what we just encountered. Think about how David moves in and out of the jungle safely."

"But doesn't having a native wife give him protection?" I ask.

"It helps, but he's well aware of where to go and where not to go, too. Some areas, stay entirely away from or you won't survive. Other places, go with gifts. Others, well, you get the picture. Anyway, now you two can write this down in your book of stories from the mission. Only one thing worries me."

"What's that?" I ask.

"I don't think Shifrah ought to go around baring her bottom like that when strangers are watching," he says, sliding quickly back into his seat and out of reach.

"You… you… know I didn't want to-to subject myself to such an indignity in the first place, Malone, and…" Shifrah sputters, eyes narrowed. It doesn't help when Malone and I start guffawing.

"What's going on back there?" Reno yells.

Shifrah's face reddens. "Never mind. Pure childish nonsense. You would think some people would be more mature at these ages. Please, Reno, get me to the nearest restaurant serving adult refreshments."

"Hey, Reno, you got everything you need to get us back to Tena?" Malone yells from the back seat, still chuckling.

"Yessir!" Reno says, momentarily turning to glance at us, and I think how unfair it is for someone to be that good-looking and be an expert pilot, too.

The Canyon

CHAPTER FIFTEEN

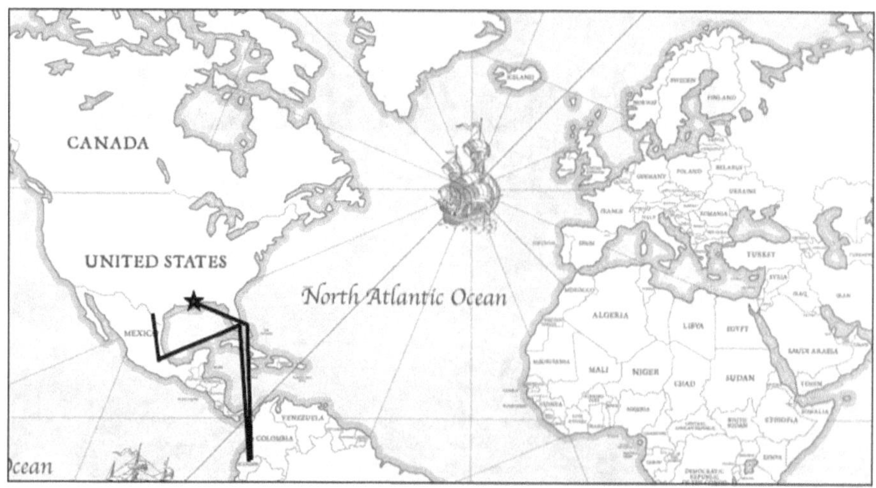

Our adventure in Ecuador has been a roaring success, that is, none of us died. Considering we were in the Amazon, one of the most dangerous places on earth, survived an encounter with warriors, and nearly had a plane wreck with a dying pilot on board, it's a pretty good outcome.

In the hospital, Jaque told us he'd be lighting candles as a tribute to all of us for the rest of his life, which I thought was terribly sweet. Finally ready to move on to the next leg of our mission, and knowing the artifact we retrieved from David is the most important one in the mission, has had us in great spirits the last few days. Malone still hasn't shown us what he got from David, but he says he will soon. Our quick clothes-shopping trip in Quito this morning before we flew out put Shifrah in an even better mood.

We're about a half hour from landing at the Miami International Airport when Reno plops down in an empty seat behind us, then leans around the side—crouching in the aisle—and starts telling us a plane story. Apparently, no one loves planes more than Reno, and his restlessness when he's not doing something physical results in his telling us plane stories.

"Hey, ladies, guess what?" Reno says. "Tomorrow, we're flying in a National Airlines DC-6. Nice planes. Very dependable. This past February, a National Airlines DC-6 took off from Miami, made a stopover in Tampa, then continued across the Gulf of Mexico on its way to Moisant Field in New Orleans. That's our exact route tomorrow, by the way. Same airlines. Same kind of plane, a DC-6."

Shifrah yawns, lights a cigarette, leans her head back on the seat eyeing him with a playful smile. "Thank you for the flight plan, Captain sir," she says, saluting, "but, seriously, let's talk about something more important. Is the prison warden letting us leave the hotel tonight to have a fabulous dining experience?"

"Afraid not. He said we're dining in the hotel tonight, but we're going out tomorrow night in New Orleans."

Shifrah snorts. "Oh, he's such a wet rag. Two times we're in Miami and not a dash of dining, dancing, or shopping. Thank goodness we're allowed out of our cages tomorrow night. I desperately want, no, I need, some of Brennen's Bananas Foster. Savannah, have you ever eaten New Orleans cuisine?" I shake my head. "No? You're in for a treat. You have to try one of my favorites, Shrimp Étouffée. It's divine. I think we should order a plethora of dishes so you can sample them all. It's essential we split a Muffuletta, too. I promise you will never want another kind of sandwich after you taste one."

"What is it?" I ask.

"It's heaven on earth, is what it is, and now, I'll tell you another story my dear Hilda told us when my family and I visited New Orleans for my sixteenth birthday. She said the Muffuletta sandwich was invented by a Sicilian immigrant in 1906, and he called it a *Roma* Sandwich, which, legend has it, later became known as the Muffuletta. Hmm. I wonder if it's true he was a gypsy? *Ce serait exceptionnel, n'est-ce pas?"*

"Did you say that would be exceptional?"

"I did because everyone knows the *Roma* are famous for their music, dancing, crafts, and cooking. But… there's another story about this sandwich. In 1924, the Perrone family claimed to be the inventors of the Muffuletta. Hilda said the dispute wasn't settled, and, frankly, all I care about is the Muffuletta exists for giving the greatest pleasure to one's taste buds."

"What's in it?"

"A delicious Muffuletta loaf is split in two and slathered with olive salad—"

"Olive salad?"

"Um-hm. You know I don't cook, but I remember olive salad as a concoction of delightfully marinated green and black olives, herbs, oregano, raw vegetables chopped into tiny pieces, olive oil, and I don't know what else, but it's delicious. Add fresh sliced ham, salami, and Italian cheeses, and *voila!* you have the best sandwich ever created by man or beast."

"I wonder if it would go over at the Dixie."

"Didn't you say the diner owner is Italian?"

"Yes, but Tony was born and raised in Texas. He's probably never heard of a, uh, a—"

"A Muffuletta."

"Shif, you darned sure worked up my appetite in a fierce way, but my legs are starting to fall asleep all wadded up here in this aisle. That pretty stewardess with the red hair has given me the evil eye a few times now."

"That'll be the day when a female gives you the evil eye," Shifrah mumbles, dragging on her cigarette.

"Y'all still haven't heard the rest of my story about the DC-6 this past February. So, anyways, that plane takes off with a crew and forty-odd passengers, runs into a devil of a storm, winds right out of hell, goes down, and no one survives. They did find seventeen bodies floating in the water real soon, but mostly, they didn't recover a lot of the rest of them."

The silence that follows Reno's newscast is broken only by the sound of Shifrah stubbing her cigarette out in the metal armrest ashtray.

"You came over here to tell us that?" I ask.

"Uh-huh, and thanks for listening. Most folks don't care a Fig Newton about airplane facts and stories. Guess I just worked up the need to spout one out since Malone's been busier than an auctioneer at a pig-squealing contest mapping out the details for our next moves. I'm a little restless with all this sitting around, especially being a passenger instead of a pilot. Not used to it."

"Did I hear you say the flight plan, the plane type, and the airline we take tomorrow are the very same as the one that crashed in February?" I ask.

"Yep."

"Count me out for flying on that National Airlines AC-60, or whatever it is tomorrow," Shifrah says.

"Aw, shoot, Shif, all the airlines are using DC-6's. American, Delta, United, National. Pan Am even started using the DC-6Bs for transatlantic flights last year. They're nifty flying machines. Safe as all get out. That 6 that went down with those forty-six souls got caught up in one of the worst storms you can imagine. Heck, they didn't stand a chance, but we're not hitting storms tomorrow. I already checked the weather patterns. We'll be safe as little pups cozied up by the stove."

His story shuts us up for the descent into Miami. The second we descend the plane steps, Shifrah and I beat a path to Malone's side. Shifrah pleads with him using all her feminine charm, and she sure has a lot of it. I'm her backup, nodding my head and keeping the proper look of fear on my face.

"Please, pretty please, let us take the train from here to New Orleans, Malone," she whimpers, clutching the material on the arm of his suit jacket.

Aside from my part in this persuasion of donning the expression of a goose about to be cooked—scared, that is—I'm thinking how I must have Shifrah show me how she does that rolling of her eyes with her lips all pursed together sort of like a fish just in case I ever need to use it. It appears it might be a good weapon of the feminine sort to have in one's arsenal. Anyone who sees it, except Malone, seems to get beguiled by it.

She looks beautiful in her pale pink, two-piece travel suit, rose-pink heels, and dark pink pillbox hat the same hue as her shoes. All of us wear our best clothes for air travel, of course, but Shifrah always stands out. Right now, she might as well be dressed in patched-up overalls for where it's getting her with Malone.

"We just can't do it, Shifrah. Flight technicalities and unpredictable people make it difficult to get all our plans to work right. If headquarters has us lined up to get a *retrieve* at a specific time in a specific way, we have no choice but to muster up and get the job done. Besides, we're already booked on a train trip from New Orleans to Arizona, and we can't afford to lose any more time. That canyon closes in October, sometimes earlier if the weather changes. If we miss our opportunity, we won't be allowed back in until Spring. Our entire mission's success depends on making sure we're in the right places at the right times."

Her face falls. She backs up, turns, and harumphs off in her miffed, fast-stepping walk toward the airport lobby. I follow her wondering why Malone doesn't share more information with us. He still hasn't shown us the artifact we collected in Ecuador, and he hasn't explained why it was so important the entire mission would have been scrapped if we had failed to get it. We know he's planning to ship it to Mr. A when we arrive in Phoenix because he said so. Will we ever get to see it?

Inside the airport restroom, Shifrah fluffs her hair and repaints her lips with jerky, mad movements. "That's it, Savannah. I can't take that man's ball-and-chain attitude another day. Tonight, we break into his hotel room and find that leather pouch. Why is he keeping the Amazon *retrieve* all to himself? I'll tell you why. It's because he wants to control everything, including us! I'm not used to these-these crazy limitations!"

"I don't know why he hasn't shown it to us yet, Shifrah, but what he said about us not taking a train from Miami to New Orleans makes sense. Looks like the schedules come from wherever that headquarters group is located, not from him. He has to do what they say. It's his job."

She pulls a tissue from her purse and blots her lipstick with fervor, then stomps across the room to throw it in the trash receptacle. In my opinion, she's angrier than she ought to be. I lean against the sink counter watching her and wondering what she'd do if she was driving an old truck down a dirt road and the engine gave up the ghost. Would she throw herself in the road in a hissy fit and wait for divine intervention? That exact thing happened to me, and I took my tools out of the backend and wired everything together to get me to the nearest filling station. Of course, she hasn't had a troop of men teaching her the basics of life as I have. No, she's a New Yorker, from the top of her coifed hair to the tip of her painted toenails.

"We're going to see that artifact on our own… tonight."

"You suppose we can finagle a key to his room?" I ask.

"That's no problem. My charms may be lost on Malone, but they won't be on a hotel clerk. We can excuse ourselves to use the lady's room at dinner tonight and do it then."

"It's terrible to be so curious we contemplate committing a crime, isn't it?"

"A crime? Us? No, he's committing the crime because he isn't being honest about everything. If we're going to risk our necks to gather artifacts from around the world, we should at least know, or see, what we're gathering, right?"

"It seems so. Hey, tricking a clerk and breaking into a room sounds like a real cloak-and-dagger operation."

"It is."

"I've never done anything that dangerous, and it's kind of, well, exciting."

"Shooting snakes and sticking your hands in gooey mud to pull out a fish with knife-sharp whiskers isn't dangerous?"

"That's just life as it comes in Texas. Most everyone knows how to shoot or club a poisonous snake to death. And catfish noodling? Well, lots of the men who savor a plate of fried catfish and some raw fun at the same time know how to do it. Not too many gals, though."

Shifrah stares at me a few seconds, shakes her head. "Well, I'm happy to be the one to introduce you to the seedier side of city life."

"Sounds kind of fun. How does it work?"

"You manipulate a key from a desk clerk by pretending you might be a dangerous but fascinating female. In other words, giving the impression you're, well, you know."

"A tramp?"

"Um, a bit loose and lonely. That makes the strongest of them your captive."

"Oh, kind of like Delilah beguiling Sampson so many times until she led him to destruction."

"I have only the faintest of ideas who those people are, but if she beguiled and deceived him for her own benefit, then yes. We'll act like we grew up on the wrong side of the tracks."

"Of course, you'll be drawing on your vast experience for that, right?"

We share a good laugh and join the men waiting for us outside the restroom.

On the way to our hotel, I'm sitting between Shifrah and Malone in the back seat. As usual, Reno's sitting up front. The silence in the taxi is heavy. Malone clears his throat. "When we get to Phoenix in a few days, we'll have a briefing and discuss our plans going forward. You already know we're headed to the bottom of the Grand Canyon for the next *retrieve.*"

"Why can't we meet our contact somewhere less dangerous, Malone?" Shifrah asks. "Making us ride an animal into a deep canyon is-is ludicrous. Can't the contact come out of the canyon, if that's where he lives, and meet us in a restaurant for coffee? Isn't that a smarter choice?"

I think I detect a momentary glint of humor in Malone's eyes. "Perhaps, but we're following orders," he says. "Okay. Reno and Savannah are both experienced horse riders. Shifrah, do you have any real horse experience?"

She huffs loudly. "Surely you remember from my background information that I spent a whole week at a horse camp when I was in the sixth grade. I'm sure I know all I need to know about riding any beat-up old mules."

No one says anything, but it's hard to keep a straight face. Any sign of mirth just won't do right now with Shifrah still riled about Malone not changing our travel plans despite her best coaxing.

"Malone, have you done a lot of riding before?" I ask.

"West Point Equestrians."

What can you say to that? Malone is a man of surprises for sure. He sighs, looks out the window. "We're staying at the Adams Hotel, downtown Phoenix, which, by the way, has a swimming pool on the roof. You two better go shopping first thing and get you some bathing suits and caps."

Shifrah snorts. "No one swims this late in the year."

"They do in Phoenix. Down the street from the hotel is a restaurant, very famous, called The Flame. We're celebrating Savannah's birthday there."

"My birthday?" I say, feeling heat crawl up my neck.

"Isn't your twenty-first birthday next week, Savannah?"

"Why, yes, but it isn't necessary to make a big fuss about it, I actually don't—"

"We're going to celebrate your birthday, our victory in Ecuador, and drink to the future success of our mission." In a few moments, he bellows out a loud laugh.

Reno turns his head. "What is it, sir? I haven't heard you laugh like that in a mighty long time."

"Oh, just thinking about how our little team of noncommissioned officers is doing all right. Yessir, we're doing just fine."

Shifrah and I share looks of complete shock.

Glory be! Malone is human after all.

CHAPTER SIXTEEN

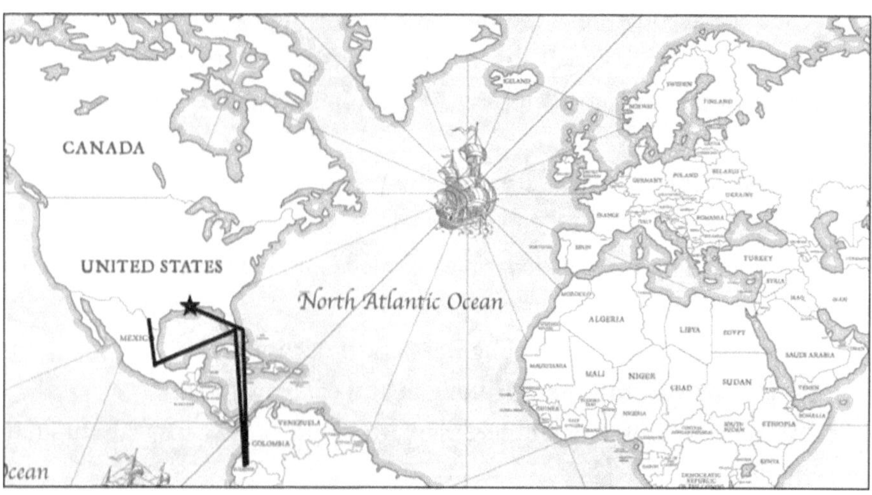

It's amazing how exciting being sneaky is. I have butterflies in my stomach as Shifrah and I excuse ourselves for our fake trip to the ladies' room to coerce a room clerk into giving us a key to Malone's room. I let out a nervous giggle as we step into the hotel lobby. "What now?" I ask.

"Watch and learn," Shifrah says with a wink. "All you do is act like you're a casual traveler in close proximity, okay?" She smiles, then loosens both her shoulders with a backward roll. She wiggles in an all-over body shake, then walks with an exaggerated hip swing toward the young man behind the counter. She clears her throat loudly as we approach. He looks up. His surprised look is replaced by a crooked grin as she approaches. I follow behind her and step to the side when she reaches the counter. I busy myself with a stack of *See and Experience*

Miami! brochures on the counter, but my eyes and ears are on full alert.

"Hi," she breathes, peering into the clerk's face. She places her elbows on the counter, bends down and forward. The clerk stares into the top of her dress and looks back up, swallowing hard.

"Can I… can I help you, Miss?" he sputters.

"How nice of you to ask. You see, I need you."

"Huh?" he says.

"I need your assistance," she whispers.

He blushes crimson. "Um, what-what do you need?"

She laughs a light, tinkling laugh, leans further into the counter toward him. "What I need…" she reaches out and runs a finger down the side of his lapel, "…is a little ol' key to my room. Silly me. I forgot mine in the room, and I need…" she fastens him with a come-hither look, "…I need…" he is leaning closer as she speaks. "…to soak my soft little body in a warm tub of bubbles." She wiggles her shoulders slightly. "I'm so exhausted. A bath will be heavenly! Please excuse my bad manners, but I didn't catch your name."

"I-I'm Larry."

"Larry. What a strong name. You see, Larry, after such a long, grueling day, I'm dying to strip off my clothes and relax. I always feel so good, so warm, after a bubble bath." She places her open palms on her upper chest, looks forlorn, sighs. "I get so lonely when I travel, you know? It's not easy to be a stranger in a city. Larry, excuse me, but would you, by any chance, have any time for a little nightcap with me later?" she says in a barely audible, winsome voice.

"Wha-what?"

"I know it's a lot to ask." She sighs. "Can I ask you a personal question?"

"Okay."

"How long before your shift is over?"

He looks at his watch. "About an hour."

"That's perfect," she purrs. She turns her face to the side, pooches her lips out slightly, her eyes locked on his. "I so hate being alone, especially in a strange city. An hour, you say?" He nods, mouth open. "I'll be waiting, Larry. That is, if you can spare a few minutes to spend with me."

He's practically drooling!

"After my bath, I'll slip into my fluffy little bathrobe so I can stir us up a couple of very dry martinis. Sound good, Larry?"

He looks like he's in a trance as he nods.

"Larry… the key?"

Larry's eyes absorb her as if she's the main course at a fancy restaurant. In a faraway voice, he asks for her room number. She tells him Malone's room number. He takes the extra key from a drawer and hands it to her. He doesn't check the register. He doesn't ask for her name. She giggles and wiggles herself through the lobby toward the elevators, stopping once to look beguilingly at him over her shoulder. I follow a discreet distance behind her.

Inside the elevator, she lets out a triumphant whoop. "Oh, gads, that was fun!"

"It's-it's scary watching you perform like that, Shifrah. You're far too good at it."

"Oh, balderdash, Savannah. It's easy. Hilda loved movies, especially those featuring the Hollywood screen sirens of the past and present. I tagged along with her to see those movies so much it's easy for me to imitate Jane Russell, Mae West, Rita Hayworth, Marilyn Monroe, all of them. It's simple. I can teach you how."

"Um, I'll pass. It really worked, though. That guy would have given you the secret formula to the world's great treasures, I do believe."

She throws her head back and chuckles. "Perhaps. I've tried a few of those tactics on Malone, as you know, but he's immune."

"Nothing so sexy as that, I hope."

"Oh, no, I would never, Savannah. I just mean I've tried to convince him using my genuine femininity, but he's a hard case. Hey, we've been gone at least fifteen minutes, right?"

I look at my watch. "Fourteen."

We step from the elevator, look both directions down the hall, and practically run to Malone's room, if you can call hurrying in those dreaded high heels *running*. Shifrah unlocks the door, and we rush into the darkness and close the door behind us.

"Where do you suppose he's keeping it?" I whisper.

"Let's check the closet and the bureau drawers."

"It's too dark. I have to turn on a lamp."

"Go ahead, but let's hurry."

As a last measure, we look in Malone's suitcase, find it, only to discover it has a small combination lock on the opening of the pouch.

"Oh, for Pete's sake!" Shifrah says. "All this for nothing."

"Yeah, and what's Malone going to say when that clerk shows up with high expectations of a grand evening with a beautiful siren?"

"He'll tell him he has the wrong room."

"Yeah, right after busting him in the nose," I say. We both laugh and hurry to the restaurant, leaving the extra key on the bureau.

* * *

The men rise as we approach the table in the restaurant. "Dang, ladies. We've put off the waiter three times waiting for you. Y'all go skin a griz or something?"

"Sorry," we both say, keeping our heads tucked down to show our contriteness and, more likely, to hide our guilty but excited eyes.

Malone says, "Next time, do your beautifying or whatever you were off doing *before* we go to eat. Got that?"

We nod.

"I was telling Reno I'll show you ladies the Amazon *retrieve* at our special dinner at The Flame in Phoenix. Reno, of course, already saw it. I meant to share it before now, but I've been buried under making sure all our travels meet up with contacts and work the right way. I want to explain it to you in detail, and I just haven't had the time yet. I think you'll find it real interesting."

Shifrah and I exchange looks. Hers says the same as mine… *we are ridiculous.*

CHAPTER SEVENTEEN

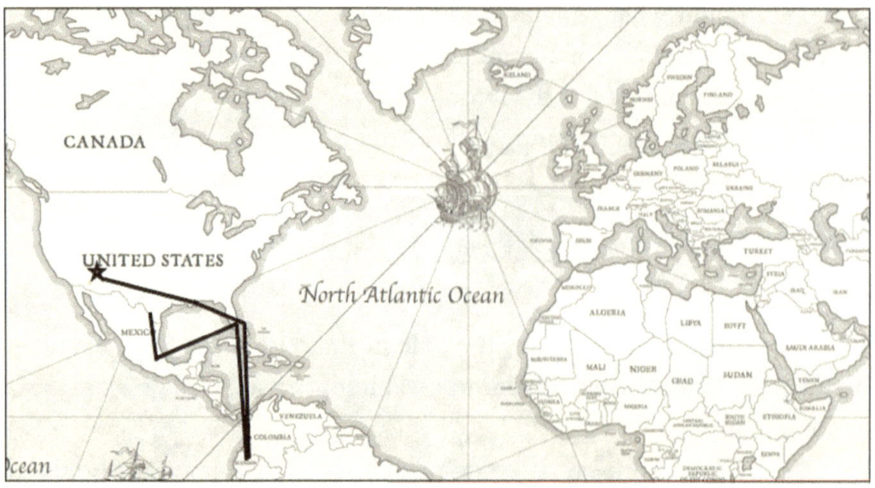

We left Miami and flew into New Orleans late yesterday afternoon, and, thank heavens, we didn't die on the DC-6 plane as did the poor people in Reno's story. We spent this evening in the famous French Quarter dining on the cuisine Shifrah told Reno and me about on the airplane ride from Ecuador. The food was everything she said it was, and now I know I'll crave it until I return someday.

It crossed my mind a few times how my mama flew the coop with that preacher and told Flora Belle at the drugstore cosmetic counter she was moving to New Orleans and never coming back. It felt odd to be in the same city where she might be if she were still alive. I know I haven't forgiven her for leaving us, so finding her is not something I've actively yearned for. I learned a long time ago to let the past stay where it belongs. It's better that way.

I drank my standard Shirley Temples all evening, and the rest of our group sampled their fair share of interesting drinks. They look a little green around the edges right now, and all of us are tired from having to be here at the New Orleans Union Station after restaurant and bar hopping not long ago. Shifrah is as grouchy as a water-soaked hen. She isn't her best in early mornings or, in this case, in the middle of the night. It surprises me she isn't in a better mood after our evening "out of the cage" as she calls it. Sometimes, such as right now, I don't understand her at all.

We're scheduled to depart at 12:30 a.m. Waiting for our boarding time, I'm a country girl in a dream as I meander around the rustic train station noting the arched entries, relishing the busy atmosphere, and glancing at newspaper headlines from the papers people read while they wait. At a little shop adjacent to a wall, I buy a cup of coffee and read a plaque on the wall beside the counter saying the train station was built in 1892 and designed by Louis H. Sullivan. Earlier, I saw a sign by the ticket window saying the station is slated to be demolished next year in favor of a complex that connects the intercity railroad services. I can't comprehend tearing down a building with so much character. If human beings can be rebuilt from the inside out, such as how I feel about myself right now, why can't the same be done with buildings? Why destroy *all the old* to rebuild the new?

Shifrah's earlier reaction to being assigned to sleep in a group sleeping car on the train instead of having private arrangements took me by surprise. Malone mentioned we'd be bunking together in an open sleeping car, and whichever one wanted the top or bottom bunk, we could work that out ourselves.

"You must be mistaken, Malone," she said. "I'm sure our arrangements are for private rooms or at least a double roomette for Savannah and me to share."

"Nope, the plan is what I told you. Bunks in a sleeping car."

"But-but, public sleeping? You mean like bums and transients sleeping on a park bench with a newspaper over their faces? My word, Malone, that may be fine for the masses, but I've never heard of such a thing for people of-of…" She flushed red, turned, and hurried off toward a cluster of vending machines, her cigarette smoke trailing behind her.

"What's got her goat, sir?" Reno asks.

Malone kept his eyes on her. "Same thing, Reno," is all he said.

Living alone and being about halfway a hermit for so many years, you would think I'd be upset sleeping a few feet away from strangers with only curtains separating us in the sleeping car berths on the train, but I'm not. Our train, the Southern Pacific's *Sunset Limited* travels from New Orleans all the way to Los Angeles in forty-two hours, so it arrives in Phoenix in only thirty-plus hours. It's exciting to cross the country on the ground so fast, so who cares where we sleep? Sitting up would suit me fine, and it appears that's what we do the rest of tonight.

* * *

I'm sorting through the brochures and papers the porter handed us when we boarded the train. "I can't believe it, Shifrah. I visited the French Quarter for the first time in my life only hours ago, and now, this *Sunset Limited* train has a lounge with the same name? It says here it has New Orleans-style wrought-iron grillwork and, listen to this, 'The French Quarter Lounge, where Sunset Pink walls set a national fashion trend.' Isn't that dramatic? This other card says the French Quarter Lounge has 'pink walls, a pink ceiling, white grillwork, and interesting people.'

"Their Audubon diner car has bird paintings on the walls painted by a famous naturalist painter, and look at this photo. It's called The Pride of Texas Coffee Shop and Lounge car with cattle brands and long-horned steer sculptures. That should make me feel right at home, shouldn't it? They weren't kidding calling it the only train with *a Southern Accent,"* I chuckle. "Want to see the photos?"

No response from her, just a stare out the window. At home, we'd say Shifrah is still *bullin'* about our sleeping arrangements, which means she's pouting. I don't understand why our sleeping arrangements are bothering her so much. I lean my head back to think. Right away, I congratulate myself for saying yes to this journey. If I wanted to look at it metaphorically, which my literature professor at college would be proud of, my world has grown from the size of a pecan into a whole section—that is, six hundred and forty acres—of pecan trees. Who will I become with an expanded world like that? Will I want to go back to Laredo and buy the Dixie? What made me grab at this opportunity like a drowning woman grasping for a tree limb above a raging river? Will I really be wealthy when the mission is over?

We eat dinner in the Audubon Room and quietly separate to go to our sleeping areas. Shifrah asks for the top bed, and I don't care a fig one way or the other. I open a book and settle in to read. Ten pages in, Shifrah's head appears upside down inside the parted curtains separating our bunks from the aisle.

"Mind if I join you?"

"Come on down."

"Aren't I interrupting your reading?"

"That's okay. I'd rather visit."

Shifrah curls down from the top bed onto the lower one. Her royal-blue silk pajamas are so bright, I almost squint to look at them.

"I can't sleep. If we talk a little while, maybe I'll get sleepy. Want half of my Almond Joy?"

I smile, and she unwraps it, handing me half.

"I'm wondering about something. You and Reno are both from Texas, but you don't have the same manner of speaking. You have that cute Texas accent like he does, of course, and some of your sayings are wonderfully funny and quaint, but mostly, Savannah, you speak very classy."

"Why, thank you. Believe me, I wasn't always this way."

"Oh?"

"You have to understand my daddy was from Georgia, so I had what I call a Texas-Georgia accent. That kind of southern drawl can flip your tongue on its backside."

"Huh?"

"Sorry, that's just slang derived from people saying Southerners talk with a slow, lazy tongue. Anyway, when Daddy passed away, I was devastated. We were so close, had only each other after Mama deserted us. I missed him so much, but I grieved my own way—alone. I decided right after the funeral I wasn't going back to school."

"But you were merely twelve, weren't you?"

"Yes."

"What caused such a decision?"

"Looking back, I think I was trying to find an identity, my place in the world as an orphan. I sure went about it in a cockeyed way."

"Tell me."

"It's kind of a long story. You sure you want to hear it?"

"I must."

"All right, settle in, as they say back home."

She tucks her legs under her like a graceful deer, takes a nibble of her candy bar.

"I suppose being allowed to help out in the diner from the time I was five made me too big for my britches. Um, that means I was puffed up with foolish pride, in case you don't know. A day after the funeral, I walked into the diner's kitchen and informed Tony I wasn't going back to school, not ever, and that wasn't all. I expected him to hire me as his full-time manager at top-dollar pay."

Shifrah shakes her head. "No wonder you were chosen for this mission, Savannah. Such *chutzpah!*"

"What's that?"

"Bravado."

"Hmm, maybe. Say, speaking of being chosen for this mission, when will you tell me about that communiqué? Where did it come from, and what was it? How was the information gathered?"

"You didn't finish your story."

"Don't change the subject, Shifrah."

"All right. It's simple really. You already know there's a headquarters team working on contacting the people who have the artifacts, right?" I nod. "Honestly, all I know is they gathered information about certain candidates for the mission, and you were their top pick. The mission was already planned, and the last thing before offering you the job involved Malone and I traveling to Laredo,

Texas, to see for ourselves how you handled yourself at the diner. We both had to personally approve you."

"But my passport was already created. That was a long shot."

"Yes, but the *powers that be* were certain you would agree. To be perfectly transparent, Savannah, they had already sent people to observe you, more than once, had already seen your school records, documented your interests, etcetera. Still, it was up to Malone and me to decide whether we felt compatible with you. You're frowning. Does hearing this bother you?"

"Well, yeah. It feels odd to know strangers were secretly scrutinizing, investigating, judging me, and I had no idea."

Shifrah pulls her knees up, studies the rose-pink polish on her toenails, polish that perfectly matches the rose-pink high heels and hat she wore on the airplane.

"I mean, how did you like it, Shifrah?"

"Like what?"

"Being secretly investigated."

"Oh, well, my selection process was different, Savannah."

"Why is that?"

"Can I tell you next time? I'm dying to hear the rest of the story about you outgrowing your breeches."

"I think you mean I was *too big for my britches.*"

"What a cute way to say you were haughty."

She sidestepped again.

"Okay, Shifrah, we'll talk tomorrow about how you came to be on this mission. I'm holding you to that."

She nods.

"Well, like I said, Daddy was gone, and my decision was to quit school and, further, I just knew I was fully qualified to be in charge of a busy diner full of grownup staff and customers. I had no doubt Tony would agree with me. I walked into the kitchen, chin up, hands on my hips, ready to tell him a thing or two."

"I can see the whole scene in my mind," she says, smiling.

"It's kind of embarrassing, but should I use my old twangy accent to tell you the story?"

"That sounds like fun."

"Okay. So, there I was standing all smug, and I said, 'Tony, now listen here. You see those fly specks hanging on the curtains by the booths from last summer? That ain't fitting in a place where people eat food. Those glass pie shelves out by the counter? Covered in smudgy fingerprints. It's downright unappetizing. The overhead fan needs scrubbing, too. Shoot, there's half an inch of grime hanging on the blades from all the frying going on in this kitchen.'"

"Was it really that bad?"

"Not at all. I was exaggerating to be more convincing. Tony was nodding like he agreed with me, so I kept going. 'It's my feeling the waitresses here ought to be wearing same-colored uniforms with starched white aprons. They do over at Cora's Café downtown, and it sure looks pleasant. We don't have to be so heathren, do we, all of us wearing regular clothes, any color, like we don't have a lick of sense in this diner?'

Since he still wasn't saying anything, just kept kneading dough on a floured board, I thought I sure had shown him how brilliant I was. I ended with, 'Something else, Tony. More schooling is a waste of my time since I already know everything I need to know to run this place. Heck, I been working here since I was five, haven't I? Now you see why I should quit school and manage this place and get paid grown-up money for doing it, don't you?'

"Boy, I was proud of myself. I was swollen up like an old bullfrog on a hot night. I expected full compliance to my sassy demands. Looking back, I sure wouldn't have put up with a little smart-mouth like that, but Tony saw through my bluster, knew it was a coverup for my pain over losing Daddy. He didn't make me manager, of course, but he gave me more opportunities than ever to learn how to cook and how to manage part of the bookkeeping. On his terms, not mine.

"He and Maria fixed up the little cabin outside their nice home behind the diner, and the staff and the regulars came as a group to move me out of the house Daddy and I had been living in and into that little cabin. Tony and Maria tried their best to get me to move in with them, but I wouldn't do it."

"You wouldn't? I've never heard of such courage in a child, Savannah."

"A lot of it was pure stubbornness, Shifrah. Anyway, Tony and Maria were smart. They used my addiction to the Dixie as bribery to inspire me to stay in school. All the regulars were in firm agreement about my education, so I finally surrendered and decided to love school, and, strangely enough, wound up excelling. Honestly, with so many hurrahs from everyone, I couldn't help myself.

"My twangy bad grammar disappeared. I became infatuated with books, geography, history. I learned Spanish and picked up a few medals in track. I earned a gold necklace with a miniature typewriter on the end for being the fastest typist at Martin High School. My adopted *dads* cheering me on at the volleyball games and track meets—ten, fifteen, or more at a time—made me the envy of the school. Of course, I worked at the diner as often as allowed on weekends, holidays, and in the summer."

"Weren't there any women besides Maria who helped take care of you?"

"Oh, sure. Some of the wives and waitresses tried to mother me through the years, but women fussing over me gave me the heebie-jeebies. I was a daddy's girl, and maybe I wasn't ready to forgive my mama for taking off with some no-account. Who knows? But Tony and the regulars were the ones I listened to and allowed in my heart. I was a tomboy when Daddy was alive, and I stayed one. I learned how to catch, clean, and debone a mess of fish. How to change tires and service engines. I learned how to shoot, hunt, and ride horses. The first time I showed up at the diner without my braids and wearing a dress before I delivered a world history speech in the school auditorium my sophomore year, everyone nearly fainted.

"I was sixteen before the feminine side of my character showed up. I got crushes on at least three or four guys starting toward the end of my sophomore year in high school, but my regulars never allowed me to be distracted. They'd teach me something new, use any ploy to keep my mind off dating. Heck, those years passed faster than all get out, and will you look at this, Shifrah? My country twang is taking me over!" I laugh, but Shifrah doesn't.

"What's wrong? You didn't like my story?"

"Oh, I loved it. Really. It's just that you've had so many tragedies in your life, and you've never let them defeat you. Quite the contrary, they molded you into someone very special. I wish I was that strong."

"But you are, Shifrah. Look, on this mission, you're keeping up with two ex-military men and a tomboy, well, an ex-tomboy. It's rattling your cage a little bit, but you have your own things to be proud of."

"Like what?"

"Like knowing how to handle yourself in public better than anyone I've ever seen. You could write a book about it! You dress like a fashion plate, and your hair and makeup—"

"All that can be learned like this," she says, snapping her fingers.

"I don't know about that. You'd better get to teaching me a little faster then," I chuckle, hoping to make her smile. She doesn't. "Um, here's another one… you finished college. You're degreed."

"Not quite. I had an interruption."

"What was it?"

Shifrah looks down. "I-I've done some pretty dumb things, let's just say that."

"Everyone does dumb things growing up. That's being a kid or a teenager. One time, I started a grease fire because I thought I—"

"No, it was more than that."

"Can you tell me about it?"

She shakes her head, fake yawns. "Sure, but not right now. I'm too sleepy. We have plenty of time tomorrow, right?"

"Um-hm."

Another phony yawn. "'Night, Savannah. I loved your invigorating story." She parts the curtain and hoists herself into the bed above mine. She sticks her head back over the side, smiles, and that's that.

CHAPTER EIGHTEEN

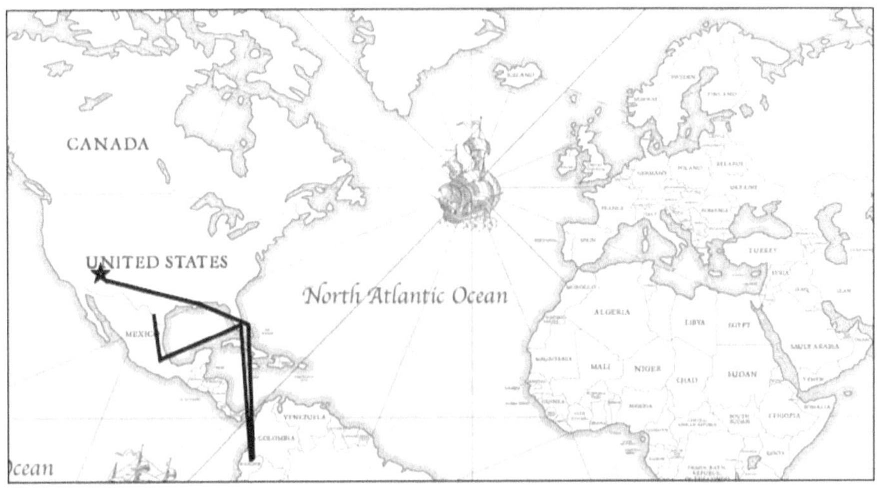

I'd rather gut, descale, and debone a hundred bony trout or work on engines with oil up to my chin than ever spend another half day walking in high heels and shopping in downtown Phoenix at Goldwater's, Diamond's, and Korrick's.

"Never, ever go shopping in flats, Savannah. That's a high school look," Shifrah told me, and that was enough to make me change from the flats I was wearing into those raised-up chambers of torture called high heels.

Before this mission, I wore high heels only a smattering of times, a fact I told her. Her reaction was a wide-eyed stare. She said, "That's beyond my logic, Savannah. I've been wearing them since I was eleven. Guess what? I saw some beautiful stilettos advertised in that little paper we picked up in the lobby. They're at a downtown store named

Diamonds. Isn't that the best name? Do you suppose David Diamond in Ecuador is related to the Diamonds who own the store here? Wouldn't that be a lark?"

Leaving the Adam's Hotel, the doorman said, "We're having a heat wave before Fall settles in, ladies. Be careful out there." He was more than right. This mid-October day gave us 103 degrees by noon. What that kind of rude sunshine does to the temperature of the sidewalks and streets we walked on is anybody's guess, but my feet now feel like swollen bricks. I've sweated through my dress at least three times, my hair is stringy, and my face looks permanently red. I'm staring at myself in the bathroom mirror in our hotel room while Shifrah digs happily through our purchases in the other room. I hear boxes opening and closing, tissue paper crunching, and, of all things, she's humming!

"Let's waste no time, Savannah," she practically sings. "You finish your toilette so I can do mine. I'm laying our party clothes for tonight out on the beds. I can't wait to see you in this after-five dress. Deep velvet blue is a stunning color for you! Our appointments at the beauty salon are in less than an hour and a half from now, and we'll need enough time to primp and dress up after our hair is done, not to mention I'm using all my expertise on your face before we go to the salon."

Her words send an electrical shock through my nervous system. "Shifrah, I hope you don't mind, but I changed my mind about the beauty shop. I'll just wash my hair here in the sink and sit under the air conditioner to dry it. It'll be fine."

"What insanity am I hearing? It's your birthday! You're going to look like a Hollywood star tonight. I already told you who you look like, and I'm designing your hair and makeup to prove it to you. Oh, you're not quite as busty as her, and neither am I, thank goodness. We certainly wouldn't want to carry around such huge bosoms, would we? I mean, what a lot of work!" She breaks out in boisterous laughter.

"Shifrah, please, I don't—"

"Nuh-uh, I'm not listening. We meet the men at six at The Flame. Oh, I'm so excited. Their eyes are going to pop out!"

At this point in our journey, Shifrah and I are friends, and sometimes, though I've never had any real experiences to compare it to, it feels as if I have a sister—a bossy, sophisticated, nice sister. She seems to know everything about my previous life, but she won't tell me anything about hers. Why is her past so private?

Right now, I wouldn't mind folding her up and leaving her inside one of those fancy ribboned boxes we brought home from the stores. My ideal birthday evening would be peeling off this sweaty dress, taking a bath, washing my hair, and dressing in casual clothes. I would go inform Malone and Reno I wanted to grab a quick bite and go to bed early before our drive to the canyon in the morning. A cheeseburger and a soft drink in a little café would be perfect for my birthday meal.

On the other hand, I must admit I love tapping into Shifrah's sophistication, and I've already gleaned a lot from her. I've gone along with almost everything up to now. What she doesn't realize is I'm fundamentally self-conscious about standing out in a crowd when it has to do with my personal self. Give a speech. Run the track. Handle big crowds at the diner. None of that bothers me, but if something tosses me into the center of the spotlight for no valid reason other than myself, I squirm and head for the door. I think it's because of growing up under the influence of down-to-earth men. Whatever made me this way, I've skirted around it so far by letting Shifrah add a clothing item or make a suggestion, which has been fun.

Tonight, thanks to my eager teammate, who apparently has made me her personal project, I will stand out, and I don't know how to get out of the whole thing. Today, she went a little crazy having me try on clothes, boldly picking out several outfits for me, including the one for tonight. I like to believe I can't be pushed around, and I can't be, but despite my misgivings, I'm flattered that she cares how I am "turned out," as we say back home.

"Savannah, have you finished your toilette?"

"Just about," I say, turning on the bathtub faucet and quietly closing the door to the bathroom.

* * *

Why can't I ever be wrong when I have a premonition? The short walk down the sidewalk from the Adams Hotel to The Flame restaurant almost ruined my life, just as I predicted it would.

After my toilette, as Shifrah calls it, she applied my makeup. She wouldn't let me look at it, a very strange experience in itself. I always said I wasn't going to wear eye makeup until I decided to wear it, perhaps never, but she declared, "We're riding on the backs of smelly mules into a giant hole in the earth in a few days, for Pete's sake. That defies all beauty rules, so why not go all out tonight, Savannah? What can it hurt for once?" I didn't have an answer, and I guess I got caught up in her excitement and shrugged my shoulders in compliance.

We took a taxi to the beauty salon, and Shifrah left me sitting in the fancy reception area with my back to all the mirrors while she "consulted" with the beautician scheduled to do my hair. Going along with someone's nonsense like this is not like me, but a part of my being was enjoying the heck out of it. Throwing all seriousness aside for once was different, to say the least. I'll say this… going to a fancy salon is nothing like visiting Jake's Barber Shop in Laredo every few months for a quick hair trim.

I was soon whisked away to a pump-up chair with my back always to the mirror, and not one, but two, and sometimes three, women went to work on my hair. Shifrah, when she wasn't telling them how to do this or that to my hair, sat across the room smiling encouragement at me from the mirror in front of her salon chair as they did her hair. When the cape was whisked off and my chair was flamboyantly spun around toward the mirror, I gasped. I barely recognized myself, and the oddest thing is Shifrah has been right all along. I do look like that movie star she keeps mentioning! What am I to do with that? The whole salon clapped while I stared open-mouthed at my reflection. My new hairdo combined with the makeup Shifrah applied, including scratchy fake eyelashes, literally made me speechless. All I could think was *I love this, and I hate this, but I love this!*

My hair is at least a shade lighter than my own blond hair with a faint glint of red now. It has different layers, and they styled it in a way that it sweeps to the side in the front and utilizes my natural waves all the way to the ends. They didn't cut off any length, but it looks longer than its regular several inches below my shoulders, perhaps because I seldom wear it in anything but a ponytail or bun.

"Aren't you ravishing, Savannah!" Shifrah said, clapping her hands and shaking her head in admiration as she stared at me. The attention in the salon turned my face purple. Shifrah rescued me by grabbing my elbow and taking us to the front. She paid, and we stepped outside to a waiting taxi. We didn't talk on the taxi ride back to the hotel, and Shifrah seemed to understand I was kind of in silent shock.

At the hotel, I dressed like a quiet mannequin, surrendering to Shifrah's touches of a certain one of her necklaces, wearing her crystal and sapphire dinner ring, spraying my arms with her Shalimar perfume, her ruffling and arranging the gauzy halo of pale-blue material at the top of the dress and making sure my hosiery was straight.

My life changed as soon as I stepped out of our hotel room.

Savannah made me pose beside a potted fern in the hallway and again in front of the closed elevator doors so she could snap pictures of me. A few people passed by, smiled, and I cringed. When the elevator doors opened, every man inside stared long and hard at us, then moved aside like regimented chess pieces. Their stares felt as prickly as running barefoot through a patch of Texas sandburs. Stepping out of the elevator, the elevator operator, a red-headed young man, put a hand on my arm. "Ma'am, are you her? Are you that lady in the movies?" he asked, and I stood there like a kid caught playing hooky.

Shifrah, frowning, lifted his hand off my arm by his jacket sleeve. "Anita Ekberg only wishes she was this beautiful creature," she sniffed in her snootiest voice. She locked her arm in mine and escorted us quickly through the lobby as if we were royalty. Me? I just hung onto that arm and let her direct us out of the hotel and down the sidewalk, but then, for the first time in my life, men whistled and yelled out of their windows from cars. I did a U-turn in the sidewalk heading back to the safety of our room, but Shifrah looped her arm more tightly in mine and put us back on the path to the restaurant.

"I-I can't do this, Shifrah. It's awful! Surely you don't like this kind of attention?"

"No, I don't like it. I love it!" she replied, not giving me an inch of room in her tight grasp. "You'll get used to it, darling, have no fear. This is your coming-out-debut. You've been under wraps for too many years."

"But I like it that way. I don't want to be the center of attention."

"It was only a matter of time. You're twenty-one years old today, and your days of refilling coffee cups and hanging out with the men in the mud to catch dogfish are over."

"Catfish."

"Huh?"

"It's catfish we stick our hands in the mud to catch."

"Oh, whatever. You know what I mean."

"I'm still going noodling when I want to."

She picks up the pace, still holding onto my arm as if it will fall off if she lets go. "What a strange name, noodling," she mumbles.

"Isn't it? They think the Scots brought the term *noodling* to the South because *guddling* is an old Scottish word that sounds a lot like *noodling* phonetically. The Scottish word means catching fish by hand, even reaching into mud or under rocky overhangs. Shifrah, can you believe the word *guddling* is used in the American classic *Kidnapped* by Robert Louis Stevenson? When I found that out—"

Shifrah puts the brakes on, almost making me fall on my face as I tilt forward on the pointed toes of my high heels. "For heaven's sake, Savannah," she says, staring at me with exaggerated shock. "Such chatter! Pleeeze don't be so smart all the time."

"I'm not. I'm interested in noodling, so of course I was interested in how it got such an odd name. It's no big deal."

"All right, all right, but for now, let's not think of it. Don't think about fish, mud, engines, or shooting snakes. Tonight, can you pretend I'm your fairy godmother and you're going to the ball?"

What if I don't want to be Cinderella?

I nod, and she raises her shoulders in relief and ushers us through the door of the restaurant.

CHAPTER NINETEEN

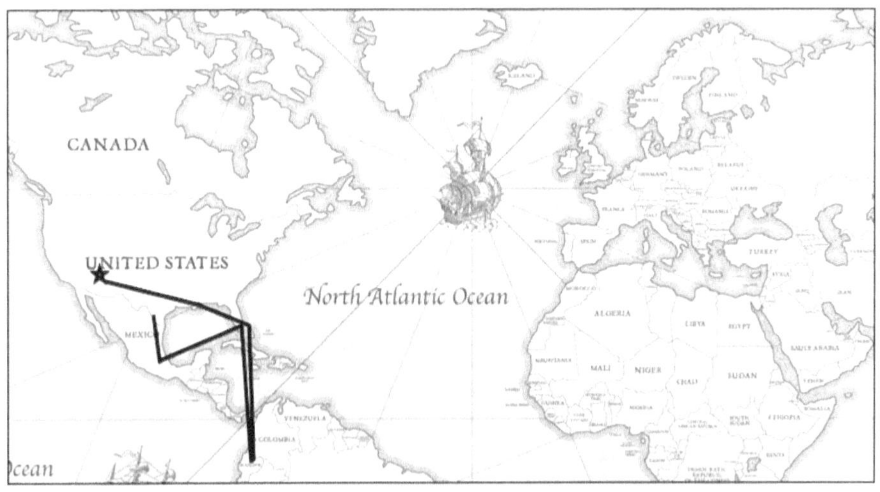

With practiced skill and precision, Shifrah speaks to the tuxedoed *Maître d'* inside. He nods and says, "Ah, yes, the gentlemen are waiting for you in our Jungle Bar. Your table will be ready shortly." He gestures dramatically, all smiles, pointing the way.

Walking with Shifrah to join Malone and Reno feels like walking the last mile to the electric chair. If Shifrah wasn't holding my hand, I'd bolt. Entering the bar area, we collectively gasp at the lush tropical plants and trees growing against the long side of the room. It looks exactly like a jungle scene from a Tarzan movie, thick like the Ecuadorian jungle, but with different foliage… friendlier looking, like in Miami.

I can't help but stare at the mesh-enclosed scene that has a waterfall with rocks covered in moss, birds sitting in the trees, and a cage holding a monkey grasping the bars and looking as if he's smiling at the customers. It's hard to imagine such a restaurant as this one existing in Laredo, or maybe, anywhere else. It doesn't smell like the rainforest with its dampened dirt and tangled greenery, but there's a definite moist, cool feeling that hits us as we walk in.

Malone and Reno are sitting at a dramatic curved bar with their backs to us, and I notice the leather pouch strap crisscrossed over Malone's shoulder. The bartenders behind the bar are visiting with the customers and stand at eye level with them. A table with four young women is close to the bar, and from the looks of it, the women are vying for Reno's attention by talking loudly, giggling, and watching to see if he turns around. Reno remains locked in conversation with Malone, seemingly unaware of them. Malone turns a half-turn to the right with a glance over his shoulder. One of the women smiles broadly, jiggles her shoulders slightly, flutters her eyelashes at him.

Is she flirting with Malone? With him being so stoic and serious all the time, not to mention he's in charge of our mission, I forget he's quite handsome in his own serious way. I don't get to think more about it because Shifrah giggles, pulls me by the hand as she glides toward the men.

She's beside herself showing off her new "creation."

She taps Malone on the shoulder. Both men turn around. There we stand, and I swear there's a spotlight shining on me from the roof by the way Malone and Reno squint, stretch their necks, exchange confused looks, then stare at me like they've lost their senses.

Shifrah clears her throat. "Gentlemen, I present to you the one and only Miss Savannah Wright of Texas!"

Both men stand up, eyes glued on me, and I am numb except for my blistering face and neck. Reno whistles under his breath, and Malone smiles bigger than I've ever seen him smile. I wobble slightly on my high heels and feel faint. Shifrah rescues me again.

"Let's go sit at that table over there until they call us for dinner, shall we?" She takes my arm and, before I know it, we're seated around a small round table with all their eyes on me.

"Savannah, Savannah, Savannah, on your twenty-first birthday, you're as flat-out lovely as a red-bud tree in full bloom. I take that back—a whole grove of those early Spring blossoms doesn't compare to your pretty self," Reno says.

"I second that!" Malone says, raising his glass in the air.

"It was always there, gentlemen. Anyone could see that. It just needed a little glamourizing and a few finishing touches," Shifrah says exuberantly. "She's the spitting image of Anita Ekberg, the actress, and I knew it the first time I saw her photo. All I did was pluck her eyebrows, apply eyeliner and eye shadow, add eyelashes, highlight her lips with that delectable Max Factor Coral Glow you see right now, and… voila! Our beauty queen emerges! Did you know this is her first time to wear any makeup other than a little lipstick and powder?"

Whoa! This is too personal, Shifrah. Stop!

Malone whips out his black-framed glasses, leans in close to me. "You know, she does look like that actress, Shifrah."

Hey, I'm right here hearing every word y'all are saying!

"What I'm wondering is how we're gonna keep the fellas off this Yellow Rose of Texas wonder, you know?" Reno says with a broad smile.

"With heavy artillery," Malone says, and everyone laughs.

"Does that mean we have to hire bodyguards now?" Reno says.

"Most certainly!" Shifrah says.

"Excuse me, I'm going back to the hotel," I say, gathering my purse and rising from my chair.

"What's wrong, Savannah?" Shifrah says, half rising from her own chair. "Are you not feeling well?"

"I feel fine, but y'all act like I'm not even here, nothing more than a-a dressed-up dummy in a store window. If that's how I get treated by fixing up a little, I won't do it again. I don't care how much lipstick you smear on a horse's lips, it's still a horse, and I'm still the same Savannah I was before Shifrah dooded me up like this."

It's as if a small tornado hits our table, everyone saying *I'm sorry this* and *I'm sorry that* and begging me to forgive them and stay for my birthday dinner. It doesn't take long for me to tuck my tailfeathers back in and settle down, since I'm not the kind to hold a grudge. Besides, missing the opportunity to see the Amazon artifact before Malone airmails it to Mr. A is not acceptable, no matter what I have to endure before that happens.

* * *

Yes, I danced a fox trot with a stranger who asked, though I wasn't very good at it, and yes, I had two glasses of champagne. I didn't think it tastes as good as a cold 7-Up, but it was bubbly and fun, and my companions were proud of me for tasting it on my twenty-first birthday. We toasted to my birthday, to our success in Ecuador, and to the upcoming mule ride into the Grand Canyon. I thought the toasting was more fun than drinking the champagne, but I kept that to myself. I guess the champagne did give me a little courage because I let Shifrah snap photos of me inside the bar and restaurant without protesting a whole lot.

We dined on chickens brought to the table on a sword and set on fire. I've never seen anything like that before, and I wonder what Tony would think of such a grand extravaganza put on for the lowly chicken. At last, our plates are cleared away, we're having coffee, and Malone places the leather pouch on the table in front of him. Shifrah kicks me under the table, and when I look at her, she rubs her hands together in anticipation of this moment.

Malone pulls out a flat, metal object and places it on top of the pouch. We crane our necks to study it. It's a metal rectangle with a rounded top. I guess it to be about seven inches wide and ten inches long. There are seven keyholes with engravings that resemble ancient hieroglyphics on the side of each one.

"Malone, what are those strange symbols beside each keyhole?"

Shifrah asks.

He holds his jaw in one hand, says, "Let's see, I think I have this right. They're ancient words from a language no longer used. Mr. A told me something about it, but vaguely. Kind of slips my mind exactly what he said."

"How could you forget something like that?" Shifrah says.

"By hearing it only once and having a lot on my mind at the same time. Anyway, does anyone want to know about this thing, or should I put it away? It flies out tomorrow."

"Tell us about it, please!" I say, a bit more dramatically than I had planned.

Did the champagne make me do that?

"Okay, headquarters calls this the *key to the keys*. Basically, it's the map, or pattern, to the *retrieves* we're collecting on this mission. You won't believe where David kept it."

"Where?" I ask.

"Inside that monkey statue. Been there for years."

"You're kidding!"

"I'm not, Savannah. The sculpture supposedly houses a terrifying monkey demon that steals the soul from anyone who messes with it, curses them and their family forever. Guess who started that rumor in the first place? Yeah. Clever as hell."

"Even the twins didn't know it was inside the sculpture?"

"No one except David, his wife, and that other guy he mentioned. He told the girls to keep you in that bathroom as long as possible so he could discuss 'important business with his visitors, but it was really to keep them from seeing how he unscrewed the top half of the monkey from the bottom half and pried the *key to the keys* loose from the bottom of the first half. He wanted it to remain a secret for obvious reasons."

"It was a horrible-looking monkey, Shifrah. A nightmare. You should be glad you didn't see it. I'll never forget the face on it," I say.

"I was too busy keeping my head the same size as it is now. Do you know what those etchings beside the keyholes mean, Malone?"

"They tell which order the keys are to be inserted, and I think I have this right, whether they turn clockwise or counter-clockwise and how many times each way."

"So, all the other *retrieves* are keys?" she asks.

"Affirmative."

"When the keys are placed a certain way and turned a certain way, what do they open?" I ask.

Malone's shoulders rise and fall as he takes in and releases a deep breath. "To be discussed later. Tomorrow, this valuable piece of our operation will be airmailed with high-security measures to Mr. A."

"Airmailed where?" Shifrah asks.

Malone doesn't answer, carefully places the metal back into the pouch, spins the small combination lock, and loops the strap over his head. He pushes his chair out from the table and gazes at Shifrah and me. "I trust with all that shopping you women did today, you have the right clothes for riding mules?"

"You're changing the subject. You aren't going to tell us anything else, are you?" Shifrah says.

"Sure. Here it is. We get a good night's rest, eat breakfast on our own, and meet in the hotel lobby at 0800 in the morning. We drive a rented car to Grand Canyon Village, ride mules into the canyon the day after tomorrow. We spend the night at Phantom Ranch in the bottom where our contact meets us and gives us our first real *retrieve,* a key. Got it?"

"What about—?"

"Did you remember to buy western boots?"

Shifrah sighs and rolls her eyes. "Yes, yes, of course, we did. We shopped most of the day, but I still want to know what the keys open and where Mr. A is."

"Sometimes, you gotta wait a month of Sundays to find out how the big pot fits in the little pot, Shif," Reno says with a twinkle in his eye. "Hey, y'all hand me that bottle so I can swig the last swallow of champagne. I kind of like that stuff."

"Sure does beat rot-gut moonshine, now don't it?" I say in my twangiest deep-southern accent, and that causes everyone to laugh, clearing the air.

"Savannah, that accent does not go with the new you," Shifrah says.

"Sure it does, Shif. She's part Georgian, I hear, since her daddy was from there. If she happens to be prettier than a Georgia peach, I'd say she can talk like one if she has a mind to," Reno says.

Malone stands up, clears his throat. Everything about him says *the party's over.* "Happy birthday, Savannah. You ladies looked top-notch tonight. I trust you won't go to this much trouble fixing up every day."

"We'll never abandon our beauty regimen, no matter what insane place you drag us to, Malone," Shifrah says, her chin lifted slightly.

"Uh-huh. I see. Well, time to go." He rapidly leads the way to the door and doesn't see Shifrah mouthing his last words with her eyes crossed. Reno and I laugh. Malone turns around. We show him straight faces and follow him out of the restaurant.

CHAPTER TWENTY

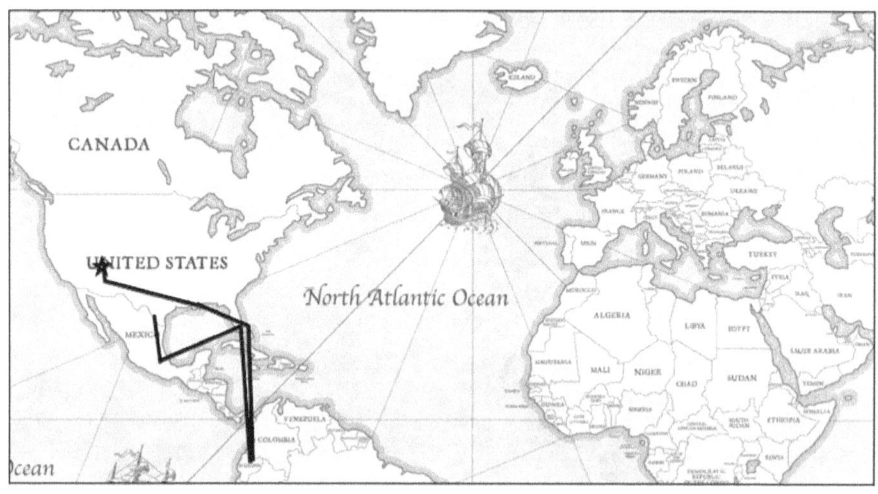

Shifrah slides silently into the upholstered chair in our hotel room and buries her face in her hands. "No, I just cannot do it, Savannah. I won't. It's terrifying. Did you look at that *thing* right outside the windows, so dangerously close and horrifying? It-it's too big, a nightmare. It's going to swallow me."

"What I see is the most beautiful *thing* I've ever seen in my life, except for my first glance at the Wurlitzer jukebox at the Dixie Diner. The sign in the lobby by the desk listed several interesting facts about that canyon. Did you read it?"

"No."

"Well, it said the canyon is a mile deep. Imagine that! From rim to rim, it's ten to eighteen miles across. The river at the bottom is the Colorado River, and the elevation here on this South Rim is about 7,000 feet. Come on, Shifrah, it's magnificent! Photos and paintings don't do it justice."

She groans. "It's a bottomless pit! I had no idea it would look so terrifying. We're supposed to ride into it on mules, and we'll probably never be heard from again. Please, Savannah! Help me get out of this."

"Outside of murder, I don't think it's possible. Malone already said no excuses tomorrow. He specifically said if we get headaches or other problems, we're still riding to the Phantom Ranch at the bottom of the canyon tomorrow. Truly, I don't understand why the contact didn't come out of there and meet us here at the hotel."

"I know why. It's because Malone won't put his foot down with that horrid Mr. A and tell him we're ladies and not roughnecks. If Malone would only try to understand… oh, I feel like the whole world is against me!"

She may feel like that, but I feel like this assignment has everything to do with the conversation I overheard with Malone saying "he" wanted us to tromp through the hardest parts of the mission. I don't feel like sharing that with Shifrah yet because she would probably want to confront Malone about it.

"At least Phantom Ranch looks nice, Shifrah. Here's a photo brochure showing little cabins snuggled underneath cottonwood trees with those massive canyon walls on every side. It looks like a wonderland."

Shifrah stares at me, groans, drops her head back into her hands.

"Reno said they have a natural swimming hole at that Phantom Ranch. It's part of the river. Fishing, too. Guess they have bait and tackle for the guests. I'm kind of aching to drop a pole in the water, if you know what I mean."

"No, I don't."

"Just a country way of saying I yearn to do a little fishing. Aren't you curious to meet our second contact?"

"No, I simply want a hot bath, a massage, and a cappuccino from Caffe Reggio's down in the Village."

"I'll bet you'll be wishing you had all that fancy pampering after we get back, not before we go."

"But mules, Savannah? Are we hillbillies? Why can't we at least ride horses tomorrow?"

I sit down in the chair opposite her and wait until she's looking at me full-on. "Ever see a spooked horse run toward a cliff, Shifrah?"

"Only in a movie or two."

"Okay, keep that picture in your mind. It's darned near impossible to stop a scared horse, even when he's running toward death and doom. On the other hand, mules understand how to pick their way down a steep hill, or, in this case, a canyon trail, and they do it with ease, almost like mountain goats. One of my regulars at the diner, Earl Parks, had a herd of mules, and his affection for them gave me a whole different perspective on the 'long ears,' as he calls them. People think they're stubborn when they refuse to cooperate, and sometimes they are, but, a lot of times, they have more *horse sense* than horses do when there's danger."

She doesn't answer. I walk over and pick up a small instruction book on the dresser and thumb through it. "This says all hats must be tied on so they won't scare the mules if a gust of wind blows a hat off someone's head. We'd better make some holes in our straw hats and thread a couple of your scarves through them."

"Rules, rules, and more rules. What else does it boss us to do?"

I flip through pages. "It says the mules are very experienced and sure-footed and they work as pack mules going in and out of the canyon a few years before they become trail mules. Even if it looks like they're walking too close to the edge of the trail, it says we can trust them because they don't want to fall any more than we do. Doesn't that make you feel better?"

"Nothing about this place makes me feel better. I'm finding out I'm one-hundred-percent *not* a country girl. The outdoors is too frightening for me."

"Give yourself a break, Shifrah. We just returned from a trip to the scariest forest in the world and now we're headed to the bottom of the biggest canyon in the world. Who normally does that? You told me when you were talking me into this that I'd go places others only dream about, and you were right."

"I was talking about some of the other places we're going to later and like when we travel to Europe on a passenger ship. Malone told me before you joined us that one part of this excursion might involve going to a castle. Can you imagine that?" She closes her eyes, opens them. "No one said we'd be in places where black alligators carry you away and monkeys scream like phantoms and you're forced to ride animals into a canyon of hell. Besides, didn't Malone ask me if I had any experience working with children this morning? Of course, my answer is a resounding *no*. I've never spent any time at all with those noisy little people. Only God knows what other hazards await us."

"Well, if the *hazards* involve watching kids, we got that one handled. They're easy, Shifrah. You just think like they do and go from there. It's fun. I did a lot of babysitting for some of the trucker's wives after I turned thirteen, so I know what I'm talking about. Lots of kiddos are in the diner all the time, and they love me."

She gives me a peculiar look, buries her head in her hands again, rocks back and forth. She's the most unlikely candidate for a mission like this I can imagine. Am I a good candidate? When will my skills mean anything on this journey?

"When will you make good your promise, Shifrah?"

"What promise?"

"To tell me how you were recruited for this mission. I want to know what skills they were looking at."

"I have to use the bathroom."

"No, you don't. Come on, what's the big secret?"

"It's personal."

"So is my life, and you know all about it."

She sighs heavily. "I-I got into some trouble."

"You? That's impossible."

"No, it isn't. It's par for the course for kids of wealthy parents. I was hanging out with a gang, er, a group of kids, well, not kids, we were all in college. Affluent, fancy cars, money to burn or do anything we wanted. That spells trouble. It did for me, anyway. I was becoming more bored and restless by the day. I had already traveled several places, had everything I ever asked for and then some. I became disinterested in my university studies, broke up with the guy I was dating. I suppose what happened was inevitable."

"What was inevitable?"

"Oh, that I'd try something different. When the idea came up, I jumped in with both feet. Nothing worked out as we planned, to say the least, and now, I can't believe it even happened. So, anyway, are you ready to go shopping in that quaint Hopi House Gift Shop we saw earlier? We have time before we meet the men for dinner. This El Tovar Hotel has a rather interesting lobby, especially if you like the Southwestern motif. Bet there's a lot of history attached to this place."

Shall I let her get away with this or call her bluff?

"Fix your lipstick, Savannah, it's faded. I'll freshen mine, too, and then we have about an hour to shop. This may be our last chance to shop before we fall to our deaths tomorrow, you know?" She smiles slightly and digs in her purse for her lipstick. She looks up. "What are you waiting for?"

"For the rest of the story."

She looks forlorn again, and I guess I have too much of a soft spot for sad people because I decide to let her off the hook. I sigh noisily. "Okay, we'll go shopping, but just know that I'm buying you some buckskin moccasins and a hand-woven Navajo shawl in the gift shop. I expect you to wear them with your fancy dress for dinner tonight or my feelings will be hurt."

Her startled look makes me laugh.

"Kidding, Shifrah, only kidding."

* * *

The cowbell on the door of the gift shop clangs again, and I look up and notice a man who looks familiar. Why? Oh, he's the man Shifrah and I saw in the Miami airport when we flew in from Ecuador, and, strangely enough, I also saw him in the train station. The same man in three of the places we've been? That's odd. I study him and notice Shifrah doing the same. She edges close to me.

"Be clandestine, Savannah. Keep your head down but your eyes up," she whispers. I nod, and we move to the leather and concha belts, chattering and pretending to be interested in the belts. The man is looking over the ponchos. I edge closer. He looks up, smiles. I return his smile and move past him. He leaves.

"Can you believe that?" Shifrah says with saucer eyes. "That man is following us, I just know it!"

"I didn't tell you I saw him in the train station in New Orleans, did I? He always wears a hat, but I've got his body type memorized. Other stuff, too."

"Not hard to do. He's built funny," Shifrah says. "Did I tell you I thought I saw him in The Flame restaurant in Phoenix, but then I decided it was my imagination?"

"Really?"

"Maybe he's another Jack the Ripper, Savannah."

"Oh, my lands. You should write novels with that imagination of yours. I doubt it's any big deal, but we better mention it to Malone."

"He gave me the creeps. Let's get out of here."

CHAPTER TWENTY-ONE

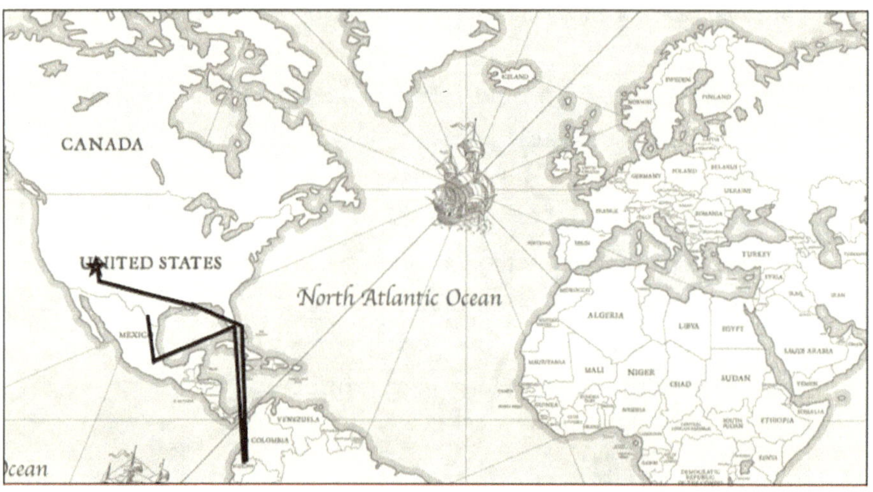

It's surprisingly cold in the early morning air as the mule guide systematically goes from mule to mule, checking everything but their teeth. He's medium-height, wearing stiff Levi's, a carved-out leather belt, a blue western shirt tucked in, and a vest over that. Cowboy boots and a hat with a string underneath it that looks like a safari hat complete his outfit for taking us into the canyon. Every few minutes, he looks up and grins at Shifrah, which seems to aggravate Malone. The more it continues, the more Malone huffs and puffs behind us.

"Damn goofy fool. Ought to keep his mind on what he's doing," I hear him mutter.

Never have I met a man as stringent as Malone, and I suppose it's his military years that make him so edgy. Reno understands Malone more than we do, and I think that's why he jumps in and starts checking the cinches, bridles, and tied-on supply rolls behind the saddles of the last two mules.

"All clear, pardner!" he says to our guide, but the guide is shooting another lopsided smile at Shifrah. An older man strides quickly into our circle and says something we can't hear to our guide. The guide huffs off with his fists clenched. Another man, dressed similarly to our guide, briefly talks to the older man, then walks past each mule, occasionally testing the tightness of a cinch or the balance of a saddle. Apparently satisfied, he turns to the group, comprised of our mission team and four other people.

"Good morning. I'm stepping in to be your guide today. I'm happy to assure you that our mules are perfectly outfitted and qualified to take you on a trip like you've never been on before." He waits for that to soak in before saying, "The Grand Canyon is the most beautiful and rugged canyon in the world, and experiencing it from the back of a mule is indescribable. Believe me, you'll never forget it. But, keep in mind, this is a physically demanding ride, and you'll need to depend on these animals to get you to the bottom and back up again. Trust them. Be confident knowing our mules are the most reliable and gentle saddle animals you'll find anywhere. They know what they're doing, so relax and allow them to keep you safe.

"By now, I hope you've gone over all the paperwork and rules, and ladies, it's nice to see you drummed up a way to tie your hats on your heads." He nods at Shifrah and me. "Gentlemen, I can't say the same for you, so you'd best be sure those hats are fitting tight on your heads. One mess up with them popping off your head, and they get crushed, rolled, and tied to the back of your saddle, and I don't give a double-dang how much you paid for them. Got that?"

Seeing Malone, Reno, and the other man in our group, all wearing cowboy hats, being bossed around, especially Malone, is a new and, I have to admit, quite pleasant, experience for Shifrah and me. We exchange subtle smiles. Malone's face reveals nothing, but he slightly nods his ascent. Reno merely grins.

"These canyon trails, including the one we're taking this morning, Bright Angel Trail, were carved out by explorers and prospectors in the

1890s. Some of the cliffs we crisscross are six hundred feet high, so keep in mind this is fun, this is exciting, but it can be dangerous if you don't follow instructions. We'll talk more about the rules as we go.

"The main thing to remember is don't let the mule in front of you get too far ahead of your mule. If the gap gets too wide, your mule will run to catch up. These are pack animals who want to be close to their pack at all times. One mule runs, the next one will run, and so on. Believe me, we don't want that happening. Keep the gaps closed. Everyone got that?

Heads nod all around. Shifrah whispers, "We're going to die, Savannah."

The guide continues. "You've noticed it's cold this morning on the South Rim. The temperature will rise as we descend into the canyon. If you read your information packet and you're wearing lighter clothing under your jackets, good for you. If not, you're sure gonna wish you'd paid attention to that little detail. Any questions?"

"How long does it take us to get to Phantom Ranch?" I ask.

"Well, we weave back and forth on switchback curves, making the ride a little over ten miles down. Usually takes us about five or six hours."

"Oh, my gawd," Shifrah mumbles.

"With all that horse experience under your belt, this should be a piece of cake." Malone says.

"Well, yes, I suppose so, but horses aren't like these animals."

"You're right. A horse would dive off the edge the first time it looked down."

The guide has been patiently waiting for our internal conversation to end. He says, "Any more questions? No? Let's mount up."

"Can I ride behind you?" Shifrah asks him. "I'd feel safer."

"No reason not to. My name's Jackson." He helps her up on her mule, and Malone mounts the mule behind her.

* * *

Swimming suits were not on Shifrah's list when we went shopping in downtown Phoenix. I mentioned them once, only to have her steer us to one department after another, but never the bathing suit area. We missed our chance to swim on the rooftop of the Adams Hotel, and, now, I find it would have been absurd to think of wearing a swimsuit in Bright Angel Creek at Phantom Ranch. After three of the other four riders from our trail ride peel off their boots and walk straight into the water with their clothes on, Shifrah and I take off our boots and socks, roll up our pants legs, and wade in.

"Savannah, my legs are permanently bowed, I just know it. Every inch of my body aches. Why we must meet a contact at the bottom of the world will never make sense to me."

I don't get it either, but I keep hashing over in my mind what Malone said to Reno when I was hiding behind the vending machines, that "he" wanted it to be rough on us. Why? All I know is headquarters, for one reason or a thousand, doesn't want this mission to be a piece of cake.

"This water feels like heaven to my blistered feet," Shifrah says. I sigh in agreement, and we both sit down in the water. It comes up to our waists, and we giggle at our impetuous behavior. "No more roller coasters or Ferris wheels for me as long as I live. I've never been so frightened, not even when the convertible was…" She stops, looks down, clears her throat. "A thousand times I was positive that animal and I would plunge off the edge to our deaths. And the dust! Why didn't they mention that? It's a good thing we had the ends of the scarves in our hats to use as masks."

"Uh-huh. What were you saying about a convertible?"

She laughs lightly. "I can't tell stories when I'm in agony. Oh, how do people survive these primitive treks? How many people have died doing this do you suppose?" She moans and turns her face to the sun, closes her eyes. "You said you rode horses a lot back in Texas. Is it as difficult as this?"

"I've never ridden a horse for six straight hours, especially down into a steep canyon, so I can't say. The day after tomorrow, we get to climb back in the saddle and do it all over again, only this time, we're going up and not down. Should be interesting. I guarantee tomorrow we'll feel like every muscle and bone in our bodies is permanently bruised. In fact, I already do."

She nods in agreement. "Please don't mention us doing it all over again right now, Savannah. That's a mere thirty-six hours from now. Do you think they have a masseuse here?"

"I'd say it's 'bout as likely as a horned toad playing poker on a Saturday night."

"What? Oh, another cute Texas idiom. Okay, I'll try to walk over and get my European bathing soap from my pack roll so we can use it on our feet and calves. It's filled with delicious, fragrant oils. So soothing. I promise you'll—"

"*Ursäkta mig!* You vhant to do soaps?" Alma, one of our trail mates with a lyrical Swedish accent, asks Shifrah.

"Um, yes. You're welcome to share it if—"

"No, no, no, pratty girl. Vee kant do soaps ahn oils en dis cricket of vhater."

"Why not?"

"You vill make pewloot! Do you vhan rilly kill fresh nahshral flewra in dis spring vhater?" Alma asks, her tone stern, eyes wide, eyebrows raised.

"Certainly not," Shifrah says.

"Din kee-ap da soap for da baht." Alma smiles, steps from the water, and trudges off carrying her pack roll and boots. Her straw hat hangs by two strings down her back.

"What was she talking about, Shifrah? I barely understood one word."

"She said soap and oils will pollute the natural flora in this spring water. She talks exactly like our Hilda from Sweden. Oh, that reminds me of a big mix-up one time because of Hilda's heavy accent." Shifrah laughs aloud. "Want to hear what happened?"

"A long as I can listen and not move a single muscle."

"Well, Mommykins was talking to Hilda as they were sorting winter clothes to be cleaned and hung in storage closets for the summer months. I was sitting nearby reading my required book for the last few weeks of eighth grade. There they were, chatting away as women do, and Mommy asked her if it was okay to inquire as to why she had parted with her husband. She said, 'O, dah. He vhas shitting on me.' I almost fell out of my chair! Mommykins says, very calmly, 'Hilda, we do not use curse words in this home.' Hilda looked so puzzled! She says, 'No. No curshes in dis home, mahdam.'

"Then, Mommy says, 'I understand he must have been an unpleasant fellow, but that's an inappropriate way to describe what your husband did to you, dear. You must find another word.' And Hilda says, 'Vhat? Duh shitting? But dat vhat he do, mahdam.'

"I was laughing so hard! I had already figured out Hilda was saying her husband cheated on her. See, they pronounce *ch* like *sh,* and Mommykins was beside herself. She reprimanded me for making light of such a serious issue, and I blurted out, as best I could, what Hilda was trying to say. Hilda clapped her hands and said, 'Yah, dat vhat he do, he shitted on me.'"

"How's the water?" Reno asks from behind, startling us. We glance at each other, our eyes wondering if he heard Shifrah's off-color story.

"Come in and find out," Shifrah says.

"Wish I could, but I better hang close to the boss. He's kind of perturbed right now. Making plans for us to leave right away." He sits down on a boulder close to the water's edge.

"Leave?" Shifrah and I say simultaneously.

"Yeah, first thing early morning after we grab some shuteye. We were scheduled to take the morning trail ride back to the rim the day after tomorrow, you know, but now, we're headed back up at first light. I do believe if he had access to any kind of communication down here, we'd be hopping on a helicopter in a few minutes."

"What changed?" I ask.

Reno picks a stem from a clump of yellowed grass, chews on it, looks off in the distance. "Well, you'll find out soon enough, so I'll go ahead and tell you our contact isn't here. He's a genuine Haveasupeenie Indian. Just found that out myself."

"What's that?" Shifrah asks, stepping out of the water and sitting on a rock along the bank. "Ew, I'm so wet and icky now. How will I ever dry all my things?"

"Strip down and spread your clothes on those rocks over there," Reno says. "The sun'll dry 'em right quick. Go ahead. We won't look," he says, smiling playfully.

She makes a face at him. "Stop it and tell us what's going on."

"Wait, let me get this straight. Our contact lives down here in the canyon, right?" I said.

"No. This is the briefing I just received from Malone. Haveasupeenies are a native tribe who call themselves *people of the blue-green waters*. He said they consider themselves the guardians of the Grand Canyon, claim they've been here since the beginning of time."

"Well, that's dramatic, but how did this *Haveasupaweenie* person get one of our *retrieves?"* Shifrah asks.

"Seems our contact was a medic in the 6th Armored Division of Patton's Third Army under Major General Robert Grow. Those boys in the Sixth were in the field almost a year, but nothing got 'em ready for, uh, well, anyways, they, uh, it's kind of confusing, but the person with the original *retrieve* passed it to someone who passed it to a woman who died right after passing it on to our contact, the *Havasupeenie*. She made him promise to keep it safe and give it to the right people. A deathbed promise. Strong stuff."

"Reno, that's about as clear as a stock tank full of cows," I say.

"Indians serve in the military?" Shifrah asks, wringing out the bottom of her shirt.

"You didn't know that, Shif? Shoot, I served with Navajos, Hopis, Apaches, Cherokee, all kinds of those fellas. No *Haveasupeenie*s, though. Native folks are tied into land and nature and love going after the bad guys. That makes 'em real patriotic about serving in the military. That Malone…" Reno shakes his head. "…he probably knows what kind of underwear Patton wears to church. What he told me just now, I mean, how does he know all that stuff?"

"Well, what was it?" I ask.

"He said about forty-five thousand Native Indians served in the last war. All branches, and that's not counting their womenfolk, who worked in offices and helped in all kinds of ways."

I whistle one of my best Hank Grimes's whistles, the one he taught me to use when we caught a bigmouth bass over twenty-four inches long.

"Hey, dang good whistle, Savannah. You call the cows home with that one?"

"I probably could, just never tried. What does this *Haveasupaweenie* serving in the war have to do with us leaving early?"

"Some facts are still classified, y'all, and some things I don't know. I can answer part of your question. Our contact sent word by letter on the mule pack train today he couldn't give us the key unless he first looked us in our eyes to believe we were honest and of a good spirit. Said he made a promise on his life to never part with the key unless the right people came for the truthful reason."

"Why wasn't he here to do it then, to look us in the eye and know we're the right people with the right spirits?"

"The note said he met with his tribal council, not telling them all the facts but telling them how important the object is. Seems they advised him to bring us to their sacred home grounds, Havasu Canyon, where, let's see if I can get this right. Oh, yeah, *the land and the waterfall summon up the truth of a man.*"

"Are you making this up?" Shifrah asks.

Reno raises his right hand, "Nope. God's honest, Shif. Malone says it boils down to this mule trip turning out to be a nature break. Now we have to ride out of here and head to a town called Peach Springs. It's not real close, a hundred miles or so. Hope y'all are good hikers, 'cause it sounds like we gotta hike the last ten miles into the canyons to get to those falls. That's what the folks inside the lodge said anyways. I'm not sure if they have pack mules for that trail or not. Guess we'll find out. Our contact gave us a time to meet him on the trail."

"You mean to say we suffered this horror all day for nothing? Nature break? Does Malone think we're Olympic athletes?"

"Nah, that's the wrong way to look at it, Shif. See, you got more than five hours of specialized mule-skinner training under your belt now, don't you? That calculates real good with that week of horse training you got as a small fry."

He ignores her severe frown, stands, stretches. "Okay, *señoritas,* meet you in the dining hall in a few hours. They tell me they serve promptly at the dinner hour. If you're not there in time, you'll miss out on the best rattlesnake stew in the country." He throws me a private wink and strides off.

"It can't be true. Rattlesnake stew for dinner?"

"Hmm, sounds a lot like someone went snipe-hunting."

"Snipe? You mean we're having snipe and snake for dinner? Are we in the Middle Ages? I can't... wait, Savannah, you're gathering up your gear. Where are you going?"

I don't turn around and look at her, or I'll burst out laughing. Besides, some questions just don't deserve to be answered.

CHAPTER TWENTY-TWO

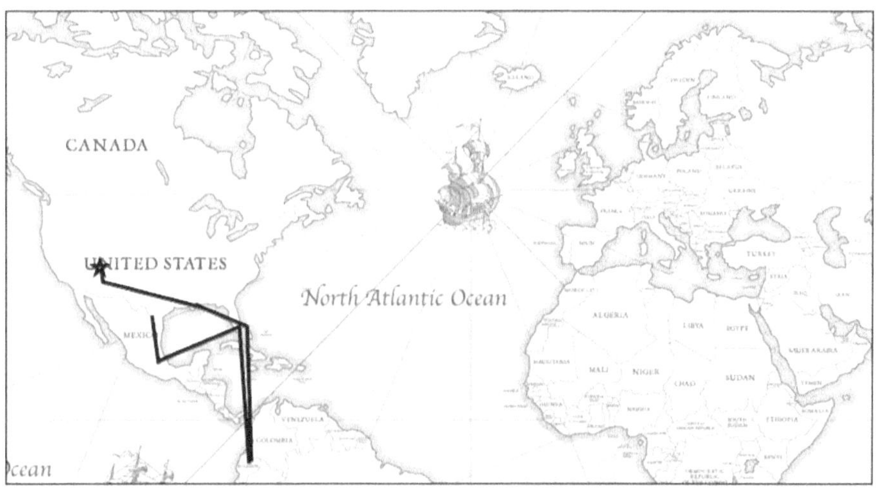

He seems to appear out of thin air. He isn't there, and then he is. He's blocking the trail about midway into our ten-mile hike to Havasu Falls. He's Native with a round pleasant face and large hands loosely clasping the reins of a mule leading four more mules with no one riding them. He shakes his head and laughs silently, his shoulders and slightly rounded belly bouncing up and down, making Shifrah and me exchange furious looks. I know we look terrible. We're disheveled, sweating tenderfeet trying to finish the physically exhausting trek into the canyons to see if we're judged worthy enough to get our first *retrieve,* and we're not taking kindly to anyone laughing at us.

"What's so funny, um, dammit?" Shifrah yells, patting her hair with both hands, then smoothing her eyebrows with an index finger.

Shifrah cussing?

She steps in front of Malone. "Perhaps you'd like to provide us with some hot water and a bathtub so we can look glamorous out here in this God-forsaken, um, hell wilderness!"

"Easy, Shifrah," Malone says, moving in front of her and stepping toward the man. We follow him, each of us almost glued to the back of the one in front of us.

"You Malone?" Malone nods. "Brought you some burritos to ride. Figured you might wanna give your feet a little rest. You guys used to hiking like this?"

"No," Malone says gruffly.

The man dismounts and easily turns the mules around in the opposite direction. He steps in to shake Malone's hand. "Nice to meet you, Major Malone. I'm Sergeant Eddie Ewing, field medic, 6th Armory division, Major General Grow. Heard real good stuff about you from, uh, you know, the Alphabet Man."

He stares at Shifrah and me. "Nice looking crew you got with you. I figure the one learning how to cuss is—"

Malone places a hand on Eddie's arm, leans in, says something we can't hear, though we're straining to do so. Eddie nods, grins in our direction. "Yeah, I get it," he says.

Malone reaches back, pulls Reno even with him. "This is Reno Taylor, Air Corp, one of my best pilots." The men shake hands, grin, look each other over.

If they had tails, they'd be wagging them.

"And these two lovely ladies are my assistants."

Shifrah snorts loudly. I manage a weary smile. Eddie dips his head in acknowledgment, swings back into the saddle and doesn't turn around. He says, "Okay, you wanna rest them tired toes, better mount up. Fresh water tied to your saddle horns. Hope you don't mind my old Army canteens. Water tastes a little metallic, but you get used to it."

"I don't know if my sore body can do this," Shifrah says, and Malone picks her up and swings her into the saddle before she can protest. Not that I think she would since she seems to live for Malone's attention. I, too, dread the climb back into the saddle, but it's all part of the job.

We ride in silence until Eddie says it's time to get off and stretch our legs. Reno disappears behind the curve of the trail, probably to answer the call of nature. Lucky men. Shifrah and I are stuck waiting for a chance at privacy to do the same. Reno returns and stands with his hands in his pockets, taking in the panoramic view of the canyons. "So, you fellas, uh, you *Haveasoopeenies* own those waterfalls we hear about and these canyons, too?"

"*Haveasoopeenies,* huh? That's a new one," Eddie says.

I figure he isn't going to answer Reno's question because a few minutes go by before he starts talking. "Yeah, things are all jumbled up right now. The government came in, stole our land, even Havasu Falls where we're camping tonight. See, that's loco 'cause we've lived along this South Rim for thousands of years. Got crops and orchards in Havasu Canyon and other canyons in the warm months. Come winter, we hunt game along the rim. Our tribe's been here since Creator planted people on the earth, or thereabouts. I think that gives us squatters' rights by any yardstick. Tribal lawyers working on it. Working hard. We'll get it back."

That shuts our mouths. What can you say when people have had their homeland stolen? The concept of identifying to land with rooted affection like that is new to me. I've never owned anything—land or home—but I'm supposed to own a diner in a few years. Do I still want to own it? I don't know.

"Hey, Reno, the name of my tribe is like *Have-a-soup-eye.* Got kidded about that soup and eye part when I was a kid. Got real good at knocking some blocks off." He chuckles. "Our name for ourselves is *Havasu'Baaja.* Hard to say for you White guys. Fellas in the Army just called me Soup. I got to where I liked it. I'd sure like to hear some of themol' boys call me that again." Eddie stares off into the distance.

"Hey, partner, I'm sorry—"

Eddie holds up a hand, smiles. "No *problema,* Reno. Like I said, I get a kick out of all the ways you *hai'iku'u* say it. Life is funny, you know? I sure didn't expect you to take me so serious, Major."

"In what way?" Malone asks.

"Oh, about the land summoning up the truth. How I had to look you in the eyes." He laughs silently, his eyes gazing out at the vastness. "I got a big laugh out of telling you guys that stuff. Truth is, my baby sister went into labor early. I got stuck watching her other two knotheads for a few days. Stopped me from heading to Phantom Ranch. I don't know why we couldn't of met someplace else in the first place, but what do I know? By the way, why did we plan to meet inside the canyon?"

Shifrah and I are all ears waiting for Malone to answer Eddie's question. He says, "Hard to explain right now, Eddie, but everything has an ultimate purpose on this mission."

Eddie looks at Malone for about a full minute, shakes his head. "Guess it's like getting orders in the military. They don't make any sense most of the time, but you do them anyways. I didn't know how to get a hold of you. No idea where you were staying, either, so I relayed a quick note over the phone to my buddy at the mail place. He wrote it down and sent it with the mule carrier headed down there yesterday. Pretty good mail service, eh? The note had a phone number on it. Figured you'd call when you got out of the canyon. I would of met you guys over there at the rim today if you did. I didn't hear from you, so I made shore I was here at the time I wrote you in the letter."

Malone doesn't respond, but Eddie's disclosure is going over like rocks for dinner with Reno, Shifrah, and me. A low-key grumbling session of growls and tongue clicks seals our shared disgust at finding out we didn't have to drive over a hundred miles to Peach Springs, drive even further to the hilltop at the trailhead, and hike with bodies desperately sore from riding mules into the canyon one day and back out the next morning.

We couldn't even talk when we dismounted from our mules yesterday afternoon after coming out of the canyon. We hand signaled each other that we were going our separate ways. Shifrah and I drank some of my BC powders for our pain, took baths, pinned up our hair—she wouldn't have it any other way—and fell asleep after drinking Dr. Peppers and eating a bag of nuts from the vending machines in the hallway. Now we find out this whole trek to Havasu Falls was unnecessary?

Eddie seems unaware of our private seething. He slaps the dust off his Levis. "Shoot, all you guys had to do was give me the code word that Mr. Alphabet—that's what I call him—gave me, and that would of been plenty. I like having me a little fun when I can, you know? After that crazy war, I figure we need that kind of stuff. Kind of cancels out them bad spirits."

"I see where you're coming from, Eddie, I do," Reno says quietly.

Eddie nods in agreement. "Anyways, my sidekick Joseph is waiting for us at the falls with your special key. He'll cook us up some good grub on the campfire tonight, help you lay out the bedrolls I brought you. Couldn't let you come to the canyon without seeing our Havasu Falls. Most sacred place on earth. A healing place. Anyone here need some healing?"

* * *

Eddie didn't tell us we'd still have to hike part of the way, and I swear my body has never been this sore. I thought I was in shape, but now I know hunting and fishing are nothing compared to riding mules for hours and hiking over uneven terrain and steep, winding trails. Malone has almost carried Shifrah the last part of our journey to the first waterfall—Eddie says there are three big ones—and she has mostly stayed quiet about it. I think she's gone into shock. I know I almost have.

We finally arrive on a butte overlooking Mooney Falls. The red rocks and turquoise water are stunning. The fresh wetness coming from the falls helps me recover as I crumple to the ground in relief. Joseph, Eddie's friend, cooks us a rustic but tasty meal of beans, fried potatoes, and frybread. We hear the briefest of facts about the *retrieve* Eddie has; namely, that he got it from a dying woman overseas who got it from someone else who got it from the original owner. That's it. That's all Malone allowed Eddie to say without cutting him off with throat clearings, coughs, and serious glances. It's frustrating because we already knew all that from Reno's explanation at Phantom Ranch.

When supper's over, Shifrah and I take Malone to the side and tell him about the man we've seen three or four times. His underreaction seems contrived to me. I notice now he's talking to Reno in hushed tones. They grow silent when I come near. I plop down close to them and watch Shifrah sitting cross-legged on a spread-out bedroll attempting some of her nighttime beauty routine with her back turned to all of us. The flickering campfire has turned all the nearby objects a yellow-orange, including her.

"I get it that you don't want to alarm Shifrah, but I think you should arm me with at least a .38 revolver, Malone. I'm beginning to believe there's more danger to this mission than you're letting on." His raised eyebrows register surprise. "Don't worry. I can hold my own, and I can prove it whenever you like. How am I supposed to defend Shifrah or myself if you two aren't around?"

"That's a big thought, Savannah," Malone says, rubbing his chin and shooting a look at Reno. "Tell you what… when we get somewhere we can do a little target practicing, I'll check you out and we'll talk about getting you set up with something. You sure you want that responsibility?"

"Positive."

The River

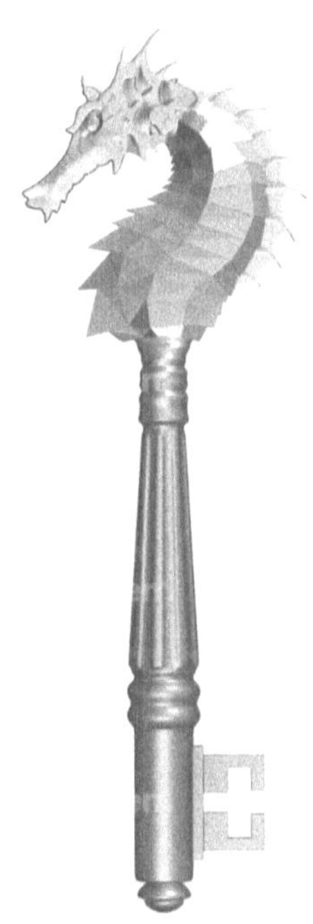

CHAPTER TWENTY-THREE

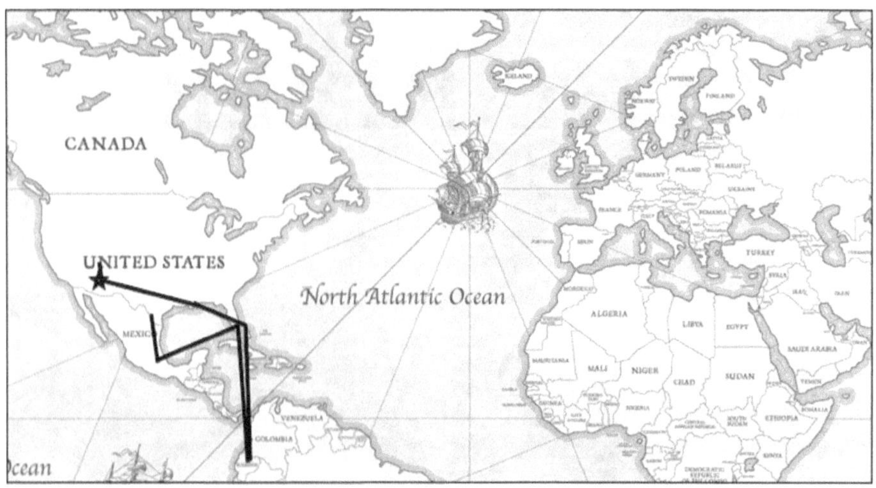

Reno stands up from sitting in the leather chair with half-circle wagon wheel arms and stretches. He bends his neck backward, forward, and to each side. He places one booted foot on a leather footstool, leans over and touches his head to his thigh. Switches legs, repeats. He places his hands on his hips and leans to the right and then to the left. "Ah, I feel circulation coming back in my ol' limbs," he says, apparently oblivious to all the females eyeing him in the lobby of the Hotel Monte Vista.

"Reno, if you don't stop, there might be an uprising," Shifrah says.

"Dang, I'm feeling energized after all that exercise we had this week. Ol' Eddie, he wasn't foofing us about those Havasu Falls. Darned pretty place, isn't it? You know, I think I got healed of all my orneriness just camping close to that turquoise mineral water. Good bathing, too.

Y'all should have gotten your toes wet at least. Now, if you'll excuse me, I'll go check on Malone and see if he's finished making calls, sending wires, or whatever else he's up to. I hope we eat real soon. This Flagstaff mountain air has me hungrier than an ol' mountain lion on a thirty-day fast."

"It's going to take a lot more than one night's camping beside a beautiful waterfall to cure that much orneriness," I say to Shifrah as he walks away.

"Don't remind me of that horrid camping ordeal. Gads, that thin layer of dirt felt like concrete underneath my bedroll. It's wonderful to be back in civilization, but, yeah, he is one handsome devil, isn't he? After the mission, are you going to give him a whirl, Savannah?"

"A whirl?"

"You know, date him, possibly fall in love with him?"

"What kind of question is that?"

"I have a feeling he might be smitten with you. I'm curious how you feel about it."

"I don't feel anything about it, Shifrah. Stop kidding around. We've already discussed how we're all colleagues and teammates on this mission and nothing more."

"Oh sure, that's the ideal, but what's the reality? Honestly, I'm a little bit jealous."

"Oh, for goodness sakes! You need to stop that kind of talk right now. Don't make me feel uncomfortable around him." She smiles, but I don't. "I mean it, Shifrah."

"Okay, okay. Excuse me for having a moment of levity. She stands and stretches. "If there really is a God, Malone will tell us we're headed to New York next. I'm dying to board a luxury liner and allow every steward and stewardess on the ship to spoil me rotten."

"There's a God, but I'm not sure he cares a hangnail about you getting spoiled rotten on your next ocean cruise. Are we really going to Budapest at some point?"

"I think so, but you know how fast things change. I don't care where we go as long as I'm at sea sipping wine, dressing for evening dining, spending leisurely hours on the deck getting pampered. I can't believe all we've had to endure. Jungles. Warriors. That terrifying canyon. Hiking for miles. How did I wind up paying such a price?"

"What do you mean?"

"Oh, nothing, Savannah. I just, uh, need a vacation."

"You said you were paying a price."

"Did I?"

She's doing it again.

I stare at her for a long minute. "You keep me very curious about you, Shifrah."

"Good. Since I'm such a mysterious woman of the world, maybe I'll get as much attention as you do these days. Everywhere we go, people do a double take, even when you're wearing just a fraction of my elegant makeup and have your hair in a simple ponytail or pinned on top of your head. You emerged from your hiding place the night of your birthday. A true transformation, and it happened right before our eyes."

"I cringe remembering all that attention."

"You deserved it. You were under wraps for years, and now you're living as the true Savannah."

"I'm not too sure about that. I still don't like being the center of attention. I will admit some of the tricks of the trade you've introduced me to are too good to let go." I look up and see Malone and Reno striding across the lobby.

"Car's loaded. We're heading back to Phoenix," Malone says when he's in earshot.

"Shifrah emits a happy sigh. "Heavenly! I'll call Daddy and Mommykins tonight. Surely, we'll have enough time to meet them for lunch, won't we? Is our first transatlantic destination England or France, Malone?"

"Neither for now. I'm glad you women bought galoshes and sensible outdoor gear in Mexico because now we're headed to the Tennessee River."

"The Tennessee River? What? Why?"

"Our *retrieve* is out that way, Shifrah."

Shifrah looks a little peaked around the gills as we pile into the rented car taking us to Phoenix. I'm on the other end of the spectrum, thrilled to be heading somewhere my daddy used to talk about. His vacations as a boy were hunting and fishing trips with relatives or close friends, and one of his favorite rivers was the Tennessee. "Which state are we going to?" I ask Malone as soon as we're settled.

"Alabama."

Shifrah's eye rolls and groans get worse. Reno turns from the front seat to look at her. "Come on now, Shif. We're heading to one of the best eating capitals in the world. Crawdaddies, fried catfish, hushpuppies. Too bad it's too late in the year to get us some fried green tomatoes and fried okra."

"Is everything fried there?"

"Not the moon pies."

"What's that?"

Reno chuckles. "You have to eat one to understand."

"Well, what's a crawdaddy?"

"Kind of a little freshwater lobster. You never ate one?"

"No, but I might have seen something like that on the menus in New Orleans. Don't they have another name?"

"Crayfish or crawfish, Shifrah," I say.

Reno grins one of his *I'm about to pull your leg* smiles that I always see but Shifrah never does.

"You're in for some good eating, Shif. Easy to fix, too. You boil the little fellers up and just ignore their pitiful hollering."

She gasps. "They scream?"

"Wouldn't you if someone stuck your hinny in a pot of boiling water?"

"That-that's horrifying to—"

"Shifrah, it's a silly fable. They don't have vocal cords, hon," I assure her.

Reno laughs aloud. "Okay, I'm pulling your leg a little. After they get boiled, you twist off their heads, suck out that good yellow stuff, then peel the tail like it's a shrimp and eat the meat."

"You're still teasing me, aren't you?"

"He's not, Shifrah. That's how many people eat boiled crawdads. I don't care for the head brine, but the meat is delicious—a little like crab and a little like shrimp. They're small, so you eat lots of them."

If she looked a little green before, it's nothing compared to how she looks now. Again, our New York girl is experiencing life in the raw around our United States. I can't help but believe it's good for her, but I'm more curious than ever how she was picked or coerced to go on a mission like this. She said she was paying a big price, so did it have anything to do with the trouble she told me she got into and that accident she *almost* mentions?

CHAPTER TWENTY-FOUR

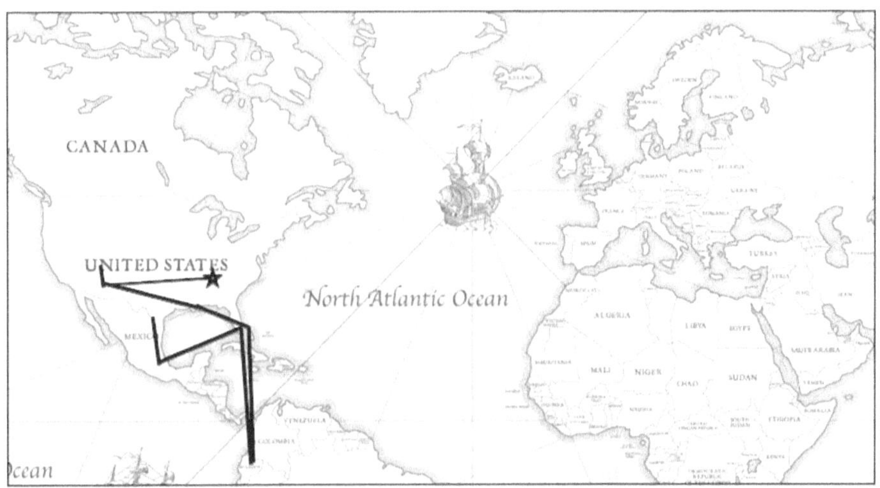

Malone is being unusually nice—or is it condescending?—to Shifrah this morning since we flew into the Birmingham International Airport on Delta-C&S Airlines. We flew from Phoenix on American Airlines into Love Field in Dallas, Texas, and then to Alabama, and Shifrah hasn't said ten words the whole time. On the way to the hotel in Birmingham, she climbed, as usual, in the back seat of the cab, and as I was about to get in next, Malone touched my arm to let me know he intended to sit by Shifrah. It surprised her, then she frowned and turned her face to the window.

"Shifrah, granted this mission's had a few rough edges," he said as we pulled away from the curb. No answer. "Before we meet up with our next contact, I'd like for all of us to go see some of the Birmingham sights tomorrow, starting early. Fact is, we need to kill a little time to keep our schedule in line. Would you like to go see the city?"

"I don't care one way or the other."

"Sure you do. Birmingham has some interesting historical significance," I say, receiving a glare from Shifrah and a nice smile from Malone.

"Says the history professor," she mumbles.

I chuckle, trying to lighten the mood. "That's fair. Yes, Professor Savannah shall tell you some of the history of this area, and we can plan our excursion tonight. Sound fun?"

She snorts, turns her head back to the window. "What can be interesting about a state that eats the brains of poor little river lobsters?"

"Funny thing about that, Shifrah. Crawdads, or crawdaddies as Reno calls them, don't really have brains. They have cells on their antennas and legs that warn them when there's danger, but they can't have any thoughts at all."

"You're a science teacher now?"

"Not at all. In my college biology class, we dissected a frog, a crayfish—which we call a crawdaddy in the South—and worst of all, a cat. It was pretty awful, and I never forgot it, the cat, I mean."

"What if you had to watch your science professor shift around the internal organs of a cadaver in your university zoology class?" she says.

"Seriously?"

She nods. "I was about to faint dead away when my friend Bradley walked me into the stairwell and lit a cigarette for me. He was always nice like that, but now... um, anyway, I never returned to that repugnant class. Still, I've never gotten the image of that body out of my head."

"I don't blame you. Naturally, I've seen dead people but never a body preserved and used by universities. Were you studying to be a nurse or doctor?"

She scoffs. "Not in a million years. One of my male friends misinformed me. He said the course was ridiculously simple, an easy class to take to build some required credits. Easy? Gads, we had classroom instruction, group lab classes, book homework, and lab assignment homework. I found out later he was studying to be a doctor, and he actually thought the zoology classes were simple. I had to transfer to a botany-bio class so I wouldn't lose my credits, but what kind of lunatics will their bodies to float forever in formaldehyde tubs?"

"How peculiar. I guess—"

"Ladies, you're squeezing me into a flapjack with all this gibber-jabber back and forth," Malone says, but his voice is light, and I can tell he's glad I got Shifrah talking to us again.

We both lean back in the seat, and soon Shifrah, apparently over her bulled-up mood, asks, "Will we be in Birmingham long enough for me to get my film developed, Malone?"

"Why, I think that can be arranged. We'll take it to a camera shop, give them a few bucks to encourage them to hurry up, and pick up your photographs when we return from Lacey's Spring in Morgan County."

"Is that where we're meeting our contact?" I ask.

"Yes and no. Mr. A has some special instructions for this leg of the trip, and you might think they're, uh, unusual. Of course, sending us to the bottom of the Grand Canyon was a tad unconventional, too."

"I don't understand it, Malone. Was that canyon ordeal merely to toughen us up?" Shifrah asks.

"Well, did it?"

"No, it made me bowlegged."

"Interesting."

"Maybe you think so, but—"

"What none of you know is I saved y'all's lives on the way to Havasu Falls," Reno says.

"You're making that up," I say.

"Nope. When Eddie gave us a break off the mules, I went around the trail bend and ran into a big ol' rattler curled up right there on the path. I was already carrying a stick, so I let him strike the stick. Then, I hooked him around the stick and flung him into the canyon. I don't think it killed him, but I know he sure as heck wished he had a parachute."

"Seriously?"

"Uh-huh."

"Good gawd, we're facing death at every turn! What do we have to do at the river, Malone, wrestle a bear?" Shifrah says.

"Not quite, Shifrah. Ever hear of brailing?"

"I've done it, sir, uh, Malone." Reno says.

"I'm not surprised. Want to explain it to the women?"

"Sure. Well, you use brails rigged out with a fringe of chains hanging down with special-made, kind of knobby three and four-prong hooks set in straight lines on the chains."

"Tell them what brails are."

"Oh, just poles or boards. See, you got these poles fixed up with chains that have hooks on 'em, and you throw those suckers over the side of the boat on the upstream side. Sometimes, they pull in about three hundred pounds of mussels each throw. While pickers pick the mussels off the hooks, another brail loaded with chain and hooks is dragged through the shell beds. Keeps you real busy till it's over."

"But closed mussels don't have mouths to grab hooks," Shifrah says.

"That's right. See, when the little critters feel the hooks on their open shell, they think it's something to eat or else something's gonna eat them. They clamp down on the hook, and that's how they wind up on the brail chain."

"Why in the world are we talking about catching mussels? Please, please tell me we're not doing anything remotely similar."

Malone clears his throat. "Here's the plan. We turn into mussel catchers on a boat for one day only. We're not observing; we're working. It'll be interesting. Different. I was told freshly caught mussels are put into a heated vat to steam them open, then they're put in a rotating shaker to shake out their insides."

"To eat?"

"No, they don't eat them."

"How barbaric! They don't even eat all those mussels they catch?"

"Freshwater ones don't taste so good, Shif. Don't worry. They don't waste 'em. They feed 'em to the hogs," Reno says.

"That whole process is merely to produce hog food?"

"No, that's the byproduct. The shells are made into buttons. It's a booming industry on the Tennessee, Mississippi, and Ohio Rivers for a long time now," Malone says.

Shifrah looks down at the buttons on her rust-colored blouse, looks up, Malone nods his head.

"Malone, please, this sounds illogical. Why must we do such a-a crazy thing?"

"Orders."

"Is our *retrieve* on the boat, or is it one of the mussel workers who's our contact?"

"Neither one."

Shifra exhales noisily, leans her head back to stare at the roof of the taxi. "Is the boat a riverboat with comfortable amenities at least?"

"Only ones I've been in for river brailing are plain ol' flat-bottomed boats made of wood. I imagine we'll be on a small one with at least two or three brails. You girls better dress in your britches to protect your legs, and wear a hat. Long sleeves, too. That sun, even this time a year, isn't friendly out on the water for a bunch of hours. Chilly on the shore, though. Say, you reckon they might have any late mosquitos?" Reno says.

"Only if it gets above fifty degrees," I offer, ignoring the frown from Shifrah. "I learned that from my daddy, not a book." I glance at her. She's staring at the ceiling. "Hey, this might turn out to be fun," I tell her across Malone's lap. The glare she throws me would shrivel a bouquet of fresh flowers, but I shrug it off. I don't expect her to understand how excited I am to see how brailing is done.

"Count me out for dinner tonight or sightseeing tomorrow," she says. "My head is starting to pound."

"Suit yourself," Malone says, and I think Malone could have spoken a little nicer to her.

CHAPTER TWENTY-FIVE

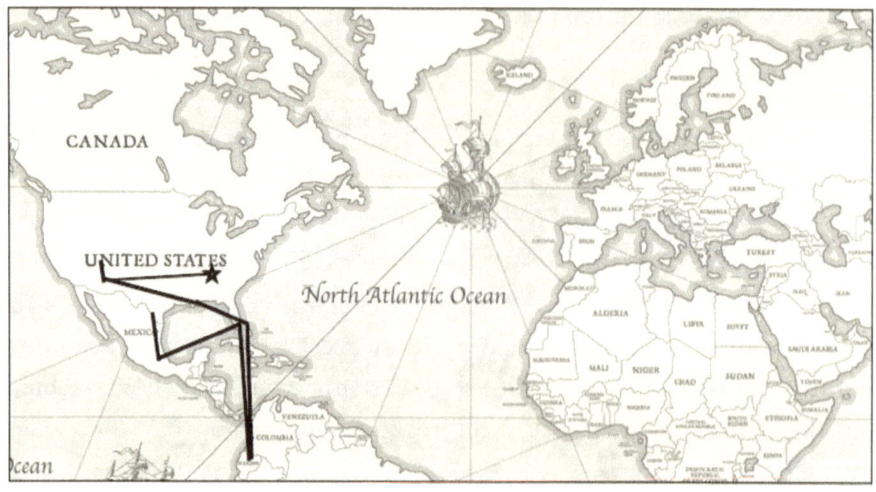

Shifrah wasn't kidding. She didn't join us for dinner last night, and she isn't going with us today to see the sights of Birmingham. Another puzzle piece revealed itself last night in the hotel room before dinner. She was resting with her fancy red ice bag on her head. Either a late-season fly or a mosquito must have bothered her because she suddenly swatted her arm and scratched at it until the sleeve of her red silk pajamas came up several inches. That's when I saw more of the scar I first glimpsed above her wrist when we were on the train in Mexico.

In all this time, she has never worn anything but long-sleeved outfits, including her nightclothes. She sat up in the bed, noticed my expression, pulled her sleeve back down to her wrist. She flipped over on her side away from me and returned the ice bag to her head.

"Shifrah, I don't mean to pry, but what gave you that scar? One time, you mentioned something about an accident. Is that where you got that scar?" She didn't answer. "Shifrah?"

"Please, hon, don't engage me in conversation. I'm nearly asleep."

"Oh, all right. Shall I bring you some dinner?"

"Might this hotel have tomato soup and rye crackers?"

"It sure might. I noticed it has quite a nice restaurant."

"I wouldn't mind having a little soup for dinner, if you don't mind going to the trouble."

"It's no trouble. Are you okay?"

"Don't worry about me."

Easier said than done. Is our trip to the river scary for her, or is there something else bothering her?

This morning after my toilette, as Shifrah calls it, I'm dressed and ready to go on our rare city-sightseeing trip. Coming out of the bathroom, I see she has pulled an armchair in front of the window. She's wearing an elegant lavender lounging suit with her hair styled and her makeup on.

"Please change your mind and come with us. We can wait while you dress."

"I can't, Savannah."

"Why not?"

"I have a lot on my mind."

"Is your headache gone?"

"Mostly."

"I'm concerned about you."

"Why?"

"You seem unhappy."

"I-I'm just trying to figure some things out." She sighs. "Savannah, you always roll with the punches no matter what, and I, well, perhaps I'm a frivolous, clueless—"

"You hush that up right now, Shifrah. You're none of those things. You grew up in different circumstances than Reno and me, that's all. And Malone, well, you know, as you like to say, he's Mr. Military Man. None of us are like him. Besides, you're getting better and better at, uh, roughing it."

"It doesn't feel like it."

"Well, you are."

She walks across the room to get her cigarette case from her purse, sits back down, lights up. "I don't understand why we are assigned to do that bracking thing. What does it have to do with our next *retrieve?"* She scoffs, takes a long draw on her cigarette. "Sometimes I feel like we're being put through odd trials on purpose, but why?"

"It's brailing, not bracking."

"What is?"

"Catching mussels in the river is called brailing."

"Oh, whatever. It's all foolishness to me."

"I haven't had a chance to tell you I pumped some information out of Malone last night at dinner. I found out our next contact is in the button business. That's at least some connection to what we're doing in Lacey's Spring. It appears Mr. A is scrambling some of the mission plans because of the mystery man we keep seeing. Anyway, Malone said after we finish brailing, we meet our contact in Savannah, Tennessee, and then we go back to Birmingham to catch our plane."

"Savannah, Tennessee, huh?"

"Uh-huh. Maybe it was named for the town I'm really named for."

"Which is…?"

"Savannah, Georgia."

"It must be nice to be named for a town or city." She turns to stare out the window at the city skyline. "Oh, Savannah, what are we doing? Malone is making us go on a crazy river excursion here in Alabama where we're forced to do manual labor, then we travel to-to Savannah, Tennessee, for the *retrieve?* See, that's what I'm talking about. It's like we're hamsters on a wheel going round and round but going nowhere. I believe Malone has lost his mind."

"I don't know the reasons, Shifrah, but I signed up for whatever orders Malone gives me. I have a lot of questions, too, but the travel and intrigue are exciting to this little country gal from Laredo, Texas. I just hope I get to utilize some of the so-called skills I was supposedly selected for. I mean, I haven't had to use my Spanish but a few times.

Oh, and my track training did get you back on the plane lickity-split when those spears were raining down on us, so there's that." I chuckle; she doesn't. "Please change your mind and come with us. We have this day off because of a schedule hitch. Who knows if it will happen again?"

She shakes her head. "Not today. Do you mind taking my rolls of film to a camera shop? Slip the guy that ten-dollar bill I put on the bedside table and give him your best sultry look. That'll make him more than happy to have my photos developed quickly. And, Savannah?"

"Yes?"

"Don't forget to reapply your lipstick after lunch. Check in your compact mirror first to see if anything is lodged between your teeth."

CHAPTER TWENTY-SIX

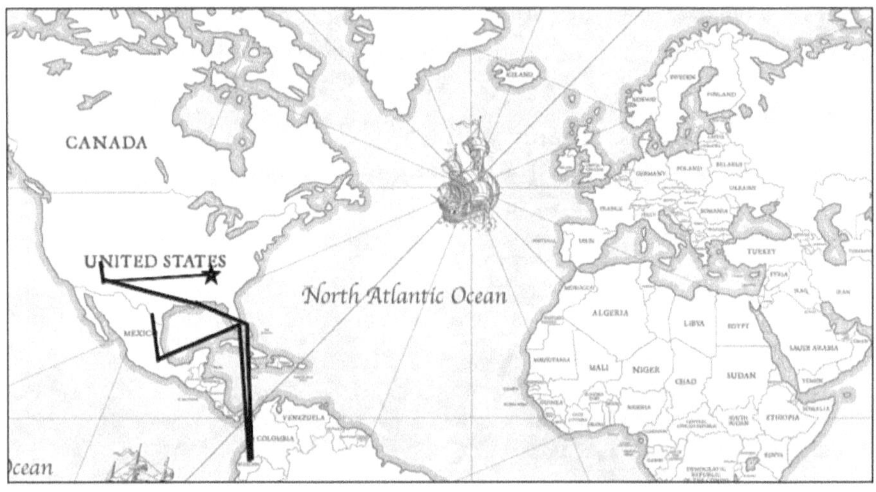

Daddy took me to a visiting carnival right before my seventh birthday. We were having the best time riding the rides, eating greasy carnival foods, and Daddy won me a big purple cat almost as tall as I was by knocking down stacked milk bottles. I had taken one lick of my ice cream cone when a weighty boy about twelve careened around the side of the tent where I was standing and knocked me flat to the ground. I couldn't catch my breath, one of my knees was scraped and bleeding, and just like that, our carefree day was spoiled.

Shifrah's mood has affected our group in a similar way. Her obvious displeasure hovers like a damp rag over us as we attempt to be lighthearted and interested in the sights of Birmingham, Alabama. We visit a museum, two factories, read plaques, learn that Birmingham is the only place in the world where all the ingredients for making iron are present—coal, iron ore, and limestone. In fact, we're proudly told by a museum attendant that iron and steel production are what caused Birmingham to exist in the first place.

"Good thing Shifrah didn't come with us," Malone says. "Can you imagine her suffering through this kind of briefing?" That makes us laugh, but it's becoming clear we've melded into a team, and having one of us missing is leaving a hole.

"She might find it interesting that Birmingham is named after Birmingham, England, and that some of the greatest scientists and inventors of all time lived in the English version of Birmingham. It says here that—"

"Savannah, Savannah… you know she wouldn't care a monkey's uncle about any of that," Malone says with a wry smile. "Now, if we were probing the history of lipstick or high heels, she'd probably perk up real quick." That causes another round of constrained chuckles. We take a taxi to the park on Red Mountain overlooking the city, a park created to house the city's most prized possession—the Vulcan Monument sculpted by Giuseppe Moretti. In a few minutes, as if we had planned it, the three of us turn and walk back to the street to hail a cab. We don't need to say it aloud, but we all know we're finished sightseeing in Birmingham.

In the car, Malone says, "This turns out to be a perfect time to check you out on a small firearm, Savannah. I made arrangements for us at the shooting range where all the city cops practice. Let's keep this between the three of us, huh?"

Two hours later, I have both a .38 revolver in my purse and the earned respect from both Malone and Reno regarding my shooting skills. I haven't lost my aim, and that's no surprise to me since I go quail and turkey hunting every year, not to mention pistol target practicing with three of my regulars all the time. I feel better knowing I can protect us if the men aren't around. After all, I've kept firearms in my cabin and my pickup since I was sixteen.

Before we get back to the hotel, Malone, says "Hey, listen, I want to tell you two something, but you can't tell Shifrah because I don't know if I can work out the logistics. Crossing the Atlantic by ship in

November and December is best, of course, and we're right on target with that. You never know, though. The weather or our timetable can change fast."

"What makes November and December the best times to cross the Atlantic?" I ask.

"Lower risk of trade winds and hurricanes. Anyhow, what I'm about to tell you has to be hush-hush."

"Our lips are zipped, sir."

"Well, you know how that little gal loves wine, right?" We nod. "If everything goes as planned, we'll leave New York Harbor for France on the next leg of the mission when we leave Tennessee and fly out of Birmingham. After a few more stops—Budapest if it works out—and one more undetermined location, we'll take the train back to Dijon, France."

"Our contact is in Dijon, sir?"

"No, but Dijon is where we're working to create a meeting place in a roundabout way."

"What does that have to do with Shifrah liking wine?" I ask.

"Rumor has it, starting in December, the Terminus Hotel in Dijon will serve free red and white wine on tap in every room."

I gasp aloud. A hotel giving out free wine is shocking, and, further, I'm surprised Malone is showing such concern for Shifrah.

"Sir, uh, Malone, you sure you got the facts straight on this one? I sure can't see a hotel giving folks free alcohol."

"Intel from headquarters, Reno. Seems they're setting barrels of wine in the attic and it's supposed to flow into the rooms through nylon pipes. It's a new concept, just being tried out, and the oddest thing is Mr. A's the one who told me about it. He wants us to go there, thus the attempt to make it a meeting place for our contact."

"Mr. A?" I ask.

"Affirmative. A little different protocol from him, that's for sure."

"Maybe he's sorry for all the pain he caused us in that canyon trek," I say. "I still don't get it."

Malone doesn't answer.

* * *

The great crisis in the world this morning has nothing to do with natural disasters or war. It's Shifrah's quandary of how to dress for a boating excursion in which she'll be pulling river mussels off hooks.

After I satisfied her fashion rules by applying light makeup and styling my hair, I donned my denim Lady Levi's, tucked my long-sleeved plaid shirt into the top of them, pinned my hair up and covered it with the same hat I used for riding into the Grand Canyon. I'm wearing bobby socks with saddle shoes I bought here in Birmingham yesterday, and my galoshes are handy for in the boat. Poof… ready!

I'm sitting here beside my packed suitcase and train case watching poor Shifrah try on multiple combinations of clothes. She finally settles on royal-blue slacks, a classic white shirt with a deep-blue embroidered yoke, a dainty blue and white striped scarf tied to the side of her neck, and black leather, single-strap flat shoes.

"You look like you're going sightseeing in Paris, Shifrah."

"Thank you. I think it turned out quite nicely."

"What I mean is… those shoes may not work."

"Why not? They look perfect with this outfit."

"They look nice, but will they hold up in a wet boat all day?"

"I can't imagine why not."

"Okay, but I suggest you plan on taking your hat and the maroon galoshes you bought in Mexico.

"Those galoshes don't match my outfit."

"I doubt you'll meet a single soul today who'll care if they do or don't."

A few hours later and ninety miles out of Birmingham, we step out of our rented car a mile outside Lacey's Spring and into a busy mussel camp on the riverbank. A nearby cluster of men lifts long poles onto forked holders protruding from two long boats near the water. The poles have a network of chains and large odd hooks hanging on them. More men are working on various-sized boats further along the bank of the river, unloading, loading, shifting, pushing, or pulling in the boats.

Many stop their work to stare at us. One man wearing overalls tucked into long rubber boots and a hat with a shallow brim walks toward us with an extended hand. "Howdy. I'm Homer. You Malone and party?" he says with a grin exposing a missing bottom tooth.

"That's right," Malone says, shaking hands. He turns and says, "This is my sidekick, Reno, and my two assistants, Shifrah and Savannah."

The man takes a leisurely, uninhibited look at us, turns and yells toward the row of tents lined up several feet from the river, "Tilly, if you wanna see the two purdy little thangs a'goin' brailing with us today, you best come a'runnin'!" He turns back to us. "If y'all females ain't a sight for sore eyes, nothing is or ever was. A good headwind might blow ya overboard if you ain't careful, though. I'll tell Tilly to cook up a bunch of vitals for tonight so's we can start putting some meat on those bones."

A portly woman with dark hair pulled back into a knot sticks her head out of the nearest tent, then steps outside. She's wearing a print dress and a full-length apron with a dishtowel slung over her shoulder. In her hands is a chipped enamel dishpan. She stops by Homer, squints, smiles big. "Homer, you shore ain't a'joshin'! They's purdy enough to be in them fashion magzines." She steps closer. "Honeys, you ain't gonna stay that fine turned out after a day on the ol' river. You shore y'all's can't stay here with me and lets them men folk do the musselin'? Land's a lot kinder on ya than that ol' water is."

"Tilly, don't go interfretting in someone else's bizness," Homer says.

She lightly jabs him on the shoulder, "Nah, I ain't tryin' to, honey. I'm being friendly, is all. See here, I got us our last go-round of them nice black-eyed peas picked out of my little garden." She tilts the pan to show us the long green pods and fresh-shelled peas inside. "I'll be makin' us a big ol' batch of 'em with salt pork and a heap of other fine eats this evenin', and y'all's might could keep me company and tell me all about them cities ya come from, can't ya? Lord knows, I don't see nothing ever day and ever day after that but this ol' river, them mussels, and these no-good men with they's brailing, divin', and toe diggin' 'quipment!" She puts her head back and guffaws, and I can't help but smile along with our friendly hostess.

Shifrah senses her one chance to be relieved of our assignment. She turns her pretty face to Malone and pleads silently with her eyes and lips, which to me, are louder than if she were banging on a pan with a metal spoon. But no, Malone resists, shakes his head.

"Thank you, ma'am, for such a nice offer extended to the ladies. I'm certain they are hard-pressed to resist your invitation, but I'm afraid we're obligated to stick to the planned curriculum."

Tilly wrinkles her nose, leans her head toward Homer with her eyes still on Malone. "What's he sayin', honey?"

"He's sayin' ya need to mind yer own bizness and let him run his household as he sees fit."

"Homer, that's not exactly what I—" Malone says.

"Nah, now, that's just the right thang fer ya to do, mister. I do the same thang myself. Tilly, you get along with whatever it is yer doin', and we'll get these folks outfitted lickity-split and in them there boats. I promise I'll bring 'em back in one piece, and see there?" He points to the sky. "It's already way up in the day, so we won't be out there longer'n three ner four hours, I reckon. You rustle us up a decent meal, and I been thinkin' we just might have us a little hoedown after supper. Yessir, believe we will. You go tell them other wives and get ol' Flint to round up the boys for us some music later on. Let's show these fine folks how we hospitable-ize down here on the river!"

Tilly's look of delight draws me in like a hummingbird to honeysuckle. Simple, hard-working folks like Homer and Tilly have always resonated in my heart. I figure it's probably my daddy's deep southern roots blazing inside my soul. I turn to our group with a huge smile, hug a surprised Shifrah, and say, "Let's get to brailing so we can get back here and have ourselves an Alabamie hoedown!"

CHAPTER TWENTY-SEVEN

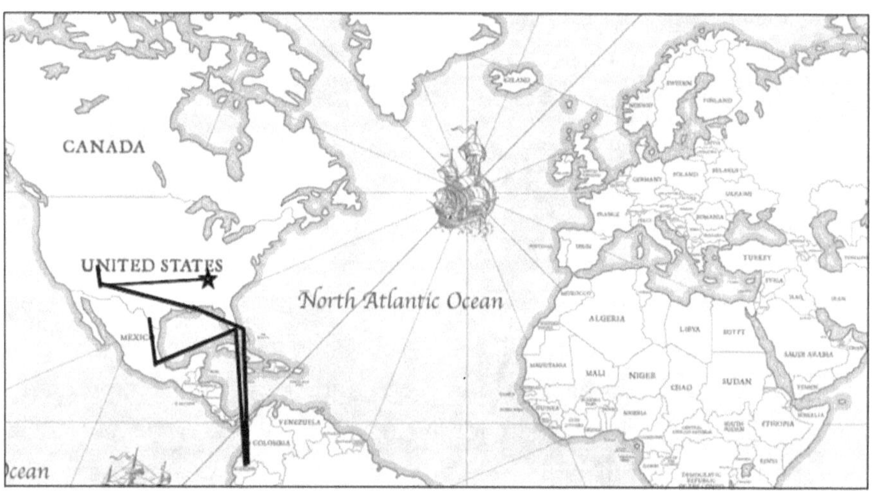

Malone dictates Reno, Shifrah, and I are to ride in the boat with Homer and his partner Slim. He departs before us in a boat with Homer's other partners, Joe and Tiny, and watching them shove off with Malone standing at the helm makes me think of Ismael on his quest for Moby Dick. The closest boat is not the one Homer takes our small crew to. Instead, he has us wait for a boat coming into shore with a net hanging from a pole already dotted with captured mussels. The other pole resting in the wooden grip on the boat has empty hooks.

"I did like Mr. Malone asks me to and got us one ready to pick right off. That's what you girls and the feller with ya are gonna do whilst we toss the other one over and drag it through a bed or two of 'em," Homer says. "Gonna be a light day, and I'm thinking we can head back to shore in no time a'tall."

The boat banks, and Homer nods for us to get in. Shifrah gives me a panicky look, and I take her arm and step us into the boat, directing her to sit on one of the cross seats. "It won't be so bad." I tell her quietly. "Remember, we eat things out of the water all the time, right? We won't eat these mussels, but they're serving a great purpose in life. Think of how many buttons you have on all your clothes, Shifrah. They have to come from somewhere."

Homer shows us how to lift and pull a mussel off the hook. Reno starts at one end of the pole; Shifrah and I start on the other. "They feel so-so wet and cold and bumpy," she says, shivering in disgust. "No one I have ever known would believe this is me, Shifrah Mandel, sitting in a filthy river dingy being relegated to pulling slimy creatures off dangerous hooks."

"This boat isn't filthy, Shifrah, it's a working boat. Men use these boats to make a living, and rivers are wet and muddy. The only worry you have right now is keeping your white shirt clean. Look, there's already a rusty mud smear by the pocket."

I watch Homer and Slim throw the other brail out and steer the boat so it's a little sideways in the water. It's obvious it would be difficult for a woman to lift and throw the chain loaded with long, three- and four-pronged hooks into the water, let alone pull it out of the water loaded with mussels. I'm glad that isn't part of our assignment.

Shifrah wipes her hands on the clean rag Homer gave her, holds her nose, and, by her expression, lets me know she thinks the boat and everything else surrounding her is repulsive. I think I understand how this seems to her, but I love messy fishing boats with bait, tackle, lines, and muddy water in the bottom. It won't be long before Shifrah's dainty, one-strap shoes will be wet. I'll try to look sorry for her, but I encouraged her to get her galoshes when I got mine out of the car while we were waiting on shore and she refused.

Picking and pulling mussels off knobby hooks and dropping them into the hold, mixed with the pleasantness of quietly rolling down a river lodged between noble, widespread oak, poplar, and sweetgum trees, lulls me into a reflective mood. My mind wanders to the Dixie,

Tony, and my regulars. I've sent them a few postcards in the last weeks so they don't think I'm dead, but I feel ashamed how I barely think of them. How is that possible when they were my whole life as I grew up? Have I become a cold, heartless person, or am I so wrapped up in my new life I don't have room to think about anything else? Was it really only six months ago I graduated from junior college and thought the best and only future for me was owning and working my whole life in a diner in a small town in south Texas?

I wipe my hands on my own torn-off rag, remove my hat, unpin my hair, and let the gentle breeze blow it wherever it wants to. I turn my face to the sunlight and contemplate how my life changed in one moment of time. Seasons change. Life-cycles change. Maybe I was like one of those little mussel larvaes living on a fish gill, and suddenly, it was time for me to drop off the gill into the river bottom to become a full-fledged mussel—time to be something else. How do they know when it's time? How did I? How does a caterpillar accept changing from a pudgy, hairy worm into an airy ballerina with bejeweled wings and a whole new identity?

And something else… what are the odds that an opportunity such as this mission would appear right when I changed from the old to the new Savannah and was apparently about to explode with boredom? Were they, the powers that be, really watching me from afar before selecting me? What do those keys, the *retrieves,* fit, and where is headquarters located? Who are the people behind the mission?

"Are y'all wondering how this boat is going down the river without a motor or without someone working the oars?" Reno asks, startling me out of my thoughts. I stick my hat back on and continue dislodging mussels from hooks. My little trip inside my head has me kind of flustered now.

"Are you laboring under a misconception that we care, Reno?" Shifrah says.

"You know, you sure can turn a word or two in the prettiest direction," Reno says. "Pure poetry."

His flattery, as usual, works. She snorts, looks away, looks back. "All right, tell us how we're drifting down this river with no motor or oars. I assumed it was the current."

"You assume right, m'lady. We have here a contraption that's been used for a long ol' time on this river. They call it a 'mule.'"

"A mule?"

"Yep, I think they call it that because sometimes mules get hitched up to the boats and walk along the shore, pulling them down the river. But this kind of mule is an underwater sail kind of a thing weighted at the bottom with a pipe. They throw it over the downstream side of the boat, the mule catches the current, and it pulls the boat down the river just as smooth and pretty as your mee-maws bread puddin'. Works just like a regular mule pulling a plow through the dirt. Clever, isn't it?"

"If one were to care about such boring things. It certainly isn't helping my sore fingers or my three broken fingernails, is it? How long before those other mussels come aboard so we can be done with this nightmare?"

"Ol' Slim says you judge it by the weight. He tests it ever little bit. I get the feeling Malone didn't want to put too much on you women 'cause Slim said again they're taking it real light today."

"Why on earth are we doing this, Reno? You know as well as I do this has no bearing on our getting a *retrieve.* Does someone at headquarters enjoy punishing us? If so, why?"

"Orders from headquarters, Shif. Guess we'll know when our mission is accomplished. We lucked out on this little deal, though."

"Why?"

"'Cause we may never go down a drunk river again."

"Drunk river?" I chime in.

"Yes'm. Drunk. See, this river starts out flowing in a southernly direction round about Knoxville, Tennessee. It goes several hundred miles or so like that, heads west here in Alabama and part of Mississippi, then dang if it doesn't make a turn and head north up to Kentucky. You ever hear of a river doing that?"

"Oh, who cares, Reno?" Shifrah says irritably.

"That's incredible," I say.

"Doggone right it is!" Reno says. "We're musseling on the drunken Tennessee River, and that's something to write home about."

"Where is home for you, Reno?"

"Ah, wherever I hang my hat, Savannah, but I claim Texas the most, of course. I was born in a little town in west Texas called Paduca, but I've roamed about everywhere before and after my hitch in the service."

"How'd you get your nickname?"

"Reno? Aw, shoot, that happened in the service. The boys and I played a lot of poker ever chance we got. Took our minds off what was going on around us. I guess I have a crazy knack for being lucky with the cards, so the fellas started calling me Vegas. Smythie, though, said I was more of a Reno than a Vegas because the town of Reno's slogan is *The Biggest Little City in the World.* He said with me flying planes, breaking broncs, and being allotted so much wild luck with cards, it made me *The Biggest Little Everything Else in the World.* So, there it was, silly as all get out, but it stuck like gum on a boot heel. Been more than ten years ago now, and I feel more familiar with it than my own Christian name."

He's pretty talkative right now. I wonder if I can get him to tell us more?

"Uh, Reno?"

"Yeah?"

"You sure do know a lot. How about sharing a little something with us, like what the retrieves open? Please?"

"Now, hon, you know I'm mostly in the dark just like you are."

"But you do know what the keys unlock."

"Savannah, I—"

"Anybody hungry for a cold biscuit with a slab a'ham on it?" Homer asks.

Reno raises his hand and quickly scoots to the front of the boat. Shifrah and I shake our heads to let Homer know we'll pass, and it looks like Homer just saved Reno from the hot seat.

"Gads, he's as tight-lipped as Malone, Savannah. They act like we can't keep our mouths shut if they tell us anything important. Hey, I'm starting to get hungry."

"Tell Homer."

"I'm not eating anything on this stinky boat. I hope Tilly cooks something edible for us. I wonder what these mussels eat."

"Plankton and algae."

She rolls her eyes. "Savannah, if you don't quit being so smart…" her voice trails off. "You know so much about history. Now, I find you're the same with science? You're too beautiful to be that smart. You need to taper off some, at least in public."

"It's no big deal. I have a good memory. I remember a lot of what I hear and read. Besides, who says we can't be smart and look good at the same time?"

"Societal norms, of course. In my world, you can be smart, but never overtly smarter than the eligible men in your own class."

"In your *own class?* Did you really say that? Let me get this straight. You lived in a castle with a king and queen and commoners like us were your servants in New York, correct?"

"Oh, Savannah, of course not. I merely meant… uh, well… I, let me think about… Oh, I don't know. You understand what I mean, don't you?"

"I really don't. In my neck of the woods, as we country bumpkins say, you're either a hard worker, or you're lazy. You're honest, or you're someone who can't be trusted. You're a good person, or you're not. That's the way we size up folks. Nothing more, nothing less."

"I've offended you, haven't I?"

I don't answer because, yes, I think she has.

"I apologize. I'm a little confused these days. What I do know is you're in a class of your own, Savannah." She manages a weak smile, turns back to stripping mussels. Something in her face tells me she's struggling as hard as I am to figure her life out.

CHAPTER TWENTY-EIGHT

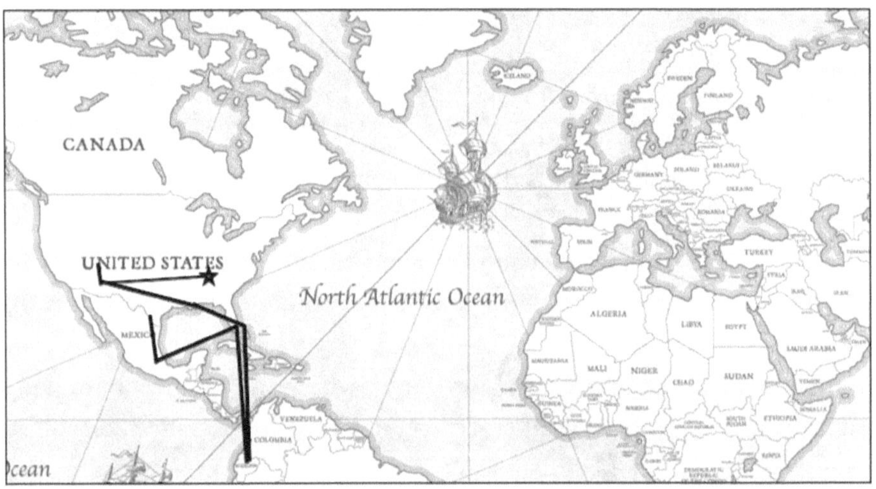

Smoke and enticing smells curl through the late afternoon air as we round the bend in the river overlooking the mussel camp. Tilly and several other women come into view, scampering around tending to pots and skillets set over grates above open fires.

"I don't think I've ever been this hungry in my whole life," Shifrah says, breathing in the rich aromas and putting a hand to her chest.

"You just left muddy fingerprints on your shirt."

She looks down, looks up, and smiles. "Oh well, what's a little mud?"

"Shifrah, I do declare, shall wonders never cease?" I say in my best Scarlett O'Hara accent, wildly fluttering my eyelashes in her direction.

"Oh, stop it. I'm trying to be more mature."

"It's working."

"What's working?" Reno says, scooting close to us and putting his arm over Shifrah's shoulders. "Say, you smell that, Shif? Bet they butchered their best hog and they're busy cooking up his snout and all the innards with onions and mustard greens just for us weary mussel pickers."

I can't help but giggle at her dismayed expression, but I don't let it go any further this time. "He's pulling your leg again, Shifrah. Pay him no mind, and never let him tell you his orneriness disappeared by the blue-green waters of Havasu Falls. I'm going out on a limb and say he has an incurable case of it."

"I didn't believe him, anyway, not for a second," she says, smiling. She swivels her head, cranes her neck. "Um, do you think Malone is back yet?"

"Yep, I spied him a minute ago forking a sample from one of those pots over the fire. He's probably fallen so crazy in love with southern cooking, he's gone off with one of those unattached females come down to gawk at the strangers in the mussel camp today."

Shifrah's fallen face surprises even Reno. He quickly assures her he's teasing and declares Malone would never run off with anyone. "He's hitched to his military past and whatever job he's assigned to in the present, don't you know? Yep, that's how it is, all right," he says, shooting me a look. The best I can figure, Shifrah is insecure without Malone around. I think she's the citified version of a total daddy's girl.

Tilly meets us before we step out of the boat, smiling and bubbling over with excitement. Little wisps of hair have fallen from her bun and curled around her reddened face. She offers me a strong arm to hold onto as I step out of the boat. I turn to offer Shifrah my hand. She steps out gracefully, soggy shoes, mud-smeared clothes, and all.

"Shoo-ie, honeys! It's so nice to see yer purdy faces again! Let me say this about that… y'all's are gettin' the bestest of our cookin' tonight. It's 'cause us wives are so 'cited for ya to be here, and we've cooked up a supper to do us all proud. Soon's we get our bellies good and full, we're having a hoedown like Homer said. Ol' Flint is tickled pink he gits to play for two new purdy girls. He brought his fiddle. Lyman brought his banjo. Shoot, I may pick up my dulc'mer if I get a fancy to.

"Now, listen, honeys. I got y'all some dishpans full of clean water and a bar of soap a piece in mine and Homer's tent. Clean towels for dryin', too. Jes don't mind the holes in em'!" She bursts out laughing, wipes her eyes with the hem of her apron. "When ya git yerselves all washed up, I'll take ya to meet our women who done and cooked their hearts out for ya and was happy to do it."

"I, uh, I'll need my hygiene case and clean clothes out of the car," Shifrah quietly says behind me.

"Yeah, uh, Reno, would you be kind enough to locate Malone for us so we can unlock the trunk and get some clean clothes?"

He salutes and takes off, stopping to smell pots and pans along the way.

Inside the tent, we silently take in the modest but sparkling clean accommodations of an Alabama mussel brailer and his wife—a simple bed, a small chest of drawers, a tiny cookstove elevated on bricks, a modest table with two water-filled dishpans on top and two wooden chairs scooted underneath. Tattered, dog-eared magazines and almanacs in a basket below a standing cabinet containing mismatched dishware complete the furnishings.

"Do people really live like this?" Shifrah says, looking all around.

"Sure. Sometimes much worse. Didn't you know that?"

"I've never thought about it. Oh, you know, if people are living in huts or shacks in some jungle or island across the ocean, that's one thing, but I didn't realize people in our own country live like this." She watches me, bites her knuckle. "I suppose this, uh, mission is the most educational outing of my life, Savannah."

"For both of us, but I'm pretty used to a whole range of people, Shifrah. Working in the diner for so many years, I saw that money and the high life don't always cause happiness. I've seen women come in dripping with diamonds and wearing mink stoles, women who could probably buy the Dixie with their pocket change. Some seem okay with their lives, but lots of them look like they bit down on a lemon and couldn't get their teeth out.

"On the opposite side of things, there's the Whitton family. They live on a little ranch outside Laredo, work their fingers to the bone barely making ends meet every year, and, I swear, those people and their four kids are the nicest, happiest people you ever want to meet. Always smiling and finding something funny or pleasant to say. If someone meets ill fortune, they're the first ones running to help and share whatever they have. I can give you example after example, but right under our noses is Tilly. Look how she lives, Shifrah, and she's literally as happy as she can be."

She exhales loudly, blowing her cheeks out at the same time. "I had no idea. Really, I didn't. Uh, say, I think we can create a modicum of privacy if we turn our backs to do our toilettes."

"My exact thought."

We don't talk while we scrub off the mud and crust of the day. Buttoning my clean blouse, I say, "Shifrah, I think we're pretty good friends now, but you've put me off every time I've asked you what caused that scar on your arm."

"A car wreck."

"In the convertible you mentioned one time?"

"Yes."

"I'm so sorry."

"No big deal. It's in the past. Okay, I'm finished. Are you ready for me to turn around? I'm so ravenous, my stomach is concave."

I'm about to comment on her lightning-fast change of subject when Reno says from outside, "Ladies, you might want to stay put for now. Tilly and the other wives said their men were beholden to clean up before supper and the dance afterward, and that's just what they're doing'!" His laugh mixes with the sound of splashes coming from the river. "Looks like the women retired somewhere else, and most of the men are going birthday-suit swimming in the cold river water. Y'all stay right there till I come tell you it's safe, and dang if I don't feel like joining them."

A few moments later, he lets out a banshee cry followed by a big splash.

* * *

Not since the spread served at Emmie Mae Broughton's funeral at the First Baptist Church of Laredo have I dined on such delicious down-home cooking. The ladies of the mussel camp prepared fried catfish, baked ham, fried chicken, shrimp and grits, thick fried bacon, steamed bass with zucchini slices and onions in foil—hot out of the campfire ashes—hushpuppies, cornbread, biscuits, collard greens, fried potatoes, boiled beets and raw onions in vinegar, and black-eyed peas with salt pork. Big pitchers of sweet tea and fruit cobblers round out the meal.

Watching Shifrah eat things she has never tried before is putting all of us in a good mood, including Malone, especially watching her eyes light up with the surprisingly delicious flavors. This meal has put me on the verge of branding Alabama cooks as good as Texas cooks, and that's a mouthful. If tonight is the contest, it's pretty darned close. With our metal plates heaped high, we're partaking with gusto.

"Must be this country air, but I can't stop eating," Reno says.

"Not bad. Not bad at all. So, here's the plan. We'll head back to Lacey's Spring after the, uh, what did they call it, Savannah?" Malone says.

"The hoedown."

"What kind of name is that?" Shifrah asks.

"My daddy told me hoedowns are the way southerners celebrate the end of the growing season. The dance is based on the movements of hoeing corn and potatoes."

"Hoeing?"

"You know what a hoe is, don't you, Shifrah?" Reno says.

"Of course, I do. It's a garden spade."

"Yeah, with a long wooden handle. The end is a sharp metal thing for chopping out weeds, busting dirt clods, and turning dirt over so the crops can breathe," Reno says.

"Works great for chopping off a snake head if you keep the blade sharp," I add.

"Oh, Savannah, did you have to mention snakes?"

I try not to laugh along with Reno and Malone, but it's hard. Poor Shifrah has been the best thing on earth to tease on this trip.

"There you guys go laughing at me again."

"No, we just think you're cute," Reno says.

"If I ever wind up in New York City, you'll be laughing your head off at me every step I take," I say. "I've never been to a place like that."

"No, you'll be the toast of the town with that face and figure, your Southern accent, and so smart and clever, too. Honestly, I don't have one friend who's ever shot a pistol or killed snakes or who knows the history of Mexican Independence Day. Everyone will fall under your spell when you come to see me, Savannah. Mommykins and Daddy, as well."

"Is that an invitation?"

She nods, and I don't know what else to say except *thank you.* Her serious comments sobered up the funny moment, so we concentrate on eating and watching the small band of musicians gather at one end of a smooth wood-plank dance floor the men laid out in nothing flat. Kerosene lanterns are placed here and there to light up the area.

When the music starts, Reno grabs my arm and we dance the Cotton-Eyed-Joe, the Two-Step, a waltz, a form of mountain clogging, and a square-dancing routine I've never heard called before but followed easily. I'm laughing and breathless when he leads me back to the tree stumps we've been sitting on. Surprisingly, Shifrah has two metal cups of sweet tea waiting for us, and she's smiling.

"You two know all the same dances," she says, "and you do them so well! Reno, how did you learn to lead so beautifully on the dance floor?"

"Aw, Shif, Savannah's just a good follower. I'm thinkin' she could follow a knock-kneed moose if he was to ask her to dance," Reno says.

The music brings back memories of my daddy playing the guitar with some of the other truckers and ranchers at the town functions and at our house. I don't let anyone see me when I wander off to have a cry by myself. Missing my daddy makes me miss Tony and all the others who stepped in to "grow me up," but one thing is dead set in my mind—I am not ready to go back to Laredo, Texas. Whatever this mission turns out to be, I want to see it to the end.

CHAPTER TWENTY-NINE

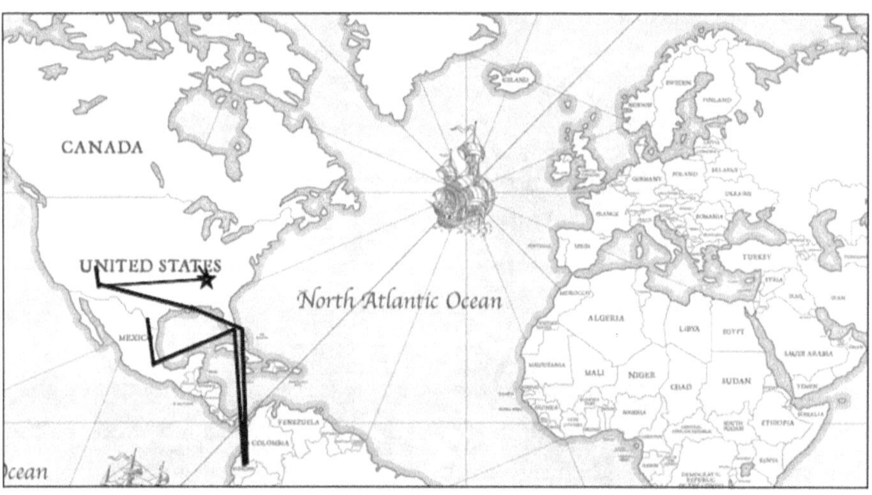

Reno had two exhausted, slightly sunburned women using his shoulders as pillows in the backseat on our late-night drive back to Lacey's Spring. In the trunk of our rented car was a small gunny sack of mussels inside a wooden box with a chunk of ice in it. Before we departed the mussel camp, Homer told us the mussels we were taking with us were the Sheepnose, Shinyrayed, and Wabash Pigtoe kind. "There's more than a hunnerd different kinds of them things in our Alabamie waters," he told us proudly.

After spending the night at Miss Millie's Home for Weary Travelers, an overnight, country-style home in Lacey's Spring, we drive the three-hour trip to Savannah, Tennessee. Following signs in town, we drive down a gravel road about a quarter of a mile before the road ends at the *Mazel Tov* Button Factory on the banks of the Tennessee

River.

"Guess it's okay to park by these old trucks," Reno says, pulling in next to an assortment of skinned-up old pickups and work trucks with barrels, wenches, and tools sticking out of the back ends. As soon as Shifrah's boot heels sink into the powdery red dirt outside the car, she clicks her tongue and attempts to wipe off the dust quickly covering the tops of her boots.

I shield my eyes from the bright sunshine and soak in the scene around us. Men shout at one another as they unload soggy baskets and tall barrels of mussels from the rows of boats banking and departing in the river. Others maneuvering mule-pulled carts whistle and cuss at their animals to back up or go forward as they hoist loads on or off the carts. Loaded carts plodding toward machinery and buildings pass empty carts on the way back to the river. A musty smell fills the air, and I love it because it reminds me of my fishing trips with the men back home. What would they think of all this?

Reno whistles. "Would you just look at those piles? Must be millions of shells." He walks over and picks one up, studies it. "Here's what the buttonholes look like," he says, holding up a shell full of perfectly round holes.

"Good thing I dressed up for this exquisite place," Shifrah says, holding a tissue under her nose.

The closest building looks like an upside-down U, reminding me of a plane hangar. It has a large, double-door opening and a small door set off to the side with a sign above it with OFFICE painted in neat capitals. A crisply-dressed man with curly hair graying at the temples and wearing glasses in wireframes emerges from the office door.

"Is it Major Malone Connor I see before me?" he asks in a heavy accent, smiling and extending his hand to Malone. Next, Reno steps up to shake hands. I've rarely seen such vigorous handshaking, but then, he breaks loose and smiles at Shifrah and me. "Ah, these are the womens you said about on the telephone, Major Connor. I see. I see." He keeps smiling at us so intently, I start feeling self-conscious.

Malone clears his throat. "Uh, Reno, grab those mussels from the trunk for Mr. Horowitz."

"Please, call me Mordi."

Reno places the gunnysack at Mordi's feet.

"And what do we have here?"

"Mussels," Reno says.

He picks up the sack and gives it a little shake. "These are your mussels from yesterday's catch, Mr. Connor?"

"Yessir, some of them. We brought them for—"

"For joke, yes?" He breaks out laughing, leaning backward on his heels as he does so. He takes off his glasses and wipes the lens with a white handkerchief he pulls from a pocket. We all trade glances, and I think we must appear foolish handing him a little sack of mussels when there are thousands of pounds of them constantly being pulled from the river.

"What shall I do with these mussels the womens strip from the hooks, Mr. Connor?"

"I thought you, uh, might make them some jewelry. Keepsakes, if you will."

"You want I should make earrings or necklace pieces for the womens? Ah, yes, I can do but not from these. Too wet. Okay to use my cured shells for making the jewelry?"

"Thank you, Mordi, but I want you to use these if you don't mind."

"Yes, I will do for you when the shells are ready, okay? Not today. Can you be waiting in town a few weeks?"

"Afraid not," Malone says. He takes the man by the elbow and steps away to talk to him alone. Mordi comes back all smiles.

"Yes, I am happy to accept this wee bag of mussels you womens stripped from the hooks with your own fingers. If that is what our, uh, our Mr. A wants, that is what he shall have! I will make you beautiful earrings and necklaces from these special mussels you bring me. And now, Major Connor, we have the business to take care of, yes?"

He signals for a young man standing nearby to join us, and speaks to him in a foreign language. The young man's face lights up as he holds Shifrah and me in his gaze. Reno glances briefly over his shoulder at us while he, Mordi, and Malone walk toward the office.

"Here we go again," Shifrah mumbles, "being treated like truant children."

I'm disappointed we weren't invited to see the handover of the *retrieve,* which makes two exchanges, including the *key to the keys,* we've missed so far. At least we witnessed Eddie the *Havasupai* handing his owl key to Malone. Malone sends every *retrieve* to headquarters instead of keeping them, which makes sense. Why take a chance of losing something so odd and, apparently, so important?

"My name is Lior," the young man says, bowing. "I am pleased to show you our exquisite button factory." He speaks perfect English with a charming accent. He's nice-looking, dressed well, and it's obvious from his perfect appearance he does none of the river or factory labor himself. When I ask him about steaming the mussels we brought with us today, he explains freshly caught mussels are soaked in cold water for three days before steaming so the shells are less brittle and the cooked insides shake out easier.

"I was listening to your conversation. Father will construct your jewelry from your own shells when they are ready. They will look especially lovely with your blond hair," he says to me.

"Why, thank you."

We walk up and down aisles watching factory employees operating button-stamping machines. Lior loves showing the factory, I gather, because he warms more and more to his subject as we continue. He holds my eyes to see if I understand his explanations about the machine gears, which I do, and lightly touches my arm or shoulder as he explains one thing after another.

"The discs are cut from the shells by those hollow drill bits before they are sanded into button blanks," he says, ignoring the smiles and shy glances from many of the younger women operating the machines. "Many button blanks are drilled from a single shell before the finishers polish the discs and use the buttonhole machines over there by the wall to drill the holes for the thread," he says.

Shifrah quietly moans behind me. I turn. "Shifrah, just think. This is more New York conversation for you. How many of your friends know anything about the buttons on their fancy clothes? Now you can tell them how the buttons come from the inside walls of mussel shells and how you personally sacrificed your fingers and fingernails one whole afternoon stripping mussels off hooks on the drunk Tennessee River. You'll have your keepsake earrings and a necklace made from those very mussels to show them, and—"

"Savannah is correct. Buttons are crucial to life!" Lior interrupts with a flashy smile, putting his arm around my shoulder to guide us down the next aisle as though we are about to observe precious pieces of art. Curious onlookers steal glances at us, then quickly resume their work as we walk the aisles. Lior is explaining the way buttons are packed and shipped and some of the exotic locations of the buyers when we turn a corner, and there stands Reno, his arms crossed.

"Time to go. Malone's waiting in the car."

Lior tightens his grip on my shoulder, which makes me turn and look up at him. He's gazing intently into my face.

"Must you go so soon, Savannah, and, uh, Shira?"

"Shira? My name is Shifrah."

"Yes, of course. As I was saying, you only just arrived. Perhaps we can have tea before you—"

"Like I said, Malone is waiting. Excuse me, partner," Reno says, removing Lior's hand from my shoulder and nudging us toward the exit.

"Thank you for the tour," I turn and say on our way out. Lior is glaring at Reno, who is looking back at him.

"That was dull and stinky," Shifrah says as she scoots into the back seat.

"I found it interesting," I say.

"Uh-huh. So… I believe Lior fancies himself quite the lady's man."

"A lot of young women were vying for his attention for sure."

"But you got all of it."

"He was just being nice. I wonder how we'll get our jewelry."

"Mordi will ship it to us," Malone answers.

"Where?"

"In due time, Savannah, in due time.

"Surely that isn't a secret—"

Malone clears his throat.

"Can we at least see the *retrieve?"*

Malone takes it from an inside jacket pocket and holds it up for us to see.

"That figure on the end looks like a cross between a dragon and a seahorse," Shifrah says.

"It does! Why are the *retrieve* keys so intricate? The last one had a vivid owl on it. Does the design have anything to do with the purpose of the keys, Malone?"

He doesn't answer, drops the key into a small zippered pouch and places it back inside his jacket.

"Another question unanswered, Savannah. Know what? The last two days don't make any sense at all," Shifrah says. "We kill our fingers stripping mussels off deadly hooks, take a pitifully small bag of wet, smelly mussels to a button factory owner not even located where we did that brawling thing on the river and who already has millions of mussels everywhere. We lowly females are sent on a boring tour through a button factory where the factory owner's son Lior falls in love with Savannah, and you guys exclude us while you get our *retrieve.* Does anyone besides me think this behavior should be psychoanalyzed?"

"Shifrah, that's outlandish," I mutter under my breath.

"What, that this behavior should be psychoanalyzed?"

"No, the part about Lior."

"But it's true. Lior fell madly in love with you, didn't he, Reno?"

I expect Reno to burst out laughing or make a joke, but he doesn't. It's easy to see he and Lior didn't hit it off. Nobody knows why that happens sometimes, how strangers immediately dislike each other, but I just witnessed a case of it.

"We're following orders," Malone says.

"What?" Shifrah says.

"You asked what was going on."

"Yeah, because our last two assignments are senseless."

"Orders are orders. That's how life is, Shifrah."

"Tell that to my bowed legs and broken fingernails. Okay, I stand corrected. It's Mr. A who's obviously off his rocker."

CHAPTER THIRTY

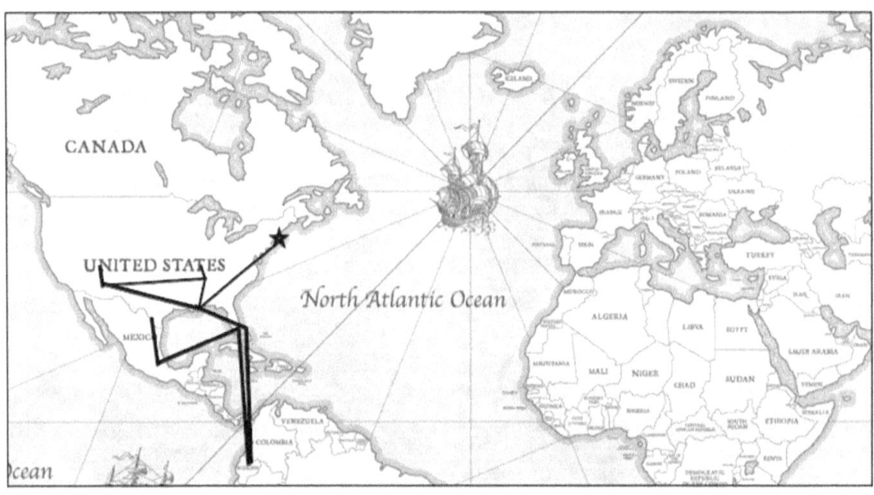

Bleary-eyed and weary is the only way to describe our lives this past week. We drove from the button factory in Savannah, Tennessee, back to Birmingham, picked up Shifrah's developed photos—which she says she won't look at until her feet touch home ground in New York City—and flew out the next morning on Southern Airlines to New Orleans. We spent a short night there, dining nicely in the hotel's open-twenty-four-hour restaurant, before flying to New York City early the next afternoon on Northern Airlines. These days, I'm constantly aware of our airline, type of plane, and more since Reno makes a big deal about every one, along with the history and capabilities of each.

We got a reprieve from our hectic schedule on our first night in New York City with an early dinner in the hotel and a much-needed full night's rest. The next morning, Shifrah loaded the two of us into a taxi to go shopping. I've read about large cities, but reading about them is nothing like riding in a cab down Broadway into Times Square. I felt disconnected from reality while I leaned out the window, looking at the lights and sights, the tall buildings, and thousands of people scurrying in every direction. A crazy thought that I might dissolve into city air and no one would notice because of the extravagant surroundings made my heart pound erratically. I popped back against the taxi seat breathing hard.

"It's all right," Shifrah said, "it's a lot to take in the first time."

We drove to Madison Square, ate street-vendor hot dogs while staring at the beautiful Statue of Liberty, and, of course, shopped. I've stopped arguing with her about how I dress or fix up because I'm starting to love it more than I probably should.

We're scheduled to board the SS America sailing to Le Havre, France, this afternoon, but, first, we're here waiting at the *Blue Stiletto* Restaurant not far from the New York Harbor to have lunch with Shifrah's parents. My small-town Texas head is reeling from all this, and I wish I could bottle up some of the excitement I feel and send it to Tony and my regulars.

Shifrah was right when she told me that life-changing opportunities come along maybe once or twice in a lifetime, if at all. I consider what is happening to me right now a once-in-*several*-lifetimes opportunity. I constantly feel giddy, but I work hard at keeping myself reserved following Shifrah's sophisticated demeanor.

Sometimes, when I'm falling asleep at night, I get confused about what this assignment is all about. Yes, I know we're picking up important keys that fit something that's important enough that we're being paid handsomely and important enough that someone is following our every move. Speaking of that, Malone took me aside in the hotel and told me to be watchful while Shifrah and I were out sightseeing and shopping. He asked, "Are you prepared for anything?" I patted my purse, and he dipped his head in approval.

Right now, I'm watching the entry of the *Blue Stiletto* and nervously sipping cinnamon tea sweetened with honey. My teammate sits as poised as a model wielding her jeweled cigarette holder as if it's her magic wand bestowing favors on the surrounding city. It's obvious she feels right at home. She's stunning in the outfit she bought yesterday. Naturally, she picked out my clothes, too, and I'm feeling nervous wearing this tight-fitting emerald green dress, black heels, a black pillbox hat with a small net protruding a few inches from the front edge. My black velvet swing coat and long scarf in green, white, and black I'm to wear wrapped once around my neck and let fall almost to the hem on each side of my coat were checked in when we arrived.

I told Shifrah I'm dressed out enough to meet the Royals of England, much too fancy to go to lunch and board a ship, but she said, *darling, it's New York, and we're off to France on a famous vessel, don't you know?* And then she laughed so cheerfully, I fell into step with her mood. Her coat is also checked in, and she's wearing a magenta dress with a wide black leather belt, black heels with a small magenta bow on top of each, gold jewelry, and the most glamorous hat I've ever seen. She called it a black-fox roller hat with a mink crown.

"Shifrah, are my clothes being paid for out of the money I'm earning on this mission? You always pay and never say a word to me. How are we affording all this?"

"My allowance from my parents, Savannah. Malone handles all my expenses and gives me cash to use."

"But what about my expenses? Are they coming from my salary?"

She chuckled. "Not at all, Savannah, you're with me. My allowance covers us both."

"That doesn't seem right."

"It's perfect. Don't give it another thought."

But I do give it another thought. I'm going to talk to Malone about it when I get the chance.

So, here we sit warned and waiting for her parents in one of the most beautiful restaurants, in the biggest city, dressed in the fanciest clothes of my existence. I say *warned* because we were instructed not to say anything about where we've been, what the *retrieves* are, or how we got them. We also can't say where we're headed next, other than saying we're off to Europe.

"Malone, you must be joking," Shifrah said when he briefed us, as he calls it, early this morning over coffee and a fruit plate. "That means I can't show Mommykins or Daddy my photos or tell them how I was nearly speared to death while partially nude, how terrifying it is to ride a mule on a narrow trail into a bottomless pit in the earth, or how I pulled disgusting mussels off hooks in a dirty dingy in Alabama!"

"That's right. You can't. Don't forget this is a covert operation, so mum's the word, Shifrah. That's an order. Don't forget, we have someone following us, and we don't want to put your parents in any danger, do we?"

"No," she muttered, her face downcast.

"Later, you can tell them all your adventures a thousand times, but we can't risk it this early. Too much is at stake. Let me say they know a few things about the overall picture, but they have the same orders as you do."

Just what do they know, and why?

Shifrah pouted and mumbled a lot afterward, but Malone said no more. Later, she confidentially told me, "He makes me so irritated, Savannah. Now, I don't get to open my photo packages until we're on the ship, and I wanted to share them for the first time with my parents. I know one thing… I'll never show Malone anything as long as I live."

I wanted to smile at that, but I didn't. She loves his attention and his approval, so her not showing him anything for the rest of her life is a dead promise. Personally, I love it that we're doing something secretive because I never have before. Will things become more dangerous as we move forward? I guess we'll find out, and I need to quit being so excited at the thought of it.

Malone is up and out of his chair to meet Shifrah's parents as soon as they enter the restaurant. He and Shifrah's father, or uncle, that is, stand across the room talking and leaning toward each other, heads bobbing, as though they are sharing confidences.

"What in the world is taking so long?" Shifrah says, suddenly bolting from her chair to practically run, elegantly, of course, across the restaurant and fall into her mother's arms. Their hugging and cheek-kissing reunion makes me smile but also feel like an outsider. Seeing her folded into her father's arms sends a pang of daddy-longing straight through my heart.

The closer they get to our table, the easier it is to see where Shifrah gets her high-fashion sense. Her mother is dressed as luxuriously as her daughter in a black coat with leopard trim and a leopard cloche hat. Shifrah gave me a hat lesson while we were shopping yesterday so I could identify which kind her mother would be wearing today. Mr. Mandel gracefully helps Mrs. Mandel remove her coat, revealing her wearing a sleek tan dress, flashy jewelry, and a fancy leopard belt circling her waist.

He removes his own heavy coat and hat and hands them to a young man standing by the Maître d'. His suit has an attractive sheen, and he's wearing a tie over a white shirt with cuffs of gold and, I assume, diamonds that sparkle across the room. My anxiety increases as I realize how seriously wealthy Shifrah and her parents are. I'm grateful they're smiling brightly as they near our table.

"Please meet my parents, Mr. and Mrs. Mandel. Mommy, Daddy, this is my dear Savannah! Let me tell you, she's a *mensch!* We're practically sisters now, and I'm having so much fun dressing her in beautiful fashions! Can you guess what movie star she looks like?"

Clasping both my hands in hers and leaning toward me with twinkling eyes, her mother says with a heavy accent, "Of course, darling, she's the spitting image of Anita Eckberg! Such a beauty you are, my dear. No wonder our *ketzeleh* has made you her *tzatzkeleh!* She did the same with all her dolls. A *shayna meydele* is my Shifrah! She kept me busy buying as many clothes for her dolls and pets as I did for her, but I didn't mind!"

I have no idea what Shifrah's mother just said, but if it means Shifrah is dressing me up and treating me like one of her dolls, I really don't like it. I'm still me, aren't I?

Mrs. Mandel doesn't release my hands, keeps looking back and forth at Shifrah and me, studies my face with a look in her eyes I'm not used to—a blend of concern and warmth. "Mommy, let poor Savannah have her hands back!" Shifrah says, laughing. "Come. Sit by me, and I'll order your favorite, a Tom Collins with lime, no lemon, right?" Mrs. Mandel nods, still smiling, and releases my hands.

Mr. Mandel steps in close and extends his hand to me. I immediately see the similarity in his eyes and Shifrah's, the unusual combination of green, brown, and gold, which Shifrah says are merely hazel. She told me he's an accountant and investor, and I guess that explains how manicured his hands and nails are. No callouses or rough edges like the ranchers and truck drivers in Laredo.

"I'm delighted to meet our daughter's traveling companion, Savannah," he says, in a rich, heavily-accented voice. He glances to the side, seems to float rather than walk in perfect timing to pull his wife's chair out before she sits.

"Mommykins, Daddy, this is Reno," Shifrah says, extending her hand in his direction. "Among other things, he's our pilot, comedian, and a complete *lobbes.*

Reno vigorously shakes hands with Mr. Mandel, nods pleasantly toward Mrs. Mandel. "Nice to make your acquaintance sir, ma'am. Uh, Shif, what's a *lobbes?"*

Shifrah and her parents chuckle as Mr. Mandel takes a seat next to his wife. "It means you're cheeky. You know, mischievous. A lot of *chutzpah* but sometimes so much it gets you in trouble," Shifrah explains, "and that's letting you off lightly."

"Well, now that we have all the introductions out of the way, who's hungry?" Malone says, waving down a waiter.

All business, all the time, that's Malone, but something doesn't feel right. He has a worry wrinkle, as I call it, right between his brows, and, frankly, his smile looks a little fake right now.

CHAPTER THIRTY-ONE

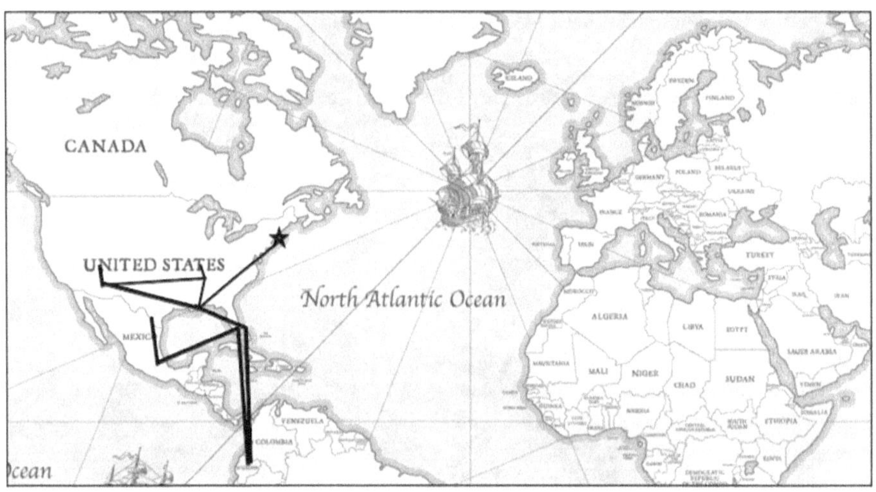

Basking in the warmness of Shifrah's parents makes me feel accepted, as if they are family members who care. Surely, she would never disappoint these wonderful people. Now I'm even more curious about the details of the story she always bypasses.

Her mother—Ruth, as she insists I call her—starts crying as soon as Mr. Mandel takes her arm to escort her outside the restaurant. She first hugs me in what we call a mama-bear hug in Texas, then touches her hand to my cheek. Something about her makes me yearn to ask her not to go. She smiles at me through tear-filled eyes, making my own eyes fill with tears.

She gathers her daughter into her arms. "My little *ziskayt,* take good care, take good care. Come home safe to us." She fixes her eyes on Malone. "Promise me, Malone, you will not let her… and when… and if…" she breaks into sobs.

"I'll take care of her, Ruth," Malone says softly.

What does Ruth mean about "when" and "if?"

With her husband's gentle prodding, she turns Shifrah loose and buries her face in a lace-bordered handkerchief. She steps into a sleek car with a driver wearing a uniform holding the back door of the car open.

The four of us watch them drive off, and I'm swept away with a surprising feeling of loss. I subtly dab my own tears and pat Shifrah's shoulder as she sobs into her handkerchief. Malone clears his throat. "They're good people, Shifrah, really good." He looks at his watch. "Okay, listen up. Our ship leaves port at 1600 from Pier 61 on West 21st Street. We can check in and embark any time now. There are a few things I need to brief you on before we take off. Let's step into that little coffee shack across the street and have us a hot coffee and a little talk.

Less than five minutes into our *little talk*, Shifrah rises from her seat in the open café and bangs her fist on the table. "I won't do it, Malone! I-I quit. I mean it. You're asking too much, and you know it!" Malone puts both elbows on the table, balances his chin on entwined fingers. His neutral expression tells me he's more than prepared to ride out Shifrah's storm.

"How could you do this to me? You know I've yearned for my time on the ship ever since this crazy assignment started. You never said one word about me babysitting a bunch of-of children on board. Are you insane? I don't even like kids!"

"It's a week or less."

"A week? It might as well be a year! That means no massages or pampering or anything restful at all. No dressing up. No nothing!"

"Nobody says you can't dress for dinner every night."

"Oh sure, dressing up to dine in the worker's dining hall. How elegant! Besides, I know I'd be too rattled to dress up after taking care of little monsters all day. And have you ever seen those horrid stewardess uniforms? They're gray with silly caps and aprons. They look like prison matron outfits and-and… thick old-woman shoes with shoelaces! I can't believe you expect such a thing of me, Malone. No, I won't do it. I have no choice but to call Daddy and have him pick me up. I can't do what you ask. Not this time."

I'm petrified hearing her say she's quitting. I can't imagine our mission without Shifrah. "Malone, let me do it for her!" I blurt out. "Please!"

"Savannah, you don't understand what—"

"But I'm used to kids, and she isn't. Let me have that job."

All of them are staring at me, and I nod vigorously to convince Malone to change his mind. He holds up a hand, turns to Shifrah.

"Shifrah," he says gently, "I understand your shock, but all of you are working on this cruise. Orders from headquarters. Did you forget about your alternative to finishing the mission?" He waits until he holds her eyes. "Uh-huh, one whole year, probably longer, and those uniforms are a whole lot uglier than what ship personnel wear, I'll guarantee you that."

Her face undergoes a metamorphosis as I watch, changing from anger to big-eyed realization to surrender—surrender as one might see in the eyes of a trapped animal about to lose its life. Her eyes fill with tears that slide unhindered down her cheeks. She scoots her chair out and around so she is turned away from us.

There's more to this than meets the eye, but I feel sorry for my friend. I don't understand the rules of this mission even though I accept them. I guess if you've never had luxuries in your life and you've always worked, you don't feel short-changed when you don't get your way. That's me, and I think Reno, as well. He excuses himself to go pay for our coffees, returns, stares at a pattern he's tracing with his finger on a small paper napkin. Malone's eyes are filled with genuine concern, and I give him credit for that.

"Malone, honestly, I would love that kid assignment. Will you reconsider and give whatever job I was supposed to do to Shifrah?"

He sighs wearily. "Shifrah, can you take dictation?"

"What is it?"

"Do you type?"

"Of course I can. I didn't care very much for it, but I think I can type about thirty words a minute if I practice first."

He looks at me, shakes his head. "That's why you can't swap jobs, Savannah. You're set to work with an author four or five days taking notes and typing them up every day with a possible break for lunch. Not sure about that part. I understand this author may call for you in the evening hours if she gets, what did she say… oh, if her muse visits. She's known to be quite strict and demands a fast stenographer when she dictates her novels. She's disembarking in Ireland, so that's the reason for the shorter employment. The last day or so on board, you'll be on call to work with any of the business forums holding meetings if they need minutes taken. You do take notes, right?"

"Shorthand."

"Yeah, that's what I remembered. Lots of corporate bigwigs on the ship might require your skills. Or not. We'll play that one by ear. You might be interested to know Mr. A himself picked that job for you. Seems he and the author you're working for have met before. Shifrah, have you decided to finish the mission with us?"

What is the "alternative" if she quits the mission? Come heck or high water, I'm going to find out.

When she finally answers, it's almost in a whisper. "Yes."

"Good. You and Savannah are bunking together on the crew level."

"Of course, that's where all the servants sleep, Savannah," Shifrah says mournfully, her back still turned. "What about you and Reno?"

"Reno's been assigned to follow and assist a high-ranking steward for important passengers—whatever they need, any time they need it."

"Hot diggity, that's gonna be a real different assignment. Hey, I might have to run off with one of those rich traveling baronesses, you know?"

Malone shoots him a quick look. "Keep your wings tucked in tighter than tight all week, Reno."

"Yessir, just joshing. I'll be straight as an arrow and twice as quick. No worries, sir."

Shifrah turns to face us. "And you, Malone? Will you be dining with the captain and escorting young debutants and wealthy widows to dinner every night?"

Malone's face registers surprise, almost shock. "Why, no. What gave you that idea? We all eat dinner together the first night at the captain's table with certain other guests. Seating is prearranged, as you know, and I, uh, we worked it out so my team could meet the captain. After that, I have my own work cut out for me, and, no, I'm not staying in first class. Don't even want to.

"One more thing, so listen up. I'm working closely with headquarters to pin down ideas and details about our spy. Don't go anywhere by yourselves. Stay among groups or crowds at all times, and when you're off duty, stay together. Reno, you're trained for this, but ladies, keep your eyes peeled and report anything suspicious to me immediately."

"Are we talking about a lot of danger?" I ask.

"Probably not, but let's err on the side of caution. Any questions?"

"When do my duties from Hell begin?" Shifrah asks.

"A supervisor will come to your room in the morning at 0500 to brief you and get you outfitted. Does everyone understand their assignments?"

All of us nod. Malone, looking relieved, tells Reno to hail us a cab. Reno steps to the curb to whistle one down, and off we head to the docks for a cruise like none of us formerly anticipated, especially Shifrah.

At Sea

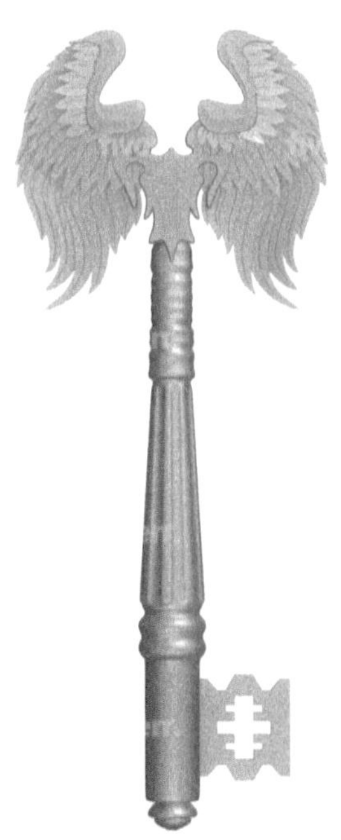

CHAPTER THIRTY-TWO

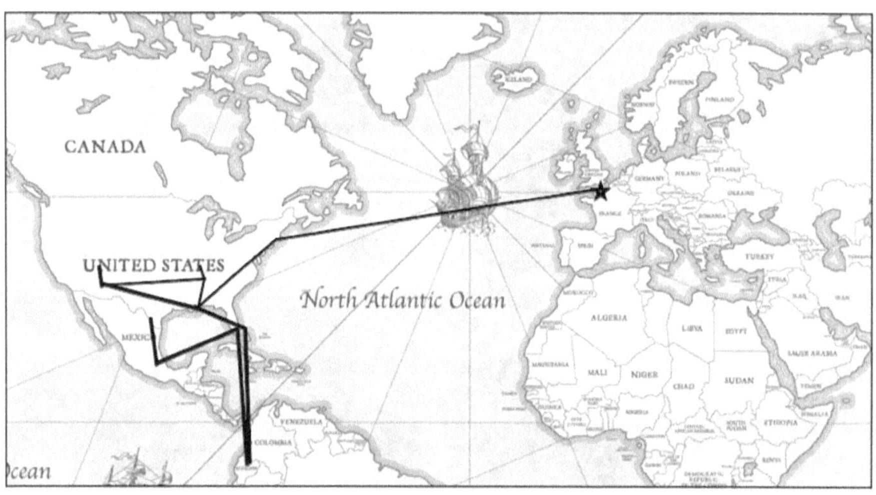

We're expected in the first-class dining room to meet the men in an hour, and Shifrah hasn't stopped crying since we were shown our *quarters* about an hour ago. She kept an icy composure during our taxi ride to the pier, while we checked in, boarded, and even when we were shown to our tiny accommodations with the exposed pipes running across the ceiling.

When the door behind the luggage porter closed, she quietly removed her gorgeous black fox hat, put it in a hat box, and hung her winter coat in the almost-not-there closet, taking up most of the closet. She fished her etched cigarette case from her purse, took three steps, and collapsed stomach down on the bottom bunkbed, weeping loudly before her face hit the pillow. She still has her cigarette case in her hand.

My main suitcase and train case are unpacked, the rest of my things stowed and stacked out of the way, and her luggage, all four suitcases and two hat boxes, remain untouched just inside the door. Our belongings take up nearly all the move-around space in our room. I'm discovering that workers on ships travel extremely light.

I feel a little guilty that I'm so excited about the jobs Malone assigned to me for the upcoming week on the SS America ship, but I can't help it. Never did I think I'd use my high school stenographer skills in such a dramatic setting. So far, they came in handy for notetaking in my college classes, but, as far as employment, I've never worked at anything or anywhere outside the Dixie other than babysitting for special occasions as a teenager. Shifrah, on the other hand, is devastated. I have to find a way to bring her out of her despair.

"How do you expect to look nice for supper, I mean, dinner, if your eyes are swollen and red, Shifrah?"

"What difference does it make? I'm a servant now. A mussel picker. A matron on a ship."

"Oh, my goodness. You're still the quintessential beauty queen. You make me fix up everywhere we go, whether we're flying into a jungle, riding mules, hiking, or going down a river unhooking mussels. Come on, girl, let's get gussied up for our first night on the SS America!"

She groans and continues to bury her face in the pillow on the narrow bunk bed. I sit on the edge beside her. "We're not servants, by the way. We're simply employees. There's nothing shameful in working, Shifrah. You'll be great with the children. You just don't know it yet."

"Not possible."

"It is. You're dreamy and young and have fresh ideas about life. That's all it takes to understand little kids' minds. They love pretty ladies, so they'll take to you the instant they meet you. Trust me on this, all right?"

She doesn't answer.

I go check my image in the tiny mirror above the sink, pat my hair, put on fresh lipstick. Shifrah's ways have rubbed off on me more than I ever thought possible. I guess that's okay, isn't it?

While I'm gazing at Shifrah on the bed from the reflection in the mirror, I get an idea. I sit down beside her and lightly shake her shoulder.

"Hey, you listenin'?" She makes a miserable grunt. "Listen up, little missy. We're talking 'bout one week—seven scrawny days. Shoot fire, Shifra, if we gotta, me and you can ride a buckin' horse while shooting the eyes out of a polecat with a peashooter for seven days straight and never miss a shot. Why? 'Cause we're tougher'n nails and meaner'n a rattlesnake with a belly full of cactus!"

"Wha-what? Are you crazy?" She rolls halfway over to stare at me.

"Yes'm, crazier'n a Grand Canyon mule wearing Maybelline mascara."

"Savannah, I swear, you-you…" she sits up, stares at my silly smile, starts laughing. I join her, and we laugh until tears run down our cheeks.

"A mule wearing mascara? That picture just-just makes me… makes me—"

"It makes you happy. Come on, Shifrah, you're stronger than this. Seven days, maybe less? They're over before they begin. Now get off this bed and fluff up so we can go eat something. That fancy little Waldorf salad we ate with your parents didn't fill up one of my kneecaps."

"How do you do that?"

"Do what?"

"Change from elegant to—"

"To backwoods?" I laugh. "Oh, trust me, that world lives inside my soul forevermore. It's my raising, you know."

"Your raising?"

I sit up straight, lift my chin in a snobbish angle, assume a fake British accent. "Perhaps I should say, it's the manner in which I was reared, dahling."

She giggles. "All right, you win. If, and I'm not promising it's possible, I can make myself presentable, I'll go to dinner with you. It is our only chance to be in a proper dining room, but I'm still so angry at Malone."

"You know he has to do whatever Mr. A man tells him to do."

"I suppose, but this? It's ludicrous. Imagine *me* taking care of children."

"You'll get through it. Say, Malone talked about an alternative to finishing the mission. Why don't you tell me what that's all about?"

She opens her train case and sets it on top of the little sink basin below the mirror, checks her watch. "I have thirty minutes to work a miracle on my face and hair. Should I change my dress, too, you think?"

She's not getting away with it. Not this time.

"No, don't change. That shade of magenta is perfect with your eyes, but look, you've put me off every time this subject comes up. How about shooting straight with me for once? Don't I deserve that?"

"Yes, of course, but, gads, I'm-I'm ashamed of it, Savannah."

"I'm your friend. I'm on your side."

She breaths out a ragged breath. "I suppose, but—"

"I can take it. Trust me."

She looks long and hard into my eyes, nods. "Okay, where do I begin? You already know bits and pieces of it. You remember my mentioning my group—a gang, if you will—of bored, wealthy college kids, right?"

"Yeah."

"All of us were of age, twenty-one or two, so I guess we weren't kids at all. One evening after consuming several Mai Tai's at the Congo Club where we hung out a lot, we cooked up a scheme, something daring, different."

"What was it?"

"A stupid plan, but once we got it into our heads, that was it. The next day we drove twenty-five miles out of the city to Tarrytown."

"Tarrytown? Where have I heard that before? Oh, yes, it was the home of author Washington Irving. I think his home was named Sunnyside."

"My dear historical, literary professor, I did not know that. No one knows that."

"Oh, okay. Please continue."

"On the outskirts of town, we parked on the side of a local filling station and waited for the perfect mark to stop for gasoline."

"Mark?"

"Target. The one we planned to dupe. It was my job to use my feminine wiles, the ones I used on the hotel clerk when we went looking for the *key to the keys* in Malone's room."

"Oh yes, the *I'm so easy and lonely* act, right?"

"Well, I prefer to call it being *seductive with unspoken promises* attached.

Anyway, it was a busy highway, so it didn't take long. Our target had a beautiful new Ford convertible, a 1951, deep blue with its white top down. After the attendant filled it up, the gentleman went inside to buy a map or something. That was the perfect setup for us. I stepped in behind him to do my little act, and Zellie's part was to confiscate his wallet while I flirted with him."

"Your friend is a pickpocket?"

"Yeah, it's crazy. Her parents own stock in some of the biggest gas and oil companies in the world, but, back then, she was constantly practicing picking pockets and shoplifting as a big joke. She picked our professors' wallets all the time. It was hilarious because she would sneak back in after class and put it in some obscure place. One poor prof thought he was losing his marbles after she did it to him three times. Soon, that wasn't enough thrill for her. She started shoplifting at some of the big stores, which I didn't approve of. She'd gotten very adept at it, and I could see it was turning into something she couldn't stop. I told you, we were restless."

"To say the least," I mumble.

"Oh, you're going to hate me after you hear this story, aren't you?"

We have a short stare. I ask myself if I'm mature enough to leave someone's past in the past. I decide, yes, I am, and I tell her so. She gnaws part of her bottom lip before turning back to the mirror to stroke powder on her face.

"So, I'm flirting my head off, as you know I can, but this man isn't what I expected. In fact, he reminds me of my own father. He politely rejects my overtures, then advises me in the nicest way that I'm too lovely and special to act like that. His smile, and the kindness in his eyes… I'll never forget it. His words have haunted me for almost two years, Savannah. If I could have backed out of the plan, I would have, but it was too late."

"Why?"

"I saw the guys through the open door by the cash register giving us the *let's go* signal. Zellie takes off, his wallet in her purse. I'm scared, so I'm right behind her. We jump into the convertible, speed off, tires squealing. Bradley follows immediately in our car, and we look back and see the man, the pump attendant, and the filling station owner all standing outside. Zellie and Skip are up front squealing and victory laughing. It wasn't fun or funny to me anymore.

"Nat King Cole's song, *Too Young,* was blaring from the radio. I leaned over the front seats and shouted we should park the car and leave it for them to find. They laughed, called me a spoil sport, a drag. Skip floored the gas pedal. We were flying down the road, Bradley close behind, when a police car pulled out from behind a billboard along the highway.

"Skip wouldn't stop or slow down, even with Zellie and me screaming at him. He'd been drinking all day, so he was hopped up past his limit. We started zigzagging across the highway, and, of course, he lost control. I'll never forget the trees we crashed into. In that flash of time, I saw them as tree monsters reaching out with limbs to embrace me into death. Bradley barely missed crashing into the back of us, I found out later, and putting on the brakes like he did flipped his car. Naturally, the cops were on the scene immediately."

Shifrah hangs her head, closes her eyes. "Skip died, Savannah, and Zellie's face is permanently scarred from going through the front window. Bradley has a permanent limp. I was thrown from the car and don't remember anything until I woke up in the hospital with severe cuts on my arm and my right thigh, lots of minor cuts and bruises, a concussion, and three broken ribs. Zellie, Bradley, and I were all under arrest.

"You might know my parents were devastated, and their disappointment hurt worse than any of my injuries. The bottom line… is we had to hire a lawyer. When I was well enough, some months later, I appeared in court. My parents acted differently after that. They still loved me, I knew that, but something had changed. My father said it was time I learned about real life, and I was given a choice, which, they said, only happened because of my father's influence and after many phone calls to who knows who."

"The *alternative* Malone mentioned?"

"Yes. I could agree to go on a mysterious trip in which I was under the total jurisdiction of Malone, whom they introduced me to, or I could serve a year, maybe eighteen months, in jail. Those were my choices. Nothing else. Of course, I chose this."

She dabs her eyes. "Drat, I can't fix my eyes if I'm going to cry again. Savannah, do-do you still like me?"

I cross the tiny space from the bed and give her a good, hard Texas hug, the kind that leaves no doubt you care about the person you're hugging. After that hug, I hold her at arm's length. "You silly little thing. What you needed growing up was a whoopin' or two, and this never would have happened. I got one from my daddy for being flat-out mean to a schoolmate for no reason when I was seven, and another one for cussing at him when I was nine. Those two whoopin's fixed me up. Anyway, the past is the past. My daddy always said, 'every path in life has a few muddy puddles on the trail, and there ain't nobody out there can say they ain't been in one or two.' In other words, we all do things we wish we hadn't, but it doesn't mean we're bad."

She dabs tears with her index fingers.

"You were already sorry while the whole thing was going on. You know what that means, don't you?"

"What?"

"It means you're good inside."

"I don't feel like I am."

"Well, start feeling like you are. I don't make many mistakes about people, and I say you're what we call in Texas *a good un.* Remember, I was already in charge of a whole slew of adults at the Dixie when y'all snatched me out of there, so I might know what I'm talking about."

"You really think I'm a good person?"

"I do."

A look of long-sought relief covers her features. "I've been so afraid if you found out about my past, you wouldn't want to be my friend, that you'd see me as a rogue."

"A rogue?"

"Someone low in character."

"Oh, for heaven sakes, Shifrah, I know what a rogue is. One misstep on a ladder doesn't mean you can't climb one for the rest of your life. You've paid your price, you're still paying it, and no one should put any more judgment on it. I sure won't, and I could never think of you as a rogue."

"Except for my parents, you're the best person I've ever known, Savannah."

"Aw, that's sweeter than tomato jam on Melba toast, Shifrah, but you won't think so if you don't hurry and paint that face so we can go eat. I'm about to get meaner than a wasp with a foot-long stinger."

CHAPTER THIRTY-THREE

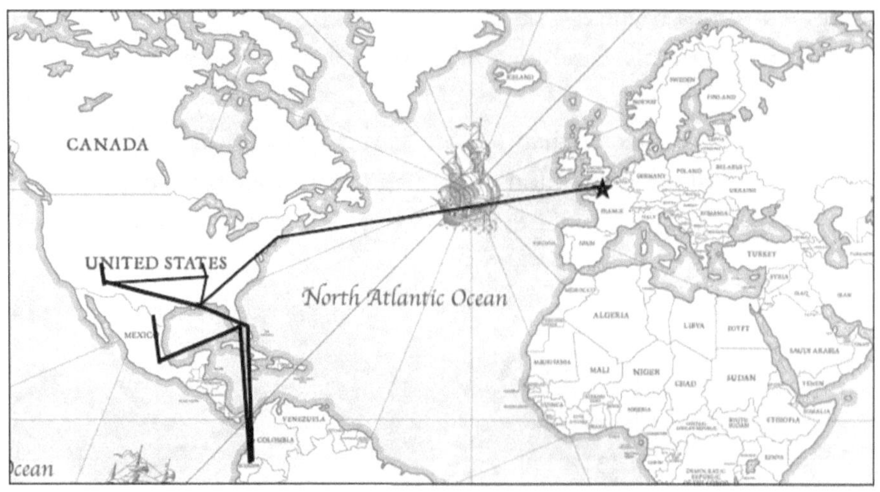

A loud knock on the door makes us jump. "I'll get it," I say, stepping carefully over suitcases to reach the door. "Who is it?"

"Your favorite bodyguard," Reno says. I open the door to his bountiful smile. "Malone sent me to escort you ladies to the dining room. Ready?"

"Do I look ready?" Shifrah says from behind me.

Reno steps in, squints his eyes. "Yep, you sure do."

"Oh, for the love of Pete, Reno, my face looks like a swollen cantaloupe."

"Naw, it looks like a fresh strawberry winkin' at the sun."

"What?"

He laughs. "I've never seen you look anyways but beautiful, Shif.

Come on now, I'm hungrier than a tick on a teddy bear. Let's get moving."

"Close the door, you *lobbes.* I need at least ten more minutes to work a miracle on my face. It won't be easy. Hey, in my pink suitcase by the wall are my developed photographs none of us have seen yet. You and Savannah look at them while I finish. They're right inside the lid pocket."

Reno and I look like confused dancers with two left feet trying to step and hop over the baggage strewn on the floor. I find the photo envelope in Shifrah's suitcase and pat the bed for Reno to sit by me. Once seated, he says, "Hey, this here's quite the luxurious bedroom, girls. Mine has four bunkbeds, one drawer and one cubby hole apiece for our things, and a closet the size of a flea's sneeze."

"Really, Reno?" Shifrah asks. That's awful. Are you used to such terrible accommodations?"

"Hon, when you've slept in a dirt foxhole or out in the open with bullets whizzing by your ears and grenades exploding and not knowing if you're gonna live or die or ever see the break of day again, anything besides that is Heaven on earth."

From the look on her face, I think Reno just opened a window in Shifrah's mind. Mine, too, for that matter. How can we ever complain about anything when we hear things like that?

I open the sealed envelope with my fingernail and pull out the photographs. We *ooh and ah* through the first batch before I realize something. "Good gracious, Shifrah! You have to see this! Oh, my gosh…"

Shifrah almost breaks her legs stumbling over the luggage to get to us. "What is it?"

"That man we saw three times. He's definitely following us. Your camera doesn't lie. Look, here he is barely in the picture frame when you're taking pictures of me in the hallway after you dooded me up for my birthday in Phoenix. All you see is a fragment of his flowered shirt and his Panama hat. Now I remember him passing by a few times."

"That must be him at The Flame, too. His hat is almost covering his face, but he has the same flowery shirt as that man in the hallway,"

Reno says.

"Let me see!" Shifrah says, practically snatching the photos from our hands. "Oh, my gawd. He's even in the background in that bar with the car name in Mexico our first night, Savannah! Dressed like a Mexican guy with that poncho and straw hat, but it's the same man. See his profile? He's been everywhere we've been, but who is he?" Her eyes are saucers. "We really are being watched, you guys."

"Yep. Looks like it, for sure. Y'all ready to go?" Reno says.

In the hallway, Shifrah and I stop two times to listen. "Am I imagining it, or did I hear footsteps?" she asks.

"On this carpet? I don't think so. I know you're spooked, but don't let your imaginations run wild. You think I can't take care of a wimp like him?"

"But what's so important about these *retrieves* that we're being followed?" I ask.

"I don't know everything, hon, but I do know a lot more is at stake here than us having a good ol' time traveling around and piling up memories while we gather those keys."

"Tell us what's at stake," Shifrah whines. "Please, Reno. We deserve to know."

"You have to ask Malone."

Shifrah lets out a growl of frustration.

"Listen, that dude looks kind of like a store-bought sandwich to me. I can take him down with one hand behind my back. We're gonna be fine."

Shifrah and I stare at one another a few seconds, take off—increasing our speed as we step outdoors and walk along the deck clickity-clacking in our heels. By the time we reach the dining hall, we're out of breath.

CHAPTER THIRTY-FOUR

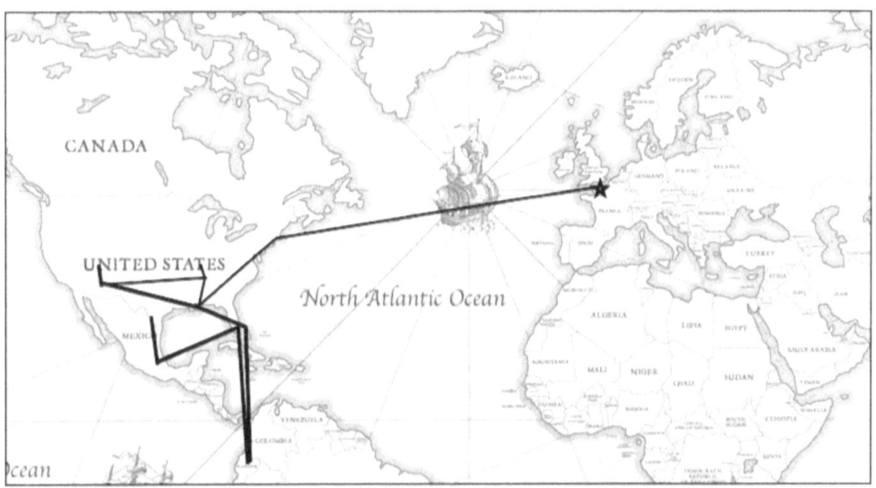

Hand-printed place cards have the three of us seated together at the table with Shifrah in the center and tourists on each side of Reno and me. Most of the people at our large round table look to be couples or tourists traveling in twos and threes. Malone is seated across the table from us beside a vacant chair. An attractive middle-aged woman with a dramatic upswept hairdo and loads of dazzling jewelry constantly engages him in conversation. Even as we make necessary polite talk with our tablemates as we sit down in our assigned places, I can tell we're still about to boil over with our news about the man in the photos.

"I'm going over there and interrupt Malone's little *tete-a-tete* with that gawdy woman," Shifrah says. She rises from her seat. Reno places a hand on her arm.

"I have a feeling we should wait, Shif."

"Why? There's an empty chair beside him. I could plop down a minute and tell him." Reno shakes his head. "Okay, then you go tell him about the pictures, Reno."

"So, if I do that, what happens? He jumps up and runs around the ship making phone calls and missing our one big dinner together.

"Reno's right. Telling him after dinner is soon enough," I chime in.

"Besides, that empty chair is for the captain. He might show up while you're sitting there getting Malone all hopped up about the pictures," Reno says.

She lets out a sigh, resettles into her seat. "Oh, all right." She takes a nibble of her appetizer, which the menu card says is Beluga Sturgeon Malossol Black caviar. Fish eggs. Not something I'm ready to try. She puts her mother-of-pearl-handled caviar spoon down, blots her mouth with the white linen napkin, mutters, "This is the worst voyage of my life."

"Come on, Shif, it isn't so bad. Look at the experiences you're tucking under your belt. How will you know how the po' folk live if you never see for yourself?"

"What's a poh foke?" she asks.

I almost spit out a forkful of smoked salmon, a fish I'm beginning to love. "He means poor people, Shifrah."

"Who in their right mind wants to know how the underlings live?" she says. She glances at us for confirmation, sees our expressions. Her haughty look dissolves, leaving a red streak across her cheeks.

"I didn't mean that. I'm terrible. I-I do care about them, but it's, um, it's new for me, all this. I've been spoiled, but I didn't know how much until I met you two. Please be patient with me while I learn how to be, well, more universally minded. Can you do that?"

Reno grins that million-dollar smile of his and pats her on the shoulder. He turns his attention back to his appetizer, which he said earlier, looks about the right size to feed a toothless beetle. Shifrah looks so gloomy, I feel sorry for her.

"Hey, you're doing okay. Everyone has to work at being better, not just you. I'm thinking about our very first conversation. Now that I've had time to think about it, I agree opportunities are rare, especially golden opportunities such as getting to come with y'all on this mission. It's changing my life. It feels like magic doors opened to a world I only dreamed or read about. But, you know as well as I do, people usually get what they get in life, and the cards are dealt to them by forces no one understands. Does a baby get to choose its parents?"

"What are you getting at, Savannah?"

"I'm talking about how we judge other people. Here's how my daddy explained it. He said we should *walk a mile in someone else's shoes before we go judging them.* So, an employee may be an underling to some, but to that employee's family, the job giving that family money to live on is nothing short of a Godsend, making he or she a king or queen to them. Shifrah, we're all just folks trying to do our best out here in the world."

Her expression reminds me of a scared rabbit about to be picked up by the neck. She takes her napkin and flattens it on her lap, smoothing it with her hand. Without looking up, she reaches for her water and takes a long drink, resumes staring at her lap. She clears her throat. "I have to, uh, to have time to think about what you said."

"I know."

"You certainly had a shrewd father, Savannah. Say, aren't they ever going to serve the entrées?"

I'm beginning to understand Shifrah. As far as I'm concerned, she's the epitome of the poor little rich girl.

The ship's captain joins us as the entrée carts roll into the dining room. His approach causes a buzz and a twitter at our table, especially among the females. He walks directly to Malone, who stands when he sees him. They grip hands, smiling and nodding at the same time. The three of us exchange surprised glances that Malone apparently knows our ship's captain very well.

"Jó estét! I am István Feher, your captain for this voyage, but you may call me Captain Stephen." He turns his place card around and holds it up for us. His first name isn't spelled anything like Stephen, but that's foreign language for you. Tall, muscular, blond, blue-eyed, and speaking in a romantic accent, he is beautiful, if that can be said of a

man. Shifrah elbows me three or four times in the ribs.

"This great man…" he gestures toward Malone "…is my hero. He is my hero because he saved me from an enemy's bullets one terrible day. I am here today as your ship captain because of Major Malone Connor."

Blond and blue-eyed Captain Stephen contrasts with Malone's dark hair and lively brown eyes. Both tall. Both are rather enchanting, if a girl allows herself to think like that. All the women at our table are thinking so. They're sitting forward, smiling excessively, murmuring among themselves.

As entrées are being served, the men sit. Captain Stephen good-naturedly answers several questions from the people at our table about the speed we're traveling, what day we stop in Ireland, if there are any storms on the horizon. There is one small one, but he said not to worry about it. He lifts his water glass and toasts to good fortune for our voyage and the happiness of the wonderful passengers aboard the SS America.

He and Malone huddle and talk as they eat their prime rib steaks with mushroom sauce, pickled beets, grilled shrimp, baked potatoes, and asparagus. When the plates are removed, Captain Stephen gently clicks a spoon on the side of his glass. "Would anyone enjoy to hear the history of our historic SS America ship?" And of course, everyone does.

Along with ice cream sundaes, petit fours, and coffee, we learn the SS America was barely out of the cradle when she was officially commissioned for war duties by the U.S. Navy in 1941 and was renamed the USS West Point. He tells us she was converted from a liner accommodating approximately twelve hundred people to accommodating eight thousand service men and women at a time.

"When her transformation was complete, all promenade deck windows were covered in life rafts, and all the other windows were also covered. Bunks were everywhere. This very room, this exquisite dining room, became the enlisted men's mess deck. The attached foyer was for cleaning mess kits. Anti-aircraft weapons were installed, and the SS America was repainted in a camouflage gray color. Oh yes, when you visit the Smoking Room and Cocktail Lounge, you can reflect on how those areas served as the officer's mess in the war."

"What's a *mess*, Reno?" Shifrah asks.

"Kind of a club where the military guys relax and spend time, eat, socialize, sometimes sleep. There's an officer's mess like Captain Stephen said used to be the Smoking Room and Cocktail Lounge. Then, there's the chief petty officer mess, and the enlisted mess."

"Well, it's an awful name," she says.

"How many war personnel did this ship transport altogether during the war, Stephen?" Malone asks.

"At least three hundred thousand altogether. With her speed and portability, she was a lady to contend with, outfoxing hostile crafts at sea many times. I'm proud to be her captain. Here's to the SS America!" He raises his water glass again and everyone raises their wine, water, or cocktail glasses to join his salute to the ship.

"Dang, that's fine, isn't it?" Reno says loudly, looking around for confirmation. That provides the chance for Malone to introduce Reno to the captain and brag about his flying accomplishments during the war. I didn't catch a lot of it because it was flagged with so many military terms and strange abbreviations, but I gathered Reno was a daredevil with extraordinary flying skills and has the medals to prove it. Handsome, humble, and a hero to boot. What a combination for some poor, unsuspecting woman is our teammate Reno.

Shifrah is drinking wine and has her eyes glued to the captain. When I teasingly ask her if she has fallen in love with him, she says, "Why not? Aren't we dancing on the edge of a dangerous mission while floating in the high seas?"

"Maybe, but don't you see that little gold band on his left hand?"

"Does it matter?"

"Shifrah!"

"I'm kidding. Keep your shirt on."

"I hope so, else I may win the undying admiration of all the men at our table."

Shifrah's shocked look makes me burst out laughing.

CHAPTER THIRTY-FIVE

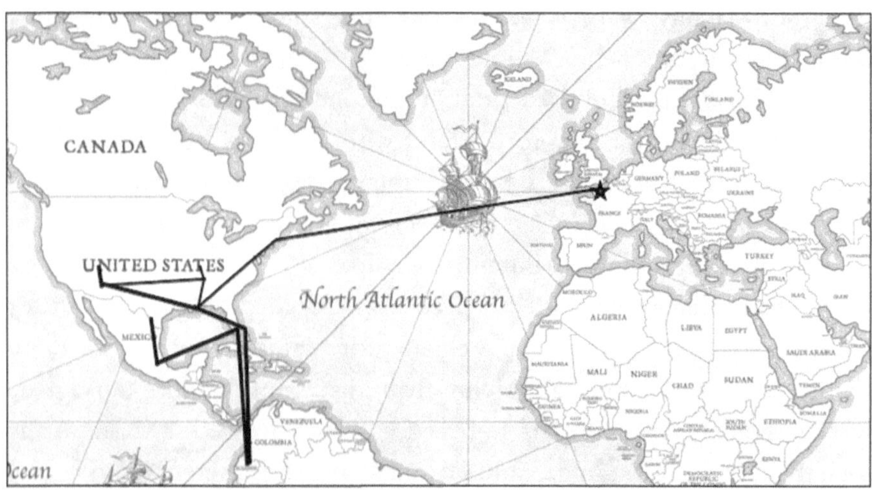

As soon as we are finished with the evening meal, Reno says, "Uh, sir, we have something mighty important to tell you." Malone waves him off. Everything about Malone seems more at ease. I suppose being out to sea has relaxed him, but I kind of suspect seeing an old friend like the captain may have something to do with it, too.

"Plenty of time, plenty of time, Reno. I want to show all of you around. It's a long day tomorrow, so you need to tuck in early tonight. I don't think Savannah has ever been inside a luxury liner, have you?"

"Never."

"All the more reason for us to take a quick look-see. Stephen told me more details you might find interesting. Unfortunately, because they were in a hurry to refit this fine ship into a Navy vessel, some of her original pieces of art and beautiful brass works were lost in the transition."

If they took away a lot of the ship's beauty, it's hard for me to tell. Gazing at the first-class main lounge, I feel emotionally stirred—a crazy feeling. I can't describe it adequately, but I feel like I'm walking, no, floating, on a cloud into another world. I suppose it's the high ceilings and the opulence of it. The huge forward doors we enter are surrounded by a gorgeous mural I could stare at for hours. Except for Europe with its thousands-of-years history, I honestly didn't know places so beautiful existed. My brief trek to New York gave me an idea of how the wealthy live, but I never imagined anything like what I'm seeing in this room floating in the ocean.

"This main lounge here was turned into a movie theatre during the war," Malone says.

"How did they do that?" I ask, finding it hard to imagine.

"By stripping out the tables and fancy chairs and mounting a big screen over there," Malone says, pointing. "Add folding chairs, and you have a theater."

"Tawdry, terribly tawdry," Shifrah says. "Can you imagine the greasy popcorn and chocolate stains on this gorgeous carpet? Maybe they pulled that out, too, and this is the new version. Anyway, Savannah, I heard this ship was entirely outfitted and decorated by women in the Hollywood deco style before it was savagely turned into a war boat."

"No wonder it's so perfect," I say softly, not wanting to break the spell the room has wrapped me in.

"Hey there, we fellas have talents too," Reno chimes in.

"Yeah, I'd like to check out some of his talents," Shifrah mutters loud enough for only me to hear.

I swat at her and give her a frown.

An orchestra is playing in the ballroom. The floor is dotted with dressed-up couples, men in tuxedoes, women in what I would guess are designer dresses. Just as I am deep into imagining Ginger Rogers and Fred Astaire dramatically twirling around the circular dancefloor, Reno says, "Hey, Savannah, think we could get those fellas to play us a lively

Cotton-Eyed-Joe?"

"Reno, you ruined the daydream I was having."

"This might ruin it even more, Savannah." Malone says.

"What?"

"They outfitted this very space with bunks for more than five hundred men when it was transformed into the USS West Point," Malone says.

Shifrah smirks, and I don't blame her. It's unimaginable.

We tour the library-writing-reading room and the gift shop, all for first-class passengers only. I was worried Shifrah might go into one of her moody tiffs after seeing the first-class grandeur, but she surprised me by not smarting off a single time. Malone told us the library was USS West Point's main toilet, eliciting another loud scoff from Shifrah.

"Strange things happened during that war. It wasn't too odd for a member of the crew to find himself sleeping in deluxe suites previously costing a hundred dollars a night," Malone says. I can literally feel Shifrah's struggle to keep her sarcastic remarks to herself about that. I'm sure she's slept in expensive rooms costing a hundred or more dollars on her other cruises, and it's understandable what a shock our present accommodations must be compared to that.

Me? I'm fine with everything as it is.

We end our tour in the first-class smoking room near the leather bar. Shifrah lights up, plops down on an upholstered loveseat, glares at Malone. "Enough with the tour, Malone. We're in mortal danger here, and you keep showing us everything we can't have on this voyage." She opens her purse, her movements reminding me of a nervous chihuahua. She takes the photographs she weeded out from the others and hands them to Malone. "That strange man is definitely tailing us, and here's the proof."

He sits down staring at the top photo. We start chattering like a bunch of magpies. "Hold it, hold it," he says. "Give me a minute." He retrieves his black-rimmed glasses from an inner pocket and rifles through the photos. Looks up. "How do you know this is the same man all the time? He's always in different garb, hats, not too many face shots."

"Malone, don't you understand women are experts in identifying the opposite sex?" Shifrah says.

"Well, I—"

"Look, this fellow has a mustache, right? Not too common in the USA right now, but not entirely unusual. This guy, though, makes a couple of big mistakes in his trimming procedures. Tell him what they are, Savannah."

"He trims his mustache crookedly. It has more space under his left nostril than his right nostril."

"I'll be a Sam Houston! You females look that close at men?" Reno exclaims.

"That's it?" Malone asks.

"No, it's shorter on the other side."

"What?"

"The higher side of his mustache, under his nose, is shorter than the other side. So, when you look at him, you're seeing a mustache raised higher and shorter on his right side than the hair on his left side."

"And you can identify that in all these photos? Some of them don't even show his whole face."

"His nose," I say.

Both men peer at the photos, holding them close. "What's wrong with his nose?" Reno asks.

"It's shaped sort of like Bob Hope's nose. See the slope in it when we have that side photo of him in the bar? Sloped."

"That's right," Shifrah says, "and he has two other peculiarities."

Malone and Reno exchange looks. "Which are…?" Malone says.

"He's unusually short-waisted. His pants seem too long, but when you study him for a minute, you see that he's quite short from his shoulders to his waist. Short body. Long legs," Shifrah says, pulling out her compact. She opens it, checks her lipstick.

"Good gravy!" Reno says. "What's the other thing?"

I smile with the superior air Shifrah and I are both relishing in the moment. "Can't you see it for yourself, Reno?" I tease.

He holds one of the photos about an inch from his eyes. "Guess I can't."

"His hair."

"But he always has some kind of hat on."

"Sure, but look along his neckline."

"I don't see anything."

"Let me look," Malone says, taking the photo from Reno. "Okay, it looks like he has thick hair."

"Bingo, Malone," Shifrah says. "Unnaturally thick, so the cut along the back would be almost the length of my index finger including the fingernail if I held it against his neck and measured the thickness of his hair."

Reno scratches his head, looks puzzled.

"Well, it's the truth. Not too many men have hair that thick in the back. Now, we haven't seen him without a hat in person or in the photos, so for all we know, he's bald on top."

Malone thumbs through all the pictures again, sets them down. "The ladies have us on this one, Reno. Pretty damn observant, I have to say." He stands abruptly. "I need to send some wires. Any other pictures of him, Shifrah?"

"Isn't that enough? He was in that Mexican town across the border where we drank gin fizzes, in our first hotel in Miami, and in the Adam's Hotel hallway when I snapped photos of our glamour girl. He was also in the bar at The Flame restaurant, and who knows where else when I wasn't being a photographer. We also saw him in that Native gift shop in Grand Canyon Village. Is he watching us now?" She looks right and left. "Most likely."

Malone scratches his eyebrow, scowls. "Reno, escort our lady spies back to their lodgings while I go talk to security. We'll be stepping up our watchfulness from here on out. Savannah, you get that, right?"

"You bet," I say.

"Get what?" Shifrah says.

"How does he know exactly where we're traveling to each time?" I ask quickly, changing the subject.

"Only one way. He's in cahoots with an insider. We have a spy at headquarters."

CHAPTER THIRTY-SIX

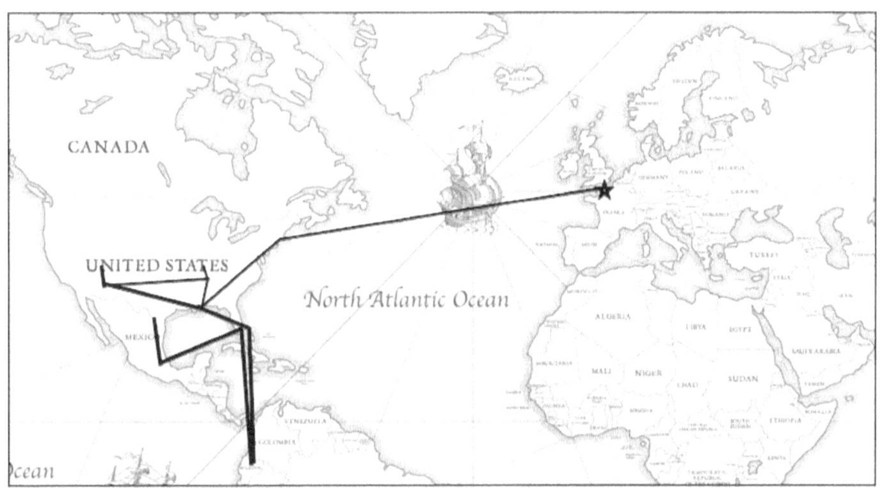

Whoever Mother Sill is, I'd sure like to give her a hug. After we returned to our cabin last night and promised Reno we'd stay put until prompted the next morning, we hit rough seas. I told Shifrah I was feeling ill, and she promptly whipped out her box of Mothersill's Seasick Remedy capsules for us to swallow. I haven't felt sick since.

This morning, much too early, a loud rap on the door turns out to be a steward announcing he has Miss Mandel's uniform. Shifrah told him to leave it by the door, turned over, and put a pillow over her head. I swung myself off the top bunk and retrieved the gray and white uniform inside a cleaner's bag on a hook attached to the outside of our door. A note was pinned on the cover saying Miss Francis Bogard would be along to escort her to breakfast and to the children's nursery in twenty minutes. I read it aloud to Shifrah.

At first, the lump in the bottom bunk doesn't move. Suddenly, it flies from the bed with wild eyes and flailing limbs. "What did you say, twenty minutes? How will I ever…? Take my travel case to the sink, will you, Savannah? No, this can't be true. What kind of world are we living in? I've never, ever been so—"

"We're used to getting up at the crack of dawn. Why is this so different?"

"Because we're on a cruise ship. I always sleep until eleven on a cruise, Savannah. Oh, dear lord, please help me!"

"I'll bet He will."

"Huh? Oh, you know what I mean. Can you find my undergarments and stockings in my fuchsia and gray suitcase, please?" She glances at the uniform. Her eyes widen in horror.

"What is it?"

"Look what's on the back!"

Hanging from the hanger down the back of the dress is a transparent bag holding a pair of dark gray shoes with a packet of new shoelaces. Shifrah looks like someone punctured her lung and air is seeping out. I have to admit they do look like a grandma's shoe choice.

"You want your feet to be comfortable, right?"

"Of all the indignities. Why didn't anyone warn me about this horrid schedule? I barely have time to put on makeup, and my hair's a fright! I knew I should have curled it under last night, but what did I do? I sat in the middle of your bed and let you tell me another wild story about turkey hunting. Oh, I'm creamed peas!"

I keep it to myself that I remember Malone mentioning the schedule three or four times last night. I get busy helping her perform part of her normal toilette. I feel like a nurse handing tools to a surgeon—deodorant, body talc, stockings, makeup, instead of scalpel, syringe, thread. It's a good thing she stopped worrying about my seeing her scars because now I've seen them all. She's acted like they were humongous, but I have a bigger one than the one on her arm on my right thigh from falling on a broken tree limb when I was ten.

In nineteen minutes, I'm zipping up the back of her uniform. A louder knock than the last one thunders through our tiny room. Shifrah turns to me for an appraisal of her looks. Honestly, she looks lovely and fresh. I think she sees what I'm thinking because she says, "Is it not too terribly bad, Savannah, or do I look positively morbid?"

I give her a big-sister smile, and mean it when I say, "You're beautiful without your finery, or with some of it, or with all of it. Now, go take care of those kids. I'll be down to check on you as soon as I can."

Another booming knock sends her hopping over the mess in our walking space to throw open the door. "You are Miss Mandel?" says a tall, thin woman dressed exactly like Shifrah and wearing a severe pulled-back bun and presenting a serious face.

"I am."

"Come with me, please. I am Francis Bogard. You may call me Miss Bogard. You will…" and they disappear from the doorway. I skip over the clutter and watch them walk down the corridor. Shifrah looks back once, and I vigorously nod and give her a thumbs up. I believe our poor little rich girl is about to join the human race as a real employee.

CHAPTER THIRTY-SEVEN

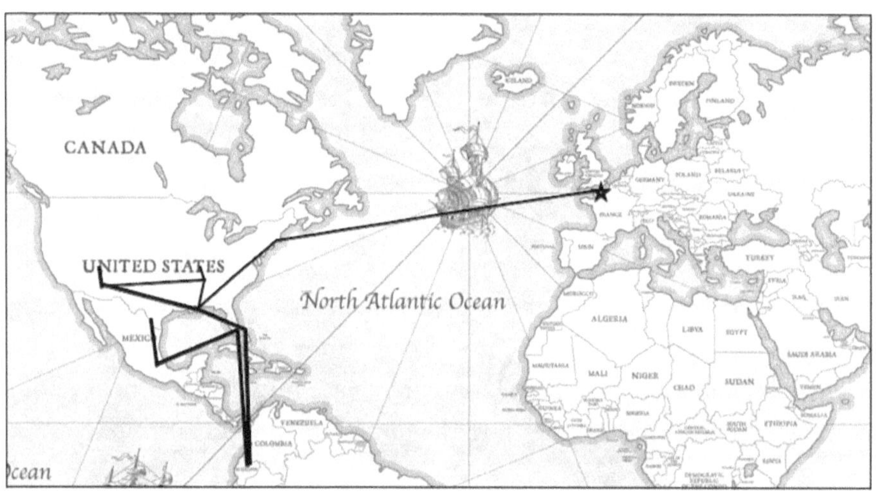

Working for a noted author like Olivia Highgard is both thrilling and odd. It's thrilling because I feel foolishly important typing the words gushing from her in torrents or streams, words that will forever live in the pages of her well-read novels. It's odd because, well, she herself is odd, or so I have concluded by this second day working for her as her scribe.

She is given to wild fits of words pouring forth so fast I barely keep up with typewriter or shorthand, followed by long spans of time in which she sits and stares at me or the ocean, either on deck or from her cabin porthole. Understandable, I suppose, since a writer surely must dredge the parameters of the brain to conceive plots and characters.

The odd part is how she smokes one cigarette after another, stubbing them out when halfway smoked with a ferocity that matches the way I've seen Bert, our cook at the Dixie, attack dirt with a post hole digger when he builds fences on his ranch.

Miss Highgard, or "Ollie," as she insists that I call her, keeps me slightly on edge, to put it mildly, especially when, with no warning, she jumps from her seat, rips the paper from my typewriter, reads it, then either hands it back to me or tears it to bits, letting the pieces fall where they may. Other times, she doesn't ask, but demands, quite fiercely that I read back some of the paragraphs I've written in shorthand. If she likes them, she sits back down. If not, she takes a pen and marks a big X across the page of my stenographer pad. At least she gives me time at the end of our session to type up my shorthand notes for her to look over when I leave.

I found a moment to ask her how she knows Mr. A, and she looked at me as though I had sprouted a second head. In the ever-more uncomfortable silence, I muttered, "I, uh, I'm sorry. I was just a tiny bit curious."

She smiled. "Tut-tut, I couldn't remember who, uh, Mr. A was for a minute. Oh, my dear girl, doesn't everyone know that debonair, globe-trotting Mr. A, as you call him?"

"I-I don't know."

She shook her head as though remembering something, still smiling to herself, resumed dictating. That's all I found out, which is nothing.

This morning, we're on the promenade deck in teak steamer chairs, sunshine barely missing us beneath the narrow striped white and amber awning. I wait as Ollie places her glass of bouillon inside the built-in cup holder on her chair and walks to the railing. We just finished working on a scene in which one of the main characters, Merrill, a dashing daredevil rake, loses his footing on a crumbling ledge and tumbles into a ravine far below.

A couple dressed for jogging pass by, followed by a slow-walking elderly man with a fancy cane. He nods pleasantly in my direction, and I return his greeting. I brush my hair away for the hundredth time, but the endless sea breeze blows it right back in my face. Far up in the sky, I see a flock of small, dark birds flying south. How can they do that with no land anywhere for thousands of miles? I'll have to look that up at the library when I have a chance.

I inhale deeply the fresh air and edge my feet and legs into the warm sunshine. We started work at six o'clock this morning, causing me to get up at five. Normally, getting up so early doesn't bother me, but Shifrah kept me awake late telling me about the kids she watched yesterday. I think I detected excitement in her voice, though she would never admit it, at least, not yet. She was disappointed I hadn't come to see her, but I explained that my author is a full-time taskmaster.

The same as we did yesterday, we began dictation this morning in her cabin, a luxuriously large room equipped with two twin beds with a plush sofa between them. One of the beds was littered with books in disarray. "Research," she explained with a wave of her hand toward the bed. She rang the bell twice for the stewardess—one ring brings a male steward—to bring us a breakfast tray with kippers, toast, cheeses, boiled eggs, and tea. I requested coffee and got it, but other than a few nibbles, the rest of the food sat untouched because of Ollie's constant dictating. I did manage a cup of coffee and a half piece of toast with a bit of orange marmalade on it. I don't recall eating orange marmalade back home, but I'm slowly acquiring a taste for it.

My typewriter was delivered to her room the night before our first day to work together, she told me, and she also requested a standing tray and a straight-backed chair. These were placed in the center of the room, I presume to allow Ollie the freedom to pace the room around me while dictating. Food was ordered in yesterday, and we never left the room until six that evening.

Ollie is still staring at the ocean, and my stomach is growling terribly. I stifle a yawn and close my eyes. The pleasant breeze and sunshine make me dreamingly drowsy. I imagine I'm traveling by ship to Europe to accept the employment offer to be a personal assistant to a wealthy earl. I am driven to his estate in a private car and ushered into a garden with fragrant roses to await his arrival. Far away, I see him galloping toward me riding a black stallion across green meadows. As he comes closer, I realize he's Malone! He waves, dismounts, turns around and… he's Reno! Reno flashes me one of his dazzling smiles and says—

"Shall I let him die, Savannah?"

Die?

"I say, shall I kill him?" a voice roars.

My eyes fly open. Ollie's face is inches from my face, eyes enlarged, her thin lips disappearing inside themselves. *I fell asleep!* "Kill who?"

"Why, Merrill, of course!"

"I, um—"

"If I kill him, I'll most certainly put a disclaimer at the end of the book stating it was my stenographer's idea. Further, I'll be sure to state your full name and address."

I stare at her, stupefied. She bursts out laughing. "Dear girl, take heart! You look as though you might melt. I'm having a bit of a giggle is all." She stretches her arms over her head, bends sideways both ways. "Five hours of this ridiculous garbling is enough, I say. Let's go partake of tea and whatever culinary delights they offer us today."

Ollie is what I've heard some refer to as a handsome woman who dresses exceptionally well but believes in the natural look. Her wavy, reddish-brown hair is cropped short, parted to the side on top. She wears no makeup other than a light coat of powder, a touch of rouge, and lip balm. Her clothes are stylish enough to make Shifrah take notice. She informed me this morning when she opened the door to her cabin that she was wearing her Chapter Eight suit today since that's the chapter we're working on. She said she bought it in Paris and it's one of her favorites—a belted, two-piece, Turkish-blue tweed suit—along with no high heels, flats only, *because I don't relish falling flat on my face if our ocean turns temperamental, don't you know?*

She watches me gathering my papers. "Are your fingers bleeding yet?"

I hold open palms toward her. "Dripping, but not gushing."

She slaps her thigh and cackles at my joke. "Oh, you are the spritely one, yes, you are. I say you might hold verbal court with our new Queen Elizabeth herself. Sad, her father passing last year, but, Tweedledee-Tweedledum, that's one of two appointments we all must attend, yes?"

"And the other is?"

"Why, our birth, of course!"

I can't help but laugh at the humorous side of my temporary employer. Unusual as she is, I like her. Of course, I've never met a real author before, let alone work for one, and I'm a little in awe.

"Come, my fair stenographer, let us get you nourished before you blow away to sea. We'll have another go at the manuscript after lunch. Then, you're free to go. Unless, of course, I send for you to type for me in the dead of night when you're in your jim-jams."

She studies my face, and I reveal no reaction to her possibly calling on me in the dead of night. Satisfied, she picks up her unfinished glass of bouillon and strides down the deck, which she told me, is made from Oregon pine wood. I follow, struggling to carry my so-called portable but heavy typewriter, my stenographer pad, papers, pens, and my purse.

We don't make it as far as wherever first-class diners eat lunch because, on our way, we run into a large, steaming buffet set up on several tables just inside from the deck. Ollie is looking it over, slowly walking along the sides of the tables and mumbling her pleasure at what she's seeing written on the little cards alongside the cloches when she notices me standing to the side balancing all my work essentials.

She strides swiftly to my side. "For gracious sake, and let us always err on the side of graciousness, why didn't you call for a steward to carry that ridiculous typewriter, Savannah?" She snaps her fingers in the air, and a uniformed steward steps forward. "Take this beastly load from my poor assistant and carry it to cabin 009."

He stares at me looking perplexed, and I feel I can read his mind.

Where do I start? This female has her things balanced under each arm, against her chest, underneath her chin, and I don't wish to get personal.

"Chop chop! I won't see this poor girl struggle another moment," Ollie bellows in her commanding voice.

He whistles. Another man in all white joins him, and my face burns with embarrassment as the two of them rush toward me and relieve me of everything almost glued to my body, leaving me feeling empty-armed and strangely vulnerable to the looks now coming our way from other diners. A head waiter appears and apologizes for any inconveniences I might have suffered and tells me he hopes I find the appetizers, salads, and soups to my satisfaction, and if I don't see an entrée I like, tell him and he will have the chef prepare something else for me. Honestly, I wish I could melt like Ollie said I looked like I was doing on the deck. Such a fuss, and I'm right in the center of it.

At last, Ollie and I are free to select our lunch. "Let's not bother with the prelude, Savannah, and simply move to the full composition," she says. I don't quite understand her analogy but surrender to her bypassing the soups and salads and guiding me to the entrée table. With her constant oversight, my sparkling white plate is soon stacked with international entrees—Baked Swordfish: À la Cubanaise, Hungarian Veal Goulash with Macaroni, Yankee Pot Roast with Corn Fritters, and a German Potato Pancake, as well as sautéed brussels sprouts and candied carrots.

"When you endure the heartache and scarcity of war, you learn to enjoy this bountiful life with all the pleasure you can muster, Savannah," she says as she points to one item after another for the chefs to dish up for us. Now, our plates look like the loaded Truck-Driver-Special platters we serve Monday through Saturday at the Dixie.

We make our way to one of the white-cloth-draped tables overlooking the deck and sea. We settle, and a waiter comes to take our drink order. I order hot coffee to keep me awake during our upcoming afternoon session. Ollie orders saffron tea.

"Saffron tea, madam?" The waiter asks in a heavy accent.

"Yes, tell your chef it's for Miss Olive of England. He'll know what to do."

"Yes, madam." He turns.

That profile!

It's him!

CHAPTER THIRTY-EIGHT

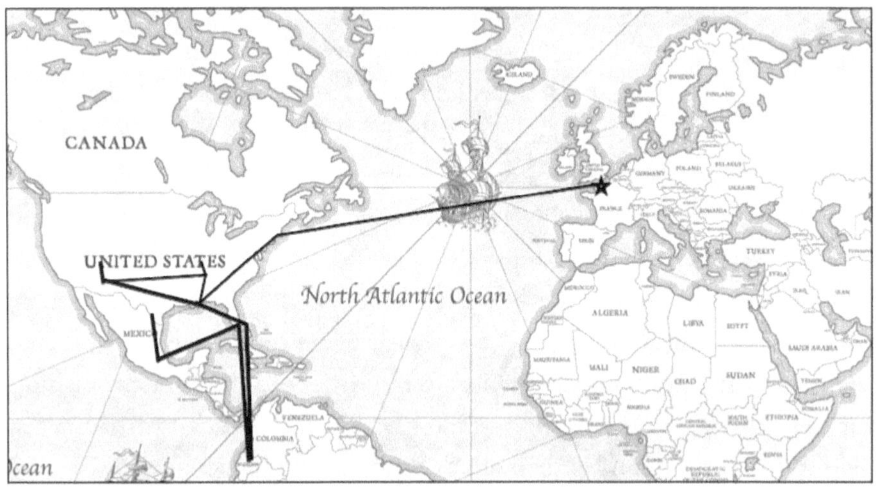

It's torture making it through the rest of the afternoon after seeing our spy, but thankfully, Ollie releases me at three o'clock. I ask for directions to the nursery, and I hurry there, suffering with the information only I know. His mustache was gone, but his nose shape and the thickness of his hair were unmistakable, not to mention his long legs and short body. I can only assume he saw me recognize him, because he didn't return with our drink order. I tried to sound casual when I asked the next waiter what happened to the previous one.

"A bit of seasickness, I'm afraid, Miss," he answered.

I want to find Shifrah and ask her if she knows how to locate Malone or Reno. How is it that we didn't figure out a way to communicate with one another during the day? After dinner, we're scheduled to meet in the crew's smoking lounge, but that's hours away.

The ship's nursery, which personnel informed me they call a *playroom*, has a small carousel, a sandbox, rocking horses, toys everywhere, and a nurse wearing all white in addition to the stewardesses watching and playing with the children. I had no idea it would be outfitted so extravagantly. Shifrah's back is to the door as she sits in a chair reading to a group of little ones sitting cross-legged on a mat in front of her.

I put a hand on her shoulder. "I knew you could do this."

"Savannah, hello, uh, yeah, it isn't nearly as difficult as I imagined. They, uh, they're actually quite smart and amazingly linear in a different sort of way and…" she smiles sheepishly, shrugs. "Are you finished for the day?"

"Yes, and guess what? I saw our spy."

"No!"

"He was working as a luncheon waiter in first-class."

"A waiter? How did he swing that? Savannah, that means—"

"Missy Mandella, is baby bear angwy when Gwoldeelocks eats all his pohwedge?" asks a small boy as he slips a chubby arm around Shifrah's neck.

"No, I can't say that he's angry, Bobby, but he might be hungry. I'll bet Mommy Bear prepares him a nice souffle or a custard as soon as Goldilocks leaves."

The little boy looks thoughtful, and I cover my mouth to hide my chuckle.

* * *

Now that I've told Malone about the spy, he's changing all the rules. Shifrah and I are keeping our present working positions, though my stint with Ollie ends in a couple of days when we reach Ireland. Reno has been switched from assistant steward to personal escort and guard for Shifrah and me. While we're busy with our duties during the day, he'll be checking on us often while also aiding Malone in talking to other crew members and the captain *to ferret out this damn guy,* as Malone puts it.

"But how did he get hired on this ship right now?" I ask.

"Maybe he clobbered someone over the head and swiped his uniform," Reno says.

"Nah, I think he's getting help from some of the same sources we are, which means travel and accommodation requests are being sanctioned by someone who carries a lot of clout with the *powers that be.* Rest assured, Mr. A is working on a plan to expose the scoundrel. Thing is, the guy knows one of us spotted him so he'll probably lay low until we dock in France," Malone says.

"Speaking of docking, I don't understand why we can't go ashore with you when we reach Ireland, Malone. I've never been there, you know," Shifrah says.

"Two reasons. One, it's a short dock. No time for shopping or sightseeing. Secondly, I'm headed to a seedy area to get the *retrieve.*"

"Seedy? You mean our contact is a criminal or a no-account?" Shifrah asked.

"People don't have to be criminals to live in the rougher parts of town. Our contact is a decorated former lieutenant in the British armed forces."

"He's British?"

"Irish. He joined with the British to fight the Nazis."

"I thought I'd heard Ireland remained neutral during the war," I say.

"The government did, but thousands joined with the British to fight. Remember that when you hear nonsense about them refusing to take sides. That riles me up. The hierarchy of Ireland remained uninvolved, but not the people. About eighty thousand of them jumped in to fight. The Irish are very fervent about right and wrong."

"That's right. Just look at our own Malone," Reno says.

"What do you mean?" Shifrah asks.

"Why, he's as Irish as a four-leafed clover, Shif. Where do you think that big ol' temper comes from… you know, the one best not to rile up?" Reno says, smiling.

She thinks about that a few seconds. "I'd think you'd at least have red hair or something, Malone."

"Black Irish." he says.

"What?"

"Black hair, dark eyes. Irish mixed with Celt or Spanish. That's the rub on my family. Now, listen up. We—"

"Wait a minute. You've made me even more curious. Why don't we all go meet this other Irish guy?" Shifrah says. "Maybe he's both handsome and interesting."

Malone lets out a weary sigh before answering. "The war did lots of things to people that others don't understand. This man is a hero, but the war damaged his spirit, his feelings. He lives alone in a scant one-room apartment, and Mr. A just about didn't find him, couldn't have if not for his connection to the bigwigs in the war offices around the globe. The poor fellow, the lieutenant, that is, was jubilant he could turn over a key he was given in a foxhole from the dying son of someone who had previously lived in Berlin."

"A German?"

"Uh-huh."

"So, he got the key, the *retrieve*, from the son of a man who had, at one time, lived in Berlin, but the son was in the war, mortally wounded while in combat, and he gave a special key to an Irish military man fighting with the British?" I say.

"That's about the size of it."

"Can you at least tell us why these keys are scattered all over the world?" I say.

"Yeah, and why are we being spied on? What's the big—"

Malone's raised arm stops our questions. "I know you're curious. I understand."

And that's the end of the conversation.

CHAPTER THIRTY-NINE

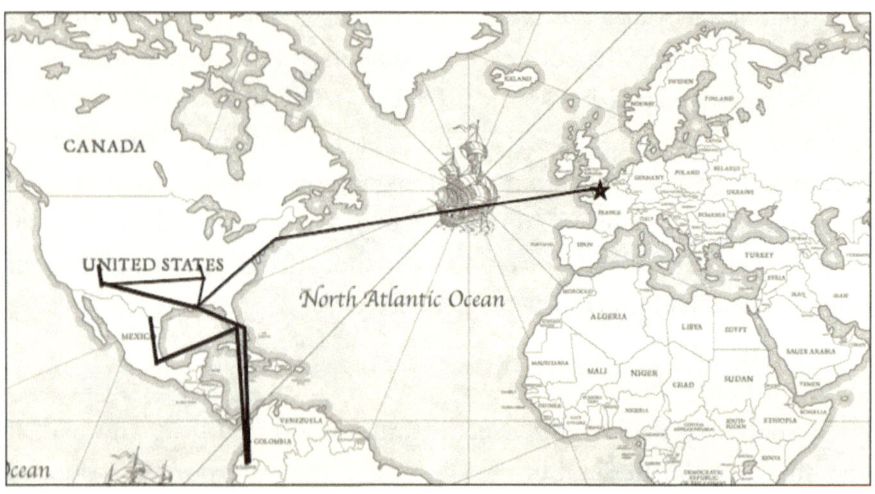

We stand at dawn on the ship's deck with other passengers watching the ones going ashore in Ireland. I expect Shifrah to gripe, but she doesn't. We watch Malone depart wearing a suit and his Fedora hat, watch him step into a waiting car, and watch the car drive away.

"All right, Ireland, Savannah and I shall return one day to explore you from one end to the other." Shifrah says, yawning. "I'm headed to the playroom now. My last day."

"Told you the week would fly by."

She stifles another yawn. "See you at lunch. Remember, my lunchtime is straight up eleven o'clock. What will you do until then?"

"Ollie asked me to come to her cabin this morning before she takes off."

"Then what?"

"It's our last day on the ship. I thought I might try to get into trouble by exploring all the different levels."

"You get into trouble? Simply bat your eyelashes and use the look I taught you. You'll be fine."

"The look?"

"Oh, Savannah, you remember. It's a slightly worried look with your lips pursed, and don't forget to roll your eyes to the side and give a little shrug of your shoulders. That makes you seem vulnerable. Men can't resist it."

I can't help but laugh out loud.

"What's so funny?"

"You are."

"Well, anyway, you aren't supposed to go wandering around the ship without Reno."

"He won't know about it."

"But—"

"Shifrah, I'm the gal who shoots snakes and helps Bert feed his mean bull. I'll be fine." What I don't say is I have my .38 snugly hidden inside my purse.

I feel a twinge of sadness seeing Ollie's suitcases all lined up and ready for carrying off the ship. She told me yesterday she plans to "hiber up" in a quaint little cottage with a thatched roof and green shutters to finish working out the rest of her novel, but, she said, "Those Irish villagers do love their pubs, and I relish a good dark ale myself. Evenings might find me wandering down the cobblestones to raise a glass with the locals, don't you know?"

She offered to hire me to disembark with her and continue working with her for six months, which, of course, I politely refused. It sounded exciting, and the money she mentioned for the task was more than I make in a year at the Dixie, but I'm working under contract with my team. I asked myself if I would have done it otherwise, and the answer was *no*. I could never resist finding out what this mysterious mission is all about.

"There you are, my saucy little stenographer. I was worried you would forget I'm departing this morning." Before I can respond, she hands me a sheet of paper with her handwriting on it. "If ever you come to London, this is how to get in touch with me. My schedule for the year is penned on the top. My address and phone number at the bottom. I would truly enjoy showing you some of England's prides and peculiarities. There are plenty of each, dare I say. Bring your little friend as well, the dainty little rabbit with those big unusual eyes. I have seen eyes that color only a few times in my life."

"Shifrah?"

"Yes. Did she tell you what her name means?"

"No, I mean, I never thought to ask."

"It has two meanings, *beautiful* and *harmony*. A lovely old-world name."

I never knew names had special meanings. Shifrah will love this!

She clears her throat. "Your payment was settled last night with that big handsome Malone Connor. I believe he was a major in the war?"

"Um, yes."

"If I were ten years younger, I'd like to *bill and coo* with that one, let's get that right."

I have no idea what to say about that, but, luckily, Ollie changes the subject immediately.

"Take note that my agent and publisher's numbers are written on the back of the schedule. They know where I am at all times. Now, I don't expect you to want to read these, but…" she walks to the bed and brings back a stack of novels crisscrossed and tied with a green satin ribbon. "I signed all of them for you."

"Of course I will read them! I'm-I'm, oh, thank you, Ollie!"

"My pleasure, dear, indeed, my pleasure."

She hands me a small wooden box with carved wooden hinges. "Here's a little something else, Savannah. I have to confess it was given to me as a present, but, dear me, do I look like I should wear *L'Air du Temps* perfume by Nina Ricci?" She chuckles. "I'm a soap and water with a hint of rose or lavender person, don't you know? This scent reminds me of you, my dear little collaborator, spicy and sweet. You'll recognize a hint of carnation, too. Of course, you know the carnation is known as a flower of distinction. Perfect for you. *L'Air du Temps,* means *the air of time,* in case you didn't know, and the doves on the stopper symbolize peace and goodwill."

"I don't know what to say. I'm embarrassed I have nothing for you."

"Tut-tut, this isn't Christmas. I'm merely bribing you into not forgetting me. They're quite selfish, these gifts."

A knock on the door, a brief hug, and my five-day stint with Olivia Highgard, famous novelist and world traveler, comes to an end. My one regret is that she didn't say more about how she knows Mr. A.

What would Tony and the regulars think of all this? The poor things have been terribly neglected by me. I did write postcards to them last night with photos of the SS America on one side, and Malone promised to mail them today from Ireland. That should be exciting for them, shouldn't it?

EUROPE

CHAPTER FORTY

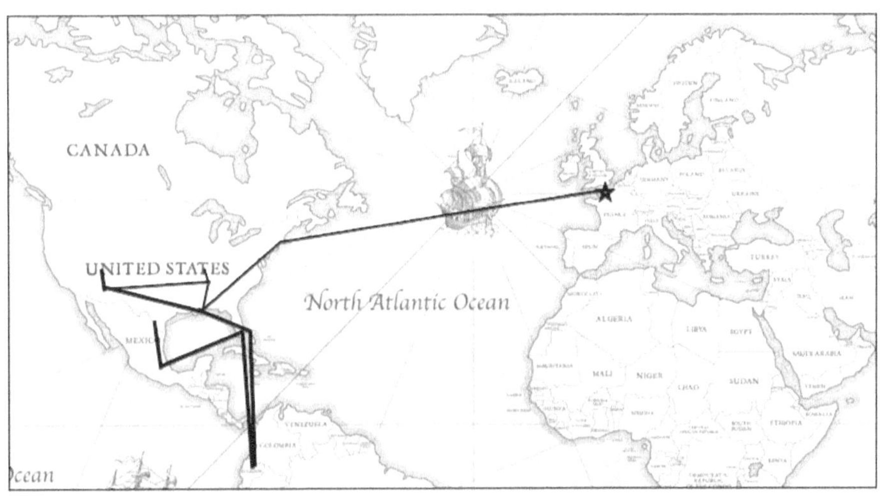

Our heads are covered in metal curlers and bobby pins when Reno bangs on the door at six-thirty a.m. "We're in France, ladies!" he announces through the door. I open it halfway, and he barges in, stops, covers his eyes. "Uh, 'scuse me. Is it safe to come in?"

"It's okay. We're finished except for our hair," I say.

"Sorry about that. I'm a little too excited. You know, my last time here was more than eight years ago. Mostly saw it from the air. Guess what? I hear we're probably going to Paris, but I'm not real sure when Malone has it scheduled."

"Paris? Really?" Shifrah grabs my hands. "Oh, Savannah, I was so afraid to hope!" She pulls the Goody spring-grip curlers from the ends of her hair and tosses them into her train case. She stops in the middle of removing her bobby pins and turns to look at us. "Guys, this is colossal! As soon as we get checked into our hotel, we'll taxi to the fabulous *Galeries Lafayette* in the very heart of Paris to shop the whole day. It has everything! *C'est manifique!* Its stained-glass dome will satisfy any of your, you know, intellectual instincts, Savannah.

"Of course, we'll need to buy chic clothes for sightseeing, and, oh, the perfume counter at *Galeries Lafayette* will be worth every hardship we've endured. Imagine all the new scents that debuted since Mommykins was last here!"

"How many times have you been to France, Shif?"

"The war messed up everything, so, the answer is never, but I know all about it from Mommykins and Daddy. It's practically their second home. I've seen hundreds of photos of the places I'm telling you about, and, Reno, you simply must convince Malone to let us stay at least two nights so we can attend the *Opéra Garnier!* Savannah, we'll shop for designer gowns and accessories for that grand occasion. Oh, how I wish we had time to have them made for us!" She sighs happily, raising her shoulders. "Before the opera, my family always dines casually at the *Café de la Paix* across from the opera house, later at a much more exquisite restaurant."

"That sounds great, Shifrah, but I have to see the *Louvre,* too. I can't be in Paris and not go there. Of course, it all depends on how much time Malone gives us. If it's only one day and it's a toss-up between the *Louvre* and shopping, I must pick the Mona Lisa."

"You would pick an art museum over shopping at *Galeries Lafayette?"* Shifrah has such a shocked look on her face, I have to turn away and struggle not to laugh. Reno picks up on it.

"Savannah, what's wrong with you? You know those glassy-eyed old painters from the past didn't paint anything as exciting as French perfume and fancy clothes," he says.

"Reno, you're absolutely right," Shifrah says, fluffing her hair.

"Dang right, I am. That ol' Mona Lisa, she's dead, isn't she?"

Shifrah looks back and forth at us. "You're making fun of me again, aren't you?"

Reno walks over and pats her shoulder. "Nah, we're just joshin' you, hon. Hey, Malone said we have a busy schedule, so we'd better hustle off this ship and get that customs business taken care of. Those suitcases ready to go?" He does a little dance, then rings the bell to bring the luggage steward.

"How much coffee did you have this morning?" I ask.

"Oh, 'bout a barrel full, but that's not why I'm so fired up. I'm just tickled to be on land again. Water's for ducks, you know? Hey, those pins in y'all's hair look real good. Shall I snap a picture and send it to the newspapers?"

"That's it. Wait outside. We'll poke our perfectly coifed heads out when we're ready to disembark," Shifrah says, shoving him out the door.

* * *

The Customs officials focus on Reno. They make him open his suitcase and his duffle bag and go through everything with stern faces. They shake and check each piece of clothing, including the pockets, and search the inner pockets of his luggage. They put their heads together, scrutinize him, and finally stamp him okay to pass through, not offering an explanation or even a smile.

"They sure give Reno a hard time, don't they?" Shifrah whispers to me during the ordeal. "Are they that jealous of his looks?"

"I don't know, but it's a good thing they don't know about all his talents. That would get him sent to prison."

Malone might as well have been a fellow employee for how they smile and send him straight through. Why, I don't know, but I'm guessing it's how he strikes everyone as someone to respect and certainly not someone to mess with. Poor Reno always gets caught in the cracks. Shifrah and I have it as easy as Malone, but I think Shifrah's coquettish behavior paves the way for both of us.

Our chauffeur, Antonius, is a merry-looking fellow, short, quite well-fed, wearing a dark-blue beret, and sporting a mustache. He tells us he speaks English, French, and Spanish. Our carefree moods disintegrate as we drive through town. I never thought a lot about the war in Europe, but now I'm seeing the effects of it firsthand. The military and the war… it's feeling as though our *retrieves* are specifically connected to both.

Antonius picks up on the somber mood inside the car. "The Americans bombed the harbor here in Le Havre," he says.

"The Americans?" I ask, shocked.

"Yes, the Germans had control of it. The Americans figured they had no choice. The whole town was blown to pieces. Six thousand people.... gone."

I'm speechless hearing that, so I concentrate on a nun dressed in black and white wearing a heavy gray coat over her habit. She pedals hard on her bicycle up a street's incline, a loaf of bread protruding from a sack in the basket behind her seat.

"War is hell," Malone says in a few minutes.

"Yes, yes," Antonius says, "The most terrible thing in the world is war. It leaves the hearts broken. Ruins the lives. Most of our buildings still have no walls. We will fix, of course, but it is slow. Someday, I am certain our town shall again be *Le Havre-de-Grâce."*

That sets Shifrah off speaking to Antonius in French. When she finishes, she says, "Savannah, just for you, I found out why Antonius called his town *Le Havre-de-Grâce*, or, as you can figure out, *Harbor of Grace."*

"Why?"

"In the past, it was named *Franciscopolis* after some king. Then it was named *Le Havre-de-Grâce* after a chapel. Hold on a minute. I forgot the name of the chapel." She discusses it with Antonius, turns to face me. "Okay, the chapel it was named after was *Notre-Dame-de-Grâce,* which everyone knows means *"Our Lady of Grace."*

"I suppose Havre de Grace, Maryland, is named after this place, too?" Malone says.

"I suppose so, Malone. Savannah, now you can't say I didn't cough up a little history for you in Europe."

"Okay, I'll remember you every time I cough."

"Every time you cough?"

"Um-huh. You said you *coughed* this piece of history up especially for me."

She smiles, resumes her stare outside. "Hey, look," she says pointing out the window at lines of men with two-wheeled carts in front of sidewalk stores mostly gutted and roofless.

"Interesting. What are they selling?"

"It looks like meats, potatoes, vegetables, fruits, trinkets, and some things I don't know, like tools or something."

"Everything you can buy from a cart," Antonius chimes in. "Do you wish for me to stop?"

"Oh, please do! Maybe they'll have fruit juices. Mommykins says the best juices in the world are in France."

Surprisingly, Malone allows us to stop and browse the wares in the carts. After poking around the wagons for a while with Reno buying a pocket knife and Shifrah buying a miniature Eiffel Tower charm for her charm bracelet "at home," she and I follow our noses to a cart selling fruits, juices, and baguette sandwiches. We stand up eating our food and taking in the scenes around us.

A woman nearby sweeps the street in front of a clothing boutique with two walls missing. Several dresses and scarves are pinned to straw mannequins placed to face the road. Everyone walking or biking has a long loaf of bread under his or her arm. It must be the natural thing to do in France, buy your daily bread. Crews work hauling clumps of concrete out of buildings, operating heavy equipment moving whole foundation blocks, and hammering rhythmically on top of new roofs.

CHAPTER FORTY-ONE

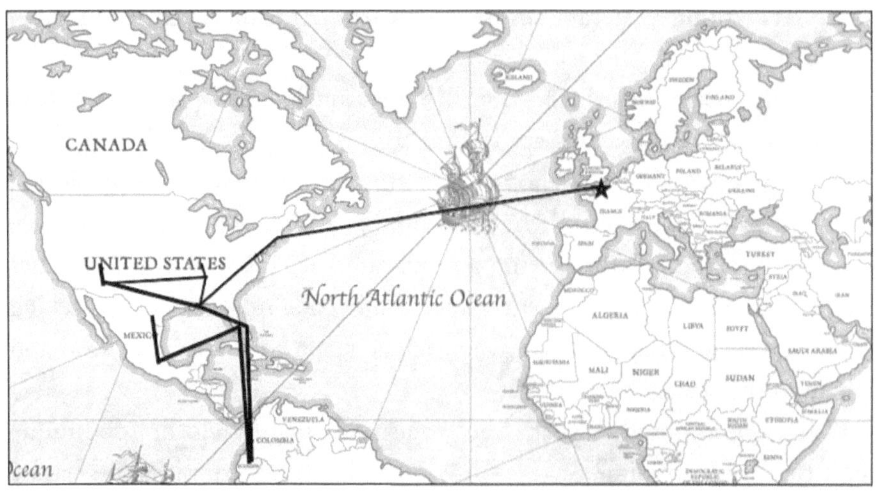

I ask Antonius, "Are those *Roma?"* pointing to one of the numerous two-wheeled buggies with arched tops we've seen along the roadways since leaving Le Havre.

"Oui, most are *Gitans,* others are farmers. It is common to see them again now that the war is over. You know, Hitler hated the gypsies, too. I think he hated everyone."

It's silent until Shifrah says, "Malone, you haven't told us where we're going next."

"We're changing up a few things so Mr. A can expose the traitor at headquarters," he says in a low voice.

"Okay, but where are we spending the night?"

"Oh, a little place down the road. We should be there any time now."

In about ten minutes, Antonius says, "We are here!"

I see a sign beside the road with words I can't read. Behind it, a scene unfolds that looks like a painting, a port village with pastoral streets and empty flower boxes hanging from the windows of tall, thin buildings. Somehow, it stirs my memory banks.

"What the heck does that sign say, Shif?" Reno asks.

"It says, *HONFLEUR, patri des artistes impressionnistes de renommée mondiale.*"

"English, hon."

"'HONFLEUR, home of the world-famous Impressionist artists.'"

"Are you kidding?" I whisper, scooting forward on the seat. "Does it mean *the* Impressionists, the real ones, like Claude Monet? Does it mean they were born here, or what?"

"Search me, Savannah, but I have no doubt you'll know the answer to all your historical questions by morning," she says.

"Thought you might like this stopover, Savannah," Malone says.

"I-I love it, Malone. Thank you for bringing us here."

The town shows little signs of destruction, unlike Le Havre. We pass a whitewashed building with royal blue shutters and a matching blue door. The sign outside the door is written in French and has a crest on it. Shifrah translates that it's a *brasserie* and inn locally owned by many layers of descendants.

"Well, one word on that sign sure does look like something else, Shif," Reno says, "something you shouldn't go putting on a public sign like that."

"It's pronounced 'brahs-rie'," Reno, not 'bruhzeer'," Shifrah says, chuckling. "It means it's a restaurant with a relaxed setting, like a pub."

Malone clears his throat. "We'll eat dinner there tonight. After we settle into our accommodations, we have time to spare today. You ladies can go sightsee all you want. Shifrah, I'm putting you in charge, since you speak French."

"Do they have any perfumeries here?" she asks, but no one answers.

Even with overcast skies, I'm enthralled with everything I see. Antonius parks according to Malone's instructions, and I find myself bounding from the backseat of the car in the same thrilled numbness I felt as a five-year-old seeing the colorful Wurlitzer in the Dixie Diner for the first time. The sun peeks from the clouds as I reach in and grab my overnight and train cases from the trunk when Antonius opens it. It suddenly hits me that I'm staring at the same seaport with its variety of small boats bobbing in the water, the same tall, narrow buildings with their rectangular windows, and the shimmers of light playing on the water that I've seen so often in Impressionistic works of art, both old and modern. No wonder I feel as if I've been here before. I have, but through paintings.

"This is St. Catherine's Quay, Old Harbor, Normandy, France," I say, mostly to myself as I rotate in a slow circle. "How can I really be here? Do you see how those buildings look like sentinels of the harbor?"

"Savannah, what are you—"

My abrupt hand in the air silences whatever Shifrah was about to ask me. I shake my head, still holding up a flat palm. "Shh," I whisper, adding a smile so I don't come off as harsh as I know I probably seem.

We wait beside the car, me in a dreamy stupor as I fill my senses with my surroundings. The damp air is cool against my face, and I smell the ocean. Malone disappears through a small door with a sign indicating it's the office for our lodgings. When he emerges, Antonius, Reno, Shifrah, and I follow him through a rustic, paint-peeling gate taller than us and into an alleyway with a worn, curved cobblestone path marked with scars of survival through decades of wear. Most of the hanging plants lining the alleyway are browned with the season, but strong vines still cling to the sides of buildings constructed of composites of wood, stone, and brick. It's like stepping into an encyclopedia photograph.

Malone stops in the bricked courtyard, looks up. "Our rooms are at the top of those stairs. Savannah, Shifrah, you're in the room to the right of the landing. We're in the one on the left."

I run up stone and concrete stairs and feast my eyes on the scene before me while waiting at the top. "Hurry and change into sensible shoes so we can go see everything," I call to Shifrah, who is staring up at me from the ground.

"For Pete's sake, Savannah, calm down. We need to freshen up and rest a little first. Sensible shoes? I'll wear my flats, if that's what you mean. Please, don't wear those atrocious oxfords. Malone, what time are we meeting for dinner?"

He finishes paying Antonius, eyes him as he departs. "No later than 1700. I want to get an early start in the morning."

"Oh, me, too! Paris is waiting for us with open arms! Don't you just feel it?"

"Tomorrow, we begin our trip to, uh, well, I'll explain at dinner. Let's not discuss our plans out here in the open like this."

"You mean we're going somewhere besides Paris next? But-but, Reno said—"

"We'll discuss it over dinner. Enough said."

Malone ends the conversation by trudging up the steps carrying his overnight case, as well as Shifrah's big overnight suitcase and her train case.

* * *

Shifrah has been grumbling ever since we started our walking tour. I finally tell her she's ruining my historical experience. She's not used to me criticizing her even a little, so it hurts her feelings. Honestly, I can't help it. The drone of her complaining about not getting to go to Paris immediately didn't mix with visiting St. Catherine's, the oldest wooden church in France, one erected by shipbuilders in the fifteenth century. Walking the narrow cobblestone streets in the oldest parts of town amidst narrow shops and buildings reminiscent of streets I have imagined in Charles Dickens' English novels and seeing sights from the old Impressionistic paintings that exist to this day was gloriously pleasant. I didn't want anything to spoil it.

She comes down with one of her headaches shortly afterward and returns to our room, which frees me to happily dig deeper into the story of Honfleur. To realize the narrow houses guarding the harbor were built in the sixteenth all the way to the eighteenth centuries baffles my small-town senses. At home, something fifty years old is considered ancient.

I meander through a bookstore with aisles so narrow I have to pass through some of them sideways. I find a book written in English about the Impressionists who adored painting this town's scenes, especially the harbor. Eugene Boudin, the book says, was born in Honfleur and is considered the *father of Impressionism.* The most exciting part to me is that he was Claude Monet's mentor. I find this by quickly leafing through the book before I purchase it.

I search for and find an outside café and order coffee, not too difficult when you point at the photos. Under a roiling cloudy sky threatening rain, I hungrily devour how Boudin taught Monet the skill of capturing natural light in its changing form. Boudin's system influenced the whole Impressionist movement, including artists like Daubigny, Courbet, Jongkind, Corot, and others who never tired of painting this town and Old Harbor in every light of every hour and in every season.

I snap the book closed and sigh. It's hard to believe I'm really here living what many would consider a lifetime opportunity. Why isn't Shifrah interested in this? Why isn't everyone? I pull my sweater tighter against the flush of cold rolling in, hug my new book to my chest, and gasp as I watch a man pedaling a bicycle along the outer edge of the café. He's wearing a large dark coat, a beret, and has the perpetual loaf of bread protruding from the bicycle basket behind his seat.

His nose, that hair… it's him!

The spy!

CHAPTER FORTY-TWO

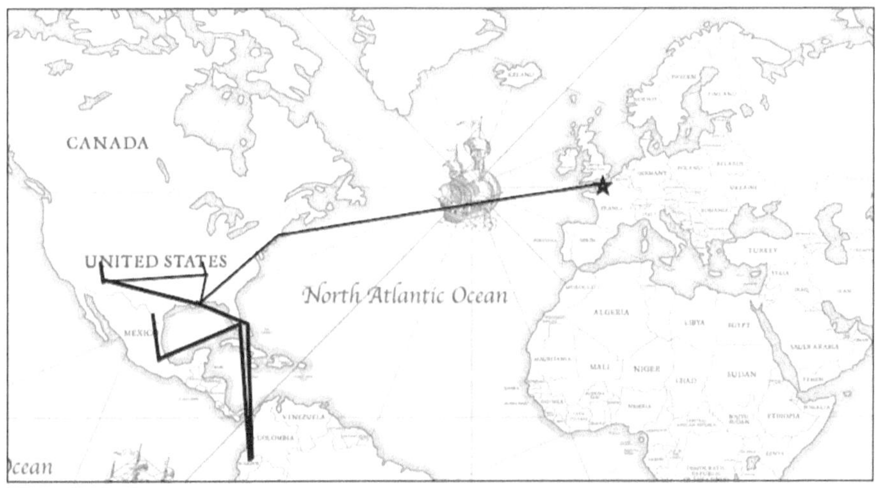

If I thought I had a chance of catching him, I'd take off running and find out where he goes. He pedals quickly down the street, around a corner, and out of sight. I glance at my watch so Malone will know exactly what time I saw him, and I'm shocked to see it's already 4:45!

Malone is a stickler for time schedules, so now I'll be late for dinner if I try to find our lodging house to change clothes and freshen up before joining them. I'll simply wear my trousers and oxfords to dinner, and Shifrah can go ahead and die of shock. Seeing the spy in Honfleur and being on time for dinner have to take precedence over how I look right now.

I wave down my waiter and ask him if he understands Spanish. He gives me a blank look. I say very slowly, *"Alguien habla español en el café?*

and point inside the café. "*Español?*" He looks at me a few seconds, then smiles, says, *"Oui,"* and flags down a young man carrying a bottle of wine to a table. Fortunately, the young man is from Spain, and though we have differences in how we speak the language, we soon understand each other perfectly. I describe the place with the blue shutters and door, and he tells me it's *Chez Bleu* and says it's about a fifteen-minute walk from this café.

I hurriedly pay and start walking. It's further than the young man said, so by the time I arrive and push open the blue door, it's already 5:25. My hair is a mess from the drizzle that started ten minutes ago, but what can I do? I immediately see Malone, Reno, and Shifrah sitting among tables filled with young boys wearing uniforms. They spot me and wave me over.

"What's this about?" I ask, pulling out a chair and nodding toward the young men.

"They're from a private boy's school in Paris," Shifrah says.

"They look too young to be drinking wine. What are they, fourteen or fifteen? Every table has a carafe of wine on it, and from the looks of it, they're all imbibing."

"Savannah, this is France. Everyone drinks wine here, even the younger generation. They think you're crazy when you order water with your meal."

"We were about to send a scout out to find you," Reno says.

"Yeah," Malone says, glancing at his watch.

Shifrah eagle-eyes me, and I look down at my dirty, scuffed oxfords that took a beating from the rough cobblestone streets and dirt paths.

"There aren't many sidewalks where I've been this afternoon," I say in my defense.

"And that's why you're wearing those trousers to dinner and have wet hair?" she says, raising both her eyebrows. "Honestly, Savannah…"

I put my head back and laugh.

"What's got you tickled, Savannah?" Reno says.

"Oh, I suppose it's more ironic than funny, but here I am in Normandy, France, the cradle of Impressionistic history. I'm drowning in the reality that I'm really here, in person, and I guess I find it funny that my big sin is that I have wet hair and didn't have time to change clothes before eating dinner in a pub. It's just me and my crazy sense of humor, Reno. See, while I was sitting in an open café drinking coffee and losing track of time, Claude Monet and a certain spy distracted me. I'm a terrible mess, I know, but please forgive me just this once."

My words settle in a few moments before Malone sits up straighter in his chair. "Did you say spy?"

"Yes, he's here in Honfleur." I describe what happened. Reno and Shifrah lean in close, absorbing the news.

Malone says. "Okay, that narrows it down. Mr. A is selectively telling certain things to certain people to ferret out the traitor. Looks like he can cross some off the list and focus on others. Good work, Savannah. I'll call him after we eat and let him know. That worked real well in our favor."

"Let me get this straight. You're sipping coffee at a café when that guy, the spy, casually bicycles by? Didn't he recognize you?" Shifrah says.

"How can you ask that when I'm wearing these awful clothes and shoes?"

"Well, yes, when you think about it, that sounds reasonable."

"I also had my loose sweater pulled over my shirt, my book on Impressionists wrapped in my arms, and, oh, there's this." I dig in my shopping bag and pull out a black velvet beret I bought at a shop close to the bookstore. "I was wearing it pulled forward and to the side."

"Why?"

"Oh, no big deal. I…"

"Tell us, hon," Reno says, his blue eyes brimming with mischief and a hint of red from the wine they obviously enjoyed before I arrived.

"It's silly, but I was kind of, um, pretending I was an impressionist artist reading a book and having refreshments at a café after a grueling, all-day painting session at Old Harbor. You've surely seen the portraits of Monet and other artists wearing berets. It's, you know, realistic."

"But your hair should have given you away."

"I had it completely pinned back and underneath my beret. It felt more genuine that way. Have you ever seen an Impressionist artist of the past with long blond hair? I took it back down when I started walking here so the rain wouldn't ruin my beret. It's a keepsake."

"You are a woman of many sides, Miss Savannah." Reno says, warmly smiling.

"A toast to our Savannah," Shifrah says, "Let's drink to her and to all the sensible people in France who say 'a dinner without wine is a day without sunshine!'"

"She's a spy spotter, that's for sure," Malone chips in, raising his glass.

"Hear, hear!" Reno says.

I don't know which is redder, my face or the wine they pour into my glass to raise in the air.

CHAPTER FORTY-THREE

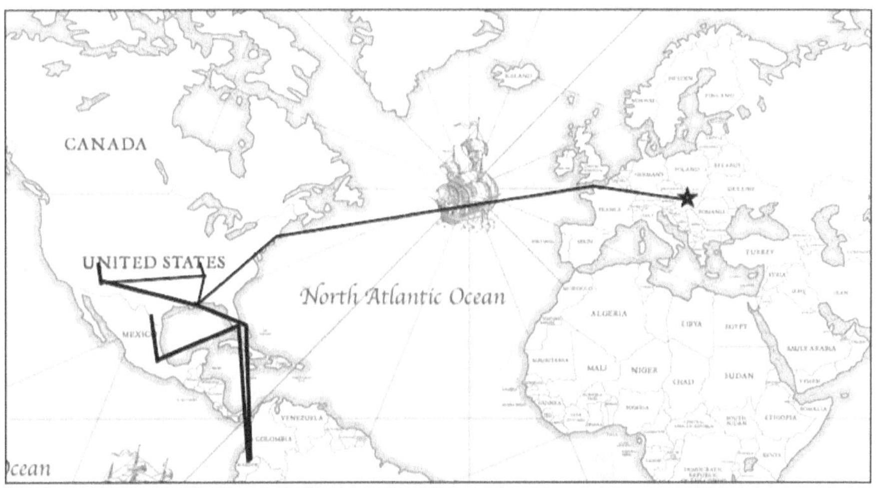

I try to burn the sight of the famous harbor in Honfleur, France, forever in my mind as I stare out the back window of the car. Our hired driver points our auto in a southern direction, and we spend a quick night in a little inn with no hot water along the way. As we drive, we see two new fads sweeping Europe—camping and hitchhiking.

People stand on the roads sticking out their thumbs like the drifters and vagabonds do back home when they're not jumping trains. Hitchhikers line the roads everywhere. My teammates think they have identified British, Danish, Belgian, Dutch, French, German, and American hitchhikers. Some carry placards with their proposed destinations written on them. Others simply wave or signal to passing cars hoping for a ride to somewhere. Every vehicle seems to have camping gear belted to the top or jutting from the back.

What does it mean? Is it joy and relief from the war being over? I don't know.

After the sun sets, we see countless campfires peeking through the trees. I enjoyed Shifrah's look of dismay when I said I wished we would stop and sleep on the forest floor with the campers.

Finally, we arrive in Nice and check into a fairly nice hotel. "Look at those posters!" Shifrah says in the lobby. "The theme for their next Carnival is *King of Toys!* Oh, how I wish it were held now instead of in February. Mommykins loves the Nice Carnival with all its color and delicacies. She's told me so much about it."

"Nice is where Henri Matisse, the famous painter, loved the most, Shifrah. I think he's still alive, but I don't know for sure. See that large plaque over the counter? It's a quote from Matisse." I get us closer and read it aloud to her.

"When I realized that every morning I would see that light again, I could not believe my happiness. I decided not to leave Nice, and I stayed there practically all my life."

"Isn't that something? Wouldn't it be wonderful to take in all the sights here? When I asked Malone if we could stay for a little while tomorrow, he reminded me we're on a mission, not a tourist trip."

"That was a little rude. When did he say that?"

"When you excused yourself to use the restroom before dinner last night."

"Well, you know how Malone is. Anyway, the South of France is another area we'll revisit and spend as long as we want."

"The more you mention us coming back to Europe, the better it sounds, Shifrah. I asked Malone why we came to Nice, and he said we're sidestepping."

"What does that mean?"

I sigh, shrug my shoulders. "I think it has to do with us outsmarting whoever's keeping tabs on us."

For the next three—or, is it four?—days, we take trains to one place after another with some of our train switches occurring in the dead of night. The interrupted sleeping arrangements, the scarcity of regular food, and the odd hours on this leg of our beleaguered journey have all of us in a less-than-jovial mood. I keep Malone's words about this not being a tourist trip fresh in my mind.

Zipping around, sometimes doubling back, and, at last, ending up in Budapest after dark, I was crestfallen to find out there was nothing to explore in Budapest. Once a city of spectacular art, architecture, and history, it is now a barely-restored victim of the war.

Our purpose in being here is the next *retrieve,* and I know our unusual travel plans have been necessary for Mr. A to weed out the traitor at headquarters, but it's still depressing to see a once-thriving, beautiful city lying mostly in ruin. Malone has remained mum about the castle where our *retrieve* is, why it's there, and if we're spending our second night in it as Shifrah emphatically believes.

CHAPTER FORTY-FOUR

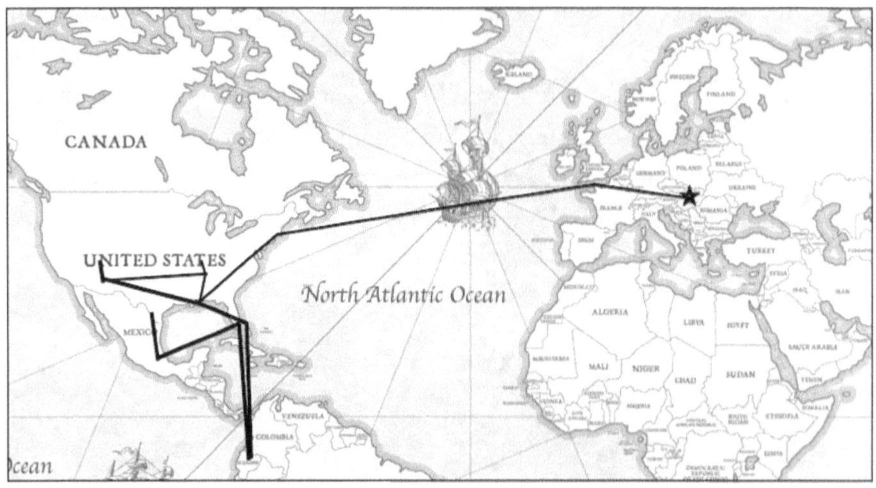

Shifrah moans, clasps her stomach, and closes her eyes. When she opens them, she might as well be standing barefoot in a patch of goatheads, she looks so miserable.

"Please tell me this is not the castle I've been dreaming of, Malone. This-this *thing* is just like the rest of Budapest, a pile of rubble!" She gazes upward. "Cranes, men on scaffolds and ladders. I-I thought, I mean, you let me believe… Oh, for Pete's sake, I should have known. Nothing on this mission is how I perceive it will be. Nothing."

She plops down on a square hunk of concrete bigger than a small car and hunches forward. She reminds me of a little rag doll abandoned in a schoolyard. I know she's tired. We all are. For once, she didn't complain when we found out Budapest offered us no side trips, not even shopping. "It won't matter, Savannah," she said last night in our modest hotel, one built in the last few years. "We'll be so pampered after our night in the castle, we'll drift off to our next destination on clouds! Wait and see."

Now, of course, her latest vision has been shattered by reality. Sitting on the concrete, she mumbles, "We missed everything important in France, and, naturally, we'll wind up not going to Paris. We've sped through exotic locations. We've traipsed like vagabonds through noisy train stations eating terrible food and never getting any real rest to arrive here in Budapest, and now..." her voice trails off. "Savannah, we'll travel anywhere we want when this idiotic assignment is over. We'll do it in style, too, believe me. I don't think I'll ever be the same after this mission."

"Maybe that's a good thing," Malone says.

Her reaction is almost a wince, but I see her recover quickly. "It's certainly not like anything I've ever experienced. Maybe, I, uh, might be somewhat more informed about life now."

"And people," I say, sending her an encouraging smile.

"Well, I've had a philosophy, science, and history teacher for a roommate."

"Stay put," Malone says, walking off toward the only man wearing an orange hard hat instead of the dark green ones the other workers are wearing. He greets Malone; they shake hands. He blows a whistle from around his neck. All work surrounding us pauses. Orange Hat picks up a megaphone.

"Kojack, go tell Mr. Wallenberg his visitors are here," he broadcasts. We're suddenly the object of stares and under-the-breath whistles. I sit beside Shifrah to escape some of the attention coming at us.

"Did you know our castle was going to be in ruins, Savannah?"

"How could I? Malone hasn't told us a thing. I guess he didn't want to face your disappointment until the last minute. You know, I assumed Hungary was spared during the war the same as Honfleur. Now, it's plain this place, this castle, everything suffered bombs, fire, and tragedy. War in Europe must have been indescribable. Aren't you curious about what happened here?"

She rolls her eyes. "Are you kidding?" She sighs, "You know I don't like discussing bad things like war, Savannah. Besides, I imagined us staying in a luxurious palace decorated in rare tapestries and paintings with a staff of a thousand bringing us delicious *pörkölt* for a first course and other paprika-saturated cuisine served on gleaming silver dishes. I wanted to drink international wines served in gold-rimmed goblets."

This is where Shifrah and I are worlds apart. I wish we could have stayed in a beautiful palace tonight, I mean, who wouldn't want that? But I'm okay with not doing it, too.

"You said something about paprika-saturated food? Is paprika a specific Hungarian spice?" I say, hoping to cheer her up a little.

"It's a carryover from when the Ottomans had control of this country. They introduced paprika to the Hungarians."

"Shifrah, I'm shocked. That's positively historical."

She tries to hide her smile. "Hilda told me. I never realized it, but Hilda was food-obsessed like you. She told me loads of strange food details."

"Yeah, like the history of Melba toast and Peach Melba."

"And the story of the Muffaletta sandwiches in New Orleans."

"And now the history of paprika in Hungary. I wish I could meet that Hilda of yours. What was that dish you mentioned earlier?"

"Pörkölt? It's a Hungarian meat and onion stew. Hilda says it's delightful served in a small bowl as an appetizer or as the entrée with freshly baked bread and cheeses."

"My stomach is growling just thinking about—"

"Up and at 'em, ladies!" Reno says, and I see Malone beckoning for us to join him. He continues talking to an elderly man wearing a brown tweed suit, white shirt, and a bowtie, undoubtedly Mr. Wallenberg, our contact for the *retrieve.* I suppose Malone is filling him in on whatever he tells everyone about us before they meet us. Mr. Wallenberg removes his glasses as we near, puts them inside a shirt pocket, and sticks out his hand. Reno shakes it, then steps aside for Shifrah and me to do the same. Mr. Wallenberg shakes my hand first, then clasps Shifrah's hand with both of his, leaning forward and smiling broadly.

Why is he reacting like that to Shifrah? What does he know that we don't?

We pick our way around tools, hunks of concrete, and dusty half-walls to follow him to a small, makeshift office. He goes behind a chipped metal desk, gestures toward two seats, then sits down as soon as Shifrah and I are seated.

"Good morning, good morning! It is always a pleasure to greet American visitors. I'm so glad all the passports and permissions could be satisfied," he says in a heavy accent. "I apologize for this destruction and construction. As you can see, our city has suffered. Unfortunately, our beautiful Buda Castle is wounded for the time being. Alas, her great assets have made her a target over the centuries."

"Her assets?" I ask.

"Oh yes." He leans forward toward us. "You see, on this hill overlooking the Danube River, she is the perfect refuge, which makes her always an object of desire for power-hungry men."

"It, uh, she's a beautiful castle. I'm sorry this happened to, um, *her,"* I say, and I mean it.

Mr. Wallenberg nods in agreement. "Thank you. Savannah, isn't it?"

I nod.

"Modern weapons are fiercer now, so callous and cold. We almost lost Buda Castle. She suffered fires from the bombs and the bullets with no water to put them out. The dome and the roof collapsed. Irreplaceable art treasures burned or buried for all time. Our great hope is to rebuild her, as you can see. At first, the Soviets were undecided if they would allow rebuilding. Heartbreaking. We toiled very hard to, uh, to assist this government to make a good decision. They have agreed to rebuild some of it."

He leans forward in his chair and rolls his eyes toward the door. "We are under communist dictatorship, you know," he rasps, not much louder than a whisper. "To the communists, 'restoration' means tearing down beautiful old buildings they deem worthless and *restoring* them into plain, modern architecture for practical use. Already, they have decided the Castle Garden and the Royal Stable will not be restored, and for no reason will they not do this!"

His face blushes red.

Such passion for this castle!

He takes a big breath. His shoulders rise and fall. "The paintings, carpets, and the precious relics of Buda Castle were the spoils of war, stolen by the Soviet soldiers when they defeated the Nazis. Were they not born with brains? Who doesn't know history must be preserved both in truth and in structure?" He looks up at the ceiling, back down. "May I share a deep opinion of mine?"

My head is nodding, and I assume we are all in agreement that Mr. Wallenberg can share anything he wants with us because he says, "Thank you. My belief is if you remove history, change it, or ignore it, civilizations can falter. History reflects the truth of life. From history, we understand our mistakes and rejoice in our victories.

"You are all young. Might I be so forward as to ask you to preserve and protect history at all costs? Never allow it to be falsely told or written, even when the truth of it is deeply painful. You will remember my admonition, yes?"

I don't know about everyone else, but I'm agreeing vigorously. I have no choice. Mr. Wallenberg has the exact same effect on me as my more dynamic college professors did. I think his fervent plea for historical truth surprised all of us. When his face changes to a peaceful countenance, I venture to ask him who is responsible for nearly destroying Buda Castle.

He waves a hand in the air. "So many, my dear. Choose any you wish. The Soviets. The Germans, the British, Americans, Hitler. Yes, he most of all. You probably know Budapest was occupied by Hitler's armies in 1944.

No, I didn't know that.

"We begged Hitler to declare our precious Budapest an *open city* so it could be saved from the ravages of war. He refused. Some will argue that he did, but the truth before our eyes does not lie. When the German and Hungarian High Command troops settled in to operate underneath the city, Budapest was, how do you say it—a sitting duck? It became the center of Hungary's military force. Of course, that brought the bombs.

"Bombings meant air-raid shelters must be built. Underneath this Buda Castle are cellars and caves. A shelter for two thousand people was built there. It connects to the Big Labyrinth under our city."

"What's the Big Labyrinth?" Shifrah asks.

"The Big Labyrinth is an underground web of tunnels. It connects to the caves underneath this castle. It was also used as a hospital in the war. Sometimes, as many as ten thousand people were inside the tunnels.

"Dang, that's a lot of people, sir," Reno says.

"Yes, yes, many people. And the war continued. What suffered? Everything. Who suffered? Everyone—two communities more than others." He looks down, then back up with a smile overshadowed by a deep sadness in his eyes.

"Come, let us speak of happier things. You are presently on Castle Hill. Buda Castle has kept guard over Castle Hill for centuries. So much history! Unfortunately, all seven bridges across the Danube have been destroyed, as was most of our city, but we who love Budapest choose to view this destruction as an opportunity to rebuild it better than before. We shall see, yes, we shall see. I wish I could accompany you to old-town Buda to see the Ruda Baths built in the Middle Ages. Someday, when we have made our city alive again, you must come back. Malone, you are leaving Budapest tonight?"

"Yes sir, that is correct."

"You mean we're not even staying here that one more night you promised us?" Shifrah asks, turning in her seat to look at Malone. He doesn't answer, but his face says *that's enough.* She slowly swivels back around.

Mr. Wallenberg unlocks the top middle drawer of the desk and pulls out a chain with a key on the end. He holds it toward the only window in the room, a dusty square high on the wall. "A very attractive key, I must say. The bull in the circle has long intrigued me. Very intelligent, that bull. Yes, very clever."

Why does that bull look like the ones on Shifrah's case?

"I am relieved to hand over this key at last." He chuckles. "You have heard the amusing story of what happened to this poor key, correct? Oh, that grandson of mine! How could I guess he—"

The phone on his desk rings. He glances at it, back at us, then holds the key and chain out to Malone, who has edged forward to take possession of our fourth *retrieve.* Malone slips the key into his jacket pocket. Mr. Wallenberg again looks at the ringing phone.

"Answer it, sir. We'll be on our way. Mr. A sends his deepest appreciation and thanks for your loyalty to, uh, well, you know who. I think you'll understand the depth of Mr. A's gratitude quite soon, sir," Malone says, talking fast and motioning at the same time for us to leave. Mr. Wallenberg smiles warmly, slightly bows his head toward us as he picks up the receiver.

Shifrah walks through the door Malone holds open for us, circles around, goes back to Mr. Wallenberg and gives him a hug as he talks on the telephone. His face lights up. He smiles as he watches her walk away. We eye her curiously as she rejoins us.

"He reminds me of someone," she says. "Malone, can I see that key as soon as we get in the car? What did Mr. Wallenberg mean about *intelligent bull?* Have you ever noticed the bulls etched on my personal cigarette case?" She chatters on nervously, looks back at the renovation crew working on the demolished castle. "Goodbye, my closest chance to live for one night as a royal princess. To celebrate my disappointment, I say we go consume some of that *black soup* they mentioned at the hotel before I die of grief that we aren't staying in a gorgeous European castle tonight."

"*Black soup?* You mean *kávé?* I'd like to see you down a cup of that, Shifrah," I say. "I hear it's stronger than Italian espresso. Besides, it might have too much sixteenth-century Turkish history attached to it to be of real interest to you."

"Says the history professor. I swear, Savannah, if you don't come up with the most obtuse facts."

"That one took extensive research."

She rolls her eyes. "When did you have time for that?"

"At breakfast. I read it on the back of our menus."

Men shouting and the sound of rock scraping against rock halts me in my tracks.

CHAPTER FORTY-FIVE

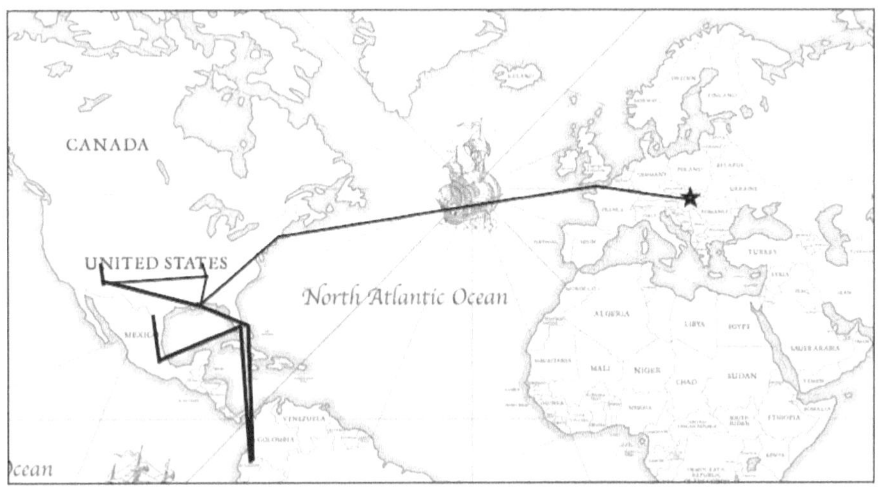

Malone hurries past me, almost knocking me down. "Back up!" he yells, and I do, straight into Reno's grasp. He pulls me further back as an avalanche of stone, plaster, and powder gushes down from above. It crashes to the floor a few feet in front of me. I lose visibility after seeing Malone draping himself over Shifrah and the two of them dropping downward. Rocks and rubble litter the area where Shifrah was walking ahead of me only seconds earlier.

"Malone, y'all okay?" Reno yells.

"Affirmative! Up high, on the left, Reno! Don't let him get away!"

"On it, sir!" he shouts, and he's already sprinting across the old stone flooring and up a partial ancient stairway where a thin, wiry man in black clothes and a black scarf over the lower part of his face is climbing a ladder leading to a scaffold encircling a section of curved stone. Men are shouting, climbing off ladders, turning this way and that.

Malone stands up, dusting himself off. His pant leg is ripped across the knee, and he's covered in plaster powder. He pulls his jacket off, gives it one strong whip in the air, bends toward Shifrah. She sits up, fluffs her hair, looks confused. I climb over the clumps of concrete and stone to get to her. Her hosiery is torn, the heel on one of her shoes, a high heel I told her not to wear, is broken off, and the top of her foot is bleeding from a long cut across the top.

Malone whisks her up and into his arms. "Anything besides your foot hurt?"

"I-I don't think so."

He fast-walks to the car where our driver is holding open one of the back doors. Without looking back, he shouts out my name. I answer. "Get in the car!" I dutifully and fearfully do what I'm told. He places Shifrah in the backseat and tells me to take care of her. He barks orders to the driver, who rapidly locks the passenger door up front and jumps behind the wheel, locking his door behind him.

Malone hands me his jacket. "Cover her up with this, and lock these back doors." The worry on his face makes me feel more worried than I was.

"But, I'm not cold, Malone—" Shifrah says.

"Wear it!" he yells, and he's gone, running briskly back through the open arches and into the work area now cluttered with workmen, their green hard hats bobbing as they collect in groups.

"Savannah, what just happened?"

I'm craning my neck to look out all the windows. "It appears we have a real bad guy pursuing us now."

"A bad guy? You mean someone did this on purpose?"

"I'm afraid so. Reno's chasing him right now."

"But why?"

"I don't know, but I do know the man Reno's after is not our normal spy."

"How could you tell?"

"He was taller and skinnier than Mr. Crooked Mustache with the long legs and short waist."

She shudders. "I can't believe it! Someone's really trying to harm us now."

"Pull Malone's jacket up tight, Shifrah. Let's not get him more riled than he already is."

"I didn't agree to go on a life-or-death mission, but…"

"But what?"

"Don't laugh, but I'm sort of enjoying this. Did you see Malone save me? Then he picked me up like I was as light as a scarf and carried me to the car. You won't believe what he said to me."

"What?"

"He said 'It's okay, baby, it's okay. Don't worry. I'm here.'"

"Really?"

Shifrah shakes her head and stares at the car upholstery on the ceiling of the car. "I had decided he was the meanest, most insensitive man ever born, and then he acts like that to me?"

"He's always had concern for you, Shifrah. You're usually too mad to see it, but it's there. Here," I say, digging in my purse, "use my handkerchief for that cut. You're getting blood all over the place. Are you in pain?"

"No, it doesn't hurt at all. Well, a little." She dabs it with the handkerchief, looks up. "What were you saying about his concern for me?"

"It's in his eyes when you're upset about something he has no control over, but it fades quickly."

"Why haven't I ever seen that?" she says, mostly to herself.

I crane my neck to see inside the construction area. "I have to go see what's going on."

"Malone said to stay put."

"Yeah, but I can't. Hey, if someone's trying to hurt us, I want to know everything. Don't you?"

"Yes, but—"

"I'll be back," I say, unlocking the door and hurrying along the path through the arches and into the scaffolded area. Right away, I see Mr. Wallenberg and Malone huddling with the man in the orange hat and four other workers. I gingerly pick through the mess on the stone floor and aspire to stay invisible behind Malone's broad back.

"I don't know how he got up there without us seeing him, sir," Orange Hat says to Mr. Wallenberg. He breaks out speaking rapidly in what obviously must be Hungarian. Three or four other workers chime in. They're all talking at once as Reno and a few other men join them. Reno shakes his head as he walks toward Malone.

"We lost him, sir. Shoo-ie, this place is like a big underground rabbit hole, a maze you can't hardly believe with crumbled rooms, bombed-out tunnels, and scorched walls. It's something else. Me and my new buddy here, János, scattered and searched everywhere that rascal had time to get to, but we didn't see hide nor hair of him. He says they're gonna form teams right quick to search this whole place inside and out. Man, let me tell you, it's spread out bigger than a Texas oilfield."

That starts another round of loud conversing until Mr. Wallenberg raises a hand. Everyone quiets down. He turns to Malone and Reno. "My superintendent of construction says this villain had to be familiar with the schematics of our construction site since he escaped so quickly. We assume he dressed in work clothes and a green hat, worked with a chisel and mallet to loosen the façade of the damaged wall up there, then changed his clothes to make a getaway." He points to where the rubble poured from. "You walked by. He pushed the loosened shale, and down it came. I deeply apologize."

"Don't blame yourself, Mr. Wallenberg. There are more factors at work here than you know. We'll get to the bottom of it."

"Are the girls all right?" he asks.

"Shaken up. A little medical needed for a cut on Shifrah's foot. Nothing to worry about."

Mr. Wallenberg shakes his head. "We will search until we find answers."

"Say, could this fella be one of your workers working here today, one that slipped off and changed his clothes before he tried to kill us?" Reno asks.

Kill us?

"Orange Hat rubs a hand across his face, shakes his head. "We took a count while four of my workers assisted you. No missing men."

"Damn," Malone says, half turning. "Oh, Savannah! What are you doing there? Didn't I tell you to stay in the car?"

I hang my head a little to look ashamed, but Reno, as usual, sees right through it. "Sir, remember Savannah wrestles Texas bulls on her day off. She's tough enough to handle this, I'm thinkin'."

Malone clears his throat, shakes hands with Mr. Wallenberg and Orange Hat, ushers us to the car. On the way, he says, "When I give you an order, I expect you to follow it. Is that clear?"

"Yessir," I say with as much contriteness as I can muster, but Reno ruins my bluff by looking back at me with a mischievous wink and a smile that tickles my funny bone. I muffle my instant guffaw, cough, and jump into the front seat of the car, something I never do. I have to or I'll start cackling out loud.

I'm finding out I have a strange sense of humor, especially in the eye of danger, and Reno has zeroed in on it. I mean, someone just tried to kill us, and I'm laughing? I don't even understand it. What would Tony and the regulars think of me in all these escapades, and why am I finding this whole journey more thrilling than the entirety of my whole past life?

CHAPTER FORTY-SIX

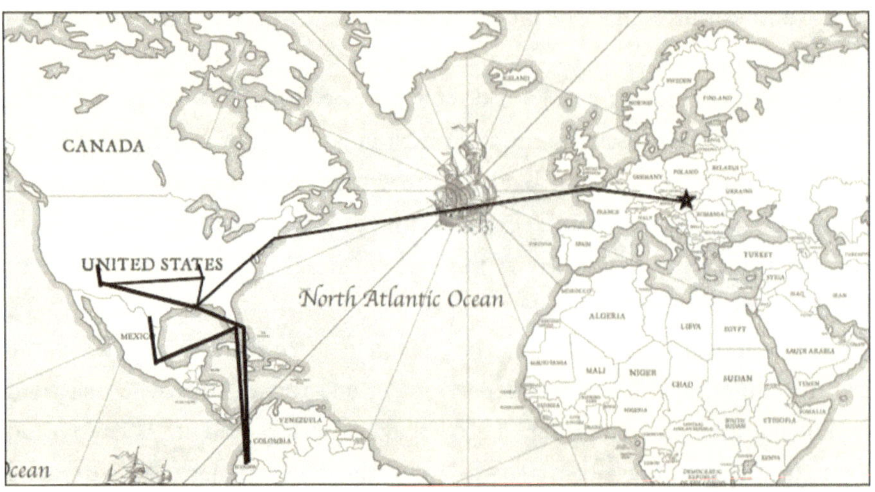

Driving to the hospital, I notice in my side vision Malone lifts Shifrah's wounded foot up on his leg. She's quiet, but I hear her thank him for *saving her life.* I tune into their conversation. He tells her we're taking a train in the morning instead of tonight so she has more time to recover. "Come hell or high water, we're headed to Dijon, France, after our next stop because I have a surprise," he tells her.

"Dijon, France? The home of Dijon mustard?"

"That's the place."

"Oh, joy! Mommykins always brings us back at least four jars of that delightful condiment when she and Daddy visit France. It's divine on a roast beef sandwich or in a cabbage salad. Savannah, I know some things about the history of Dijon mustard you'll enjoy."

I turn in the front seat. "I don't know if I can take it, Shifrah."

"What?"

"You spouting off more historical facts. I'm still a little weak in the knees from hearing you tell me about the Turks and paprika."

"Paprika? Isn't that the red stuff women sprinkle on the top of their tater salad to make it look pretty, or is that chili powder?" Reno says.

"In Texas, it's usually chili powder, Reno, but Tony also used paprika for his potato salad and pea salad garnish for all the city dudes. But Shifrah sharing the history of Dijon mustard may make me pass out from shock."

"Oh, stop it. I studied French in school, so my parents supplied me with booklets and brochures from France. The ones about Dijon mustard got me an A in my French class after I wrote a paper and gave a presentation on it."

"All I know about it is that we had to start keeping it on hand in the diner after so many travelers asked for it, especially to go with their ham or bacon sandwiches, and sometimes on the side when they ordered grilled or fried chicken. I like it okay, but Tony and the rest of the Dixie crew stick to their old-fashioned yellow mustard."

"Well, do you want to hear my interesting facts or not?" Shifrah says.

"I'll die if I don't," I say.

"Dijon, as you probably already know, is the capital city of the Burgundy region. The ancient Romans started the whole thing by planting brown mustard seeds with their grapevines to give them nutrition. I think phosphorous is the main thing the seeds provided for the soil around the vines. Anyway, monks kept doing this for eons of time, then, some smart guy started combining the seeds with the sour juice of unripe wine grapes instead of with vinegar, which was already being done."

"Unripe wine grapes?"

"Uh-huh. I think it's called vuhjuice or verjuice, something like that. Supposed to be as sour as lemon juice. So, Dijon mustard is now made with brown mustard seeds and verjuice or, sometimes, brown mustard seeds and Burgundian white wine, and it all started with the Romans."

Reno and I clap our hands. Malone joins in.

Shifrah's cheeks turn pink. "Are you guys making fun of me again?"

"We're admiring your story," Malone says.

"That's right, Shif. You turned into a regular little historian first time out of the chute!" Reno says.

"Okay, okay. Um, Malone, do we pick up our fifth *retrieve* in Dijon?" she asks.

"You might say so. I'll know more in the morning. We have two more *retrieves* to gather. That's the facts regardless of that fool causing havoc at the castle."

"So, Dijon is next unless that changes tonight when you talk to Mr. A, and the last one isn't Paris, is it? I did so want to go, Malone, but I understand we have to change our plans now that we barely escaped death."

What? No sarcastic jabs? No whining or loud sighs? She understands?

"I wouldn't say we barely escaped death, Shifrah, but we came too close to being seriously injured. I'll be working on the phone tonight with Mr. A, spreading out the maps to see how best to finish up. He and his, well, his closest ally at headquarters are working with the last two contacts. At this point, the core of headquarters is being run mostly by the two of them and a handful of their most trusted. "

"Malone?"

"Yes?"

"Haven't Savannah and I been patient enough that it's okay for us to know more about the mission? I mean, I was almost buried under a wall of plaster. Don't you think I at least deserve to know why?"

I turn to see Malone's reaction, and what I see is he and Reno exchanging glances. Malone looks past Reno out the window. His shoulders rise and fall in a large sigh. He starts talking while still staring at the scenery outside.

"Surely you know I've been operating under confidentiality orders from day one. Those orders do not allow me to reveal a lot of details.

Reno knows some of them because, whether you realize this or not, he's my point man. Reno has been armed, as have I, this whole time. We knew to expect some trouble with so much at stake. When the time comes, soon now, all of your questions will be answered. Not by me. By Mr. A."

"Mr. A?" I ask.

"Affirmative."

"We get to meet Mr. A?" Shifrah says.

"He and others. After we gather all our *retrieves*. Hey, how's the foot doing?"

Shifrah and I stare holes in each other. We need no words to agree we're both shocked by Malone's disclosures. He's changing the subject, so that means no more questions right now.

"Wha-what did you ask me?" she asks.

"I asked if your foot hurts."

"It's kind of sore. The worst part will be if I can't wear high heels for a day or two." She smiles good-naturedly. "Of course, you know how tough I am."

"Tougher than nails is our Shif!" Reno spouts, causing an all-around, relieved chuckle, clearing the air.

"Thank you for asking about my foot, Malone."

What am I hearing? Malone throwing himself over her to save her from the landslide and carrying her to the car grew her up about five years' worth?

"Is it all right to ask about some of our options… I mean, what place we might go to, other than Dijon, for the other *retrieve*?" I ask.

"I have to discuss these latest developments with Mr. A, of course, but I'm quite sure we can work the schedule to proceed to Venice in a matter of days, Savannah. I don't know yet if that will be a contact point or if it will be another diversion."

"Venice, Italy? I've always dreamed of being rowed through the canals and lagoons by handsome *gondoliers!* How romantic!" Shifrah says.

It's quiet in the car until our driver announces we're at the hospital, which looks like a low-slung, whitewashed house with a red cross painted on the door.

CHAPTER FORTY-SEVEN

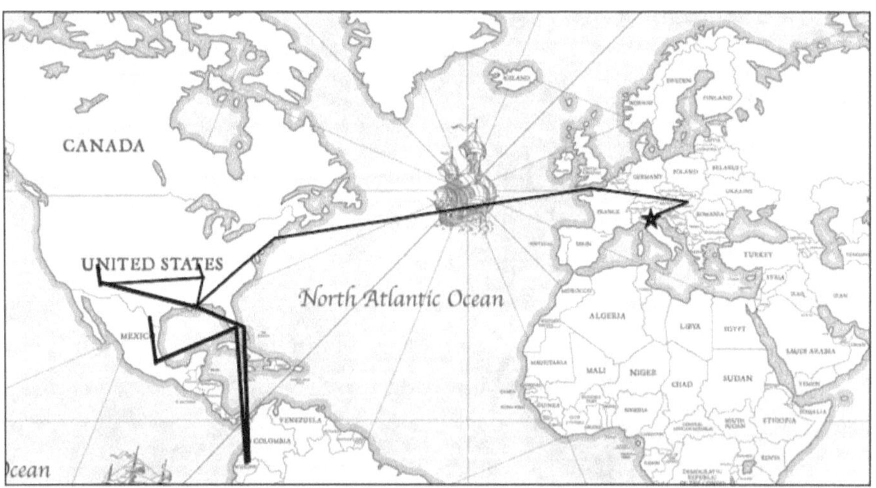

Venice is everything I imagined it would be, including our hotel. I'm in awe as soon as we're shown our suite at the *Hotel Acque Antiche* in Venice, but Shifrah takes it all in stride. "At last, a room that befits us perfectly!" she exclaims. She tips the bellboy after he leaves our luggage where she points.

I walk around gently rubbing my hand across tapestries hung on the wall, flocked wallpaper, thick wood columns with intricate cutouts, and an arch that separates the bedroom and sitting room. The sitting room has low-slung, cushiony furniture placed on Persian rugs. Various urns, gold-framed mirrors, and paintings are throughout the room. It opens to a small, private terrace overlooking the famous Ancient Bridge and the canals of Venice, scenes I have often seen in paintings and photographs. Because of Shifrah's sore foot, our suite is on the ground floor, which I love because it's only steps away from historic Venice.

On the reverse side of the sitting room is the bedroom. The twin beds have gilded French Provincial headboards outlining tufted burgundy velvet. I rub my hand across the marble top of one of the nightstands and admire the golden lampstand sitting on the top. It supports three small, fringed, accordion-pleated lampshades. Muted designs in burgundy and gold are on the wallpaper on the wall behind the bed, and exotic woven rugs decorate the floor.

I sigh and throw myself back on the wine-colored bedspread hemmed with twilled amber fringe. This room, this hotel, the glistening Venice waters right outside our room crown the idea of a world I never imagined seeing. Is it any wonder I felt my small-town world closing in on me right before I met Shifrah and Malone? Will that world be enough for me when this job is finished?

Shifrah orders hot spiced tea and a small cheese and fruit board from room service. While Malone checked us into the hotel, she and I stepped outside and stood by the canal watching the *gondoliers* dipping their constant oars into the waterways. Many were flirty toward us as we stood there, and I'm wondering if I can handle all the attention we get in Europe. The men seem bolder here than in the States, or is it because Shifrah has me so dooded up all the time?

I wish it were summer, but even in late fall, the scene around us is magnificent. Malone warned us not to take any excursions this afternoon for two reasons. One, it might make us late for our early dinner, which he said involves a surprise guest. He hinted we might get a few answers to some of our questions, and that alone was enough to make us adhere strictly to his orders. The second reason he gave was that he doesn't want us going off without him or Reno until he can figure out some things.

We sit on the patio in our jackets watching the *gondoliers* smoothly operating their *gondolas* under cloudy skies. A pleasant fragrance is in the air, almost like watermelons. We're quiet until Shifrah says, "It looks as though Venice remained untouched during that nasty war. Aren't you glad?"

"I'm more than glad. It's so beautiful, it's hard to believe it's real. I think we're staying here a day or two, right?"

"I hope so, but you never know. I desperately want to ride in one of those *gondolas*. Uh, Savannah?"

"Yes?"

"Do you honestly believe we'll get a lot of our questions answered tonight?"

"Maybe more than we want."

"What do you mean?"

"I've been thinking lately how the truth of our mission seems to be built on the back of that terrible war."

"Yeah, when you put it that way, maybe I'd rather stay ignorant."

"If I weren't so curious, I'd agree. You do realize all the *retrieves* have been held by someone who was in the war or close to it, don't you?"

"I guess so."

"Eddie, the *Havasupai* Native, for example… he got his key from someone overseas while serving in the military. He mentioned General Patton that night by the falls, didn't he?"

"Yes, but our second key was that button factory owner, the man with the black and gray hair and wire glasses. Wasn't he too old to have been in the war?"

"Maybe, but he was from Germany. Germany, Shifrah! The hub of the whole war in Europe."

"I only know his nice-looking son had a charming accent, spoke perfect English, and fell madly in love with you."

"Oh, for heaven's sake. Why do you keep saying that?"

"Because it's true, and I think it bothered Reno."

"That's so silly, I won't even bother answering it."

"Savannah, sometimes, you are so naïve."

I scoff and roll my eyes, but the fact is, when it comes to relationships, I am naïve about men. My regulars made sure of it. "Well, anyway, our third *retrieve* was held by an Irishman who became an officer who got his head messed up while fighting with the English, right? More war connections."

"What about your handsome jungle man you thought looked like

Clark Gable? Was he in the war?"

"I don't know, but he didn't have a key, just the *key to the keys* in that hideous monkey statue. I'm talking about the keys, the *retrieves.*"

"Well, I'll never forget that sweet Mr. Wallenberg and the lecture he gave us about history, not to mention the key he gave us with the bull etched inside the circle on the end. That shocked me more than anything else. That bull is similar to the ones on my cigarette case, and that gives me the shivers, Savannah. Am I somehow connected to this mission?"

"I have no idea, but have you noticed how everything seems connected to the war? I don't know Mr. Wallenberg's connection, but we met him in a ravaged city with a bombed-out castle suffering the after-effects of the war. Think about it. We've gathered items from the Ecuadorian rainforest, Arizona, Tennessee, Ireland, and Hungary. Now we're going back to France for our fifth *retrieve.* Who knows where the sixth one is? Do you remember the *key to the keys* had seven keyholes? Malone said we're retrieving six keys, not seven, so where is the seventh key? I have to say this mission has turned into quite a mystery."

"Didn't I tell you Malone said Mr. A has the seventh key?"

"No, you didn't. When did he say that?"

"I think it was in Phoenix before we went to Alabama."

"Where was I?"

"Hmm, let me think. Oh yeah. We were waiting for dinner, and you went to buy some postcards."

"Well, thanks, Shifrah. That's kind of important information to forget to tell me."

"I'm sorry. Anyway, we know those keys unlock something. Do you remember Reno's slip of the tongue our first night in Mexico City?"

"You mean when he mentioned unlocking something, and Malone shot dagger-eyes at him?"

She nods.

"Uh-huh, so, what do they unlock? A vault? A warehouse? A house? A trunk? Whatever's inside is valuable enough for someone to go awol at headquarters and not mind if he harms us in the process," I say.

"Summed up perfectly. You think we'll get to see what's in that secret place?"

"I sure hope so."

She smiles, sips her tea, and watches the waterway. After several minutes of shared silence, she says, "What are you thinking?"

"That several men I know of in Laredo went off to war, but I don't remember hearing them talk very much about it. Of course, there's Leon. We never met him before he came to town, but rumor has it he returned from overseas duty and flat out left his family in Austin, a wife and two little kids, and moved to Laredo. He bought a little shack, and I do mean *shack,* outside of town by the train tracks. He comes into town to get groceries, sometimes buys a cup of coffee at the Dixie. Keeps to himself, orders his coffee, hunching over the cup. He gets up and leaves without a word, his money on the counter. I'm beginning to understand why he's so sad."

"Sad?"

"Uh-huh. It's like a mist of gloom surrounds him. I always feel it. What did he see, and what truths hollowed him into the ashes of who he was before he went to war?"

"Now, that's spooky," Shifrah says, shivering.

CHAPTER FORTY-EIGHT

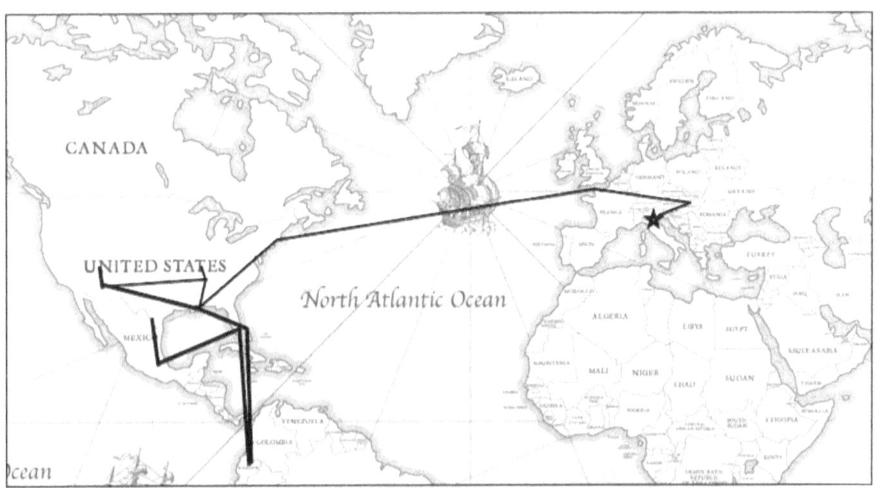

A slim, well-dressed man wearing peculiar glasses rises from the table as soon as we're escorted by the Maître d' into the restaurant's private dining room. He looks about Malone's age, clean cut with brown hair and even features. He watches us through lenses tinted in purple as Malone steps close to him. They shake hands energetically.

"Malone, Malone, Malone. I have no words except *thank you.* I knew if anyone could pull this off, it was you." He gives Reno, Shifrah, and me *the up, down, and sideways,* as my daddy used to say. "Everyone looks like they survived and thrived. Of course, none of us had any doubt you would get the job done, Major."

"You should hold off until I finish the mission. Two more *retrieves* to go, and we still don't have those culprits lined up all the way."

"We'll get there. Anyway, the spoils will soon be properly dispersed, yes?"

"You bet, Jonathan. Hey, let's get you introduced to my team. You and Reno have gabbed on the phone, and if I'm not mistaken, you know a bunch of the same military personnel, right?"

Reno quicksteps to Jonathan with his hand out. "Yessir, it's an honor, Captain," Reno says. "A real pleasure."

"Likewise, Reno. Man alive, you left a wide streak in the skies, buddy. They tell your stories all through the ranks. All I have to do is mention Reno, the pilot in the Fighting First Air Corp, and here comes another tale of wonder! How many medals did you rack up?"

"Aw, shoot, just a few."

Jonathan throws his hands in the air. "Modest, too, huh, Malone?"

"That's one of the things I always—"

"Any chance of us getting invited to this party sometime this evening?" Shifrah says, looking a bit slighted with her chin held at that certain raised angle.

"Oh, uh, sure. Jonathan, meet Shifrah." He pushes her forward and stands back. Jonathan steps close. "I've heard so much about you, Shifrah. It's a pleasure to finally meet you."

"Thank you. This is Savannah, my best friend," she says, turning and pulling me forward by the arm.

Something about Jonathan seems distantly familiar. I think he reminds me of someone I've seen at the Dixie. All those faces for so many years, yet I still think I've seen him somewhere.

"How about we have a seat and order up some drinks?" Malone says.

"I second that," Shifrah mutters, pulling out a chair. I settle in beside her. She leans her head toward me and whispers, "Get a load of those purple lenses."

The door opens and two waiters enter. I start to order my usual Shirley Temple, change my mind, and, to the surprise of my team, order a glass of house champagne. Jonathan overhears my request.

"A glass? Let's have two bottles of *Dom Pérignon,*" he says to the waiter standing next to him. Soon, we're sipping champagne and sampling shrimp canapes and goose liver pinwheels. I inwardly laugh at how my life has changed in the last months.

"Malone, as you know, we've followed this mission every step of the way. It's been interesting, to say the least. Captain Taylor, you always do us proud at headquarters, not to mention how many times you split our sides laughing!"

"Aw, Cap, I just aim to please," Reno says.

"Captain Taylor? Both of you were captains in the Army?" All three men look at me with blank expressions, as if they can't grasp such a lack of knowledge.

"Affirmative, Savannah," Malone says at last. "Thought you knew that."

"I knew you were a major, but Reno never said anything about his rank. Of course, we didn't know about Jonathan, either. So, you work at headquarters, Jonathan? Is that how you're connected to our mission?"

What follows is a strange lapse of silence highlighting the fact that no questions will be answered merely because we ask them. Were my questions rude? Malone shuffles position, looks at Jonathan.

"Quite a team, eh, Jonathan? My noncommissioned female officers have done me proud, no lie." All three men look at us, all smiles, heads nodding, and it feels like Shifrah and I are outside a glass window looking in at people who know the secrets to everything while we know nothing.

"I think they've done a commendable job of traveling all over the world and…" he looks at Shifrah, "enduring a few hardships along the way, yes?" He leans back in his chair. "Ladies, with your permission, I would like to share a story with you. A story of survival and, as we say in the States, a story of true grit. It isn't a pleasant one, and I apologize for that."

Shifrah raises her hand. "You have a question?"

"You can say that again. Do you work with Mr. A, whoever that is? Why can't we know who—"

"Shifrah," Malone says in a low tone.

"Malone, don't we deserve to know anything? We're always left in the dark."

"Yes, but—"

"It's okay, Malone. Her curiosity is understandable." Jonathan smiles at her. "The story I tell you now will answer a few of your questions, and the rest will be answered very soon. Can you bear your curiosity a short time longer?"

"I, maybe, okay, yes." She sighs noisily, elbows me in the ribs. Why, I don't know, but I think it's because she's a little bit intimidated by all this military brass and their obvious camaraderie. I know I am, especially since I don't know what they know.

"Thank you. I appreciate your patience." He pushes his hors d'oeuvre plate to the side, entwines his fingers, and places his hands on the table. "We went through a heck of a war this last time, a war that changed the world, cultures, people, life as we knew it. How did one man, one ideal, change a whole country, and then the world, in one terrible segment of time? No one knows the exact answer to that, and perhaps, no one ever will," Jonathan says.

Shifrah grabs my hand under the table. As we discussed earlier, this whole mission revolves around the Big War. From our shared look, we both wish it didn't.

"David Diamond. What did you think of him, Savannah?"

"You want to know what *I* thought of him?"

Shifrah leans forward. "She thought he was delightful, intelligent, and as handsome as that movie star Clark Gable. She was smitten with him, and if he hadn't been married—"

I dig my elbow into her ribs and clear my throat.

"I thought he was charming. I was impressed with his intelligence, his manners, and his devotion to his wife."

Jonathan nods approvingly. "I understand from a very good source he was a self-proclaimed, lifetime bachelor until meeting his wife. Pursued by duchesses, wealthy widows, and young ingenues, he resisted them all for the sake of his career in medicine and—you may not know this—also in law. His wife Alwine must be very special. It's a shame you didn't get to meet her."

"But why is he in Ecuador?" I ask.

"That's exactly what we shall discuss after dinner." He rings a small bell beside his plate, and here come the waiters again. One goes around refilling our glasses, and the other begins taking dinner orders.

* * *

Malone and Jonathan do most of the talking over dinner with Reno piping in with a side story or a humorous anecdote. They laugh good-naturedly, their heads huddled close. It's making Shifrah and me feel like fifth wheels. She isn't complaining, and I really believe her near collision with that wall of plaster changed her, along with Malone's overt concern for her safety.

I'm trying to figure out those strange glasses Jonathan's wearing. I'm guessing his eyes were damaged in the war. I've seen a man wearing pink lenses because of an eye disease, and Elmer Coates in Laredo wears amber-tinted glasses for some reason. I've never asked him why, but it has something to do with a car wreck. When dinner is cleared away, coffee served, and Shifrah and Jonathan are both smoking, I get brave enough to tell Jonathan I've never seen such colorful lenses before.

"Aren't they unusual? They change the color of everything." he says, smiling, and that was that. In a few minutes, he stubs out his cigarette and leans both elbows on the table. "If I have your permission, I'll now continue my story about David Diamond."

Shifrah says, "Go ahead. Too bad I wasn't invited into that spikey-roofed hut to meet him." She sends a semi-offended look in Malone's direction. "Now I suppose we're about to learn he's a very important person to this mission."

"Absolutely he is, and all of our contacts are important, Shifrah. I hope I can stay with your team long enough to discuss that further. As I mentioned earlier, David's story isn't pretty, but it's relevant to the purpose of the mission, and, as you saw for yourself, it has a good ending. David is living exactly where and how he wishes to live these days. Before I begin, would anyone care for a *digestif?*" Jonathan asks.

"This country boy wouldn't know a *dee-jes-teef* from a side of beef, Jonathan," Reno says. "Is it edible?"

"A *digestif* is an after-dinner drink such as brandy or cognac that supposedly aids digestion, Reno," Shifrah says.

Again, her level of sophistication is impressive. I give her a thumbs up.

"In that case, I'm just fine like I am."

"Anyone?" Jonathan asks, and the rest of us shake our heads.

"I'm still enjoying the champagne," Shifrah says.

"It is delightful, isn't it?" he says, smiling. "All right, to continue our story, David practiced as a medical doctor in Berlin under his long-time assumed name, Dietrich Detzer, until 1936. That was the year doctors of his religion were barred from practicing medicine in German institutions."

"Because of his religion? How stupid!" Shifrah says.

"I agree. Nevertheless, David relocated with thousands of others to Budapest, Hungary, to continue his medical and law practices. He found a rich cultural life there, but it wasn't perfect. Nowhere is perfect for people of certain religions or cultures, but, I am told, it was full of art and science and dreams. Scientists, artists, movie makers, craftsmen, authors… those were the people of Budapest."

"It's in terrible shape right now, but we saw lots of encouraging rebuilding," I say.

"You have to excuse her; she's nuts about history, art, and a million other things," Shifrah says, blowing smoke circles toward the ceiling.

"I enjoy history, too, Savannah, and I find it tragic what has happened to our world, especially in places like Budapest. So much has been lost. When David moved there, it was a different place for most of the war years until Hungary, an Axis member, fully aligned itself with Nazi Germany. The Nazis brought their usual antisemitism and discriminatory legislation against the Jewish people. If you enjoy allegory, I'll say the situation changed from gray to black beginning in March 1944.

"After the March occupation, severe persecution followed lightning fast. Restrictions. Rules. Citations. It wasn't long before apartments, businesses, and homes were confiscated. Literally stolen.

Hundreds of families, now homeless, were sent to the *Kistarcsa* transit camp. In another few months, Hungarian authorities ordered all Budapest Jews into designated buildings throughout the city, buildings marked with Stars of David."

Jonathan turns his gaze on Shifrah and me. "To be frank, I detest discussing war atrocities with civilians, especially those from the States who haven't been exposed to this kind of mayhem. Do I have your permission to continue?"

"Jonathan, Shifrah and I have been sheltered from the facts the whole time we've been gathering *retrieves.* We're adults. Whatever you say to help us understand the mission, we want to hear it, right, Shifrah?"

She doesn't answer, holds her empty glass toward Malone, who is sitting next to the bucket holding the chilled champagne.

Shifrah, you'd better say yes!

Malone hands her glass back to her. She sips and sets it down.

"Shifrah?" I say.

She sits up straight in her chair and fixes Jonathan with an eye lock. "Look, I didn't survive spears thrown at my derriere, riding a mule into an endless hole in the earth for hours and hours two days in a row, ruining all my fingernails pulling slimy river mussels off grotesque hooks, traveling in working-class wearing a drab uniform and old-woman shoes on a luxury liner, and barely missing being squashed by rubble in a wrecked castle to be too timid to hear what this is all about."

"Hot diggity, our little Shifrah has grown up on us, Malone!" Reno says, and the look on Malone's face I equate to a parent's pride when his kid wins a game. I pat her on the arm and wink my approval at her.

Jonathan smiles and nods. "Commendable indeed. You women have endured enough experiences on this mission to write a book, yes?"

We nod.

"Still, the truths of war are brutal, so I apologize in advance." He takes a long drink of water, dips his head toward us, which I take as an acknowledgment that we just signed up to hear what comes next. "The Nazis overtook Budapest in March 1944. Conditions continued to spiral downward. One travesty led to another, each one worse than the last.

Finally, more than twenty-five thousand Jewish residents from the suburbs of Budapest were herded into Auschwitz II-Birkenau's killing camp."

"Gads," Shifrah mutters under her breath toward me. "He wasn't kidding."

"You mean it went from the occupation to stealing all the residences and businesses to herding them into confinement, and then to sending thousands to killing camps in a few short months?"

"Affirmative, Savannah. Hungarian authorities stopped those deportations to Auschwitz in July of that same year, which saved some citizens, but not nearly enough. David had already been sent to Auschwitz II. I wonder, did any of you happen to see the tattoo on his arm?"

Malone and Reno nod.

"Tattoo?" I ask.

"You may not know about those tattoos, Savannah, but they were a large part of the captivity process for prisoners in camps. In this camp, Auschwitz II-Birkenau, prisoners selected to be sent to the gas chambers were not tattooed or registered. Anyone they chose to be a *work slave* was tattooed with a number. More than four hundred thousand serial numbers were assigned at the Auschwitz camps."

The dark thing I saw on the inside of David's arm was a concentration camp tattoo, something I barely knew existed.

"We are grateful that David was tattooed and positioned inside a special squad of prisoners known as the *Sonderkommando*. This squad had one horrendous purpose, and that was to dispose of the corpses of the murdered prisoners. They didn't kill them, just disposed of them. Sometimes, it was members of their own family."

The silence in the room is heavy.

"The *Sonderkommando* were given better food than the other prisoners. More rest, kept as isolated as possible. They were front-line witnesses to Hitler's mass murder of anyone he considered inferior human beings. He wanted to eliminate not only Jews, but *Roma,* people with physical abnormalities, anyone with handicaps or mental problems, Soviets, dissidents—all of them had to be eliminated to fit his psychopathic *cleansing* of the world.

"When it started to soak in that Germany might lose the plan for world domination, the killings increased—an eleventh-hour effort to hide the sins of their evil regime. A few members of the Birkenau *Sonderkommando* recorded their experiences in writing and buried their documents under the grounds of the crematoria. I have read them, and it's-it's rough."

"What's a crematoria?" Shifrah says.

"The place where they burned the bodies after they died or got killed," Reno says.

"Oh," she says, looking puzzled and distressed at the same time.

"With their human dignities ripped away, the Birkenau *Sonderkommando,* of which David was a part of, planned a rebellion. Certain female prisoners smuggled small amounts of gunpowder from the munitions factory in the camp for them. The plan was to blow up the gas chambers and the crematoria to cause a confused distraction, possibly leading to escaping.

"Unfortunately, their plan was thwarted. Word was passed along secret channels that the SS planned to eliminate most of the *Sonderkommando.* You see, human elimination was the only thing Hitler understood as he experienced defeat. An uprising broke out in the camp. A bloody, terrible revolt. More than two hundred and fifty prisoners were killed, another two hundred wounded. The women who aided in smuggling the explosives were executed. David was shot twice but managed to escape during the rebellion wearing an SS uniform."

"How on earth…" I manage to say through an almost closed throat.

"How? Determination. More than we can possibly imagine, Savannah, and, might we surmise *Providence* had a hand in this, as well?"

How I wish I had known all this when we met David.

"Fevered, injured, almost dead with infection and the after-effects of humiliation and horror as a prisoner, he was assisted in his journey to Ecuador by a network of courageous people and admitted to the hospital in Quito. That's where he met his future wife, Alwine.

"Did the Nazis destroy the entire Jewish population of Hungary?"

Jonathan blows out a noisy breath of air. "Well, when the Germans invaded, there was an estimated Jewish population in Hungary of 825,000. Between May and July, more than 434,000 were deported to Auschwitz, where most were killed upon arrival. In Budapest, many still lived in closed ghettos. If they didn't have protective papers—almost impossible to get—they also usually perished. As the war was ending, it's estimated at least twenty thousand more were shot along the banks of the Danube, many of their bodies simply tossed into the river. Hitler and his henchmen were vicious madmen during the last days."

"Jonathan, the Major, I mean Malone, may know this but he hasn't told me yet. Since David was sent to that camp in Poland, how did he keep the *key to the keys* safe while he was gone, and did he personally go back to Budapest to take it to Ecuador?" Reno says.

"That's another interesting story, Reno. A subject for next time, yes?"

"What next time?" Shifrah asks.

"Malone and I will be hashing out the answer to that while you relax and enjoy the rest of your evening."

"How do you know Malone?" Shifrah asks. "I mean, how did you meet?"

Silence.

"What branch of the military were you in?" I ask.

"Army."

"You have an accent. Where are you originally from?"

"And who is following us and why?" Shifrah asks.

Malone holds up a hand. "Okay, okay, that's sufficient. We'll meet in the hotel restaurant in the morning at 0800. You're free to do whatever you wish right now, but if you leave the hotel, take Reno with you. That's an order." He looks at his watch. "It's still early, and I hear the shops around the hotel stay open on the late side. See you at breakfast."

"Come on, Savannah, we've been dismissed," Shifrah says, a bit of her snobbish tone returning. Reno walks out with us. She asks me halfheartedly in the hotel lobby if I want to go shopping.

"I think I want to sit on our little patio and stare at the lights reflecting off the water. I need time to adjust and make sense of what I just heard."

"Reno, I'm with her. We're going to our room. No shopping this time."

"Roger that, Shif. You ladies change your mind, have 'em ring me up in the lounge or in my room. I'll come a'running."

We watch him walk away. Shifrah grabs my arm, turns a concerned face toward me. "Oh, Savannah, I've led such a sheltered life. I-I didn't know those awful things were going on, did you?"

"A little bit, but not to the extent I just heard. I guess we were too young to realize what was going on. I sure don't remember people talking much about it. I saw newscasts when I went to the movies, but it was always how we were winning the war or how we won the war, not about the mass killings and brutality we just heard about. You aren't the only one who's lived a sheltered life. It looks like most of us back home have, too. When I think of all the bombed buildings we've seen since we disembarked from the SS America, how the city of Budapest and the beautiful Buda Castle were in ruin, and-and hearing about the innocent people who did nothing wrong… well, it's hideous. How lucky were we to live in our own country?"

"I know, I know, and I have the creepiest feeling my mysterious past is catching up with me. I never bothered to think about it until now, but I'm suddenly so grateful I was adopted by Mommykins and Daddy when I was three years old. My gawd, I'm only now realizing, I mean, what do you suppose happened to my other family, to Daddy's brother and his wife, my mother? Where were they sent? Did they suffer? Um, Savannah… you do realize I'm Jewish, right?"

"Of course."

"You never said anything."

"Why should I? Remember at dinner on the ship I told you a baby has no choice of where it is born, who its parents are, how poor or rich they are, or anything else? Well, that's just how it is. I wouldn't care if you were cousin to a rooster and descended from a lost tribe of elves with pointy ears. You're you. That's all I care about."

"You're the greatest person, Savannah, my best and truest friend.

Almost like a teacher to me."

"That works both ways, dahling," I say, raising my chin parallel to the floor and assuming my best and newly-acquired snooty look."

We chuckle, relieved to claim a shred of humor after the terrible reality we heard in that private dining room. We join arms and walk to our room.

CHAPTER FORTY-NINE

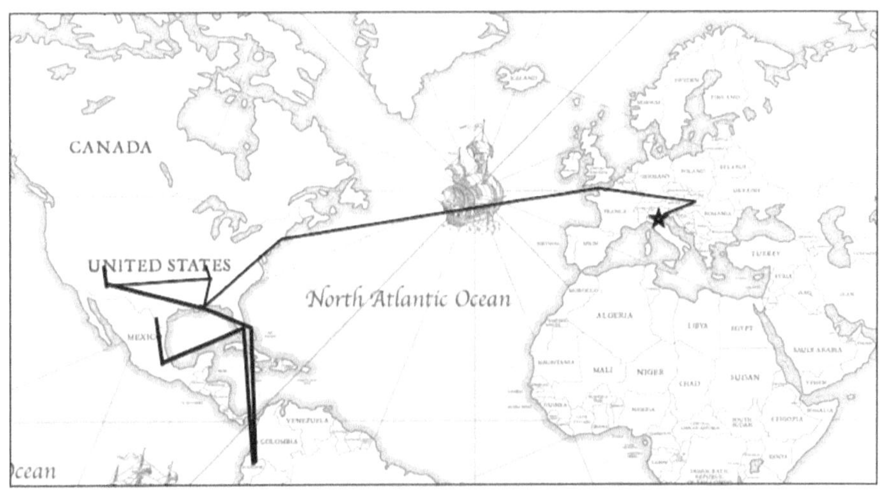

My eyes pop open to darkness broken by pale light seeping from a large square at the end of a room attached to where Shifrah and I are sleeping in twin beds. Where am I? I sit up in the bed and rub my face. Are we in France or Hungary or…? I swing my feet to the floor. Think. Think. Oh, yes, Venice, and the square across the room is light coming through the curtains covering the double French door entry to our patio overlooking the canal.

Why am I awake?

I don't know, but I'm not sleepy now. Perhaps leafing through our tourist pamphlets will help. I pad into the sitting room and curl up on the sofa. Shifra could sleep through a tornado, so it won't bother her if I turn on a light. My hand on the lamp knob, I see, from the corner of my eye, movement. Behind the curtains is a shadow. Is someone taking a shortcut through our private patio? The shadow is moving slightly but doesn't move away from the doors. I hear a scratching sound.

Someone's trying to break into our room!

I run back to the bedroom to use the phone beside my bed. My hands tremble as I dial the hotel front desk and ask in my lowest voice to be connected to Reno's room. He answers after the first ring.

"Reno, someone's breaking into our room!" I rasp.

"Patio or hallway?"

"Patio."

The phone cuts off. I put on my robe and cinch it tight against the impending danger. I retrieve the pistol from my purse and place it in the open drawer in the nightstand. I shake Shifrah awake. She moans, and I lean down and whisper in her ear, "Don't make any noise." She sits up, pushing her sleeping mask onto her forehead.

"Why are you bothering me?" she asks groggily.

"Shh!" I point toward the curtains. She squints, sees the shadow outside, gasps.

I cover her mouth with my hand and whisper, "Reno's on his way. Here's your robe."

She grabs my arm. "Oh, my God, Savannah, it's the killer!"

"Hush! Put your robe on, and I'll—"

The shadow melts quickly away. I race to peek through the curtains. Can't see. I open one side of the patio doors and stick my head out. Reno is chasing a wiry man in dark clothing. He jumps into a waiting boat. I hear the motor as the boat disappears down the waterway. Reno stands looking after them, turns and jogs toward the patio as I fling open both doors. An unpleasant, almost sewer-like odor seems to be coming from the canals.

"That danged scoundrel had it all planned out," Reno says. "Had someone waiting in a motorboat. By the looks of him and how fast he runs, I'm thinking he's the same fella who dumped that plaster on us in the castle. Get inside and lock those doors, hon. Be back in two shakes with Malone. Don't open your doors to anyone but us, you hear?"

"Don't worry. I won't," I mumble, and I'm surprised at how shaky my voice sounds.

I lock the patio doors, inform Shifrah we're about to have a spur-of-the-moment meeting with Reno and Malone, and watch her skedaddle off to the bathroom to fix her hair and whatever else she thinks should look perfect after being terrorized in the middle of the night. I put my pistol back in my purse.

* * *

"One good thing is Mr. A should know exactly who his traitor is now," Malone says. His legs are doubled up like a crane at a child's tea party as he sits in one of the low-slung lounging chairs in our suite's sitting room. He's fully dressed, not a hair out of place. I asked him about it when he first came to our room and he said he'd been burning the midnight oil with Jonathan and hadn't been to bed yet.

"You know, I had misgivings about putting you girls on this bottom floor, but Shifrah's foot…" He takes a big breath, shakes his head as he exhales. "Damn."

I wait for Shifrah to tell him we're not *girls,* but she doesn't. She's sitting on the floor not far from his legs. It's easy to see how much he represents safety to her—a daddy's girl through and through.

"Did anyone notice the canal smelling, well, kind of awful tonight?" I say.

"Happens at low tide," Malone says.

"Why?"

"Just the way it is. Nice at high tide; not so nice at low tide. Also depends on the weather and wind. Anyway, Savannah, you have your, uh, your security measures intact?"

"You bet, Malone."

"What security measures?" Shifrah asks.

Malone ignores her question. Stands up. "Okay, Reno'll be camping out down here on the couch, so get some shuteye." He checks his watch. "It's quarter to one already. First light, we check out of here."

"And go where?" I ask.

"We'll see."

"Where will you be while Reno's here?" Shifrah asks.

"In my room making phone calls. I'll finish the night, what's left of it, snoozing on the floor down here."

"The floor?" Shifrah says, her eyes wide.

"Nah, I'll sleep on the floor. The old man should get the couch," Reno says.

"Thirty-three is an old man?" Malone says.

Reno dons his teasing face, says, "Oh yeah, you remember that field tactic drill—"

"Stop joking, you guys. This is serious. Savannah and I almost got kidnapped or-or killed."

"Right, which means we should be told what's going on here," I say.

Malone stands up. "Soon. Very soon."

"Before you go, I have a question about Jonathan's eyes. Were they injured in the war?" I say.

"You might say that," he says, departing, leaving Shifrah and me staring at the closed door.

"Uh, ladies, any chance of borrowing a fancy nightie gown?"

Our heads whip to the side and there's Reno smiling that luxurious smile of mischief that defines him more than anything else.

CHAPTER FIFTY

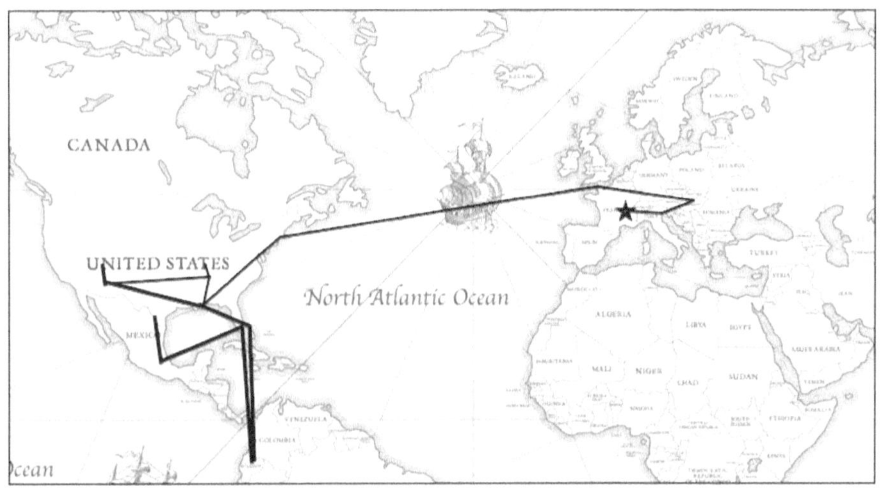

I suppose it's normal when a group has been through experiences together for any length of time, they might feel a little intruded upon if someone else joins them. Jonathan, we were informed over breakfast at another hotel than where we were staying here in Venice, is riding with us by train as we return to France. At least, part of the way, Malone said.

We're standing under bright sunshine but cold air here on the platform at the Venice Santa Lucia Train Station waiting to board, and I think we're all feeling, at least Shifrah and I, somewhat strange about, well, everything. Knowing someone is definitely out to get us and hearing brutal truths about the war… it's a lot. Shifrah is dealing with the unknown ghosts of her past, and I haven't made up my mind what I'm going to do with the rest of my life. The saving side of it is that we're approaching the retrieval of our fifth *retrieve*—always exciting—and Malone still hasn't told us where the sixth and final one is.

Shifrah has retreated into a kind of fragile silence. She looks like a movie starlet standing quietly in her winter-white sheath, deep green high heels and purse, and full-length coat in the same green as her accessories, which she calls *hunter green.* It's her first time back in heels since her foot was injured, and if she's in pain, she's not showing it. *Anything for beauty* is Shifrah's motto every day of her life.

I could tell Malone felt bad telling her we had to leave Venice pronto, no time for *gondola* rides or sightseeing. The disappointment on her face made me promise her we'd come right back here as soon as the mission was over and ride on every waterway in the city.

"Promise?" she'd asked halfheartedly, and I crossed my heart.

Over breakfast, Malone said, "Things are moving fast. We have a hefty train ride to Dijon where we spend one night in the Terminus Hotel for the, uh, the surprise I mentioned. Then, we take a train to Luxembourg. After that..." he glances at Reno. "...Berlin."

"Luxembourg? Berlin? Why are we going to Germany?" Shifrah asks.

"To meet with Mr. A for the final steps in completing our mission."

"Is Luxembourg the new place y'all came up with last night?" I ask.

"It is. Our late decision means the contact for the sixth *retrieve* has to work out some details before meeting us there. Thankfully, we've finalized plans for our other contact with the fifth *retrieve* to meet us at the hotel in Dijon. In fact, as we travel there, so is she."

"She? Where is she coming from?"

"Originally, Florida."

"Why didn't we get the *retrieve* the two times we were in Florida?"

"She was visiting her sister in California both times, goes for three or four months every year. Anyway, the rest of our plans have been scrambled after that episode last night. The traitor has been pinpointed, but Mr. A is laying a trap to be positive. Serious business."

"Who's meeting us in Dijon with the *retrieve?*"

"The widow of the original person possessing it."

"And who—"

Malone sighs and I see the weariness in his face. I act like I'm zipping my lips, and he smiles and nods.

A dark cloud has appeared and graced us with rain spatters. Shifrah and I retreat under the overhang while they finish loading the passenger luggage on the train. She hasn't been the same since the accident in the Buda Castle, and the changes are quite striking. She still emits a delicate air, but her sarcasm and streak of conceit—or was it entitlement?—have mostly faded away.

Reno is still himself, ornery, capable, and so good looking he creates a female stir wherever we go. Of course, he teases us that he's secretly fighting men off Shifrah and me *left and right*. "What? You don't see me engaging in hand-to-hand combat behind your backs? Well, you just aren't looking close enough. I gotta spin my head in a complete circle to watch for trouble, and I disappear every little bit behind a corner to give those rubber neckers a thrashing," he jokes.

Have I changed? One thing I've thought about a lot since leaving Laredo is that the Dixie Diner will always mean the world to me, especially Tony, Maria, and my regulars, but I am not sure I'd be happy simply owning a small diner in a small town. What shall I do with my life, then? I don't know yet, but I do know I'm anxious to find out what all those keys unlock.

I fix a contemplative stare at the train stopped in front of us, letting myself get caught up in the dramatic sounds of train whistles, screeches of steel upon steel, the scratchy loudspeaker announcements, and the tangible excitement on the faces of the travelers.

* * *

"Mind if I join you?" Jonathan asks in the dining car of the train.

"Please, do," Shifrah says. "I have many questions I want to ask you."

"And I may have a few answers for you."

"In that case, sit down quickly," I say, smiling.

He looks around. "Malone and Reno will be here in a few minutes.

What do you say we move to that one round table over there before someone else claims it? I think we'll all fit better."

Malone and Reno show up as the waiter passes out menus. "Just strong coffee for me," Jonathan says.

"Aren't you eating?" Malone asks.

"I have a dinner I have to attend."

On the train?

After we order, Jonathan places his elbows on the table the same way he did in the restaurant's private dining room. His purple lens glasses are a bit of a distraction, but he can't help what happened to him in the war.

"I heard about the intruder last night," he says.

Shifrah groans. "It was terrifying."

"I can imagine. That's why we've made sure you've been surrounded by the best of the best during the mission."

I know he means Malone and Reno, and I agree. I say, "It's still a little unsettling knowing we've been watched from the time we left Texas and crossed the bridge into *Nuevo Laredo*, and then this second guy—"

"Second guy?"

"The first man who followed us from *Nuevo Laredo* onto the SS America and to France is not the same man in the Buda Castle or the one who ran down the waterway and jumped into the boat."

"Don't even bother asking them how they know that kind of stuff, Jonathan. Trust me, they could spot a speck on a frog's spotted back with him jumpin' across the pond at midnight," Reno says.

"Reno and I think the man in the castle is the same man who tried to break into our room last night, right, Reno?" I say.

"He sure could run like that last fella," Reno says. Seemed about the right size, too."

"I see," Jonathan says. "Let me comfort you with this… it's doubtful there will be any more attempts to-to…"

"To what? Is someone trying to deter us or are they trying to murder us?" Shifrah asks.

Jonathan is quiet a few seconds. "I'm not sure I have the exact answer to that, Shifrah, but I don't want you to worry, okay? Further, all your questions will soon be answered."

The waiter arrives with our beverages. When he's finished serving, Jonathan says, "I'll start where I concluded last time and answer Reno's question. You see, when David left Berlin to live in Budapest, he had two crucial items in his possession—the *key to the keys* and one of the seven keys that fit into the *key to the keys.* As the Germans moved in, he saw the writing on the wall. Unable to leave the city, and fearing the worse, he handed the two items over to a trusted colleague for safekeeping, a Swedish professor of medicine he knew from attending medical school in Berlin. They had remained in close contact from those early days, and that colleague is the main reason David chose to relocate to Budapest in 1936."

"Wasn't his friend fearful of the Nazis, too?" Shifrah asks.

"He wasn't of the same religion as David."

"And he didn't care if David was, um, Jewish?"

"A great question. What I have found is most learned men of science are interested in a person's mind, his expertise, and his character. They don't usually care about his race, his religion, or his creed. That's the best part, the human part, of science, in my opinion.

"David's friend, the professor, was, is… a loyal friend, and he kept the *key to the keys* and the key safe when David was sent to Auschwitz, never knowing why they existed or what they were for. David had written sealed instructions on how to return them to-to, uh, Mr. A or his counterpart if he never returned."

"Savannah and I don't know what that *key to the keys* or the keys are for. Why not enlighten us right now?"

"Shifrah," Malone says in a low voice. "Let the man talk."

"At least tell us how the professor managed to keep those things hidden in a city filled with crazy Nazis turning the town upside down and the-the bombs and all that."

"As a point of interest, when you reside in a town full of caves and caverns, it's easy to hide things. However, the professor was not on any endangered list, he being Swedish and not connected to any political parties, so he still had the freedom to be a human, unlike so many others. Here's another revelation you might enjoy, Shifrah. You remember the elderly gentleman, your contact at the Buda Castle?"

"Who could forget Mr. Wallenberg?" she says.

"He's the one I mentioned—the retired professor of medicine and David's truest friend from medical school."

"Really? I thought he was a building manager or a museum curator," I say.

"He retired from medicine and teaching long ago, but he wears many titles."

"No wonder I felt like I was in a college lecture hall when he *talked* about the value of history. Of course, he's a professor!"

"I'm wondering why David didn't go ahead and get the *retrieve* when he went back to fetch the *key to the keys,*" Reno says.

"An interesting story about that, Reno. A little history first, if you don't mind."

"Savannah sure won't mind, will you, Savannah?"

"Not in the least."

"Well, maybe I mind because you're telling too many stories and not giving us any real answers," Shifrah says.

Jonathan sends a tolerant smile in her direction, continues talking. "Hugo Wallenberg, your contact at the castle, is a first cousin, a few times removed, to a great wartime hero, Raoul Wallenberg, the Swedish diplomat whose work with the War Refugee Board in Budapest saved countless Hungarian Jews. Raoul Wallenberg distributed hundreds of *certificates of protection* to the Jews. Do you remember I mentioned those certificates yesterday, how they saved many but were not plentiful enough to save multitudes? Raoul Wallenberg is a great and righteous man who saved many people from death."

"And we need to know that because…?" Shifrah says.

"You'll find out in a minute. After David escaped Auschwitz and made his way to Ecuador, we got word he was alive and preparing to return to Hungary to retrieve the items he left with Hugo Wallenberg, his friend and former professor. He was adamant about never returning to Germany. Many expatriates of Germany feel that way, and it's understandable, of course. His injuries were extensive, but when he was able, he returned to Budapest. Hugo, the distant cousin of Raoul, was recovering in the hospital from an emergency appendectomy. At the hospital, he told David where in his home to find the *key to the keys,* and he explained he didn't have the key because of an oddity."

"An oddity?" Shifrah says.

"Yes, Hugo's daughter and young son were at his home on vacation from South Africa when Hugo was taken to the hospital with a ruptured appendix. The child was a bit of a snoop, as some children are, and he plundered his grandfather's bedroom. He found the key behind a slightly loose stone in the fireplace and became so fascinated with it, he took it home with him. His mother didn't discover it until he—"

"The kid stole the *retrieve?*" Shifrah exclaims.

"We prefer to think of it as a childish prank rather than a theft. Hugo's daughter realized the importance of keeping the key safe after her father became upset when she called him and told him of his grandson's folly. True to her word, she brought the key back to her father when she returned for another vacation a year later, too late for David to get it when he came from Ecuador to pick up the *key to the keys.* Odd set of circumstances, for sure. We're grateful to have recovered it at all. So, that's how Hugo had the key.

"Shifrah, I wanted to explain about Raoul so you would know all the connections I'm about to tell you. This next one might be a little shocking."

She puts her hand over her heart. "What is it?"

"Hugo Wallenberg, the man you met in Budapest, Raoul's distant cousin, is also related to the Hilda of your childhood."

"Hilda? Our Hilda?" Shifrah closes her eyes and puts a hand on her forehead. "What are you saying?"

"Hilda is Hugo Wallenberg's sister, so she is also a cousin to Raoul Wallenberg. Hilda and her former husband moved from Sweden to the United States in the early1930s. Years later, she was living in New York City and needed a job. I believe her husband had left her."

"No, that's not what happened. She threw him out for-for…" Shifrah looks at me, "…for shah-ting on her."

"For what?" Malone says.

"Cheating. He cheated on her." We share a look remembering the story of how Hilda's pronunciation of *cheating* shocked Shifrah's mother.

"Through our interconnections and communications, we learned of Hilda's situation and helped her obtain employment with your parents. I believe you were about thirteen when she was employed in your home."

"But that means my parents and Hilda, they know of Mr. A?"

"That's right."

"For Pete's sake, why didn't I know any of this when I met Mr. Wallenberg, Malone?"

"It wasn't the right time," he says.

"No one tells me anything! Why didn't Mommykins tell me? If my parents know Mr. A, then Mr. A must have known my other father, and…" She lights a cigarette, takes a sip of her tea. "This isn't fair. You know that, right?" she says, staring a hole in Malone.

He nods, looks innocent.

Shifrah draws hard on her cigarette, blows out angry puffs. Sighs. "So, Hilda and Hugo are siblings," she mumbles. "No wonder he felt so familiar to me. Would it have hurt to tell me that before?"

Jonathan drains his coffee cup and stands. "I understand this is hazy information, Shifrah, but soon, everything will be clear. If you will excuse me, I must gather my things to get off at the next stop. Enjoy your time in Dijon and Luxembourg. Remember it's cold there and in Berlin this time of year. Please take care to bring adequate clothing."

"Aren't you coming with us to Dijon?" I ask.

"Unfortunately, my schedule doesn't allow it, Savannah."

"But—" Shifrah sputters.

"Until we meet again, I bid you all goodbye." With a gracious smile, he exits the dining car, leaving Shifrah and me to our jumbled thoughts.

Malone coughs. "Uh, ladies, a little change of subject. Jonathan left this for you. It's in French and English both. Mr. A sent it." He reaches inside his leather briefcase and pulls out a book, hands it to Shifrah. She reads the front, hands it to me. Her expression is unreadable, almost blank.

"It's a tour guide book to French cities, Savannah," she says. "Right up your alley."

"From Mr. A?"

"Affirmative. There's a guide to Dijon in there, too. Since we get one free day there, that guide might come in handy. Shifrah, you okay?" Malone says.

"I'm tired. I'm going to the passenger car and close my eyes for a while."

"You haven't eaten," I say.

"I'm not hungry. See if they can wrap it up for me, or… no, never mind. You all share it, okay?" She stands. Both Malone and Reno politely stand until she walks away. We watch as she opens the door of the dining car and disappears through the vestibule.

Malone steeples his fingers, holding them in the air. "I knew the conclusion of this mission would be tough on her, Reno. It's not nearly over, either."

"You're right, sir."

"Well, if that's the case, why not let her know the truth?" I say.

"I have orders to follow."

"I was kind of wondering how you know you can trust Jonathan."

"He can be trusted because he's the reason I'm on this mission."

"He is?"

"That's right. He and I go way back. All the way back to the war."

CHAPTER FIFTY-ONE

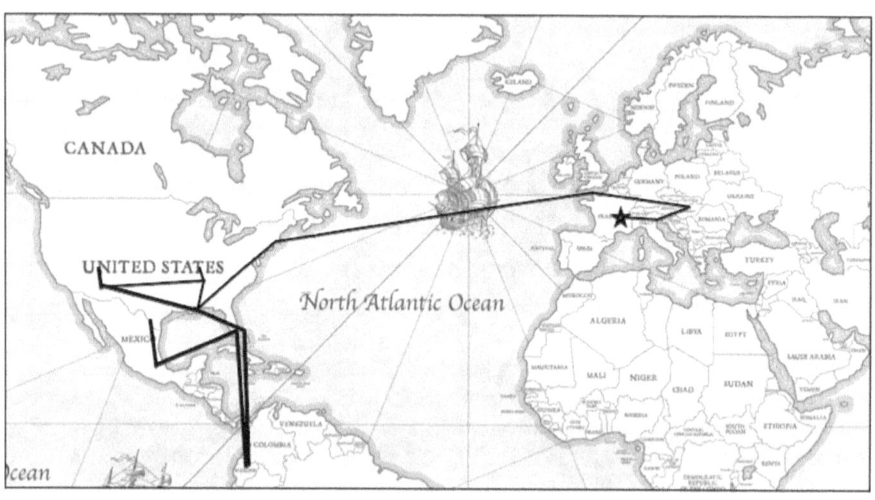

Entering the lobby of the Terminus Hotel in Dijon, Shifrah aims for the concierge desk. We follow like a string of cutout paper dolls attached to her back. She asks, I presume, if they serve wine in the rooms.

"Oui, mademoiselle."

"Le service en chambre, oui?"

"Oui, mademoiselle, aussi par les robinets des chambres."

"Es-tu sûr?" Shifrah asks.

The concierge smiles. "*Très populaire, mademoiselle, surtout avec des stars de cinema comme vous!*"

"I'm beginning to make out some of what you said, Shifrah. French and Spanish have some similarities," I say.

"Well, I sure can't. What're y'all talking about, Shif?"

"He said it's true—wine is available through faucets in our bedrooms, and… he thinks I'm a movie star. Malone, are you responsible for this?"

"I can't take credit for anything but getting you here. Mr. A thought you and Savannah were due for a nice surprise long about now. They started this, uh, this wine thing a few weeks ago, December first, but we've known about it for a while. I told Savannah and Reno about it in Birmingham, but they didn't believe me either."

"Yeah, I kinda thought a screw or two had popped out of your noggin when you told us," Reno said.

Shifrah's lit-up face right now is the first "sign of life" I've seen on it since Jonathan told us yesterday that Hilda and Hugo were sister and brother. I'm guessing hearing Jonathan's sordid war details about David and then realizing she's personally connected to the reality of our mission has silenced her into deep thought.

I've been thinking a lot, too. Obviously, Shifrah was sent to live with her uncle and aunt in New York to keep her safe from a world gone mad. Thinking about what must have happened to her real parents and how difficult it had to be for them to part with her must be painful. She hasn't wanted to talk about it, which is fine. Some things are too private to speak out loud, and I understand that more than I probably should.

Coming here to Dijon was a lifesaver, I think, for all of us. When Malone told Shifrah in the car from the train station that red and white wines are pumped right into the rooms in the hotel where we had reservations, she said, "That's the silliest thing I've ever heard, Malone. You must think I'm simple-minded or totally naïve to believe such nonsense."

"Nah, he just thinks we all fell off the turnip truck," Reno said.

"Turnip truck?"

"It's a country saying, Shifrah. Pay this mischievous man no mind at all," I told her, nodding toward Reno.

Now, we know Malone wasn't kidding. Only in Europe, I suppose, where wine is equal to water. It seems crazy, but *es lo que es*. I feel our serious moods lifting as we stand here in the lobby.

"I guess we better get checked in so we can taste this crazy French idea for ourselves," Malone says. "Can I trust you two to imbibe conservatively enough to meet us for dinner in two hours at 1700?"

"Don't worry about me. No matter how many times Shifrah insists I taste her wine, I don't care for it," I say.

"I, on the other hand, promise nothing," Shifrah says, but she's smiling, and it's sure nice to see it.

Shifrah taste-tests both the red and white wine as soon as we get to our hotel room. "It's certainly not a *Giacomo Conterno Monfortino,* but it's a fun idea, and for free, it's not bad," she declares.

"I'll stick to my Shirley Temples," I say, ignoring her eye roll.

Not long after we're seated in the restaurant this evening, Malone is paged. When he returns, he's accompanying a sweet-faced woman I guess to be in her sixties. Malone introduces her as Chana Levy as Reno rises from his seat.

"Please be seated, young man," she says, all smiles, in a lilting accent. Reno introduces himself, Shifrah, and me and waits for her to sit down before he takes his chair. I have to admit that country boy has exquisite manners.

"Chana is on an ocean cruise, but we arranged to have her meet us here in Dijon. It's been a crazy mess," Malone says, rolling his eyes toward Chana as the two of them share a chuckle. "At one point, we were scheduled to pick up the *retrieve* from her in Florida, but things happened, and we shuffled and reshuffled until we worked it out."

"You're currently on a cruise? Will you be able to join your fellow passengers again?" Shifrah asks.

Chana giggles, her eyes shining. "Oh, Malone, he's such a *mensch!* He worked things out for me to rejoin my group in Southampton. Of course, my two sons will be attending the party—"

"Would you care to order a drink, Chana?" Malone says, louder than usual.

Chana looks surprised for a second, then nods. "Oh, yes, now I remember, Malone. Yes, I'll have some Schnapps, please."

Hmm, Malone stopped her from telling us something. What was it? Maybe she'll let something slip later.

Chana, as she insists we call her, is charming and talkative during dinner. While we're waiting for dessert, she takes a small velvet pouch from her purse. She opens it, pulls out a key, and holds it up for us to see.

"It's gorgeous," Shifrah says, holding out her hand. "May I see it?"

Chana places it in Shifrah's outstretched hand, doesn't let go, "Shifrah, I pray you find peace with every portion of your life," she says.

Shifrah looks puzzled. "I, um, thank you. I hope you do, too."

"I only wish my Jankel was here to meet you."

"Jankel?"

"My late husband, darling. He would find you enchanting." Chana glances at Malone, who is clearing his throat loudly. She smiles, raises her shoulders, and puts a hand in front of her mouth, letting go of the key with her other hand. "I beg your tolerance. I do chatter on sometimes."

But not nearly enough!

Shifrah examines the key, running her finger over the dove holding an olive branch in its beak at the end of the key. She glances at me, and I feel like I know what she's thinking; that is, *why would this contact's deceased husband love to have met me?*

* * *

On our second and last night in Dijon, a crazy thought hits me just as I'm falling asleep. Maybe I'm not thinking straight, or perhaps I'm overstimulated. Who wouldn't be after seeing historical arches, gates, and ancient churches like the Saint-Michael Church of Dijon, the one with the sculptures carved into the outside arches? Inside that church, I felt like an ant crawling beneath the tall arched walls. The Palace of the Dukes housed so much historical fodder, I almost became overwhelmed, especially inside the *Musee des Beaux-Arts* with its collections of art and antiquities.

With our limited time, we had to choose which things to go see, predetermined from our new tour guide book from Mr. A, and whether we would be walking or taking taxis. I know one thing. I'm coming back to Dijon, Paris, and Venice when I'm not on someone else's timetable so I can see everything there is to see.

Why am I so restless tonight? I search for the bag of macarons I bought this afternoon and help myself to one, then sit in the chair across the room and look out the window at the fading lights of Dijon. Today, we walked, rode, pointed, and gasped through museums, courtyards, and stores. Well, Reno and I did. It turns out, he enjoys history and geography, a fact I didn't know until today. Shifrah and Malone mostly waited for us by sitting on the numerous benches placed throughout the city, on the edge of a fountain, or on a parapet as Reno and I listened to the plentiful guides give details of each place. I noticed Shifrah and Malone conversing and laughing a lot, and it was a pleasant sight.

Interspersed with our sightseeing was shopping and more shopping so we, as Shifrah, said, could "refresh our wardrobes." The men stuck to us like glue, heads swiveling this way and that. I asked Malone if they were expecting trouble, and he said no, they were merely erring on the side of caution. They were so attentive, they followed us into a dress shop and made themselves comfortable in the two chairs outside the dressing area.

"What are you guys doing?" Shifrah asked.

"Getting ready for the fashion show," Reno said, grinning.

"Out!"

"What?"

"You heard me, out! We're not models on a runway. We don't want any men around when we step out here to see ourselves in the full-length mirrors."

"But—"

"Come on, Reno. We can keep an eye on things right outside the door. I need a cup of coffee anyway," Malone said.

Shifrah shuffled us back to the hotel by three o'clock to partake in a special Burgundy wine-tasting and cheese class. Accompanying the cheeses were little white fluted bowls Shifrah called *ramequins* filled with the world-famous mustard Dijon is known for.

I wish I cared for wine, but I don't. Shifrah says it's an *acquired taste,* but I don't know about that. What I do love are all the cheeses we tasted, especially dipped in a little bit of Dijon mustard and eaten with flavorful squares of bread. I can't pronounce the French names of the cheeses we sampled, but one was called Monk's cheese. Those made from goat's milk were different from any I'm used to, and I wondered what my rancher regulars at the Dixie would think of me eating goat cheese. They'd probably laugh me out of the diner.

Speaking of my other world, I mailed a slew of postcards to everyone from the hotel in Venice, so at least they know I'm alive. My world back in Laredo, Texas, seems like a dream now, and this one feels real. What does that say for my future?

Anyway, if I don't quit rehashing all we saw and did in Dijon, I'll never get to sleep. Shifrah and I are packed to leave for Luxembourg in the morning, and we're scheduled to meet Mr. A in a matter of days. With all that said, exhausted or not, an idea is playing around the edges of my mind. If I were to let myself concentrate on it, I'd be up all night, and that's just not acceptable.

The Bulls of Bashan

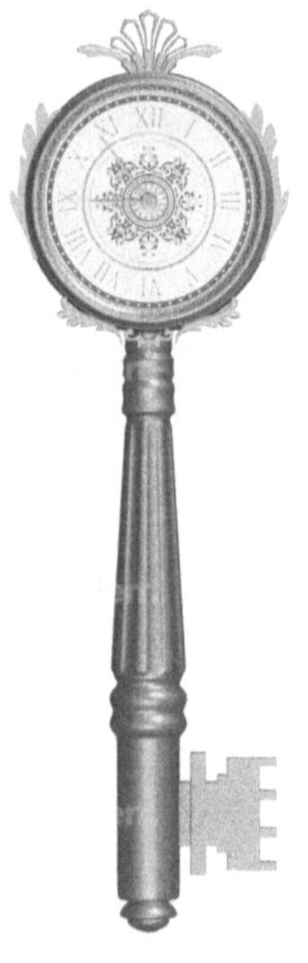

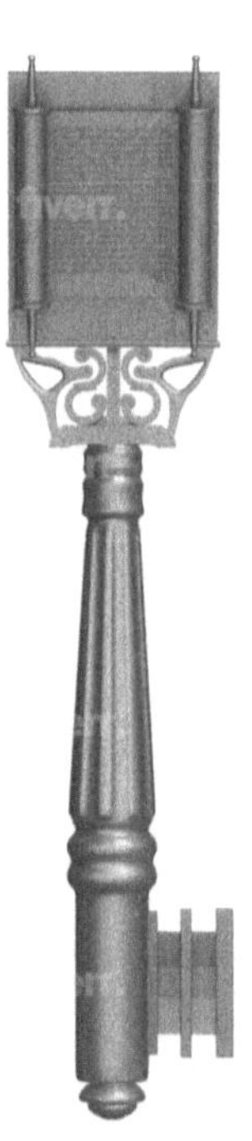

CHAPTER FIFTY-TWO

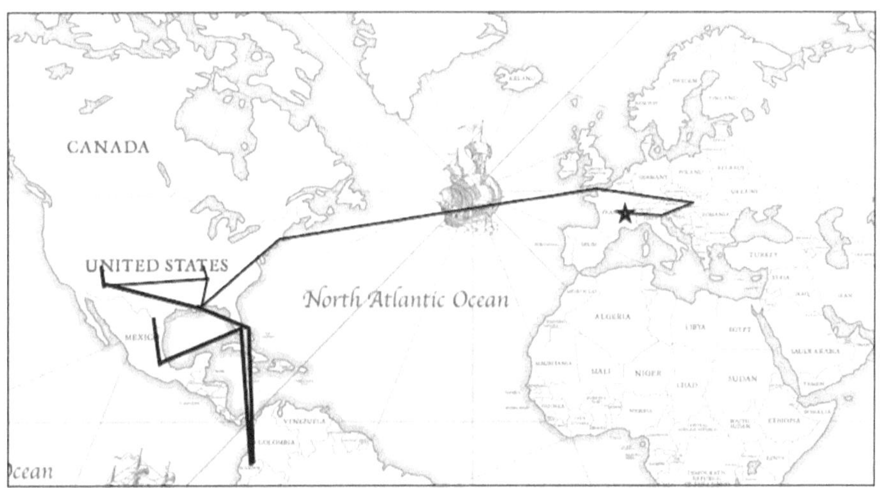

Travelers seem enshrouded in that special magical air surrounding people in the last stretch before Christmas. The frosty air, the excitement of nearing the end of our mystery mission, and Christmas decorations everywhere we look are intoxicating. Our beautiful new clothes, including new coats with matching gloves and hats, have Shifrah and me high stepping, or, I should say "high clicking," in our high heels through the invigorating cold air outside the train station. I wouldn't have believed how much I've grown to love shopping and dressing up, but it's true. Shifrah's fashion obsession has rubbed off on me.

Boarding the train, Malone says, "As soon as you two are 'squared away,' meet us in the dining car for a status report on the peculiar political protocol of East and West Berlin."

Shifrah laughs. "Sure, we'll do that as soon as we understand what you said."

"Just a little history lesson. It's important."

Making our way to the dining car, she says, "Why do we have to hear a history lesson when I'm in such a festive mood?"

I shrug nonchalantly, but secretly, I'm excited.

We join the men and exchange small talk until the conductor takes our tickets and a waiter brings menus. It's ten in the morning, we had croissants and coffee at the hotel, and the only thing that sounds appetizing to me is a glass of fruit juice. My order causes everyone to order the same thing.

"After the war—" Malone begins.

"Must you discuss that horrid war so early in the morning?" Shifrah moans.

He shrugs. "You'll appreciate having some background when we get to Berlin the day after tomorrow. As I was saying, when the war ended, the Soviets got control of the Eastern parts of Germany. Our allies, that is, France and Great Britian, along with the United States, now occupy the Western parts of Germany. Whether the citizens want it or not, the Soviets have installed communism in East Germany. Conversely, West Germany is being rebuilt as a capitalist democracy."

"Why do we have to know this?" Shifrah asks.

"Because it's important for you understand some of the elements we're dealing with in Berlin. Thank God that Olympic Stadium is in West Berlin with the Britons in charge or we'd have a hell, uh, a heck of a job finishing up our mission."

"Stadium? Did you say stadium, Malone?"

"I did."

"We're going to a stadium?"

"Very likely."

Shifrah pulls her cigarette case from her purse, places it on the table in front of us. "First, one of our *retrieves* has a bull on the end of it, and now you say we're going to a stadium—two things etched on my cigarette case. Is this the moment you give me some well-deserved answers?"

"You have no idea how many times I've wanted to tell you things, but it's not for me to say. Just understand that over the last eight years, searches were endlessly conducted, countless strings were pulled, palms greased, years of tracking, and multitudes of disappointments on the road to making this mission, our mission, viable. We aren't the only ones in this, not even close, so I need you to hang tight a while longer, Shifrah."

"All right, Malone," she says in a soft tone, and Reno and I exchange surprised glances.

Shifrah calling "calf rope" that easily?

Malone drinks his juice, scoots the glass aside. "The city of Berlin is divided just as is the country of Germany. Berlin represents the dichotomy of a country taken over and split by two opposite factions. One side, the West side, is still called Germany, and the other side has been renamed the German Democratic Republic—a real joke naming themselves anything with the word *democratic* in it, because it's far from that. There are a lot of disgruntled people being governed by that Socialist Unity Party.

"What is a Socialist Unity Party?" I ask.

"That's what they call their government on the East side. Their dire working conditions, restrictions, and suppression of personal interests is causing general unrest. I see you're yawning, Shifrah." He smiles a patient smile. "It's true you don't *have* to know this, but it's better to be cognizant of how life is for the residents there. We Americans have no idea what it's like to live under communist rule, or how it would feel if they, say… divided New York City into two cities and one was ruled by a communist regime."

"That isn't even a credible comparison, Malone. That would never happen in our country."

"Aren't we lucky then? Others haven't been so fortunate. Berlin was savaged during the war, and one side, at least, is slowly poking its head out of the mess and trying to rebuild. People by the millions were homeless, their fortunes and families ruined. We've never had to run for our lives into bomb shelters, watched our families dying, stand all day in a bread line—"

She holds up a hand. "You're right. I'll try to be more understanding."

Is this the same Shifrah I know?

"What I don't understand is why they, the German citizens, didn't oust that monster before he ruined everything. Didn't they see or care about what was happening all around them?"

Malone nods. "A valid point, Savannah. The way I see it, sometimes a ripple slowly becomes a wave, then a bigger wave, and before you realize it, it's turned into an uncontrollable tidal wave. More definitely could and should have been done, and history will reveal the whole sordid picture in time. I'm just saying we shouldn't judge everyone by one yardstick. Germany is like a wounded animal right now. It's important not to throw the baby out with the bathwater."

"Which happens to be a German idiom from way back," Reno says, and we all stare open-mouthed at him. He grins. "One of my grannies is German. Want to hear that little ditty in German?"

"You're kidding, aren't you, Reno?" Shifrah says.

"Schutten sie das baby nicht mit dem bade aus."

The loud clickity-clack of the wheels on the rails melts into the train's lonesome whistle as Shifrah and I gape at Reno for at least half a minute. "Did you know Reno speaks German?" I finally ask Malone.

"Ja," he says, and we all laugh.

"Aw, shoot, I don't speak it fluently, but I know enough to get us a place to sleep and some chow if no one speaks English. Probably won't ever be necessary. Y'all notice how everyone speaks lots of languages here in Europe?"

"I've noticed, and I don't understand why we aren't taught more languages in our schools," I say.

"Me neither. Course, I do speak English, a smattering of German, and real good *hillbilly*."

"Savanah, too! She can switch from her sophisticated persona to a country person just like that," Shifrah says, snapping her fingers.

"Country person? You mean a country bumpkin, don't you?" I ask

Malone shifts his position and clears his throat, which means it's time to get serious again. "Okay, we'll be in Berlin the day after tomorrow. Jonathan is meeting us at the station and taking us to our hotel. In the meantime, we meet our contact at the hotel in Luxembourg. I hear Luxembourg has mighty good *Öennenzop* and regional beer and wine."

"What's *Öennenzop?"* I ask.

"Onion soup."

"You'll love it, Savannah. It usually has a crust on top, and it's served with cheese toast." Shifrah says. "So, Malone, when do we meet Mr. A?"

"Two days."

CHAPTER FIFTY-THREE

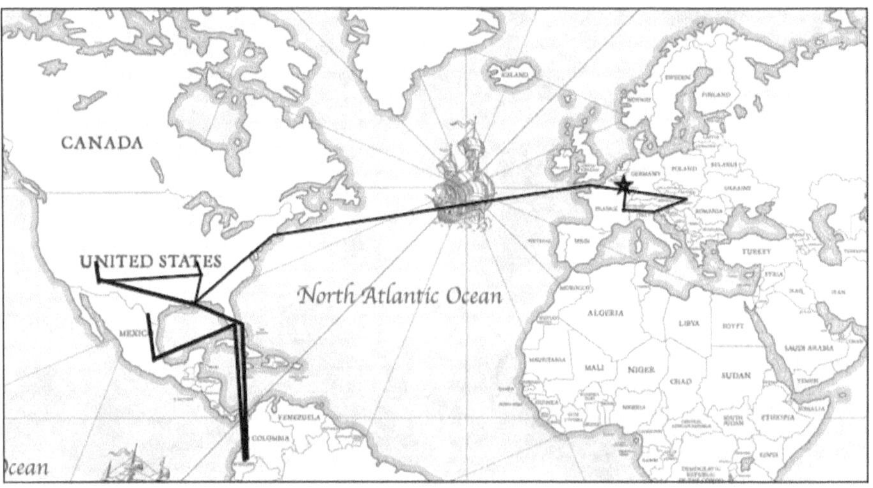

Staring longingly at the water, I say, "Darn it, Shifrah, we should have bought swimming suits and caps when we were in Phoenix."

She gives me a look that I know means *I can't go swimming with scars,* and to that, I reply with my own look, *nonsense!* She sighs.

"How did you find this unusual place, Malone?" she asks, changing the subject of our silent conversation.

"There was a lot of damage to Luxembourg during the war. When I heard about them building this place to help revive the tourist trade and bring in more funds, I figured why not be comfortable while we're here," he says.

We arrived in Luxembourg in the late afternoon and checked into a hotel that had Shifrah and me shaking our heads in disbelief—a newly built Moroccan-style hotel with an enclosed, central patio with a tiled swimming pool in the center, shiny green potted plants everywhere, and exotic Persian rugs on the marble floor. Beautiful flowering vines climb around the arches leading to the guest rooms, and a tiled mural of an ancient Morrocco city graces a wall leading to a restaurant. The pool looks warm and inviting, especially with large, puffy snowflakes falling lightly outside the partially steamed-up windows.

Malone checks his watch. "Our contact, Mr. Schweitzer, should be here in about an hour. We'll meet right here in the lobby at 1800. Looks like a nice place to talk over there under those curtains with the fountain and all those little benches."

"We aren't going to dinner with him?" Reno asks.

"We'll grab something here in the hotel restaurant later. He's catching the train back to Switzerland tonight. Busy man. Owns a clock and watch shop in Zurich, has seven sons, and a slew of little grandkids. We're lucky he agreed to come. If not, our entire Berlin schedule would have been thrown off."

Shifrah scoots us off to our room for "refreshing our makeup," but I think she has something on her mind. I was right. She quickly checks her hair and lipstick, sits down in one of the chairs in our room. "Are you scared of meeting Mr. A, Savannah?" she asks.

"Not scared, but I do feel a little nervous about it. He's always been this unknown person behind the curtain, sort of like the wizard in *The Wizard of Oz*, and now…"

"That's a good comparison—the wizard behind the curtain. I don't really know how to feel anymore. What's the meaning of the bulls on my cigarette case and on that key? Then, Malone says we're going to a stadium. Why do I have a stadium on my case, too?"

I sit down beside her. "When you first showed it to me, you said you were told it was a map to your future. I don't know what's going on here, but I think you might be on the verge of unlocking the mysteries of your life. Didn't you say your parents wouldn't allow any discussions about how you came to live with them or anything about the war?"

"Yes, it was *verboten,* and I didn't really care. Now, I do."

"There has to be a good reason why they didn't say anything about your past."

"Maybe, but this mission grows more peculiar all the time. I know I chose to go on a strange quest with Malone being in charge of me instead of that dreadful alternative, but I didn't know it would tie my past and present together in a knot. When I was in the hospital after the, you know, the accident, Daddy told me he pulled a lot of strings to *allow* me the opportunity to go on this escapade with Malone. Anyway, can you imagine me in a prison?"

"No."

"Neither can I. Anyway, Daddy wouldn't tell me any of the details, even after I said I would do it. Shortly after that, he and Mommykins took me to dinner at their fancy yacht club and that's where I met Malone. Daddy was completely tight-lipped about everything, no matter how much I pleaded to know more. I felt like I was jumping off a cliff wearing a blindfold. I begged Mommykins to save me, or at least tell me some details. She cried her heart out, but she wouldn't reveal a thing."

"That's a mystery, for sure."

"I know. Now I'm feeling betrayed by my parents. Why didn't they tell me anything about my past?"

"I don't have all the answers, but I do know with all my heart they love you. It shows in their words, even the way they look at you. If they've been silent about your past and about this mission, it's because they had to be for reasons we don't know yet."

"Maybe. Honestly, who am I, Savannah?"

"You are our Shifrah, that's who, and you are about to find the missing puzzle pieces of your life. Let's get excited about that."

"Excited? What if I find out my other family was tortured and—"

"Shifrah, listen. I don't doubt you're going to hear some unpleasant details. It only makes sense, considering what we've heard so far, but all the hurt will fade in time after you get to see the whole picture."

She looks up. "You think so?"

"I do. Look, I'll never know why my mama up and left a little five-year-old girl who adored her and a husband who always bent over backward to please her. Why would a woman do that? Boredom? Lust? Stupidity? And she left without a backward look, never a postcard, note, or anything else to explain her leaving us. Who does that, and why? I will always be hurt about it deep in my heart, but I've learned to cherish all the good things in my life.

"It seems likely you'll find out the whole story of your family and why things unfolded as they did. The *why* is so important because I believe it holds the magic of moving forward, not a little, but completely."

"I'm such an idiot, Savannah. You've been through so much grief, and all I do is think of poor little Shifrah and how she might hear some facts that hurt her little feelings and make her uncomfortable. I'm a fool."

"You are not."

"You're the only adult of the two of us."

"That's ridiculous. It's normal to be… uh, you know what? We're sitting here saying this and that, and we can sum it all up by saying we've become true loyal friends like David Diamond and Mr. Wallenberg."

Her eyes are sparkling. "That's true, isn't it? You know what? They broke the mold when they made you."

"Was I built in a factory?" I say, smiling. "However I came to be, I'm glad there's only one of me. I couldn't handle two. Hey, there's something I've kept a secret—a conversation I overheard between Reno and Malone when we were in Miami the first time. Are you up for hearing it right now?"

"I'm all ears, but why didn't you tell me before?"

"I was afraid you'd let the cat out of the bag and say something to Malone. Everything's different now."

"You didn't trust me?"

"Oh, I've always trusted you, but you were a bit of a spoiled one back then."

"Don't you mean I was a spoiled brat who expected the world to keep me comfortable and in style every step of the way?"

"Not at all."

"Well, what did you hear?"

"I heard Malone saying someone, and I don't know who but I

suspicion that it may be Mr. A, wanted you and me to wade through the hardships of this mission. Malone was upset about having to take us to the rainforest, and he was getting the feeling that *he*—whoever that is—wanted us to tromp through some tough times. That's why Malone said we had to stay in the planes. He told Reno that would keep us out of danger."

Shifrah stands, hands on hips, "Really? Does that make sense to you?"

"Without knowing more… no."

She huffs out an irritated breath.

"Anyway, look at it like this… we're living inside a mystery novel. You can be Sherlock, and I'll be Watson, and our personal mission is to find the reasons for everything in the world!" I chuckle and she at least half-way smiles. "Now, let's get properly primped so we look as gorgeous as any detective duo should look, right?"

"I think I've created a monster."

"Just call me Frankenstein."

"Frankenstein is the name of the doctor."

"I know. So, which one of us is the doctor and which is the monster, or are we both?" I laugh my most evil laugh and step in front of the mirror to reapply the new lipstick Shifrah picked out for me to wear today.

CHAPTER FIFTY-FOUR

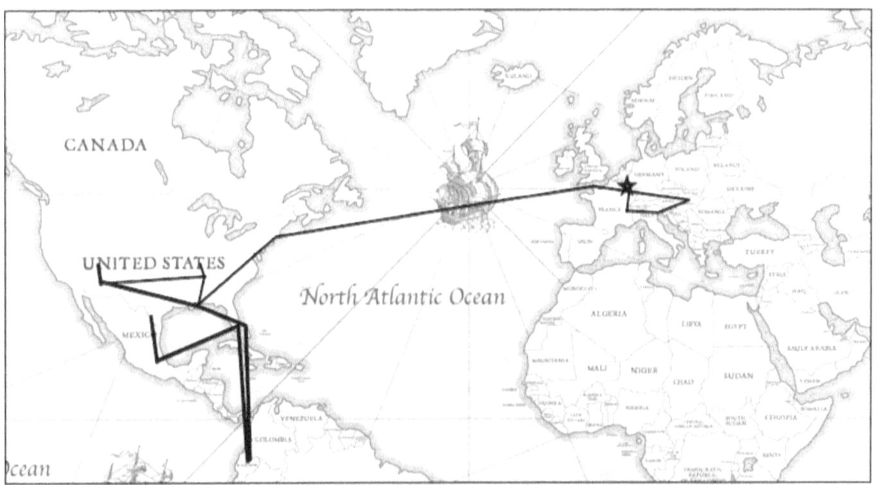

Shifrah and I would have changed into slacks before going to the hotel restaurant if we'd known we'd be sitting on the floor underneath a short-legged table laden with food. As it is, we had to sit down sideways before extending our legs underneath the low table. I keep accidentally poking Reno's crossed legs with the tips of my high heels. He suddenly pulls off my shoes and puts them beside him.

"What are you doing?" I ask.

"Saving my shins!" he replies with a smile.

"You ladies want to go back to your room and change? Damn, I had no idea they'd carry their Moroccan theme this far and stick us on the floor to eat dinner," Malone says.

"We're fine," Shifrah says, and again I'm shocked at how well she takes inconveniences lately. I would love to change my clothes, but I figure if she's being such a good sport about it, I can be, too.

Dinner so far has been exotic, but I will never get used to eating *couscous* and other foods out of a shared bowl with my fingers as some of the other diners are.

"Our train to Berlin leaves at 0700 in the morning, so it's an early call," Malone says.

"Can I see that *retrieve,* I mean, the key again, Malone?" Shifrah asks.

He takes it from a small pouch inside his jacket, hands it to her.

"I guess this one has a clock on the end because Mr. Schweitzer is a clock and watchmaker?"

"Sounds reasonable."

"He was the most nervous contact so far. Well, of the ones Shifrah and I got to meet. I mean, compare him to Eddie, the *Havasupai.* Now, that guy takes life as it comes," I say.

"Coming to Luxembourg was hard for him. As I said before, war does crazy things to people's minds. The way I understand it, he and his family barely escaped from Germany to Switzerland… had some harrowing experiences along the way."

"That explains why his eyeballs were rolling around in a circle and he was in such a big hurry to leave," Reno says.

Malone nods. "That's about the size of it. Finish your, uh, what's this stuff called?"

"C*ouscous* and *tagine,"* Shifrah says, "and it's divine."

"Right. We have a full day tomorrow, so let's finish up."

***

Cold air hitting the back of my head partially wakes me up. I turn over and snuggle deeper into my blankets. More cold air hits my face. I open my eyes. The fringe on the heavy drape over the window in our hotel room is moving slightly. Why is the window open?

A chill runs up my back. I silently slip my hand into the open drawer of my nightstand and clutch the .38, slowly roll onto my back, lift my head. I gasp as I see the outline of a man holding a limp Shifrah crossing the room.

Why doesn't she wake up? flashes through my mind, and I realize she's been drugged or knocked out. Adrenaline surges through my veins in waves.

Get it together! You know what to do.

I sit up as I say in my gruffest voice, "Put her down, or I'll shoot." The outline momentarily halts, then sprints to cover the distance to the window.

"Stop!" I scream.

He doesn't.

I aim and hit his right thigh, praying Shifrah's legs are out of the way. He cries out, drags his leg, nearly reaching the window with Shifrah still in his arms. My head is ringing from the sound of the shot. I aim again. His right arm takes the next bullet.

He drops Shifrah and races to the window. He climbs through, leaving part of the drape dangling out the open window. I get there in time to see a bulky man limping quickly through the street and around a corner. I close the window and rush to Shifrah. She's out cold. I switch on the lamp. My ears are ringing; my head feels like its full of churning hot cotton.

Heavy banging shakes the door. My heart is in my throat as I approach the door. No peephole. More banging. "Open this door or it's coming off the hinges!" Malone yells. I throw it open. Malone rushes in like a madman, his clothes askew, his hair mussed. "Did I hear shots?" he yells, then spies Shifrah on the floor. "What the hell happened?" he shouts as he hurries to her side. His voice sounds faraway.

"A man… came through the window. I-I shot him. Twice. His leg and his arm."

"Didn't you lock the window?"

"I did, but…"

"Honey, oh honey, it's okay. It's okay," Reno says, taking the pistol out of my hand, spinning the cylinder to an empty slot, and placing it on the dresser. He folds me into his arms. "You're shaking like a leaf, you poor little thing. You sure showed that rascal who not to mess with, that's for dang sure." Reno is bare from the waist up. Despite my highly emotional state, my face burns from being hugged so intimately. He backs up, places his hands on my shoulders, and gently pushes me into a chair. "I have to check the street, hon. I'll be back shortly. Malone, I'm on my way out," he says, disappearing out the door. He walks backward back into the room.

"What you do to my hotel?" says an angry man wearing a skull cap and a nightshirt over baggy pants. "Did I hear guns? Did I?"

"Hey, Ali Baba, a man broke into this room and assaulted our womenfolk. Get out of my way," Reno says in a harsh tone I've never heard him use before.

The man jerks his hat off, turns a horrified face toward all of us. "Broke in your room?'

"Yeah, through the window," Reno answers.

"I will coming with you!" he says, and the two of them are gone.

"Damn nation! Looks like he knocked her out with his fist," Malone says, lifting Shifrah onto one of the beds. She groans. I shake my head to get some sense into it, then go to the sink and wet a washcloth for her head.

"Wha-what happened? Why are you… you looking at me like that, you two? Why aren't you dressed, Malone? Did we have a car wreck?" Shifrah sputters.

"Keep your head still, Shifrah," Malone says, not too gently. He's angry. I'm sure I will be, too, as soon as I get all my faculties back.

"Shifrah, are you okay?" I ask softly, deliberately counteracting Malone's brusque manner.

"I think so. My chin feels funny, and I have a killer headache."

Malone swears off to the side. Stands. "Give me the facts, Savannah," he says, walking toward the window. He pushes the curtain out of the way. "Hells bells, this cheap little lock wouldn't keep a fly out. He busted it by pushing on it. That's all it took."

"Savannah, what is he talking about?" Shifrah says. She starts to sit up, winces, lies back down.

I'm shaking so bad, my teeth are chattering. I take a deep breath and tell myself to calm down. "I awoke to see a man carrying you through the room, Shifrah. I ordered him to stop. He didn't. I shot his leg. I told him again to stop. He didn't. I shot his arm. He dropped you on the floor and jumped out the window. That's it."

Her eyes are like saucers as she wiggles into a sitting position. "You-you shot him? Where did you get a gun? How did you know what to do? Oh, my gawd, he was stealing me? Why me?"

"Shh, it's okay," Malone says. "Lie back down; you're safe now. I armed Savannah a while ago for backup—one of the smartest things I've done on this mission. Good work, Savannah." The respect and gratitude on his face fill my soul, and I stop shaking.

Reno returns with the news that the man is nowhere to be found. "Blood's everywhere outside the window and down the street. I followed it until there were no more street lights and I couldn't see a blasted thing," he said.

"All right, let's grab the girls' stuff and take it to our room, Reno. We're all bunking together tonight. You and me sleep on the floor, that is, if we even get any shuteye. Now we know a lot more than we did."

"Like what?" I ask.

"Exactly who the traitor is and, uh, a few other things," Malone says, glancing momentarily at Shifrah.

He doesn't have to say it aloud. All of us know for a fact Shifrah is the target.

CHAPTER FIFTY-FIVE

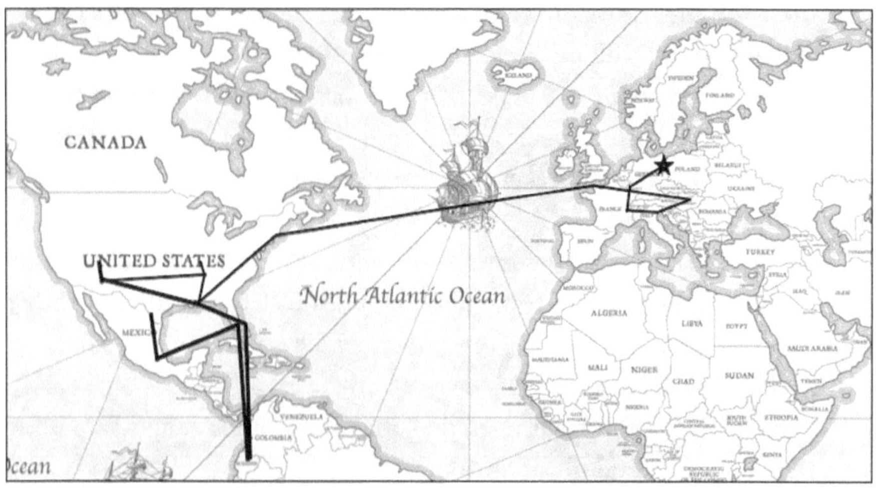

Jonathan is the first one we see as we step off the train this afternoon. He's dressed in a suit, vest, tie, and a long coat. Except for his odd glasses, he presents quite a flamboyant figure standing on the platform smiling heartily at us, his breath hanging in the cold air.

"Still wearing those purple glasses, I see," Shifrah mutters behind me.

"Shh," I whisper. "He can't help it."

"Good morning! Our car is waiting to take you to your hotel. We have big plans for tonight. I-I'm so sorry about your hotel experience. Terrible thing. I hope your train journey was pleasant, at least," he says, gathering us into a group. We walk a short distance and step into a touring car with three rows of doors and a back hatch. After helping the driver load our luggage, Reno jumps up front, his favorite place, and

Jonathan holds the door open for Shifrah and me to scoot into the seats behind the driver and Reno. He and Malone sit behind us, and our luggage fills up the last portion of the long, black car.

I notice another black car pulls out in front of us, and our driver follows close behind it. "Are we following that car?" I ask.

"Security measures, Savannah," Jonathan says. "Another one in back of us."

I turn to look, but I can't see over our piled-up luggage in the back of the car.

"You mentioned big plans for tonight, Jonathan?" Shifrah says, pivoting in the seat.

"Yes, Father has planned a big evening for everyone in his Berlin home."

"Your father lives here?"

"Part of the time, yes. I lived in the house we will go to tonight until I was sixteen."

"Where else does your father live?"

"France, Istanbul…"

Shifrah locks eyes with me. Jonathan is assuredly from a wealthy family. She's amazingly recovered from our nightmare in Luxembourg last night. I think Malone's attention is like a balm to her spirit. For myself, I've had to do a lot of private soul-searching. I've never shot at, let alone hit, a human before. Malone's and Reno's accolades have helped a lot, but the image of it stays with me. My ears took a long time to quit ringing, too, but they'll be okay.

We see some of everything outside our windows as we drive to the hotel. New construction. Reconstruction. Buildings. Shops. Cars, buses, taxis, bicycles everywhere. Berlin is a very busy city.

Jonathan says, "You've heard of the Marshall Plan? It has helped West Berliners reconstruct, but many of the buildings of historical and architectural importance are waiting for funding. Who knows if they will be restored. From what Father tells me, the citizens desperately want some of their favorite landmarks returned to them even if they must wait a long time—places like the *Neues Museum,* the *Konzerthaus…* many others."

"What is that pitiful structure over there?" I say, pointing.

"*Haus Vaterland.* Fatherland House. A tragic story, one of thousands. This building was once part of the popular *Potsdamer Platz.* It housed dance halls, cinemas, cafés, a Japanese Tea House, an American Wild West Saloon, a Turkish café, and lots more. Plans to restore it were shattered this year, only this past June to be exact, when it was set on fire by East German workers protesting working and living conditions in East Germany. Now, it is a sad, gutted ghost."

"That's terrible," I say.

"War is terrible. Okay, the hotel I have selected for you is less than a mile from my old neighborhood. When I was a boy, I rode my bicycle, played soccer with my friends, ditched my piano lessons near where the hotel is. My childhood home was surrounded by many trees and land, yet it was near schools, synagogues, churches, and shops.

"The Nazis stole our home for administration and war planning after Father, uh, he… anyway, Father restored it when he reclaimed it. Not a trace, not a fingerprint of any of those bas—, I mean, the former occupiers, is now found in those walls or halls." Jonathan's voice fades as he stares out the window.

"You grew up here, but you speak English so well," I say.

"My boyhood is a lifetime ago, Savannah. The United States is my home now."

"Where did you live in America?"

"Chicago." He clears his throat. "I'll pick all of you up at 1630, er, 4:30 p.m. Sunset comes early in Berlin in December. May I suggest you rest before this long evening?"

"What shall we wear?" Shifrah says.

"I encourage you to be comfortable."

"How many people will be there?"

"Quite a few."

"Dinner and…?"

"Cocktails, dinner with musical accompaniment, and a private presentation after dinner."

"And Mr. A will be there?" I ask.

"Yes."

"And you want us to dress comfortably, say in rag-tail shirts, slacks, oxford saddle shoes, and bobby socks?" Shifrah says.

"Shifrah, be nice," I say under my breath.

She laughs. "Jonathan, *comfortable* to Savannah and me for an occasion you mentioned means evening clothes suitable for the opera in Paris, that is, if one were ever allowed to go to Paris." She sends a playful, raised eyebrow look at Malone, who receives it with an innocent shrug. Shifrah is right. I wouldn't be caught dead dressing *comfortably* at such a gala event, an event that sounds fancier than any I've ever attended.

They resume talking behind us, low tones, which perks up our ears again. We turn to face one another, and, with eye movements, indicate we plan to listen to every word they say.

"Malone, we never had any doubt you could pull this off. Your handling of the travel plans, the retrievals, the women—it's remarkable. Now, mission accomplished in less than a year after we sat at that table in New York and brainstormed with blood, sweat, and tears."

"Surprisingly few hitches, which says a lot for the team we assembled. Reno was the perfect fit, for starters."

"Someone mention my name?" Reno says from the front of the car.

"Negative, Reno," Malone says. "Just hashing out a few details."

Shifrah and I lean as far back in our seats as possible to continue eavesdropping on their conversation.

"Mr. A was right about, well, he was right about all of it, especially, well, you know. Tough going at first, but improvements showed up. Pretty big ones," Malone says.

"I'm picking up on that. Quite remarkable. Good thing you had an extra shooter, too." Their voices drop so low we can't hear them until Jonathan says, "Ah, here's the hotel. Remember, I'll be here at 1630. Part of our security squad is staying here in full alert at the hotel."

"Roger that."

The driver parks. Malone and Jonathan open our doors for us to step out. As soon as the driver and Reno unload our luggage and give it to a bellhop, Jonathan gets up front, waves, and is gone, his car pulling out behind the other black car. The black car following us parks, and four men wearing black suits, white shirts, and black ties get out and stand by their car.

"Are they with us?" I ask.

"Yeah. Let's, uh, get inside. Reno and I will come to your room to escort you to the car this evening. Don't use room service for food or drinks. Call us, and we'll get whatever you want. Don't go out of your rooms. That's an order," Malone says.

CHAPTER FIFTY-SIX

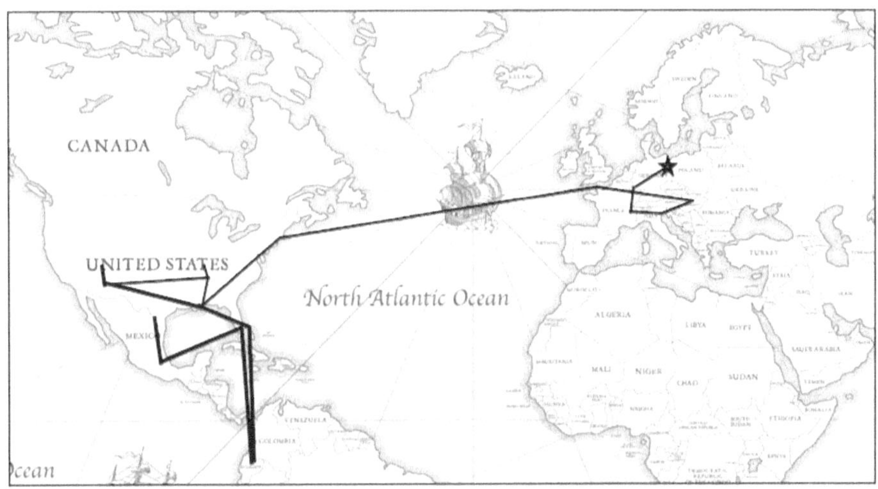

Jonathan points, and four heads swivel to take in the fiery sunset rays engulfing the famous Brandenburg Gate visible from the car window. "When you walk through the columns from this side, which is West Germany, you are in East Germany," he says. "There is talk that both West and East Germany will restore this famous gate to its original grandeur, but we shall see. Talk is easy; action is, well, something else."

"It's otherworldly with all those golden beams shooting out of the sky and covering it," I say, glad that Malone told us a brief history and present status of Berlin because I would be in the dark if he hadn't.

"Looks kinda like the front of a religious pamphlet, doesn't it? Those rays coming down and all seems like God's saying, *You folks quit your bickerin' and fightin' down there. Just look at all the damage you're doing.*"

Normally, Reno saying something like that would make us laugh or comment, but it hits a delicate chord this time. The silence in the car makes me start worrying about my evening outfit. I look down at my coat covering everything to my knees. Can I just leave it on at the party? I glance at Shifrah, who happens to be looking right at me.

"Don't even think about it," she says.

"What?"

"You can't leave your coat on. You and that dress will give a beautiful surprise to Mr. A and everyone else who's been pulling our strings while we dance through this mission."

How did she know what I was thinking? "Are you calling us puppets, Shifrah?"

"Almost."

"It's just that this dress is so, you know—"

"Gorgeous? And, hmm, maybe sexy?"

I feel the heat jumping onto my cheeks. My dress is a replica from the new movie that came out this past August, *Gentlemen Prefer Blondes.* I haven't seen the film, but Shifrah has, and she was beside herself when the owner of one of the dress shops in Dijon told us she was also a dress designer and had duplicated five of the outfits Marilyn Monroe wears in the movie for a special fashion show in Paris. On the walls were movie posters with certain fashions circled in red crayon.

"You'll look fabulous in any of them, Savannah. You and Marilyn Monroe have the same complexion, and you're both blondes!" Shifrah gushed, her eyes twinkling like stars in a winter sky. When the shop owner brought out the bright orange dress she'd copied from the movie, Shifrah went crazy. "Savannah, look! Ruched chiffon!"

"What in the world is that?"

"It's a-a, let's see, how do I describe it? They use a certain technique to create a fabric with a rippled look. You know, gathering, pleating, all that, and it accentuates body curves. They use ruched fabric all the time in those spectacular Hollywood gowns."

I've never seen myself in anything like the dresses I tried on that day. Form-fitting, more low-cut than I've ever worn before. Shifrah literally talked the designer out of the dress I'm wearing right now. I felt like a child standing there as they bargained back and forth in French until Shifrah clapped her hands and squealed. "We got it! You're wearing the bright orange ruched chiffon gown with the scarf worn horizontally across the front of your neck with both ends hanging down your back."

The shoulder straps, as well as a line running vertically down the front of the dress concealing a zipper, are trimmed in crystal beading. It's form-fitting to the knee, then it flares. Thankfully, it doesn't fit me as tightly as it fits Miss Monroe in the movie posters because I wouldn't have worn one that tight. How did she ever sit down in it, I wonder?

Shifrah's diamond earrings and one cocktail ring are all I'd let her accessorize me with for tonight, and I'm wearing a pair of clear high heels with a rhinestone strap and a matching evening purse only big enough for a tube of lipstick, a folded twenty-dollar bill, and a tiny comb.

I almost wish I could throw everything off and jump into my dungarees. I say *almost* because part of me is excited to shed my coat and show off this famous movie dress. I can't believe the transformation I've gone through by being Shifrah's companion and friend these past months.

I'm still going noodling for catfish sometimes, get that straight, says a part of my mind, and I literally answer with *sure, but, afterward, I'm dressing up and sipping a glass of champagne!*

"Savannah, are you mumbling to yourself?" Shifrah asks.

"Oh, it's just a little inward fight I'm having with myself."

"Anything I can help with?"

"No, you've done quite enough already," I say, patting her arm.

Shifrah is decked out in a full-skirt evening gown in pale aqua with a dramatic sheer glittering aqua scarf shawl and matching jewelry accessories that look like the magazine pictures I've seen advertising Tiffany's of New York. She looks radiant.

Right now, we're covered in our heavy warm coats, and our teammates have no idea the length Shifrah has gone to fixing us up for this event. I believe she went a little overboard to compensate for whatever difficult facts she may learn tonight when we meet Mr A.

That's my guess, and I feel anxious for her. She kind of shrugged off last night, our scariest moment of the mission. Malone's concentrated attention since then seems magical for her.

We drive down a straight, tree- and lamppost-lined driveway toward a lit-up home at the end that looks pretty much like a castle in my humble opinion. Shifrah grabs my hand and flashes me a look that seals our mutual excitement.

"Jonathan, I'm sorry you had to grow up so shabby," Reno says, and all three men laugh.

"Reno, wealth is a commodity about as stable as quicksand and as satisfying as saltless meat," Jonathan replies.

"I'll try to remember that hunk of wisdom when I lose my first zillion bucks," Reno says.

"Look at the cupola, Savannah," Shifrah whispers, and I barely know she means the rounded dome protrusion in front of the house shaped like a fancy silo with arched windows. Architecture isn't something I've ever thought much about, but, lately, since coming to Europe, and because Shifrah knows a lot about it, it has flagged my interest.

"I suppose you know what style to call that wonderous house, Shifrah? You've known a bunch of them so far."

"Not exactly, but…" she taps a finger on her cheek. "I'd have to guess it's a combination of baroque and neoclassical."

"Good heavens, how did you know that?"

"It's buried in my psyche. My friends have all been from wealthy families, some ridiculously rich, owning homes like that one plus more in other locations. One time, we all took a trip to… oh, I'm starting to babble, aren't I?"

"Don't worry. I understand." We chuckle nervously as the car slows in front of the house and waits for the car in front of us to unload. When we stop, every door of the car except the driver's door is opened by men wearing black tuxedos. Their dark green half-vests cover only their midriffs and have two rows of gold buttons, one on each side. White shirts and green bowties complete their elegant look, and now I do feel as if I'm arriving at a real castle.

I take Reno's offered arm and step around the car toward a strip of green carpet running from the driveway to an open entry sparkling with light. Music pours through the doors like a vaporous ribbon, filling the cold air with excitement. Jonathan salutes in our direction before taking the steps to the front door in an energetic stride and disappearing inside. Uniformed staff stand prominently at the door as greeters. Behind them, I see a tangle of men, women, and maids with trays crossing this way and that. From what I can make out so far, Shifrah and I may not be too overdressed. Thank heavens for that.

"Reno, I'm afraid this is too highbrow for a little country gal. I'm not sure I belong here."

"Hush that kind of talk," he answers under his breath.

"I have half a mind to ditch these heels and go find myself a fishing pole."

He laughs. "If you did, I'd come find you."

I glance sideways at him, but he's looking forward.

Before my shoes touch the carpet, Malone and Shifrah come from the other side of the car, arm in arm. She's wearing her icy city-sophistication look with an uplifted chin and a detached expression, and for the first time, I see it as a protective shield, a way to hide insecurity. That revelation puts me instantly at ease. After all, people are just people, and money doesn't make them higher or lower than anyone else.

"Reno, you feel like skipping the rest of the way to the door?"

"Huh?"

"Just pulling your leg, or am I?"

"Well, hon, they might think we drove in from Cow-Patty College if we did that."

I flash him a big smile, tighten up on his arm, and march us toward our purpose in a faster pace, skipping once to make our strides match.

CHAPTER FIFTY-SEVEN

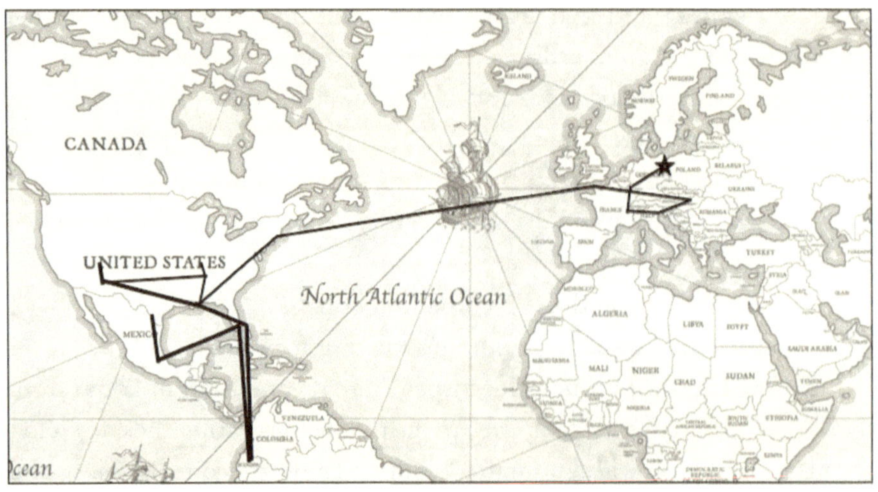

Most assuredly, as Shifrah once said, I'm Cinderella arriving at the ball, and I hope I don't turn into a pumpkin when I reveal my orange dress—typical nonsensical thoughts I have when I'm overwhelmed by my surroundings. We're ushered inside with smiles and slight bows.

"No, thank you," Shifrah says, when a doorman tries to take her coat. She takes Malone by the arm and beckons for Reno and me to join them as she maneuvers us to the side of the doorway. "I think it's nicer if our own gentlemen help us with our coats this evening. Malone, would you do me the honor, and you, too, Reno?"

They look puzzled for a moment before Reno says, "Why, I'm most gratified to be of assistance. It's good experience for when I begin my new life as a butler and coat wrangler."

"What?" we all say, then laugh because it's Reno being the cutup he always is. He starts to help me, and I put a hand on his sleeve. He follows my eyes to Shifrah.

"Malone?" she says, unbuttoning her coat. He moves behind her and pulls her coat off, turns and hands it to a man waiting to take it. He tells him the name to put it under, turns back, does a doubletake as he looks at Shifrah. All of us do. She pivots slowly in a circle, and I admire for the hundredth time her ease and sophistication in public.

"Man oh man oh man, Shif, if you aren't the star at the top of the tree! You're too fancy to hang out with ol' Malone and me anymore. Wait here while I call an agent in Hollywood to come pick you up!"

"Thanks, Reno, but I better stick around one more night to hear all those deep mission secrets you guys have been hiding. Why is Savannah still wearing her coat?"

"What? Oh, sorry, Savannah."

I give one last beseeching look at Shifrah. She shakes her head. I undo the buttons down the front of my coat, and I might as well be naked for how panicked I feel right now. Reno walks behind me, removes my coat, and I nearly black out as my bright movie dress is revealed to my team and onlookers who immediately stop and gawk at me.

Why did I do this? It's too much!

Reno's mouth gapes open. Malone stares without blinking, and I feel lightheaded. Shifrah steps in and takes my arm. "Can you believe this beautiful creation is real? This dress is famous in a movie that came out a few months ago, and she wears it perfectly!"

"Shifrah, uh, I may need to go sit down," I say, feeling woozy.

"Huh? Oh, yes. Savannah and I have barely eaten a morsel all day. We'll join you later after we scavenge hors d'oeuvres and wine."

"No wine," I say, and I wish Malone and Reno would stop staring at me. Shifrah whisks me away through clusters of dancers and waiters, and the air from the movement of us hurrying across the room cools my hot face.

"I should never have let you talk me into wearing this dress."

"You'll be fine once we get something in your stomach. Do you want some seltzer?"

"Does it keep you from fainting?" I ask, keeping my eyes down to avoid the gaping from strangers.

"It fixes everything. Oh, look, Savannah, a beautiful full orchestra at the end of this gorgeous ballroom. What a grand party! I haven't seen anything this fancy since I left New York. Isn't it heavenly?"

I don't answer or take my eyes off the floor. Shifrah stops us in our tracks, waits until I look at her. "Savannah, listen to me. You're going to be stared at whether you're wearing your Lady Levis or an intoxicating dress. Just accept it. It's the way things are, and you can't let the attention of others ruin your fun. We're going to nibble and drink and maybe dance a little, have dinner, and then we get to hear all the secrets they've been keeping from us. Don't we deserve some fun after all these months of secrecy and danger?"

That snaps me out of my bashful spell. *Did I forget the purpose of this evening?*

"I'm acting like a child on the first day of school, aren't I?"

"It's okay. You're still not used to who you really are. I've had years of experience, and you're brand new at it."

"You're right, but I have a question. Tell me what changed in outer space that has you drilling logic into me instead of the other way around? Isn't that my job?"

"Perplexing, isn't it? Imagine me giving you advice, Savannah!"

Reno walks toward us with a plate loaded with hors d' oeuvres. "You women are standing there sightseeing and all, so I figured you might need something to tide you over while you're doing it, especially since you say you didn't eat today. Follow me. They have some real nice chairs and tables set up by the windows. Those waiters and maids are walkin' around with all kinds of drinks, so we can snag what we want from one of them. That heated eggnog I got a whiff of sure smelled nice, especially with the cold weather outside."

"He can't stay away from you, can he?" Shifrah says under her breath as we follow Reno to the edge of the room.

"You need some food, Shifrah. Your brain is melting."

We settle into plush green chairs surrounding a small polished table near a window at least twenty feet high. Small bowls of floating red and white roses decorate our table and all the ones around it. I glance outside. Snowflakes drift lazily toward the pavement in the glow of the lampstands.

"Where's Malone?" Shifrah asks, looking around.

"I think him and Jonathan are talking to Jonathan's dad right now. He says most of these folks are leaving after dinner. Seems they're long-time friends and acquaintances he hasn't seen in a while. Our private meeting later is with a select group."

"And who is in that select group, Reno?"

"Shif, if you aren't about as curious as a kid in a toy store."

She takes a bite from a tiny crustless sandwich and looks full at Reno. "So how about indulging me for once. Who are they?"

"I'll just act like I'm Malone and say, 'All in due time, sweetheart, all in due time.'"

"He doesn't call me sweetheart. Not yet, anyway."

"Shifrah, are you two…" and I stop talking because of the look on her face. Reno doesn't say anything, which means what? He turns his chair away from us as if he's giving us privacy to discuss this.

That nagging thought playing around the edges of my mind lately… is it true? "I, uh, how long has this been brewing?"

"Well, you know we all agreed to remain strictly colleagues for this mission, and I think we accomplished that. Now that we're at the end of it, I can admit I fell for Malone when Daddy first introduced us in New York. Couldn't you tell?"

"I suspected it a time or two, especially lately, but you had me convinced you thought he was unfair, insensitive, a *wet shirt*."

She smiles. "He hurt my feelings a lot, that's for sure. He was always so gruff and cross with me. You'd think I would have cooled off after being treated like that, but I never did. Now, don't get all psychopathic about this, okay? Nothing is solid yet, but I think I know two things for certain. Well, kind of for certain."

"What are they?" I ask.

"I'm pretty certain, I think, maybe he cares for me, too."

"You don't know for sure?"

"Let's just say I have a strong feeling about it. The other thing I, uh, think I know is he thinks he's too old for me, which, of course, is preposterous. Mommykins is eight years younger than Daddy, and they're perfect together. Malone's barely thirty-three, and I turn twenty-three in a few weeks. He's not too old for me, but what does age matter anyway? It doesn't when you love someone."

"Did you say *love?*"

She nods. "All I'm waiting for is a sign he feels the same."

"How do you propose to get that sign?"

She smiles. "I have my ways."

"Reno?" I say, but his wave of the hand in the air with his back turned says he is not getting involved in this conversation.

I'm reeling. This opulent home, the no-expenses-spared party, my gorgeous movie-star dress, the expectations of meeting Mr. A and learning the secret purpose of our mission, and now, Shifrah confessing her love for stoic, all-business, Mr. Military himself?

I cradle my head in my hands for a few moments, look up and see Jonathan, Malone, and an elegantly dressed man with a slight limp headed straight for our table.

CHAPTER FIFTY-EIGHT

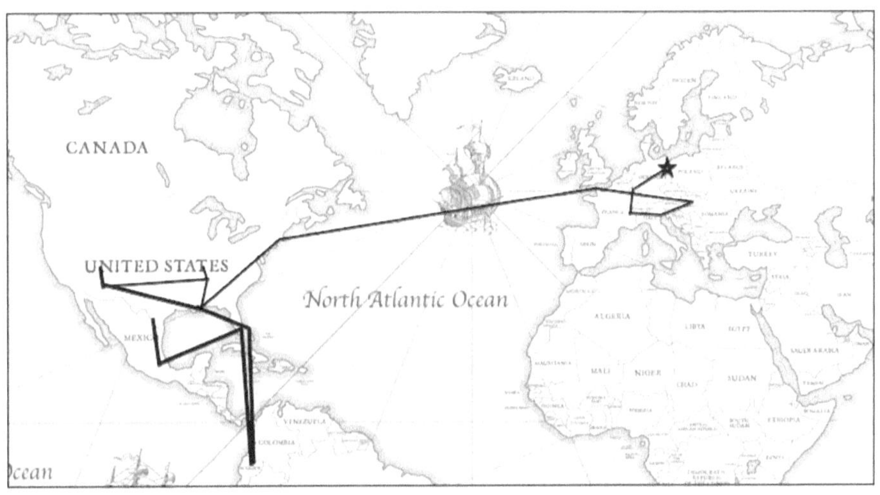

My emotions are bouncing around like, as my daddy used to say, *a marble in an empty shoe box* as the three men approach. Reno stands up right away. Shifrah and I quick-glance at one another.

"Father, meet Malone's team—Savannah, Shifrah, and Reno," Jonathan says when they stop at our table.

Reno thrusts out a quick hand.

"I am thrilled to meet you, Captain Taylor. Jonathan tells me you've done a spectacular job assisting Major Connor these past months," he says in a thick accent.

What's wrong with me? First Jonathan, and now, this dapper gentleman looks vaguely familiar, too?

"It's been my pleasure, sir," Reno answers, sits down.

That was quick. Reno is usually more talkative… and funny.

Jonathan's father turns a pleasant face toward Shifrah and me. I don't know what to do other than keep smiling and mentally note his unusual forest-green dinner jacket and try to guess his age. He has a streak of gray hair across the top of his dark hair and gray at the temples. Maybe fifties? Should I shake his hand? I stick my hand out. He takes it, kisses it, smiles into my eyes. No one has ever done that before. He lifts one of Shifrah's hands from the table and kisses the top of it. Is this a German custom or…?

"A long-awaited pleasure, ladies. Welcome to my home. I am sorry I cannot stay and have more conversations with you. I forced Jonathan to bring me over here to meet you, but, alas, I have last-minute preparations to see to. We shall meet later."

"Thank you for hosting this beautiful party at your home, sir," I say, unsure of what protocol I'm supposed to use in this situation. He nods pleasantly, turns, and the three men walk away.

"What in the name of all that's sacred was that about?" Shifrah says. "Jonathan's father is elegant, for sure, but why are we using his home for the private meeting later? It's a perfect place to entertain, but doesn't something feel fishy to you? Besides, have you ever seen Malone so regimented?"

I let out a deep, held-in breath. "I don't know anything about anything, Shifrah. Kissing our hands? Are we royalty?"

"Oh, that's just a *frou-frou* greeting, hon. It happens all the time in the upper echelons. Well, I guess we'll get our answers, to quote Malone, *in due time.* Reno, if you'll excuse us, Savannah and I need to find a powder room to freshen our lipstick after this snack."

"Don't let her fool you, Reno, she'll make us thoroughly check our teeth to be sure there's no food stuck in there, dab powder on our noses, make us pinch our cheeks to keep them rosy, be sure every hair is in place, and then and only then do we get to freshen our lipstick."

"And what's wrong with that?" Shifrah says, rising from the table.

Reno rises, too. "Y'all sure do a lot to look like movie stars, don't you? Say, there ought to be a little boy's room close to the little girl's room, oughtn't there?"

"Are you talking about little girl and little boy nurseries?" Shifrah asks.

"He's talking about the ladies' and men's bathrooms," I say. "Reno, are you tailing us this evening?"

"Nah, not really. Just making extra sure y'all are safe."

"But why here? I noticed the doormen thoroughly checking the register and the invitations as people arrived. Besides, have you seen all the armed security here?"

"Hey…" he smiles, "…who wouldn't want to make all the fellas jealous by escorting the prettiest girls at the party all over creation?"

He and that smile… I don't doubt it's his ticket to get away with about anything and everything.

* * *

The lingering traces of scented pipe tobacco, oil-polished wood, and fresh flowers saturate the library we've been ushed to after a delicious but too-formal-for-me dinner. This room appears to be an annex to the main house with a stain-glassed mosaic wall so beautiful it's hard not to lose myself in it.

With Reno closely watching over us during the cocktail party, seated beside us at dinner, and now with he and Malone sitting on each side of us at a Viking ship-sized mahogany table, the evening has taken on a serious tone for Shifrah and me. We've asked Reno questions he won't answer. We've speculated until we ran out of questions we want answered, and now, here we are in this room at this table sitting in tall leather chairs and waiting. Waiting for what?

The thought that I literally shot a man tries to again fill me with anxiety, but my common sense won't let it. If I hadn't shot him, what would have happened to Shifrah? I glance down at my tiny, fancy purse. No room for a pistol. It's the first time I haven't had mine with me since Malone handed it to me in Alabama.

Jonathan sits beside an empty chair at the head of the table on our left with a stack of papers in front of him. Waiters or butlers, I don't know which, have asked us which *digestifs,* coffees, or teas we want, and

I'm happy with my glass of iced water. Shifrah isn't having anything, isn't even smoking her one Turkish cigarette after her meal. By the time the waiters serve us beverages, she announces that, so far, there are twenty-one people sitting at the table. I'm guessing she's occupying herself with mindless things so she doesn't concentrate on what she may hear later.

"I think I'm seeing the same security guys who were inside the hotel with us," I say.

"Where?"

"Crisscrossing in front of the two open library doors. Wonder why we need them here when this place is loaded with security."

"Yeah, we've been surrounded ever since we arrived in Berlin. Honestly, I don't mind." She places her palm over her bruised chin.

"How's your head?"

"No headache, thank God."

Jonathan nods, and the two doors to the library are pulled closed by a butler. Jonathan looks around the table, seems to mentally calculate who is here and who isn't.

"Good evening," he says, smiling broadly. "I know how difficult it was for some of you to attend tonight, and, let me say, we appreciate your extra efforts. This evening, this conclusion, almost defies logic, does it not? It consummates a twenty-year secret, a secret some of your loved ones went to their deaths protecting, a secret lying right under the noses of our mortal enemies. That makes our victory much, much sweeter, agreed?"

A general buzz of assent goes around the table. Heads bob in agreement.

"Where's Mr. A?" Shifrah whispers across me at Malone. "And don't tell me I'll know *in due time*. Please."

Malone looks as if he's about to answer her question, but stiffens back to attention when Jonathan starts talking again.

"We have so much to talk about, but let's start by acknowledging the mission team who went around the world to gather our *key to the keys* and six of the seven keys that fit it, sometimes at great risk to their personal safety. They traveled by plane, train, ship, and automobile to

Ecuador, Ireland, France, Hungary, Italy, Luxembourg, not to mention the States. Oh, one more mode of transportation involved mules, I do believe." He grins at Shifrah. "Major Malone, will you please stand and introduce your team?"

Everyone is beaming at us with such heavy admiration, it makes me wonder how my life in a small Texas town was supposed to prepare me for a moment like this. My throat is scratchy, and my lips feel dry enough to crack open.

"Affirmative, Jonathan." He stands and gestures toward Reno. "My right-hand man here is Captain Thomas "Reno" Taylor, World War II flying ace of the Fighting First Air Corp and one of the youngest legends of the skies. He's at home in any cockpit, hanging on the back of a bucking bronco, playing guitar, or hitting dead on any target he aims at. He's a pleasure to work with, and his crazy sense of humor took the edge off any challenge we faced." Reno partially stands, nods toward everyone, sits down.

It's strange seeing him so docile and serious this evening, and why didn't I know he plays the guitar?

"Next, the lovely young lady in the very bright orange dress is Savannah Wright."

Oh no, no, no…

"Savannah came to our team with several years of experience dealing with every type of person while working in a South Texas diner in the United States. She was promoted to main manager of that diner before she turned twenty-one. Experiencing many personal hardships and loss, she weathered the storms of life with courage and fortitude. She speaks fluent Spanish and has intellect decades beyond her age. Oh, it seems she can also hotwire a stubborn engine or sprint down a track field in record speeds. She's college educated, a top-notch stenographer, and, just for the record, she recently worked seamlessly with a famous author on the SS America while sailing to Europe.

"Last but not least, Savannah added another level of security to the team with her firearm knowledge. Let me tell you… this girl can shoot!" He starts clapping, and now everyone is clapping. If jalapenos had been sliced open and rubbed all over my face, it couldn't burn more than it does right now. I look down to hide the bashful tears running down my cheeks.

Shifrah whispers, "No tears. It ruins your makeup," which helps me regain control. That's our Shifrah, all right, always worrying about our looks no matter what.

"The other female on our team is Shifrah. She's the fashion plate of our group, the champion of *haute couture,* a word she doesn't think I know. She dresses herself and Savannah in outfits befitting a Paris runway, as is evidenced by how outstanding they look tonight."

If Malone looks at her face right now, he'll know how she feels about him.

"Shifrah speaks fluent French, and she good-naturedly kept all of us in good humor with her New York City survival skills in the middle of the Ecuadorian rainforest, as well as in the biggest canyon in the world, the Grand Canyon. She turned out to be a good sport amidst the rigors of this mission, and… for the record, you might want to ask her about her, uh, her experiences in that jungle when we emergency landed with our nearly dead pilot."

Now, Shifrah is blushing as the participants applaud.

"Our mission team went through some odd, sometimes dangerous escapades, learned a few lessons along the way, and, well, I'm proud of having worked with each and every member of this team. They don't come any better. Back to you, Jonathan."

"Let's hear it again for the mission team!" Jonathan says, standing up.

Everyone stands, claps. Thankfully, Jonathan soon calls the meeting to order again. My face is sore from staying red for so long.

"All right. Very good. Very good," Jonathan says. He drains his coffee cup, sets it down. "The mission team, all except Major Malone, knows who I am about to introduce as 'Mr. A.' The rest of you know well who this man is, a man who has devoted his life to the *Bulls of Bashan* Project, to the *Bulls* themselves, and to their descendants."

Shifrah whispers, "Did you hear that, Savannah, the *Bulls of Bashan?* Descendants?"

"As many of you know, the man I'm introducing shared many of the same sorrows as you in the terrible war. His wife was fatally wounded in an airstrike while waiting for him in England. Unfortunately, he had been arrested as a war criminal for secreting his personal affairs out of Germany to Amsterdam and the United States. He survived the rest of the war in a concentration camp, an experience permanently affecting his body but not his spirit.

"For the past eight years, he has tirelessly worked to locate and lay the foundation and means for gathering the keys that unlock the secret place you are all aware of. Frankly, it was an impossible task, and I can't begin to understand how it finally all came together. Some of those keys changed hands at least three times, some were on the battlefield, and one was in the hard-won, secret possession of a dear and brave woman gasping her last breaths in a concentration camp infirmary. Was locating and retrieving all our keys impossible? Yes. Yet, we did. And so, without further delay, let us all welcome Mr. A, or, as most of you know him, Aaron Mandelbaum, the man I call with great affection… my father."

CHAPTER FIFTY-NINE

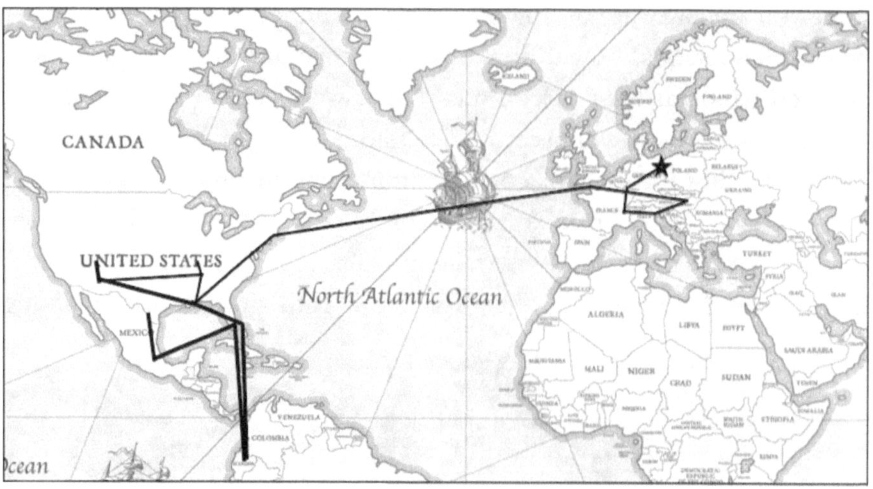

The doors open and in walks the gentleman in the forest-green dinner jacket. Under the man's arm is a long, slender case of polished wood. He and Jonathan lightly embrace, Jonathan sits, and Mr. A continues to stand and smile. Everyone is standing, applauding, giving him a hero's welcome, but I feel a little lightheaded.

Shifrah leans over me and fixes Malone with a severe frown, "For Pete's sake, Malone, would it have hurt you to mention we already met Mr. A himself?"

He makes hand gestures indicating she should keep her eyes upfront.

"Please take your seats," Mr. A says. He places the long case on the table. His eyes glitter with tears as he scans the room. "This night, and your presence here, warms my soul. In this room, we are *mishpocha,* we are family. We are united in our hearts and in our goals." He turns to look at us. "Thank you, mission team. We are grateful you did the leg work to help us fulfill a project of promises that began in 1933 Berlin and culminates this night, tomorrow, and hereafter. Jonathan, is the first slide ready? Dim the lights, please."

The first image on the wall is the *key to the keys.* The photo is old, but the metal object looks brand new, obviously photographed before it was marked by time, travel, and living inside a ferocious monkey sculpture.

"Please notice the Amorite words beside the keyholes. The Amorite language, for those who do not know, is a lost Semitic language, discernable only by a few talented philologists of ancient languages. We have the meanings of these words written in code and stored in three places. They tell us in which order to insert the keys, as well as which direction to turn them. Some must be turned twice or thrice, perhaps once in one direction, and then twice in the opposite direction. This was a brilliant design by one of our original *Bulls,* Jankel Levy, who is, sadly, no longer with us. It is wonderful to welcome his two sons from Florida, Noah and Caleb, tonight. Next slide, Jonathan."

Up on the wall flashes a photo of all the six keys we retrieved, and one I've never seen before. It's a beautiful key with what looks like a scroll on the end. They are inside a velvet-lined, open box I recognize as the box now in front of Mr. A.

"And now you see the keys, the *retrieves,* our brave mission team traveled around the world to retrieve. It was important to us at headquarters to have Major Malone in charge of the team because of his outstanding military record, his astuteness to detail, and, lastly, because of his deep friendship with my son, Jonathan. The women, well, that is a topic for another time, but you can trust they were perfect choices for this mission."

"What's that supposed to mean, *we're a topic for another time?"* Shifrah whispers to me. "Surely he won't mention the real reason I was on the team, will he?"

I shrug my shoulders because what do I know?

Gasps around the room snap our attention back to the wall where we see two photos of a sculpture of bulls, horns and heads thrashing mightily in the air. One photo is from the side, and one photo is from the top of the sculpture. I quickly count seven bulls. The bulls are an exact replica of the bulls etched on Shifrah's cigarette case, not to mention the one on the end of the key Mr. Wallenberg gave us. She leans horizontally across me, tugs on Malone's sleeve. Her pretty face is a mixture of fright and confusion. "Malone?" she says. He places his palm against her cheek, leans down and whispers loud enough that I overhear him, "Hang tough, hon."

"Everyone in this room knows at least some of the details of how the *Bulls of Bashan* Project came to be, why it was implemented, how it survived, and how, at last, it shall be fulfilled. For those who do not know, would you like me to expound a little?"

"I definitely want you to," a woman says.

"My daughter doesn't know the whole story, Aaron. Please explain it for her benefit," says a mustached, bearded man sitting beside a young woman across the table from us.

"My father is reluctant to say anything about Berlin or the war," says a familiar voice with an accent. "I wish to know more."

Shifrah and I lean forward and see the son of the button factory owner sitting on the same side as we are, three seats down from Malone.

"Savannah, your lovesick man is here," Shifrah mutters under her breath. Before I can chide her, he sees us, smiles broadly, waves.

"Let's see, what was lover boy's name?"

"His name is Lior Horowitz, and please stop making up fictional stories."

Mr. A is talking, and I focus in to catch up. "…how this project was born. I apologize it isn't a pleasant story. Shall I continue?"

Yeses and raised hands around the room affirm we are about to learn the truth of what our mission was about. I'm so excited, I shiver.

"Oh, here we go," Shifrah mumbles, leaning against me.

"Twenty years ago, in 1933, seven dedicated Jewish men representing different districts and families came together to work on a solution to the mayhem pouring down on them. I was one of those seven men. Each of us had a deep sense of impending doom after Hitler was appointed Chancellor of Germany in January of that year. By March, the first concentration camp opened—Dachau. At that time, it was mostly filled with Soviet prisoners, criminals, so-called political dissidents, but it was another ominous sign to us.

"In April, our Jewish shops and businesses were boycotted, shattering many financial foundations. Next, the Laws for Reestablishment of the Civil Service were established, barring Jews from holding positions in civil service, in universities, or in state positions. The venom of antisemitism was spreading like wildfire, burning paths through our lives, our families, and our livelihoods. Each day brought more shocking news and tribulations. Lifelong friends and neighbors shamed us, ignored us, cut us out of their lives."

Mr. A points to one of the walls of books in the library. "Do you love books as I do? Most of my book collection was stolen from me. I don't know where it was taken, but any book written by a Jewish author was burned, even the most respected university texts or books of beautiful poetry. Heaping piles of them were eaten by the Nazi flames. It was…" Mr. A looks up at the ceiling, sighs "…very tragic.

"These atrocities led to August 1934, the pinnacle of when Hitler proclaimed himself *Führer* and *Reichskanzler*, that is, Leader and Reich Chancellor of Germany. All the armed forces, willingly or not so willingly, swore allegiance to him. He had already purged the leadership of the SA and any other political opposers. There were none left to dispute his rise to absolute power. He became unrestrained in his hatred for anyone outside his disillusioned image of the Aryan race, or of anyone rebuking his lust for power." Mr. A leans forward, stares at us with wide eyes as he says, "He became a self-appointed God."

Reno leans in to us, whispers, "This is a little tough. I'm here if you need me."

Mr. A takes a drink of water, confers with Jonathan mouth to ear, continues. "Our small band of seven underground men was hard at work behind the tragedies unfolding around us. We desperately wanted to help preserve what rightfully belonged to our neighbors, our friends, our own families. We were collecting, making detailed accounts, noting family ties, evaluating worth, and storing everything in my cellar in this very house. With my many connections, I, my wife, and my sons were relatively safe for a brief time, but conditions worsened each day. How do you bribe someone when they can easily and legally murder you and take everything you own? Yes, that was becoming the reality."

His last words cause a ripple of chatter among the guests.

"Bashan. Many of you know from your studies that Bashan is an ancient Biblical place in the northern section known for its thick forests and rich pastures. In Hebrew, it means *fertile, stoneless ground.* In the *Sefer Tehillim,* David, the son of Jesse, describes being surrounded by opponents who are *like the bulls of Bashan.* The bulls were remarkable for their size, strength, and fierceness. According to some of our ancient Hebraic beliefs, the mighty bulls of Bashan may have represented *the sons of God* who had authority over the world's nations. Is it any wonder why the bulls of Bashan were chosen to represent those seven men who refused to fully surrender?

"They became our symbol, our pledge, to fight the domination of Hitler. We hungered to be like those bulls—strong, fierce, unwavering! The Bulls of Bashan sculpture represents the original seven men, the *Bulls.*"

"Did you hear that, Shifrah? The bulls represent seven men," I whisper excitedly. She rotates her head slowly, looks at me with a blank expression.

Mr. A removes his glasses, takes a handkerchief offered by Jonathan.

Poor man!

"Father, perhaps we should allow drinks to be freshened and a comfort break?"

"Yes, of course."

Jonathan nods to an elderly butler standing in front of the library doors. He opens the doors, speaks to one of the men in the black suits and ties standing outside the door. Conversation breaks out around us. Chairs are scooted out. Some walk out, I'm assuming to use bathrooms or stretch legs, others light cigarettes or pipes and stand in small huddles talking. Shifrah lights a cigarette, leans her head against the back of the chair.

"You okay, Shif?" Reno asks.

She doesn't answer. I exchange a worried look with Reno, then Malone. The pieces of the mystery are being sorted out, but will Shifrah be all right when they click together?

CHAPTER SIXTY

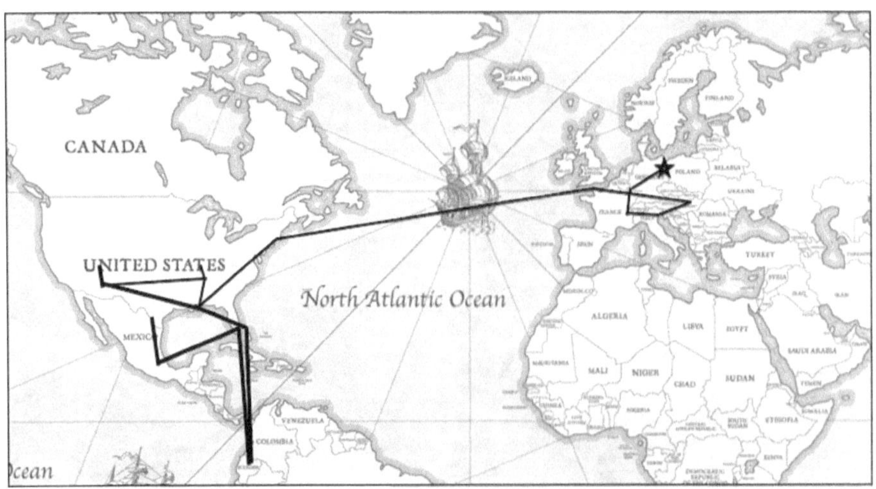

I scoot my chair out and stand up to stretch. "Shall we go freshen up, Shifrah?" She shakes her head while still staring at the ceiling.

Shifrah miss an opportunity to primp in a mirror?

"Ah, hello again, dear Savannah," Lior says from behind me. I turn, and there he is, standing too close, smiling, scrutinizing my cleavage. "*Mein Gott,* my eyes are injured from your beauty!" he says, moving even closer to me. I lean slightly backward against the back of my chair.

"Um, yes, hello, Lior. I don't see your father. Did he come with you?" I try to extend a hand for him to shake, but I can't because he's standing too close.

"How's about giving the lady a little space, Mr. Horowitz?" Reno says, physically wedging himself between us. Lior's face turns stony as

Reno inches forward, causing Lior to back up. He pokes his head around Reno.

"Can we step away for a moment, Savannah? I have something very crucial to discuss with you…" he says, glaring at Reno, "…privately."

Reno puts a hand on Lior's chest. "Hey, buddy, you know what I think—"

"Reno, I'll take it from here," I say, scootching out from behind them. "Coming, Lior?" He shoots a triumphant glower at Reno, offers me his arm. I don't take it. I look behind my shoulder at Malone, Shifrah, and Reno watching us. They don't understand this side of me, that I'm no pushover when it comes to cooling the heels of an aggressive suitor. My regulars at the diner taught me well.

Outside the library, Lior says, "Rude lout! He acts as if he owns you. It's good you intervened, Savannah. I was captain of my boxing team in college, you know. He was this close to getting his nose bloodied!" He holds up two fingers to show me how close Reno was to danger, and it's all I can do not to smirk. He doesn't know how close he came to having his face rearranged, or worse. Lior reaches for my hand, kisses the back of it.

What is it with these European men?

"Savannah, my fair Savannah, I have not been able to get you off my mind. Ever since you came to our factory that wonderful day, I have dreamed of when we would see one another again. I do wish, and I know you can understand, that you weren't showing quite so much of yourself to the men here," he says with a brittle smile, pointing at my dress with the side of his hand. Reacting to my immediate frown, he says, "No, no, no… not important. We can discuss such matters at a later time. I have so much to tell you, and there is so little time. I must take many shortcuts if you don't mind. Is that all right?"

"I suppose so."

"That's generous of you, my dear. Oh, how I crave more time to-to become acquainted with such a woman as you. Young people deserve that kind of time, don't they? Ah, Savannah, merely saying your name fills my heart with gratitude that Father allowed me to represent our family at this rendezvous. I understand that your, uh, your mission is coming to a close. That sets you free to do as you wish, yes?"

I nod.

"Then, it's perfect! Such exquisite timing. You see, Father, Mother, and I are scheduling a grand European tour this summer, and we are extending an invitation for you to join us. We shall see all the outstanding sights of Europe together. Sailing and swimming in the South of France, strolling the banks of the Danube, visiting the City of Love—Paris—and so much more. And, Savannah, let me say that my parents are very understanding. They will give us time and space to be alone to dream and plan as much as we wish. Have you been to Venice, my sweet? My favorite restaurant there highlights the—"

I put a finger to my lips and say, "Shh, Lior."

"What is it?"

"Please take a breath."

"I'm simply so excited, my heart is racing!"

"This is a lot for me to absorb."

"Of course, it is. You must pardon my impetuous behavior. I could not leave Berlin without sharing my heart with you, my lovely Savannah, and you are so tightly hemmed in by that brute. That is what makes me tell you so much so quickly."

"Brute? You mean Reno?"

"I do. He's an outlandish boor."

"Lior, listen. Thank you for your invitation. It's very kind of you and your parents to include me in such an extravagant tour of Europe. It's true that our mission is ending soon, and I am certainly free to do whatever I want afterward."

"Which is why—"

"I'm sorry, Lior, but Shifrah and I have been making our own plans for traveling afterward."

"Shifrah? Your other female companion?"

"Yes."

"But she is of no importance, Savannah, not when you consider our future together. This tour is our opportunity to become well acquainted and, dare I say, intimately involved? If you will allow me, I will show you how life can be when you are genuinely happy. We were made for each other, my love. Surely you cannot refuse an opportunity—"

"Just a minute, Lior. Are you saying you've already decided my future?

"Our future, my sweet, but—"

I scoff. "I'm sorry, but the truth is, I don't share your feelings. I'm sure you're a very nice person, Lior, and I'm flattered, but—"

"Savannah!"

His commanding tone just *bristled the hair on the back of my neck,* as my daddy used to say when he became instantly angry.

He smiles, reaches to touch my cheek. "Dear, I apologize for my harsh tone, but you must understand how much I adore you already. Yes, it seems unnatural, I know, but can we argue with fate? Given time, you will feel the same. Of all the women I've known, you are the one I pick to share my life with. Isn't it wonderful? My family is a wealthy family, Savannah, and, well, I wanted to save this surprise for a more intimate time, but I'll rush ahead and tell you. Our family on my mother's side is related to the former royals of Germany."

I literally see his chest swell as he says this.

"Naturally, it is good fortune to marry into such a family as ours, especially if one has no real connections in life."

"Connections?"

Lior nods. "I confess I did a bit of research on my own, and I don't want you to worry that you have no parents or even about your past as a waitress. It matters not in the least to me, and my family is more modern-thinking every day. Our love will show them—"

I literally let out what sounds like a hen cackling over a new egg. I slap my leg, put my head back, and guffaw.

"What is so humorous?"

I take a deep breath, regain my composure enough to say, "You are, you pompous buffoon!" and I start cackling again.

"Pompous buffoon? I'm afraid my deep revelations have put you in a state of shock. I never, uh, Savannah, my-my dear, I choose, yes, I do, never to remember those words coming from your lovely mouth. I-

I forgive you."

"Oh please, Lior… please remember those words to your dying day!" I break out in more raucous laughter, notice Reno walking through the open library doors. I beckon to him with a big, unladylike arm swing. As soon as he nears, I slip my arm through his.

"Lior, meet my fiancé, Captain Taylor—decorated war hero, sharp shooter, and the most un-pompous man I've ever met. He could have any woman he wants, but he chose me. Can you believe a man with those accomplishments would want an orphaned, unconnected, lowly waitress such as I?"

Lior's face reddens as an emotional storm blows across his features.

"One last thing, and I hope you never forget this. Reno and I don't take kindly to people with their hind ends jacked up so high and mighty they need a ladder to use the toilet, do we, Reno?"

"Uh, no, no, we sure don't! And that goes double!" he says, edging closer and turning his beautiful blue eyes on me. "Sorry, buddy. You lose. I win." He spins us around and fast walks us through the doors and back to our seats. Malone and Shifrah are sitting up straight in their chairs as we near the table.

"Reno, thank you, thank you, thank you for saving me from that prideful man. He's connected to former royalty of Germany, don't you know?" I say in my snootiest tone of voice. "And he was getting his semi-royal gloves dirty by falling in love with a lowly former waitress with no parents or connections. Further, I was to be eternally grateful for his benevolence. You know what else? He shouted at me, shouted my name, as a reprimand for my telling him I was not interested in his proposal."

"That jackass! I'm gonna go bust his nose just for propriety's sake."

"Settle down, Reno," Malone says sternly. Reno presses his lips together. His fists are knotted.

"Reno?" Malone says, and Reno pulls his chair out and sits.

"Lior actually thought you would marry him?" Shifrah asks.

"Uh-huh, and I was supposed to fall on my face and thank him for the honor, me being of such humble background and all."

"Well, I must say I told you so, Savannah, but what a classic snob he turned out to be! Good thing Reno happened along."

"If he hadn't, I might have forgotten my own manners and taken him down in a headlock. I thought about it. I'm pretty good at it, you know."

"He has no idea what I still might do to him," Reno mutters.

Malone leans over. "Not worth it, buddy. Besides, he *is* the son of Mr. Horowitz, an original *Bull* in this project, right?"

"Yeah."

"Um, I noticed it looked kind of deserted outside the library. Have most of the regular people departed?" Shifrah says, attempting to change the subject.

"I wasn't paying any attention," I say. I lean down and give Reno a brief hug. "Thanks again, Reno. You saved me before I did something that may have embarrassed us. I hope you don't mind the story I made up. I wanted to discourage him forever, and being engaged to someone he hates seemed the best route."

Reno doesn't look up.

CHAPTER SIXTY-ONE

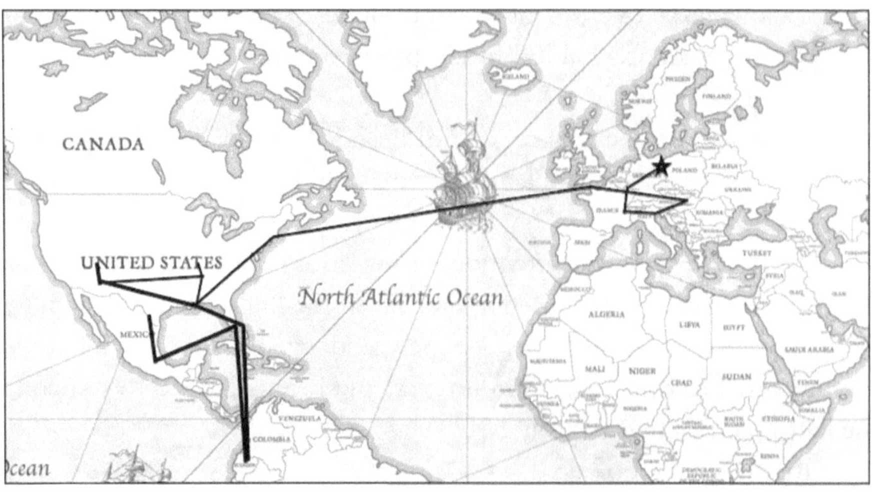

Coffee, tea, water, and brandy have been served, and the doors are once again being closed. A younger butler standing inside the closed doors has replaced the older gentleman. Jonathan brings us to order by tapping his spoon on a coffee cup, "It looks like everyone is back. We won't keep you much longer. I want to assure you again that the ledgers with the records of exactly what belongs to any certain family, person, or group will be checked and rechecked by several experts with witnesses in attendance.

"Every family document, genealogy, land grant, mortgage, piece of jewelry, monies, coins, precious stones, photographs, art, every single object, was documented and logged, even a thimble that was precious to a *bobe,* a grandmother, desperately wanting it passed down to her progeny. It was all the dear soul had left after being plundered by the

Nazis.

Keep in mind that your family genealogies were written down and stored in the secret place, as well as triple-recorded in code books secreted to Switzerland, England, and the United States. In other words, we have checked and screened every family member or designee in attendance tonight as thoroughly as if each were a grain of sand underneath the Hale Telescope.

"Those of you notified previously will meet with me and our attorneys at the specified bank at ten a.m. in the morning for signing and notarizing all necessary paperwork. Later, after you receive notification of their impending arrival, your items will be shipped securely to you wherever you designate or, in the case of funds, sent to the financial institutes you choose while you are here. The dispensation will occur after the sifting, sorting, and in one case, melting. Be patient, please. Our time is finally at hand, and we want to be certain everything is handled by the books.

I wish I could cheer or clap, but any sign of jubilation would be disrespectful with such heavy emotion filling the room. I turn to Shifrah and whisper, "Have you ever heard anything so horrible and incredible at the same time?"

Her gaze is locked on Jonathan and Mr. A, her cigarette a long ash in the ashtray. She whispers, "I just want to know why those bulls are on my cigarette case."

"I have a feeling we'll know soon."

"Father, are you ready to continue?" Jonathan says.

Mr. A nods, asks for the lights to be dimmed.

"Jonathan mentioned *melting,* and I wish to explain that. Please look again at the sculpture in the slide. It was painted dark with a water-based paint, then sheened to look like bronze. In reality, it is the totality of all the pure gold we collected and melted from our friends and families. Again, we are indebted to Jankel Levy, an original *Bull* and master sculptor and jeweler for creating this beautiful piece of camouflage. Take note that a record of the exact weight of every contribution, to the smallest gold wedding band, forged into this statue is recorded in two ledgers.

"You can turn on the lights again," he says. Mr. A sips from his coffee cup. "I am returning to our history for a moment. As we continued to gather items, our sense of foreboding deepened. How long could the treasures so dear to the owners be hidden safely in my home? And, of course, we were still collecting, sorting, and recording. As time passed, a soldier of any rank had full authority to break down my door, kill us or throw us in the streets. Can you understand our anxiety?

"Secretly, dangerously, we began moving items to odd places—walls, attics, cellars, banks, vaults, barns, houses—but no place was safe for long. So many times, we were nearly caught. So close, but, every time—a miracle! We pulled it off! Again and again." Mr. A pauses, scans the group. "Do you suppose we had a little help?" He points his index finger toward the ceiling and smiles.

I can't believe how much I'm smiling back. I glance around and see attendees wiping tears, others smiling, still others wearing grim expressions or no expression at all. My smile slides off my face. Mr. A's narrative involves their own loved ones, and I can't imagine the pain some of them are experiencing.

"Miracles. We believed in them, accepted them, and we were grateful. Out of the blue, our grandest miracle came, a miracle which made Hitler's dream come true. Berlin was awarded the designated city location for the 1936 Olympic Summer Games instead of Barcelona, Spain. For us, it was like golden cherub wings floating out of the heavenlies.

"We speculated that Hitler's arrogance would become our paragon, our great chance to hide our treasures where they would never be discovered, and… we were right! His delusions and illusions of grandeur overtook him, and, of course, the current stadium and all the surrounding buildings and grounds were not good enough to show the world the glory of the Nazi regime and its supreme leader. He ordered the stadium to be demolished and rebuilt. *Meshugana!* A crackpot! But his pride worked beautifully in our favor.

"The stadium…" Shifrah mumbles. I glance at her. She looks pale.

"Werner March. Have any of you heard of him? He was appointed chief architect for the new construction of the Olympic Stadium, the

Reichsportfeld. The work began in March 1934, and it constantly fell behind schedule. Threats to the construction companies caused them to hire fifteen hundred workers. Still not good enough! Soon, the number of workers rose to more than two thousand. All the better for us. How did we find this out?" Mr. A smiles. "We had our ways, oh yes, we had our ways."

"More than five hundred building companies were hired to make Hitler the preening prince of Germany with his grand *Olympiastadion.* The hirers were told to *employ only deserving workers of German nationality and Aryan descent."*

Both Mr. A and Jonathan laugh aloud. Mr. A says, "Ha! Do you know how impossible it was to check thousands of workers to ensure they had not a drop of Jewish blood? In another time and place, yes, it was done, but not when the *Fuhrer* was whipping and beating the Steed of Construction to a full sweaty gallop!"

"You'll have to forgive my father. He loves to make wild comparisons. Metaphors, similes," Jonathan says, shaking his head and smiling. "He means Hitler was in a very big hurry to complete the *Olympiastadion* and the surrounding grounds."

Mr. A continues. "His haste provided our solution. We had help. Lots of it. Four faithful workers related to two of our original *Bulls* were brought into our scheme after being sworn to secrecy. How do you trust them? You include them in the spoils, of course! After the secret hiding place was created, the treasures were carted in under lumber, inside buckets, in between panes of glass, among old pieces of plaster being hauled here and there. Tarps were the best. That is how we hid our Bulls of Bashan sculpture, wheeled that huge thing into the stadium right under their Nazi noses!"

"But what is the secret place?" I blurt out, immediately clamping a hand over my mouth. "I'm-I'm so sorry."

Reno whispers, "Settle down, girl, or I'll have to calf rope you," which doesn't help my sense of embarrassment.

"Don't apologize, Savannah. I get too excited and start explaining every detail in my stories. Jonathan forgot to remind me to hurry!" He smiles, refills his water glass from a nearby pitcher. "Let's jump to the most important part so all of you can go to your hotels and rest before tomorrow's big day, yes?

"The renovation called for the fields to be deepened by ten meters. That's more than thirty-two feet. Imagine the digging! Imagine the refurbishment and the possibilities of areas no longer used except for girding and structure."

"That's right, and the *Olympiastadion,* the *Reichsportfeld,* was built on top of the foundation of the stadium and grounds erected for the 1916 Olympia games, which were canceled because of World War I," Jonathan says.

"And tomorrow, when the last key has been turned, the door will open to the secret hiding place containing our remnants of the heart and much, much more," Mr. A says.

"How will you carry all of it?" someone at the end of the table asks.

"Yeah, and where are you taking it?" asks a woman sitting next to Reno.

"We have high security and armored trucks at our disposal. The goods will be taken to a secure location to begin the task of sorting and recovery. All the arrangements are set. Now, please, come and see for yourselves these magnificent keys designed and forged by Jankel Levy twenty years ago to fit the *key to the keys."* Mr. A unlocks the wooden box on the table, opens the lid, and holds it up for everyone to see.

Jonathan stands, "That concludes our private meeting. We are thrilled you shared this evening with us, a special offering from us to you in remembrance of all who have sacrificed and worked on the *Bulls of Bashan* Project, especially to those no longer with us. Remember to meet me at the appointed time and place tomorrow."

Several attendees go forward to shake hands and chat. Two men in black suits come to stand behind Jonathan and Mr. A, arms draped in front in what my speech teacher called the fig-leaf position.

I scoot my chair out, yawn, and start to rise.

"Keep your seats," Malone says.

CHAPTER SIXTY-TWO

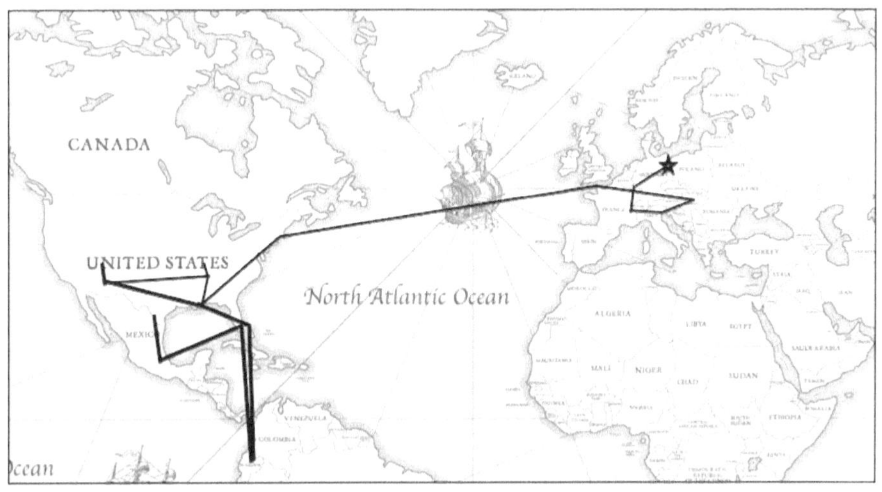

We sit, in my mind, like crows on a fence waiting for the corn to ripen. Malone and Reno are too quiet for my comfort. When the last of the attendees walk out, the library doors are again closed. The butler, who left two times while Mr. A was talking, is the younger man who joined us earlier inside the library.

Mr. A and Jonathan pull out seats opposite us at the table. Shifrah whispers, "They better tell me what's going on or else."

"It's about to happen," I whisper back.

"Did you enjoy the presentation?" Jonathan asks. The doors to the library open and in walks one of the black suits. Mr. A and he go aside and talk privately. Black Suit leaves.

"The main squad is leaving, Father?" Jonathan asks.

Mr. A nods, "Squads one and two. We're fine with Squad three."

He settles in, gazes at me. "Savannah, I admire your enthusiasm! The exact details of the hiding place are still classified except for this small group right here, but now that we are alone, I can tell you what you asked."

"Oh, you don't have to, Mr. A. I-I'm fine not knowing. I just lost myself in your story and got too excited—"

"But I love it, my dear!" His smile almost makes me cry—fatherly and kind—reminding me of my daddy. I manage to smile, but I feel tears hovering near the edge of my emotions.

"Here is how it came to be. The new plans for the stadium didn't call for destroying all the former structures because of time constraints. Below the ground where columns of concrete were placed inside an area already finished out but no longer needed other than for support features, one certain very large column has a hollow center. On the backside of that column facing an unused wall is a discreet door painted the same gray as the column. Can you guess where that door leads? It leads down concrete steps to another door that can only be opened by affixing a certain piece of metal—a shield with seven keyholes in it—to the front of it. The shield attaches to holders in front of seven drilled holes, each one a keyhole with a type of combination. The keys must be placed and turned clockwise or counter-clockwise in a certain order as explained in a forgotten Semitic language. Behind that door is a room that used to be a section of the old stadium's basement. Tomorrow at daybreak, my security teams, your team, Jonathan, and I will intrude upon that room for the first time in all these years. Daybreak is when my British colleagues have cleared the way for us."

"We're beholden to you for allowing us to go with you tomorrow, sir," Reno says. "I was hoping we'd get to."

"It's my personal pleasure, Reno, and I think it's time you call me Aaron."

Reno grins, salutes. "I'll try, sir, but once I get a name—"

"Or a title," Malone says.

"When I get used to saying *sir* or calling someone a name, it sure is hard to get my mind and tongue lined up to change it. I'll try, Mr. A, uh, Aaron."

"Father, ready to continue?"

He nods. "As Germany lost its soul to a crazed dictator, families made decisions that tore them apart, but any flicker of hope was grabbed with desperation. Our *Bulls of Bashan* Project gave us hope for a possible future time when we would live free again, but what of our own children's safety in those terrible times?

"My son Jonathan was sent away from us when he was sixteen. Oh, how his mother and younger brother cried! My cousin in Chicago, God rest his soul, agreed to sponsor him. It was typical for families to send the eldest son out of Germany to preserve the family name provided they had a sponsor to support them.

"He didn't want to go. He refused! Many noble men gathered at our home to tell him they were trying to do the same thing with their sons. At last, Jonathan went to Amsterdam and on to the States in 1937. I can't forget waving to him the last time at the railway station, and…" Mr. A's voice breaks. He looks away.

"Father, I'm here now. I won't ever leave you again."

Shifrah abruptly stands, places her palms on the table as if she might spring forward, leans toward the two men opposite us. "I don't mean to be rude, but enough history and family stories. Mr. A, did you know my original parents? What happened to them? Who gave me my cigarette case? Was my father one of your original *Bulls*? Where is he? Dead? Am I an orphan?"

It's an awkward moment, and, from the look on his face, I'm guessing Mr. A wants to reveal Shifrah's life in his own way. He glances at Malone. Malone clears his throat, puts folded hands on the table. "Shifrah, as a favor to me, can you be patient a few minutes longer?"

She glares at him. "No, I can't! Why do I have a cigarette case etched with the *Bulls of Bashan* and the stadium that Hitler, that Great Idiot, rebuilt? Are the symbols on the edges of the case another key on how to use the keys? Why can't you just tell me the truth?"

Malone puts a hand on her arm, holds her eyes with his. The power that man has over her lately is impressive. She sighs noisily, sits down frowning. I understand how she feels, how everyone is feeling, and I feel terrible for all of them.

"Okay, I'll make this fast," Malone says. "Mr. A wants you to know a little more background, so let me say I met Jonathan before the war. We won't bore you with the details, but they involve Intelligence, D-Day, and all of that. I don't suppose you've heard of the Ritchie Boys, but that's what Jonathan is, a Ritchie Boy, trained at Camp Ritchie in Maryland. Jonathan, is it okay to talk about this?"

"Sure. We're all, uh, friends here. Just hit it light, okay?"

"Will do. See, when Germany declared war on the United States, German citizens living in America were declared *enemy aliens.* Thankfully, Congress reconsidered and allowed many of those so-called *enemy aliens,* many of them the young men sent to America by their families to escape Hitler, to enlist in the army. Believe me, Jonathan, and others like him, were frothing at the mouth to pay back a regime that had victimized them and tortured or killed their families. Jonathan tells me it was rocky, though, because most of the American-born soldiers and even officers, a lot of times, were suspicious of German GIs."

"It was rough," Jonathan says, shaking his head in remembrance. "Then, as Father says—a miracle!"

I think if I could see behind his purple lenses, his eyes would be shining.

"The war planners at the Pentagon soon realized the German-Jewish men in uniform were the ones who knew the enemy best, their language, foods, customs, and how they thought because, well, they were German also. Even better, our hatred of Hitler exceeded that of the average soldier. A lot of what we trained for and did is still classified, but thousands of us received top-secret training along with our field training. We were quickly made U.S. citizens and shipped overseas to fight, survive, and interrogate. That's briefly who I am."

Shifrah jumps out of her chair. "I'm happy for you, Jonathan, really I am. I-I'm sorry, but I can't take this anymore. I never get my questions answered, and I'm-I'm…" She bursts into tears and turns away. Malone is instantly out of his seat and whispers something in her ear. She nods. Malone turns to us, says, "Excuse us a minute." They walk to the far end of the library with Malone bending to talk to her as they go.

"I think she's holding up pretty danged well, considering," Reno says.

"She's a trooper," I offer.

"Of course, she's feeling low," he says.

"Who can blame her?" I ask.

"Look what she's been through."

"Amazing strength."

Mr. A has been turned around watching them. When he turns back, his cheeks are covered in tears. "Jonathan, it is time," he says.

"I agree, Father."

The seriousness of their words and faces causes Reno and me to shut up and sit quietly, respectfully. This is a moment belonging to Shifrah. We're almost intruding by being here. She needs our support or we'd excuse ourselves. All this we communicate to each other without opening our mouths. I didn't realize we could do that, but we did.

When Shifrah and Malone return, she is so much recovered, I again marvel at his influence over her. There's no denying she trusts him explicitly. As soon as she settles into her chair, Jonathan says, "Shifrah, thank you for your patience through this ordeal. Father and I have only a few more things to explain to you. Why? Because we want you, no, we need you, to understand the whole picture."

She nods, leans into Malone.

Jonathan smiles at her. "I was sent away to a foreign country, and my younger brother Peter died from Scarlet Fever the next year. He was ten years old. My parents were forced from their home by Nazi occupiers, their friends were killed or shipped to concentration camps. They never knew what the next hour might bring.

"After *Kristallnacht* in Germany, Austria, and in the Sudetenland, hope basically died. It's known as the *Night of Broken Glass*, a night of unspeakable terror. Hundreds of synagogues were destroyed, several thousand Jewish shops looted, thirty thousand Jewish men rounded up and sent to concentration camps. That was 1938, only one year after I left Germany and very soon after Peter died.

"Father got Mother safely smuggled to England only because he was paying everyone off and had information on some of the officials that could send them to prison. That was how he had survived so far. Alas, before he could join Mother, he was arrested and branded a war criminal for sending his wealth out of Germany. That part was true, but several more trumped-up charges were tacked on. It was a conspiracy of the officials he had the goods on, and it got him sent to *Buchenwald.* Later, my mother was killed in a bomb raid, and none of us got the chance to tell her goodbye."

It's quiet in the room, and I hate myself for complaining about anything ever. My life has been a bed of roses compared to these poor people. "I-I'm so sorry for your losses, Jonathan… Mr. A," I say.

"I-I am, too. Did you suffer many injuries in the war, Jonathan?" Shifrah says softly.

"I made a full recovery."

"Except for your eyes, of course. That's too bad."

Jonathan glances at Mr. A, who nods. Jonathan takes off his glasses "Shifrah, I've been wearing these purple lenses so you and Savannah couldn't see my eyes."

"Why?"

"Look closely." He leans forward, and so does she until they are a few feet apart over the table.

"They look fine to me. They're brown. No, wait. They're hazel. Like mine. They even have that black circle around the iris, and that's rare they say, but…" she recedes back into her chair with frightened eyes.

"It's true. You are my little sister, Shifrah, and our eyes are identical. I know this is shocking, but please, open your heart and hear the facts. The pain we suffered sending you away when you were three years old was nearly unbearable. You were the joy of our worlds, so funny and jolly, bursting with life. So cute. So trusting. We couldn't bear to think of a tragedy befalling you. Letting you go was the hardest thing we ever did. We were heartbroken, but at least we knew you were safe and protected."

Mr. A wipes his eyes with a handkerchief. "My daughter, please forgive us. My brother, your uncle, and his wonderful wife have loved you as their own beloved child, and I did not want to cause any problems. They wanted to introduce me to you as your uncle after the war, but my mind and emotions were, were… not well after-after everything. I was prone to burst into uncontrollable tears at the slightest provocation. It took some time for me to regain control, but know this… I have followed every moment of your life before and after I was released from *Buchenwald.*"

"Shifrah?" Malone says softly.

She doesn't answer, continues to stare across the table at Mr. A and Jonathan.

"Do you want a glass of water?" I ask.

She doesn't seem to hear me. She looks faraway, mumbles toward Malone, "Why was I sent on this mission?"

That's her first question? She's definitely in shock.

Malone coughs. "There was a joint discussion with Aaron, the Mandel's, and Jonathan. I threw my two cents in, too, but, remember, you had two choices, hon. You chose the mission."

"The details for the mission were completed a short time before your, uh, your recovery from the accident. It was originally to be only Malone and whoever he selected," Mr. A says.

"That would be me," Reno says.

She stares off in the distance. "Let me get this right. After I got into trouble with the law, everyone wanted me to experience life outside my ivory tower, to go through normal hardships, and then, to later discover I have a living father and brother in charge of everything?" Nods all around. "Congratulations… mission accomplished," she says, her voice shaky but angry.

"Yes, my little Shifrah. That is correct," Mr. A says. He leans forward with tears on his cheeks. "How could I let my little girl go to jail after that horrible accident? It's unthinkable. Your father—my brother—and I were outraged at such a notion. Alas, we both knew you were headed for more trouble if you didn't experience life in a different way. No, you didn't have to ride mules, take care of children, or pull mussels off nets to complete this mission, but those were our tactics to help you see beyond your privileged life.

She looks down at her cigarette case. "When did I receive this case?"

"I sent it to my brother after Jankel designed it. He kept it for you until you were older. It represents our entire scheme, and yes, those etchings in the corners do tell the order of the keys."

"I see. So, tell me how Savannah was chosen. Was there really a contest of candidates?"

"Shifrah, that's okay. It doesn't matter right now," I say.

"No, it does, Savannah. Everything matters," she says, turning wet eyes on me. "I want the whole truth."

Mr. A sniffs, dabs his eyes. "I will tell you." He looks at me. "Savannah, there were other young ladies we considered for the mission, but you were always our top choice. I knew about you. In fact, I have watched you grow up."

"Me?"

"Let me explain. Jonathan stayed in the military until he retired last year. I traveled often to the States to see him. He was stationed in many places—Virginia, Alabama, California, Arizona, Texas. One time, I stopped to eat at a diner in Texas and saw the most precocious child, oh, thirteen or fourteen years old, seating customers, taking orders, calling the orders out in code to the cook, serving, working the cash register. She was a ball of energy! I was enthralled with her, and so were the locals coming in teasing her or talking about her grades and sports events. She answered everyone, never missing a moment of her duties, always smiling.

"After that, I stopped in three or four more times over the years, once with Jonathan, and always pleased with what I saw and heard. I learned you went hunting every year and sometimes bagged the best turkey or the most quail. Your firearm skills were important to us, as well. Dealing with this amount of treasure and money, trouble was imminent.

"I learned about your love of fishing, your education, and much more from merely sitting in a booth and watching you and hearing your customers talk to you. Though we did consider others, you were the most accomplished. I always knew if we could get you, you would not only be the perfect companion for our Shifrah, but also the perfect match for the team."

"What about me? Did you ever check on me?" Shifrah asks in a small voice.

"My darling girl, I have watched you from the sidelines in New York since 1946 at any public event where it was feasible. My brother and Ruth—your parents, yes?—kept me informed so I could watch you from afar at an opera, a ballet, a play. Your tennis matches? I saw many of them.

"I've sat in a malt shop with a newspaper in front of my face watching you feed coins in one of those colorful jukeboxes, hearing your laughter as you teased with your friends. Once, I sat at the far end of a long bench in that building, what was it? It had the impossibly high ceiling and the marble tiles. Yes, the Abstract building. I wore sunglasses and pretended to read a book while you were slumped over waiting for your music lesson. So many sighs! I take it you did not grow to love the violin?" he chuckles.

"Before I went to *Buchenwald,* we constantly received word about you… when you started school, lost your first tooth, learned to ride a bicycle. I wanted to hold my little girl in my arms so many times, but we did not want to confuse you. We didn't want you to know of our terrible wartime experiences. And, too, my emotions took time to heal. Can you try to understand, my dear daughter, my *bubbeleh?*"

I start doing what we call back home *breaking out blubbering*, even more so when Shifrah walks around the table and dissolves into Mr. A's arms.

CHAPTER SIXTY-THREE

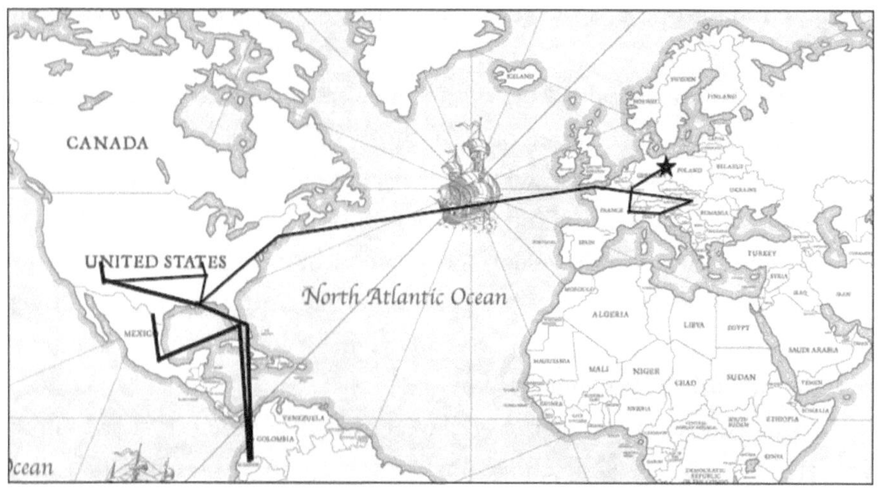

The tender moment between Shifrah and Mr. A is shattered by the library doors bursting open. Five armed men dressed in black wearing skull caps and scarves wrapped around their noses and mouths stand in a V formation inside the room. The newest *butler*, obviously a fake butler, closes the double doors, locks them, strides toward Mr. A.

Mr. A shouts, "What's the meaning of—" He is interrupted by a hard slap across the face by the fake butler. Everything blurs as I see the men spread out toward us and Jonathan shoving Shifrah to the floor. I am being aggressively pushed downward by Reno's arm and leg as he literally stuffs me underneath the table. His legs disappear. Shifrah and I stare at each other in shock, and I try to wiggle closer to her. My tight gown makes it almost impossible, but the looseness of it from the knees down helps me move slightly. Around us are shouts, thuds, glass crashing, legs darting by the table.

A gunshot! The elegant glass chandelier crashes on top of the table, spraying glass everywhere. Arms reach under the table and grab Shifrah. I grab one of her hands, which is all I can reach, and hold on as hard as I can. I scream as she is pulled from my grasp. Her shrieks fill the room. Adrenaline boosts me up on all fours. I stick my head out and see a war zone, or how I imagine one would be.

Fake Butler is restraining a struggling Mr. A at the end of the room. Thousands of broken glass shards from the two Tiffany lampshades and the chandelier are everywhere. Four men are in hand-to-hand combat with Malone, Jonathan, and Reno. The other intruder has Shifrah in a neck lock, which instantly makes me furious seeing her delicate neck under the grasp of a large man with muscular arms.

A gun fires, and the man tussling with Reno crumples forward. Reno steps from behind him. Malone shouts, "Twelve o'clock, Reno!" Reno dips to his haunches, pivots, shoots a man leaping through the air toward him.

Jonathan scoots across the top of the table on his belly and strikes the man wrestling with Malone in the head with the butt of his pistol. The man stands up lightning fast, aims his gun at Malone on the floor. A shot from Jonathan drops him.

"Jonathan, behind you!" Reno shouts. Malone rises from the floor and shoots. The man falls to the floor, blood gushing from his stomach.

"Drop your guns or the girl dies!" the intruder holding Shifrah shouts in a heavy accent very similar to Mr. A's. Fake Butler roughly tosses Mr. A aside. He and Shifrah's captor walk backward toward the door, Shifrah in front as a shield. Fake butler unlocks the doors.

"You won't make it past my security squad," Mr. A yells.

"We already did, old man," Fake Butler says. "How do you think these guys walked in here? They said they're musicians putting on a special show for Mr. Mandelbaum! Bad decision sending your other guys home. I've been serving this puny crew complimentary drinks with sleeping powders and hallucinogenics the last thirty minutes, drinks courtesy of Aaron Mandelbaum—a most congenial host! They're lame as lambs. Tell them to shoot, and they'll shoot their own feet off." He laughs.

"Silence!" yells the man holding Shifrah. "If you want her alive, pay attention. Keep your daybreak plans at the stadium. Instruct your armored truck drivers to go to the address I send to you right before they drive away from the stadium. I don't want any of the paperwork. I warn you, if you sic any of your rats or the police on us, she's dead. Don't make a mistake. We'll have eyes on every move you make. Deliver the goods where I tell you, and she lives.

"Have you lost your mind, Ab?" Jonathan shouts.

"Shut up, Jonathan. Do exactly what I say, or you'll never see your sister alive again."

"And you think all this carnage was worth it? Four men critically wounded or dead? What the hell are you really after?"

"Am I *meshug?* The Mayan book, of course."

"It's written in a lost symbolic language."

"You forget how filthy rich I'll be when I cash in those treasures. That much money buys a hundred moth-eaten philologists. Maybe I'll save myself the trouble and sell it on the black market."

"Oh, Ab, Ab, I should have had you arrested two days ago when I found out you were the traitor behind it all. You betrayed us, stole information, spied on our team, and perhaps now, I think, you don't care if you kill all of us. I had mercy on you," Mr. A says, his voice quivering. "I told you to leave us and never return. Your foolishness shamed your dead father enough, and for that, you will always suffer. Despite your trespasses, I promised to send you the inheritance your father left for you as an original *Bull* of Bashan. Now, see what you have done, Absalom, son of my dearest friend! Your father weeps in his grave because of you!"

Have you ever seen a flash of light appear at the side of your eyes, one so fast you think you imagined it? That's how the next second unfolds as Reno's rolled-up body crashes into the legs of the men and Shifrah. In the next half instant, Malone and Jonathan throw themselves over them until they are one big mesh of Shifrah and five men. Grunts, thunks, and shots are fired, followed by silence.

"Shifrah? Jonathan?" Mr. A calls in a trembling voice.

"Reno? Malone?" I say, my lips quivering.

Silence.

I scream and run toward the heap of humans on the floor, stop in horror. Blood is pooling underneath them on both sides. Jonathan rolls over, takes a knee to rise. The front of his clothes is embedded with glass slivers sparkling with blood. Malone groans, stands. He rubs a hand over his face, bends to pick up Shifrah, who, by her limp posture, has fainted, or worse. All of them are a bloody mess. Malone carries Shifrah to the leather sofa near the wall and lays her out on her back. Mr. A and Jonathan follow. Malone feels her throat.

"Is she…" Mr. A says.

"She's alive. I think she fainted." Malone says. He does a quick rub down of her legs and arms, rolls her over, checks her back. "No wounds."

I watch all this as if I'm in a trance. I turn and see Reno's body entangled with the fake butler and the one they called Absalom. Blood is everywhere. No one is moving.

"Malone!" I scream. He turns his head. "Reno is…" I bend over in anguish. "Reno, please, please…" I start wailing like a hysterical bawl-baby. I edge closer and squat beside him, an impossible move in my tight dress. I tilt all the way over with my arm and cheek against the floor. How Reno would have laughed at that, but now… I struggle into a sitting position and scoot as close as I can to him. Malone and Jonathan move in closer, their shoes crunching over the glass on the floor.

"Reno, oh, Reno, I've never known anyone like you. I-I can't imagine my world without you in it, and now, now, you're gone! Oh, Reno." I blubber, nose dripping, face drowning in tears. "You made me laugh every day." I sob, grabbing the end of my gown to wipe my nose. "You were so-so handsome and kind. So accomplished. I'll never meet anyone like you, and—"

"Tell ol' Reno what else is in that sweet little heart of yours," he says, suddenly sitting up and causing me to jump out of my skin. He shakes his head, turns it both ways as if he's letting water out of his ears after swimming. "Think I got pistol-whipped in the head and lost consciousness for a second or two," he says.

"How-how long have you been conscious?" I ask.

"Oh, long about when you said you can't figure your world without me in it."

"Reno, you gave us a scare, bud," Malone says. "You all right?"

"Right as rain, sir. Kind of rum-dummy is all. Dang, that was exciting. Hold on a minute, sir, while I tend to a little unfinished business."

He stands up, pulls a glass shard out of his arm, and bends to lift me up by my waist. He stares into my face so directly, I feel a little weak. "I loved all those things you said over my dead body, Savannah. You crying your pretty eyes out for me like that? Well, dang, it warmed my heart. You know what? I love you, too, darlin'. Wanna get hitched?"

The absurdity of what he said hits me like a sledgehammer in the face. "Wh-what? Are you really alive, and-and, are you still out of your mind?"

"I sure am, on both counts."

"It's about time," Shifrah calls from the sofa.

"I-I don't know what either of you is talking about. I'm—"

"We're talking about how crazy I am about you, you silly goose," Reno says, pulling me into his arms.

EPILOGUE

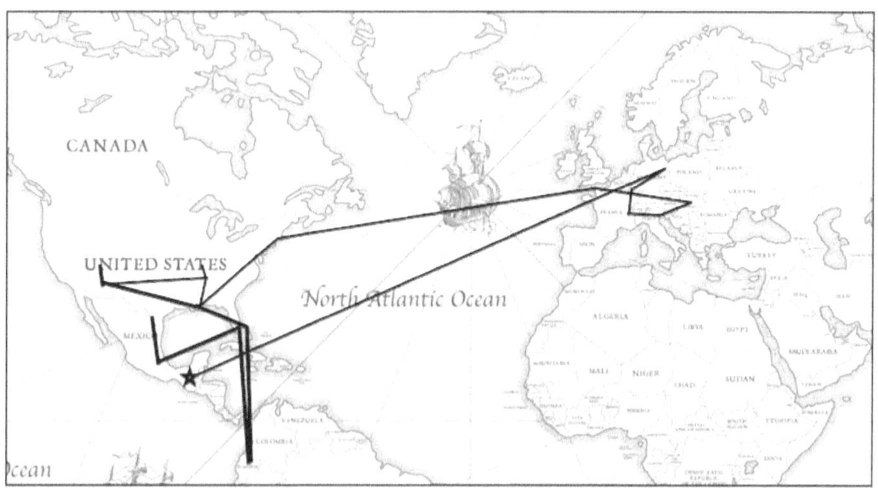

TWO MONTHS LATER…

Bullets whizzing through the open canopy of our boat hit the tangled jungle vines on the other side of the river, a strange muffled sound. "Get down, Savannah!" Malone shouts. I duck and roll onto my stomach. I see Shifrah already lying prostrate on the boat floor. I lie still until the shots and shouts end, listen to the sound of a motorboat fading into the distance, leaving behind the usual pungent odor of black smoke from a leaky engine.

"Anybody hurt?" Jonathan yells.

"A-okay back here," Malone says, raising an arm.

"Roger that," says Tiny, our oversized lookout man occupying the back of the boat.

Reno makes his way from his lookout spot near the front, squats beside me. "Dadgum river pirates, hon," he says, holstering his pistol. "Second bunch since yesterday. For all they know, we're carrying a load of toads, but they gotta go and stir up a ruckus anyways. You okay, punkin'?" He touches my hand, and my stomach goes haywire with butterflies. I admit I have a weakness for those blue eyes and that infectious grin, and, honestly, is that my fault?

Mr. A and Jonathan confer with Howie and Bruce, the men Mr. A brought from his own security squad to keep us safe from thugs, wild animals, or any other pest—ghost or real—standing between us and our present mission.

Malone assists Shifrah off the damp floor, and Reno steps to the rear of the boat to dig in a knapsack for more DEET. "Anybody else need some more of this kick-em-in-the-pants skeeter stuff?" he says.

I raise my hand. The ambitious mosquitos on the river have caused Shifrah and I to almost bathe in DEET, which is loads better than contracting malaria from their constant attacks. Interestingly, our river guide doesn't use any bug propellent and claims he never gets bit.

"Aye, señor y señoritas, I am greatly favored by *Kinich Ahau, Dios Maya del Sol,* our Mayan God of the Sun. He loves me. Do not anger him or *Ah puch, Dios Maya de la Muerte,* our Mayan God of Death, when you assault their sacred jungle secrets."

HOLD IT RIGHT THERE…

What has us rolling down the Usumacinta River between Mexico and Guatemala into the dense Lacandon Jungle in the heart of the ancient Mayan kingdoms in a patched-up but durable river boat with a canopy top and a boatful of gear?

The answer is Mr. A's ancient Mayan *book* from the secret room in Berlin. In actuality, it's a strip of bark paper about the size of two men-sized palms with ancient drawings and symbols, but it's something that unscrupulous men were willing to lie, steal, and kill to own. It was gifted to Mr. A by none other than the famous American epigrapher and archeologist Sylvanus Morley because he, Mr. A, helped him finance an expedition to Chichén-Itzá in 1923 and 1924.

"A marvelous man, Sylvanus. A most entertaining fellow, reckless and smart, and, as I found out later, an American spy during World War I," Mr. A told us before the mission. "He said this little scrap of a book wasn't anything exceptional, but I suspect he knew it was and gave it to me because we became such good friends. Later, a colleague deciphered it and declared it a treasure map to untold amounts of gold and jewels hidden in the southern regions of the Usumacinta River and the surrounding jungles."

So, here we are, our team—larger now—working together, avoiding catastrophes, looking out for each other as we navigate the *River of the Sacred Monkey.* I'm finding danger and adventure are strangely addictive, and, further, that the richness of each day seems to leave no room for tomorrow's worries.

Are we couples now? I'll leave that for you to figure out.

What, then, does the future hold?

That's a big question.

All I know is I'm a long way from Laredo, Texas, but my heart feels right at home exactly where I am.

~ The End ~

About The Author

Jodi Lea Stewart is a fiction author who centers her themes around the triumph of overcoming adversity with grit, humor, and stubborn tenacity. Her writing reflects her life beginning in Texas, relocating as a youngster to an Arizona cattle ranch next door to the Navajo and White Mountain Apache Nations, and as a young adult, resuming in her native Texas. Growing up, she climbed petroglyph-etched boulders, sang to chickens, bounced two feet in the air in the backend of pickups wrestling through washed-out terracotta roads, and rode horseback on the winds of her imagination through the arroyos and mountains of the Arizona high country.

Leaving her studies at the University of Arizona in Tucson, she moved to San Francisco, where she learned about peace, love, and exactly what she didn't want to do with her life. Since then, Jodi graduated summa cum laude with a BS in Business Management, raised four children, worked as an electro-mechanical drafter, penned humor columns for a college periodical, wrote regional western articles, and served as managing editor of a Fortune 500 corporate newsletter. Her lifelong friendship with an eclectic mix of down-to-earth people, cowpunchers, intellectuals, world travelers, country folks, and the Southern Gentry inspires Jodi to write historical and contemporary novels featuring the piquancy of life anywhere in the world.

Jodi Lea Stewart's Social Media Contact List

https://jodileastewart.com/
https://www.youtube.com/@jodileastewart/videos
https://www.youtube.com/@jodileastewart
https://medium.com/@jodileastewart
https://www.facebook.com/jodi.lea.stewart
https://www.linkedin.com/jodileastewart
https://jodileastewart.com/blog/
https://www.instagram.com/jodileastewart/
https://www.pinterest.com/jodileastewart/
https://x.com/jodileastewart?mx=2

Other Titles by Jodi Lea Stewart

Silki, the Girl of Many Scarves Series:
- *Book 1: Summer of the Ancient*
- *Book 2: Canyon of Doom*
- *Book 3: Valley of Shadows*

Blackberry Road
The Accidental Road
TRIUMPH, A Novel of the Human Spirit
The Gold Rose
The Bulls of Bashan

Progressive Rising Phoenix Press is an independent publisher. We offer wholesale pricing and multiple binding options with no minimum purchases for schools, libraries, book clubs, and retail vendors. We offer substantial discounts on bulk orders and discounts on individual sales through our online store. Please visit our website at:

www.ProgressiveRisingPhoenix.com

If you enjoyed reading this book, please review it on Amazon, B & N, or Goodreads. Thank you in advance!

www.ingramcontent.com/pod-product-compliance
Lightning Source LLC
Chambersburg PA
CBHW030240030726
47493CB00023B/265

* 9 7 8 1 9 5 8 6 4 0 7 5 3 *